DUST BOUND

BOOK ONE IN THE FAEPOCALYPSE CHRONICLES

CLEMENTINE FRASER

ISBN 978-0-473-56271-7 (Paperback)

ISBN 978-0-473-56272-4 (Hardcover)

ISBN 978-0-473-56273-1 (Epub)

ISBN 978-0-473-56274-8 (Kindle)

ISBN 978-0-473-56275-5 (iBook)

Interior illustrations created by author using purchased illustrations from Shutterstock and Canva, modified using the Sketchbook app.

Cover Art & Design by Fantasy & Coffee Design

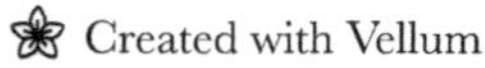 Created with Vellum

ALSO BY CLEMENTINE FRASER

Siren's Call

To my parents.

Thank you for your unending belief, encouragement, and love. I am who I am because of you.

CHAPTER 1

Carcasses of fallen buildings lay swallowed by Fae Dust as Adelia Lark picked her way over the rubble. Swirls of grey powder clouded her view of the deadlands. She blinked away the film with an impatient sigh. The acrid scent of rust seeped from skeletal metal rods, and she tugged her scarf over her face to shut out the metallic tang—too much like blood.

So much blood spilled when the Fae first came.

As she kicked over a twisted piece of steel, scanning for anything useful, she wondered when she'd become immune to the desolation. If Auckland had been her hometown, maybe she'd find it harder. But she was one of the lost ones.

Fifteen years. Nearly half her life had been spent in broken ruins and confined spaces. Every so often she wondered what the rest of the world was like. If the Fae destroyed it like they had New Zealand, she had no way of knowing. The Fae saw to that when they sent their Dust to smother and destroy. *All of us are on our own, now. Some of us more than others.*

Her gaze darted toward the old hospital buildings forming the ramshackle compound of Newhaven barely visible through the Dust. She pressed her lips together and stretched her neck.

Ryder will have a fit if I stay out here much longer.

Her fingers curled around her knife, dislodging the gritty powder on the blade. Very little was left in the deadlands to scavenge now. But Ryder needed a new breathing mask, and small pieces of forgotten metal and wire lay hidden, waiting. Her gaze lit on a leaning crane, crushed against the side of a building. She sheathed her blade, her fingers smudging grimy lines on her trousers. *If I climb high enough, I can use the binocs and scan more widely.*

Dust skimmed over the ground as she strode towards the crane.

Ryder could wait. He'd appreciate it in the end.

Deep cracks scarred the road in front of her. She stretched her leg across a crumbling rift, one hand resting on the wreck of an old bus for balance. Ryder filled her mind. Strong arms and broad shoulders that carried the burdens of everyone in Newhaven. The smile that would turn to a grimace when she walked in too late, a fierce glint in his hazel eyes. Her mouth quirked up. Funny how he still tried to tell her what to do. He should know better.

Blue light pulsed through the gathering Dust, lighting up the distant compound and leaving a burning afterglow. Hollow fear rang through her. *Shit.* The Fae.

She tumbled to the ground. Debris shifted as she scrabbled under the carriage of the old double decker.

Sucking in shaky breaths, she kept her eyes on the rusted metal above her and willed her pulse to stop racing. Distant sirens from the compound rang in her ears. Tension drilled into the base of her neck. *No. Breathe. Let go.* Tears slid down her cheeks. *Stop. Breathe. You're safe. Safer here than at the compound near Fae eyes that see too much.*

Her breathing slowed, and she rubbed the silvery scars on

her arms, burning heat prickling under her skin. *Damn Faeries. They already came this year. They already came...*

Fae magic filtered pale blue through holes in the metal panels of the bus. It would be so easy to stay hidden, to keep herself safe. Ryder's crooked smile came to mind, and her breath caught in her throat. Visions from her past clamoured to escape—Fae claws and pain. *I can't stay safe when he might be in danger.* She ground her teeth together and rolled over, creeping out from under the bus. Ashen powder swirled around her arms and legs with every inch she crawled forward, until she swam through clouds of grey.

She pushed herself upright then fumbled in her pack for the binocs. They weren't great. Unlike other models, they didn't filter Dust from the visuals. Unlike other people, she didn't need them to.

Tattered buildings came into focus as she trained her gaze on the three wings of the central compound. People stood at the edge of the large crater where the fourth wing of the old hospital once stood, before the Fae threw their mountains down on the earth. Three Fae hovered over the gathered people. Blue shimmers surrounded them and cast stuttering shadows on the ground. Scorched, bare dirt covered the long-dried blood of those caught in the first attacks. Her heartbeat spiked, and she looked away from the rubbled ridge around the crater.

Several thousand were in their community, but only a couple hundred gathered in front of the Fae. They shuffled forward, eyes on the sky. Children clung to those who stayed at the back of the crowd, unable to leave now the Fae had spotted them.

The brittle casing of the binocs shifted under her fingers as the images in her head battled with the images filtering through the lenses. *Mia. Sitting on the sofa with her son. Staring at the door, willing it to stay closed.*

She forced her gaze to shift the other way. To the lights. To the Fae. Blue swirls distorted the image, but after a moment, the lenses compensated for the glare. The Faeries came into sharper focus. Her stomach twisted, and her vision shook as her hands slipped on the case. The Fae hovered just above the crater, bright multihued wings catching the breeze, shimmering in and out of focus. Bile rose at the back of her throat. She swallowed through a dry mouth. *They can't see me from here.*

She dropped the glasses and rubbed her eyes. They'd come already this year. Surely no more children would be taken. Her trembling fingers stuck in her hair as she brushed it off her face. They must be here for something else. But dread coiled in her stomach, and her thoughts turned to ash in her mind.

Movement snared her attention. She peered at the compound. Ryder strode toward the Fae. Whipping the binocs back up, she focused on his face, taut and grim even from here. Under control. Like always. He crossed his arms and faced off against the hovering Fae.

Arguing.

He was arguing with them.

Her heart jumped into her throat. The Fae moved closer, blue tendrils twisting from their outspread arms into the crowd. Ryder gestured sharply, and the gate guards shifted to stand in front of the gathered people. Fluttering wings spread out, and a Fae garbed in red descended until it hovered directly in front of Ryder, a good head taller than him. Whatever it said seemed to change his mind. His shoulders slumped, and the blue tendrils retracted, pulling children with them. Her lip trembled.

A Taking.

Addie turned away, and shoved the glasses back in her pack. Ryder could have died, but at least he tried to stop them. No-one else did anymore.

Fine grey powder fluttered onto her cheeks and arms, dusting her hair, turning dark strands into ash. The Dust was falling faster now, almost like raindrops. She scrambled to her feet, shaking her head to clear it. Fingers tightening around her pack straps, she gritted her teeth. Time to head back. The Fae didn't stay long once the Taking ended. *The old tales told the truth. The Faeries do steal children, and when they return them, they're never the same.* Clambering over a car enveloped by Dust, she ignored the prickling of the scars running down her arms. *Never.*

She jumped onto a fallen column, a Romanesque pedestal peeking above shattered concrete. Her pack slipped, and she hoisted it higher on her shoulder, scraps of wire and dead electronics tumbling around inside—not as much as she'd hoped to find, but maybe enough to fix Ryder's mask. She drew up her hood, shutting out the world. Broken pieces of people's lives lined her path as she trudged home.

Dust thickened as darkness gathered.

Maybe Ryder is right. Maybe I do stay out too long.

She strode through the small area of land surrounding the compound, cleared of ruins but still dead and grey. Shadows shifted close to the gates. She squinted, her hand sliding to her knife. A figure loomed from the darkness, scattering grey powder like mist. She jumped back with a curse and caught her heel on the uneven earth, tumbling onto her backside. Pain shot through her leg, and the shadowy figure drew closer.

"Sorry, Sorry, Addie-del"

She sighed as relief washed over her. There was no mistaking the jittery voice of her old friend.

"You should be, Jasper, you gave me a hell of a fright, old man. Give me a hand up, will you?"

Wiry fingers grabbed hers and pulled. Jasper's bird thin appearance hid surprising strength.

Dust clung to her trousers, and she gave up brushing it off. "At least you were the only one who saw me squeal like a pig and fall on my arse."

He grinned, wrinkles softening his sharp gaze. "Addie-del does dig and delve, bits and bobs and scrips and scraps."

She reached for her pack. "Not much today, Jasper. Only a few wires and pieces of rubber. It might be enough for a mask."

His blue eyes flashed through the Dust. "Five score and ten, tearing it down, building up again, find it, find it, in the hand!"

Her mouth twisted in a small smile, hidden under her scarf, and she shook her head. "I'll try again tomorrow, but I can't promise I'll find anything." She fidgeted with the edge of her sleeve. "You saw them come?"

He spat on the ground. "Fae fly flo, they come, they go."

She turned her eyes to the dark buildings, not able to put it off any longer. Her voice quiet in her own ears, she asked, "Who did they take?"

Jasper sighed, his voice bereft of its usual frenetic hum. "The youngest Chang girl, Mia's son, and Tamahou. All gone, all gone, all gone."

Her eyelids fell shut on the pain as she caught it and tucked it away with all the rest. Opening her eyes again, she pulled down her scarf, shaking off fine grains of grey. It was dinner time, and cooking aromas escaped from the residential block, battling with the ever-present musty smell of ground-in dirt and too many people. *Just as well so many people died when the Fae first came. We'd be even more crowded otherwise.*

"Where's Mia?" she asked.

A blunt reply came from over her shoulder, the rumble of Ryder's voice making her heart leap. "I asked Doc to sedate her when she wouldn't stop screaming."

Addie kept her eyes on Jasper. "What do you think, Jasp? Necessary or convenient?"

It was always disconcerting when Jasper's eyes twinkled. It reminded you much more went on behind them than you thought. He grimaced at the man behind her then stretched open his wrinkled eyes to show bloodshot whites.

"A tisket a tasket, all the lemons in a basket." He winked at her and glided away.

A huffed laugh floated over her shoulder.

"He agrees. Had to be done. The quiet was just a bonus."

His breath warmed the back of her neck where her scarf rode up. She jerked around to face him.

"You know your worst fault, Ryder? You always think you know best."

He smiled down at her. Dust powdered the short scruffy strands of his coppery hair, and her fingers curled with the urge to brush off the fine grains.

"Not a fault," he said, "just a fact. You know your worst fault, Lark? You always stay out too damn late, and you don't follow procedure."

She raised her eyebrows and glanced away. "That's two."

"Good counting. Why were you out so late?"

Her pack slipped down the worn fabric of her coat again as she hunched her shoulders, refusing to look at him. "Looking for stuff. Rubber, wire. You mentioned you needed a new mask."

"Lark—" His voice trailed off, and she risked a glance. Taller than her by nearly a foot, his long and lean frame exuded strength. Except for now, when he exuded exasperation. His face had that familiar look again, like he didn't know what to do with her. Of everyone in the compound, he was the only one who called her by her last name instead of Adelia, like he thought she was a fragile bird who should stay safe in a cage. Though she was now twenty-seven and their age difference didn't seem like so much anymore, one look from him and she was fifteen again—stumbling into the compound, desperate for safety and acceptance.

Muscles aching, she fought off a frown. Yeah, she stayed out too late. But she didn't need the buddy system—the only life she risked was her own. The only reason she came back at all was because she didn't want them sending someone out after her.

Dust shuffled off the worn leather of her boot as she kicked her foot against the ground. "Jasper and I'll see what we can do with what I found. If you'll excuse me, I'm going to go find Mia now."

His eyes flickered green in the dull glow of the gate lights, and he grabbed her arm as she brushed past.

"You heard about the other kids?"

She frowned at his strong hand encircling her forearm. He didn't budge.

"Yes, I heard about all three of them. What do you want me to say? That it sucks? Because it all sucks. We both know that, and we both know it won't ever change." Poor little Lily would be so frightened. So would Matt. Maybe Tama, being older, would look after them. Until he couldn't. Her eyes prickled, but it was easier to glare than cry. "Can I go see my friend now?"

He held her for a fraction longer, then let go, his fingers brushing over the straps on her wrist as his hand drifted down.

"It isn't like I can get you to do anything anyway. Why ask?"

She smiled, her lips twisting. "Because asking is polite, and I'm a paragon of good manners."

He laughed, stepping back and crossing his arms.

"Good luck trying to escape Doc's tender mercies. Some of us realise you're never worse for wear no matter how much Dust you roll in, but she'll never believe it."

Addie grimaced. That was exactly why she tried to avoid the medical centre as much as possible, no matter how much she liked Doc. No escaping it this time though. With a little salute, she strode away, avoiding the impact crater, as she always did, and suppressing a shudder at those who walked blithely across it.

"Lark."

She glanced over her shoulder.

"We have two weeks before the Fae return." A muscle flickered in his jaw, and resignation slumped around his eyes.

Memories pushed against the wall in her mind, and her scars burned.

CHAPTER 2

Addie stripped off her boots, coat, vest, and scarf before entering the heart of the medical centre. The one time she'd tramped Dust into the clinic, Doc had appeared like an avenging angel, white lab coat flaring, and swept her out.

Her stomach cramped, and she wiped her palms down her trousers, sweat tracking through grime. *I can do this. For Mia. I can at least try.* Vibrations from the generator filled the silence with a low, familiar hum. She focused on the sound washing over her and waited for her pulse to slow. Shaking grey powder from her braid, her gaze lit on a faded sign asking her to Be a Tidy Kiwi. She hesitated then scooped her clothes from the floor where she'd tossed them, folding the vest and coat carefully and placing them on a chair. The red bricks of the old hospital peeped through peeling green paint. Flakes of colour clung to her hand as she turned the door handle.

The clinic beyond glistened, rigorously kept clean from the ever-present dust and grime that seeped into the rest of the compound. Anahera Rongoa bent over a notebook at the far end of the small room, dark curls bunched up in a messy knot at the back of her head, a few strands drifting down over the frown on her usually smiling face.

"Hey, Doc."

Anahera eyed her from across the room, raising a brow at the pack half hidden behind her legs. Addie shrugged, her mouth screwing up. She tossed the bag to the ground behind the door and walked through.

"How's she doing?"

Anahera grabbed a clipboard and pushed a button above the counter. The door snicked shut behind them. "About as well as you'd expect. She's still under sedation and should come 'round in about an hour." The doctor smiled, a twinkle dancing in her brown eyes, and strode towards her. "Plenty of time to check you out."

Addie stepped back, bumping into a metal trolley. Her hands gripped tight onto the handle. The scratched steel was cool against her too warm palms.

"Yeah, about that. How about we don't and say we did?"

Anahera's jaw tightened. "No, Adelia. It's been over two years since your last medical check, and you're spending longer periods in the Dust. Maybe you look okay, but I've seen what that stuff does to people. I'm not just talking about the fatal incidents. It's a slow decay. You need to make sure you keep up with medicals."

Addie shifted her weight, inching close to the gap between the trolley and the door. Closer to a chance at escape. "I think that's my choice."

Anahera shook her head. "Actually, no. Mandatory medical checks are in our compound manifesto and council rules. Everyone who has contact with Dust has one check-up a month. Minimum. You know this. If not for Ryder, I would've gotten the council to order you in ages ago."

Addie's eyebrows went up. *Really? Wonder what he's up to.* She eyed the clipboard. "Can we make a deal?"

Anahera picked up a small bag, bulky with implements of medical torture.

"Do you realise I don't need to make deals?" the doctor asked, "I can rescind your permit for going outside the compound."

A smile pulled at Addie's lips as she remembered all the times Doc stood up for her against the compound council. "Yeah, but we both know you won't. So, what do you say?"

Anahera flung her arms wide. "Fine. What do you want?"

Her hand twisted against her leg. "I want to make a new mask, but I need a filter. So far, no luck finding one. I wondered if you have a few spares."

"A mask? Are you finally going to wear one?"

"Not for me. For Ryder." She tried not to mumble. Doc's eyes twinkled and Addie fought down a blush.

"Okay, e hoa. You let me check you out, and I'll give you a filter. It's an old one though. You'll have to fix it."

She let a smile escape. "I can do that. Thanks."

Despite Doc's gentle hands, she flinched from the metal instruments. Her legs twitched, and she had to force herself not to run. The doctor's mouth pursed as she darted a glance up from her tattered stethoscope. Addie breathed through the roiling in her stomach, counting the dots on the linoleum floor to focus her mind on anything but the panic.

After minutes that dragged like hours, the long metal prodders finally lay wrapped and hidden in faded nylon. She let out a breath, coming slowly back into herself, and risked looking up.

A wry smile twisted Anahera's mouth but left her eyes alone. "You spent years in the Dust as a child and turned up at our gate dirty but unblemished. I always wondered about that. Dust doesn't affect you, does it?"

Addie hunched her shoulders, stuffing her hands in her pockets. "Not much. Sometimes I cough."

"A cough. People come in here with blindness, burning

skin, nerve damage. You get a sniffle. You ready to tell me why?"

"I would, but I have no idea why." Her fingers curled in her pockets. *Truth. Of a sort. No reason to feel bad.*

Anahera frowned, her brown eyes dark and her jaw tight. "Do you have any idea how many tests I could run? Perhaps we could find a way to help others fight against the Dust. You should have told me before."

Ice burned her blood. She leaned back against the cabinet top and gripped the cool metal, using the pressure to help subdue her pulse into something resembling normal.

"No tests." Her voice rang flat in her ears. She avoided the glance Doc shot at her. "Sorry, not happening. I let you check me out, but that was the only thing in the deal. There's nothing in the compound manifesto saying I have to submit to tests. Nothing about me can help anyone else. That's the truth."

Anahera gazed down at her feet, her hands holding the ends of the stethoscope draped around her neck. She sighed. "Okay, you're right, I can't force you to be tested. But you should. If not for others, for yourself. Push against the Dust too long, and it will come back to bite you. If you change your mind, you let me know, alright? After all, we can't rule out the possibility that you could help others unless we run those tests." Fierce eyes snared Addie in an intent gaze. "Newhaven only works the way it does because we all pull together."

She nodded, her heart still fluttering.

"All right then. I'll grab the filter from storage and leave it by your bag. Go visit Mia, but then you need some rest. Dust or no Dust, you're skinnier than ever, and those dark circles under your eyes tell me you aren't sleeping."

A smile played on Addie's lips. "Yes, whaea."

Anahera's eyes lit up. "Oh, come here."

Her muscles pulled tight as the other woman grabbed her shoulders in a quick embrace. She tried to ignore the steel snaking through her spine as she made herself lean into the affectionate hug.

Doc stepped back and picked up her pouch with a smile. "Alright, go do your thing." Walking out, she left Addie alone in the clinic.

Addie released her death grip on the counter, flexing her fingers as painful pins and needles shot through her hands. *White walls. Screaming. Silence.* Wiping her palms, she took a shaky breath. The machines were silent, but she eyed them anyway. She straightened her shoulders.

Time to face Mia.

GRIEF CARVED deep lines into Mia's pale face. Her eyes stared at the ceiling, unfocused, drenched with tears. An ache filled Addie's chest—burning weights dragging at her heart. She stretched out a trembling hand, smoothing chestnut strands from her friend's forehead, tucking them behind her ear. Mia's loss flooded out in silent, relentless sobs. Addie blinked away her own tears.

Words died in her mouth, fleeing her brain. Nothing she said would be enough. When Addie's brother was killed, people tossed soft phrases around as if the words could've brought Beckett back or stopped the pain from consuming her world. Words never helped. She climbed up on the thin bed and curled around Mia, ignoring the twinges as her friend gripped her hand so tightly her bones ground against tendons.

Exhaustion dragged at her eyelids and her body sank into the hard mattress. Her eyes flew open when Mia spoke.

"They took him, Addie. They took him, and I couldn't stop them. I couldn't help my little boy. He screamed. So loudly. My hands held on so tight. But they slipped. The monsters flew off with him." A broken shell emptied of tears, her lifeless voice whispered from a face too drawn and blank. "I don't know what to do. Tell me what to do."

Addie's arms tightened around her shaking shoulders. "There is nothing to do but wait. Waiting is the hardest part." She shifted to ease the twinge in her chest. *Not strictly true. Waiting is probably the best part—hope still exists in the uncertainty of waiting.*

Her heart constricted as she thought of Lily's parents, their grief. Then tears sprang to her eyes as she thought of Tamahou. The teenager was a foundling—discovered as an infant outside the compound, next to the Dust-burned bodies of his parents. No family was left to scream when he was taken, no-one grieved for him. She brushed the wetness from her cheek. Not true. He was one of them, even if he never felt like it. Her gut twisted. Tama was more like her than she cared to admit.

"Will you help Matt?" Mia asked. "When he comes back? Do you promise to help my boy if I can't?"

Echoes of the past filtered through the door in Addie's head. *Screams, burning pain, shattered mind.*

She blinked them away, kissing the head of the one person in the compound she considered family. "Always. I will always help him." She would do what she could to help them all. Not that it would make any difference.

❧

THE HOSPITAL DOORS closed behind her. Cold air brush across her heated cheeks. Her shoulders slumped. Face in her palms, her mind tangled in the past. A hand landed on her shoulder and her eyes jerked open.

"You're jumpy, Lark."

She turned to face Ryder. "You're too quiet. Learn to clomp around on those big feet so we can hear you coming and head the other way."

"Nice. Here, thought you might need this."

He held out a thermos, his eyes warm in the harsh light spilling from the doorway, his lips turning up. Her own mouth twisted to stop a smile peeping out. She unscrewed the lid, releasing the rich scent of nutty tea into the night air. Lush, warming aromas dove straight into her mind, tugging out memories of her mother and a cosy kitchen. But her mother's warm drinks had never been made from scrabbled weeds and herbs and nuts saved from a blanket of Dust.

Her eyes prickled. She glanced up at Ryder. "Thanks."

"You're welcome. How is she?"

She poured the tea into the faded thermos lid then took a cautious sip. Hot. Not scalding. Perfect.

"Mia's how you might expect her to be. She'll be better tomorrow when she starts waiting for him to come back. She'll be lying to herself, imagining him being the one child in a million who's brought back scared but unharmed."

Ryder frowned. "Bit harsh, Lark."

"It's the truth. Let her have her hope. It will be gone soon enough."

She sipped and focused on the warm liquid rolling around her mouth, trying not to remember the terror on her brother's little face as he screamed out for her seventeen years ago. As she ran and ran and couldn't reach him. As Fae magic took him from her. She swallowed, wishing the warmth could wash away the pain.

Ryder sighed and reached out to rub her arm. Her skin tingled where he touched it, and she held her breath.

"We all have demons, Lark. Don't let them win."

Her gaze darted to his face, strong and reserved. Mia had told her a little about his past, but he never said anything about it.

He smiled, taking a step backwards. "I hope the tea helps you sleep."

Ryder walked away, his long strides purposeful as he began

his nightly patrol. Funny how everyone wanted her to sleep. She drank the rest of the tea and screwed the cap back on the thermos.

Ryder waiting to check on me, giving me tea, telling Doc to back off on the medical checks. Odd.

She kicked at the dirt. Ryder probably still saw her as a fifteen-year-old girl, stumbling in from the Dust. Anything else was another foolish hope she should've squashed years ago.

Only tea. That's all it is.

In her mind, his eyes danced. She cradled the warm thermos to her chest as she walked back to her unit.

CHAPTER 3

Sirens blared, cutting through the quiet afternoon air and echoing around her small room. Addie's hand froze in the middle of pointing at the metal casing now falling from Jasper's grasp. Prickles burned along her scars, driving their way into her tightening stomach. A flash of sorrow flickered on Jasper's face. His head cocked, and his hands shot up.

"They come, they come, they buzz and they hum, and they leave all broken behind them."

She picked the casing up from the floor, smoothing the wires dangling from it, letting her pulse slow. Thirteen days. They'd come back a day early. Her fingers pressed into the rough metal. She shut her eyes for a moment. "I guess we better go out then."

Her gaze went to the hospital as she trudged towards the crater, heavy lead filling her veins. *Mia should be here.* She shook off the thought, guilt knotting in her gut. Last time Addie saw her, Mia had been laying semi-catatonic, refusing food.

Grey clouds roiled in a darkening sky. Memory flared to life. *Screaming. Loss. Alone.* Stones slipped underfoot as her vision blurred with unwanted images of her mother's fear-stricken face staring as Addie rose higher and higher into the air, carried away in a vice like grip. She stumbled, righted herself, and stretched back aching shoulders, her fingers curling into her palms. *I'll be there for Matt, in whatever shape he comes back.*

A small group converged on the impact crater, quiet and shuffling, staring at the sky. She slipped around silent people, eyes fixed on the ground, trying to still the ragged breaths pulling at her chest. The burly back of Paolo the bartender filled her vision like a shield, and she stopped directly behind him.

The air thickened. Dry and brittle crackles of energy flickered through a growing blue glow. Ryder strode to the head of the crowd. People made way for him, settling as he passed, his very presence a reassurance. Broad shoulders strained at his shirt when he crossed his arms. His head lifted to face the heavens from which no angel would come. Coldness seeped into her heart. *Even Ryder knows he can't help them.*

As if her eyes drilling into his back tugged him around, he turned and motioned her to him, brows lowered over eyes glinting in the blue light. Heat rushed to her cheeks. Breath hitched in her throat. Paolo stepped aside, and she shoved her hands into her pockets as she brushed past him to take a place at Ryder's side, where a lieutenant might stand. Anahera smiled, and no-one else blinked an eye. *Since when did I become a second in command?* She caught Ryder's sideways glance and straightened, leaving her hands clenched in her pockets.

The shimmering blue light disappeared, melting into Dust. Her heart beat a warning against her ribs as the Faery appeared, its billowing orange gown and silver wings filling the sky. Her fingers trembled, clutching at the rough wool of her scarf to cover the bottom half of her face. *Surely the Fae won't sense anything. So many years have passed.*

The Faery floated down into the silence. It hovered above the ground, wings beating in a pearlescent shimmer. Coiled blonde hair struck Addie as out of place, something belonging to a figure skater, not a creature of nightmares. Its shifting ocean eyes raked the courtyard, lingering on faces. She shut her eyes. Turned her head as its gaze drifted over her. The Fae spoke, and its voice ripped straight into her mind, a harsh melody exposing old wounds. Her stomach flipped. Bile rose in her throat. Eyes flashing open, she stared at the ground, pushing the sound out of her head.

"The Taken will be returned. A Testing will be carried out in one moon cycle. All must attend."

The Fae didn't wait for a reply, spreading gauzy wings and drifting into the sky. Long orange drapery floated lazily like flames in the Dust. Its arms spread out until they were level with the silver wings at its back, and three bodies appeared out of nowhere.

And so it begins again.

Blue light twisted through dark clouds, and the Fae vanished. The bodies thudded onto the ground, sending eddies of Dust bursting into the air. Ryder stalked past her, jerking his head for her to follow him into the impact crater. She clenched shaking hands. Willed her feet to move. *Just a bit of earth. No danger. No Faery. Just a bit of earth.*

Ryder went for the two in front. She strode past him to kneel by the smallest form, curled on the dead earth. Images of her brother's torn body played in her mind, and she blinked away tears. She reached out to brush off the silvery webbing shrouding Matt, and her eyebrows drew close as her hand trembled.

Teeth pressed together, she tore the sticky strands off with harsh strokes to expose his small, white face. His pulse beat strongly in his neck. A deep, shuddering breath shook her. She wouldn't have to tell Mia her son was dead. Yet.

"Tama and Lily are alive." Ryder said, "Matt?"

Her throat swelled, and she nodded, not trusting her voice.

Ryder turned away, gesturing to Doc and Paolo to bring the stretchers.

She brushed a lock of hair off Matt's face. *Maybe this time will be different.*

Ryder's voice rumbled through her thoughts. "He's awake!"

She froze, staring at Ryder. "He can't be."

"He is. Doc! Tama's awake!"

Ryder put a hand under Tama's shoulder and helped him sit up. The teen's eyes blinked rapidly. Silver webbing clung to his brown skin like cobweb. His expression crumpled as if he was about to cry. She didn't blame him. Her stomach churned, and breath rattled in her tight chest. Burning pain tracked down silvery scars. Doc ran towards them, Paolo struggling with one stretcher over his shoulder and shouting for someone to bring the other.

She dragged her gaze away and slid her arms under Matt's small body. Pushing to her feet, shaking off hands that tried to help, she carried him out of the impact circle.

⁂

Cool evening air wafted in through the open door of Addie's quarters, sending shivers up the back of her neck. She hunched her shoulders and curled her hands around the mug, breathing in the steam. Peace didn't come when you chased it, and the tea was just tea tonight. She shuddered, and ran her fingers over the cool ridges of her charm necklace, her mind wandering. Mia's screams rang in her ears, remembered pain sitting in the back of her mind. She bit the inside of her cheek and tried to let the physical pain drive away the anguish echoing in her head. *Each step towards the ward as heavy as a death march, the small body limp in her arms.* Her fingers tightened on the cup, and her lips pulled down. She swigged a mouthful of tepid liquid. *Mia running towards her until her knees buckled and she crumpled to the floor, wailing.* She shoved the mug across the table. Resting her head on twisted hands, she forced breath into her chest—so tight every pulse of her heart pushed against her skin. The cool metal of the necklace wound around her fingers, and she tried to change the pictures in her head.

The sound of rushing footsteps brought her eyes up. Paolo's wife, Eva, burst through the door, her treasured pearls swinging over her buttoned cardigan, and blurted out, "They've gone wild, you got to come. They're trashing the place."

She frowned, tucking her charms back under her shirt. "Who is? Have you called Ryder?"

"He's the one who sent for you. The kids in the ward are out of control."

The chair fell over as she leaped up and out the door, sprinting to the medical unit. Her heart raced in time with her thoughts. *No. No. No. Not again.* A scream pierced the air, guttural, like a wounded animal. She skidded around the corner, crashing into a group of people gathering outside. Clutching at a strong arm to restore her balance, she glanced up at one of the gate guards, Craig, his skin pallid white around fixed eyes and tight lines radiating from his mouth. Her heart sank. Who was she trying to fool? Of course it was happening again. All of it.

"Go home," she said. Her voice grated harshly from a raw throat. "You'll only make it harder. Go away."

She pushed herself off Craig. Stumbling backwards, she glared at the gathered people, daring them to stay. When her back touched the door to the hospital, she fumbled at the handle, turned, and walked into chaos.

Plexiglass cordoned the ward from the main hallway. On the other side of the wall overturned monitors lay in shattered heaps. Eleven-year-old Matt swung an IV-line stand, sweeping neat packets of bandages and medicines to the ground. The glass shuddered as a blood pressure machine rebounded. Lily reached down to grab another missile. Their raw, guttural cries didn't belong in such young bodies.

She dragged her gaze away, pushing back on a door in her mind.

Xiyu Chang shouted at Ryder, her voice rising in panic, demanding he let her through or do something to help her daughter. Mia stared through the glass at the children, her eyes wide and her medical nightgown open at the back. Addie walked over to her and tied up the drawstrings. *For heaven's sake, could no-one think of the woman's dignity?*

Xiyu hit Ryder in the chest, and he thrust her at Anahera. "Make her calm down or send her out."

Addie stroked Mia's shoulder and turned to face Ryder as he stalked over to her.

"The kids have been like this for about ten minutes," he said, his voice tight and eyes shadowed. "Ana couldn't calm them down. I thought they were going to turn on her, so I pulled her out. Any ideas?"

She frowned, chewing on her lip, fingers tugging at the bottom of her sleeve. "Where's Tama?"

"Over there"

She followed his gesture. The teen sat hunched up in the corner, his arms around his head and his knees drawn tight to his chest, rocking. *Alone.* She blinked, a burning weight settling in her heart. *No one cried for him.* Rubbing at her arm, she stared back at the tormented children on the other side of the wall.

She'd have to go in.

She didn't want to.

Addie glanced at Ryder. He seemed to think she'd know what to do. Foolish as it might be, she didn't want to disappoint him. Mia shuddered and began to cry, little whimpers hiding the depth of her pain.

Tucking hair behind her ears, Addie nodded.

"I don't know if it will work, but I'll see if I can calm them down. Perhaps they just need a different face."

He shrugged and waved her towards the door. "Give it a go. If you think they're going to turn on you, signal. Then we'll have to sedate them, no matter how much their parents hate the idea."

She understood why. Having your child awake, even if they were screaming and out of control, seemed better than a coma shrouding them with deathly stillness.

Unless you knew why they were screaming.

Her eyes darted to Tama again. His lanky frame shuddered, and her fingers curled into her palms. *Nothing I can do now.* Somewhere deep inside her head, a twelve-year-old girl cried with him.

Ryder held the door handle. "Ready?"

"Go."

She slipped through, and the door clicked shut behind her, the snap of the lock drowned by the crash of metal instruments hitting the floor and the children's screams. Worse were the expressions on Matt and Lily's faces—fear, not rage, contorted their features and drove them to destroy the things their sore and violated brains saw as threats. She knew that feeling.

She paused for a moment before walking into the centre of the room, away from the machines and medical tools, her hands spread in front of her. Lily whirled on her then stopped, panting. Confusion creased her forehead under her straight black fringe.

"It's okay. It's just me. You know me. I'm Addie. I won't hurt you. No-one is going to hurt you here. You are safe."

She didn't tell them to stop. No-one liked being told what to do.

Lily glanced at Matt, who stilled and faced Addie with a screwed up, hurt look on his pale face. Interesting, they seemed to be working together.

"Matt, you know I would never hurt you."

His face puckered. "You didn't stop them. You let them take us. You all let them take us."

The ache in her heart wasn't just for them. The past

swirled in her thoughts. *Lost. Alone. Abandoned.* The scars on her arms prickled fiercely, and she flexed her fingers. "I know. It was wrong. It's always wrong. But you are here now, and I will help you. If I can."

"How?" Lily's young voice rasped. "How can you help us?"

She shook her head. "Honestly, I don't have a clue. I can do it more easily, though, if you're not tearing the place up."

The children gazed, as if for the first time, at the chaos surrounding them. Lily bit her lip. "Will Doctor Rongoa be very cross with us?"

She shook her head. "No. She doesn't know what's upsetting you, but she doesn't blame you. None of us do."

Maybe she should use softer words, endearments, maybe move to hug them, but she lost that part of her long ago in the deadlands. She could only go with what she knew. Her blunt words and still figure appeared to be working. The red light in their eyes faded, dying away as fear dulled to anxiety.

She risked moving a step forward, her hands lowering. "Come on, let's get you out of here."

They shuffled to meet her. Then, in tandem, their eyes rolled back in their heads and they dropped to the floor, like puppets whose strings had been cut. She threw herself down next to them, feeling their pulses flutter.

Anahera rushed through the door. She checked their pupils and sat back on her heels, shaking her head. "I can't tell until I've done more tests, but I'd say both of them have slipped back into their comas."

Xiyu screamed, her wails punching the air. Addie wondered who held Xiyu back as Ryder came to a stop behind her.

"Lark, what happened? What did they say?"

She pushed herself to her feet, exhaustion dragging her muscles downwards. She met Ryder's eyes briefly. The skin around his lids pulled tight, and his irises darkened to a murky green. Her gaze drifted around the room. Anahera and her assistant lifted the children to the remaining upright bed. Xiyu sobbed and pushed against Paolo's steady arms while Mia leaned on the glass, silent and still. Tama stood in the doorway. The shadows in his eyes and the firm set of his jaw made her breath catch. *Like looking in a mirror.*

She rubbed her face and let out a sigh as her hands found her hips. "They said we didn't stop them being taken. That we let the Fae do it. They're right. It's wrong, and we allowed it to happen. They're traumatised. In pain. Can you blame them for releasing it?"

"Pain? Did they say they're hurting?" asked Anahera.

She shook her head and kept her eyes on Ryder. "No. But anyone can see they are. We didn't stop the monsters from tearing them away. They were as good as dead the moment they were taken away. And we let the Fae do it."

Ryder's jaw tightened, but he didn't look away. She finally let her hands fall to her sides and walked out, ignoring him as he reached out for her.

It would all happen again, and there was nothing she could do to stop it.

CHAPTER 4

It was no surprise Paolo's bar was so full tonight. Sometimes deadening your emotions was the only way to carry on, and if that came at the bottom of a bottle of fermented roots, well no-one here judged. Leaning against the wall, Addie took another sip of her drink. Warmth from the bite of smoke seeped into blood chilled by screams and hospital rooms, pushing back dark thoughts struggling to escape. The sip turned into a slug, and she grimaced.

Voices and music cloaked her in a welcome cocoon. Humans might have lost everything when the Fae came, but god damn if they didn't find ways to make instruments and art and fight the grey desolation with their vision.

The band played Mia's favourite song. Her hand gripped tighter on her glass. Not that anyone else knew it was Mia's favourite. Music pulled out happy memories of Mia belting out old classics in her house, dancing around with Matt. A small smile tugged at her lips even as her eyes prickled. *Odd, being here without Mia.* She took another swig.

Kira and her new girlfriend waved at Addie as they walked past to the pool table. The engineer might not be exactly a friend, but she was more of a friend than most. And her warmth encompassed everyone in a fuzzy blanket. Addie swirled the empty tumbler and tore her eyes from Kira's happy face. Not good to get too close to people. Except for Mia. It never ended well. A sigh escaped her, and she shut her eyes.

When she opened them it was to a fresh glass of the house smoke appearing under her nose. Paolo waggled his eyebrows as he explained Keegan paid for it. Heat flashed into her cheeks at the thought of her old boyfriend buying her drinks, and she passed Paolo her empty tumbler. She fixed her gaze on his twinkly eyes and steadfastly avoided glancing at the men clustered around the bar.

Chill air cut through the muggy room as Ryder strode through the door. All eyes turned to him, and she ignored the urge to stare as the grim set of his face relaxed into an easy smile. Muted greetings, strong handshakes, and offered drinks slowed his progress through the room. *Damn. He's coming over here, bringing more questions I can't answer.* She took a swig. *No point walking away, stubborn bastard will just follow.*

He stopped in front of her, the faint scent of soap mixing with the smell of alcohol. Her bottom lip pulled through her teeth before she masked it with another swig. Copper strands in his hair glinted in the warm light and broad shoulders in a dingy white shirt filled her vision. She craned her neck to look up at him, fighting against an unwelcome sensation of small-ness. A muscle shifted in his jaw, and lines creased around his shadowed eyes. She leaned back and looked out the window, away from the fixed gaze boring into her.

"We need to talk." His voice rumbled, and her heart sped up.

"You are talking."

"Really? Come on Lark, what's going on? Why do I get the feeling you know something about what's happening?"

She clenched her teeth. Too many answers to choose from and none she wanted to tell him. The window opened onto a grimy courtyard where Paolo kept the bins, not a pleasant vista but better than meeting Ryder's eyes as he loomed over her. His arm came up, blocking her view as he leaned on the wall behind her, hemming her in. She sipped again, swirling the bitter smoke round her mouth before letting the fiery liquid slide down her throat. Despite the once white shirt stained grey with Dust, Ryder and his lean and muscled arm right in front of her face was a big improvement over the courtyard. She let her eyes drift over his tanned forearm, a dragon tattoo just visible before slipping under a rolled cuff. Her fingers tightened around the cold glass. *I could keep this up all evening.* A sigh escaped him, breath grazing her hair.

"Fine, have it your way," he huffed, and pushed himself off the wall. "You should get it into your head, I'm not trying to make trouble for you." He crossed his arms, and the cold rigidity of his expression twisted her insides. She rolled her shoulders and sank against the wall. This was ridiculous. She was an adult. But she slouched like a sullen teenager anyway.

"The thing is, Lark," his voice was quiet now, gentle, and she bit her lip. "This isn't about you. It's about Tama, Matt, Lily."

She tried, but she couldn't stop the twitch at the corner of her eye. She knew he saw it when his frown cleared and he smiled. *Bastard.*

It's a hell of a thing, having a conscience.

Refusing to meet his eyes, she turned her head away. Her forehead crinkled. Keegan was strutting toward them, the twinkle in his eye not as charming now at twenty-seven as it had been at twenty. She looked back to Ryder, her eyes fixed on his collar, willing Keegan to go away.

"I'm not talking to you here," she said.

"Fine. We take the discussion upstairs."

Upstairs. To his rooms. She flicked a frown at him, supremely conscious of Keegan standing right behind him, and Ryder grinned. "Don't worry Lark, no-one's going to think anything of it." He winked. "They'd be too scared to."

He walked past her towards the door, scooping a bottle off the table. Keegan hovered, eyes darting between the two of them. Lark shrugged and trailed past him, her mouth twisting and her cheeks flaming as his face fell. Ryder paused at the bottom of the staircase to let her catch up, staring at Keegan until the younger man turned away. Her stomach flipped.

He leaned on the doorframe, knocking off more of the peeling paint. As she reached him, he asked softly, "Or are you the one who's scared?"

She scowled at his raised brows and stepped heavily on his foot as she walked past him up the stairs.

Dim lighting pooled around the door at the end of the narrow hallway, and she paused until Ryder ran up the last couple of steps. A worn carpet runner swallowed the sound of her boots. Her pulse rushed in her ears, muting the music filtering through the floorboards. The handle slipped under her fingers. She pressed her lips together and shouldered her way through the door. Pale blue paint covering a scruffy concrete floor reminded her of the old school room, just with cosier furnishings.

She sat on a chair, turning it away from the low metal bed under the window. Ryder's lips twitched. He spun the other chair and sat with his arms resting across the top, smoke bottle sticking out to the side.

"So, shoot," he said. "What's the deal? What do you know that you don't want to tell me?"

She stretched out her legs, flexing her feet in her boots. "I know lots that you don't, Ryder. Want to narrow it down?"

"No games, Lark. Tell me about the kids."

She leaned back, hearing her spine pop against the back of the chair. Sitting up with a sigh, she lifted her gaze back to Ryder, his eyes glinting gold. "It isn't how it normally is. You know that yourself. They come back, they lie in a coma for a week, two tops, and then they die. This, the whole waking up screaming and trying to trash the place thing, that doesn't happen." Muscles in her back tensed, cords of remembered pain shooting up into her neck. She blinked away the images crowding her head. "Tama, awake, talking, walking around. None of this is what happens when the Taken are returned."

"That much I know. Now tell me why you're watching Tama like a hawk but not speaking to him. Why they calmed down when you went in, and why, when you went back just now, you placed charms of some sort around Matt and Lily."

She sat up straight, pulling her legs in, glancing at him under lowered brows. "You notice a lot, Ryder."

"It's my job. Now spill."

She pressed her lips together and tried to swallow, her mouth dry. Her nails scratched over the glass. The smoke would help, but she didn't want to look weak. She tried to keep her face still and pushed the words through parched lips.

"Since you notice so much, you might have picked up I didn't say it never happens. That it hasn't happened before."

His expression didn't change. But his arm tensed on the back of the chair, and his fingers tightened around the bottle. "You've seen this before?"

"When I was younger. Part of a different community. Didn't end well." Maybe she did need the smoke. She gulped down another shot, relishing the burn that pushed the lump in her throat away.

"How did it end?"

"The Testing. You haven't seen a successful one, have you? Because you've never seen them returned like this. The Fae will come, they'll test the kids, they'll take them again, and then they'll check everybody else."

His eyes widened. "Everybody? Old folks too?"

Jasper flashed into her mind, and her heart sank. "Everybody."

His brows drew together, and she glanced away, watching

his hands as he rolled the bottle between them. "The Testing didn't seem so bad when it happened before. I mean, sure the whole thing's invasive and creepy, but it's over fast. And no-one seems to be hurt."

"Because the people they're testing are either in a coma or as good as. When they're awake, when they find what they're looking for, that's a different story."

His eyes locked on hers.

"And what is it that they're looking for?"

She took another swig, realised only the last dregs remained, and frowned at the glass. "Haven't you ever wondered, Ryder, what they want with us? Why they bother with the Takings and the Testings? We live like rats in a hole surrounded by cats. They brought Dust to the whole world. Why would they even let us remain? They need something from us. That's what they're looking for."

"I'm gonna ask again. What is that?"

She glanced up from under her eyelashes. "You're so sure I know. Why is that?"

"Because you're a well of secrets, Lark. You're the only one who's seen a successful testing, the only one who's seen the Taken like this, and you're the only one who can spend all day in the Dust and be fine."

Always the different one. She sighed, frowning at her empty glass.

"I don't know what they want with us. All I know is that we're in danger if they ever find what they're looking for." *Truth. Of a sort.*

He pushed off the chair, twisting the rickety frame round to where it was before. Her scalp prickled under the weight of his gaze.

"I wish you trusted me, Lark. You can't see it, can you? No one here cares if you're different, if you have secrets. You're one of us. I hope you don't forget that."

She stood more slowly, ignoring the hand he put out to

help her to her feet. She hadn't had that much to drink. "I won't forget. You asked me to trust you, and I do."

He quirked his brows at her, and she bit her lip. "I do, Ryder, really. I need you to trust me too. If I can help these kids, I will. Whatever it takes. But I don't know anything that will help."

Burning pain, soft wings, a white room. Blinking the visions away, she shrugged. "I'll tell you if I think of anything. I'm going to bed now."

He grabbed her arm as she walked past him, sliding his hand down to hold hers firmly. Butterflies took off in her stomach. She clenched her jaw and kept her face still.

His expression softened, and his eyes flickered warmly in the yellow light of his room. "I don't know what you went through before you came to us, Lark. I've never asked, and I won't now—that's your story to tell when you want to." She turned away from his eyes, and her glance fell on his large hand wrapped around hers. His thumb stroked over her wrist, and she hoped he didn't feel her pulse jump.

"I meant what I said. You belong here. You don't have to fight all your battles alone."

The fierce light in his eyes sent warm tingles down her spine, but a cold chill in her heart quenched them. *He doesn't know what I have to do. He can't.*

She disentangled her wrist and stood back, her hand going awkwardly to her opposite elbow. "Thanks. If I have a battle, I'll call you. 0800-Dial-a-warrior."

He smiled a little wryly and stepped back as well. "Never doubt. You call, and I'll answer. Goodnight, Lark."

Ignoring the impulse to move towards him, she nodded and headed back to the stairs. "Goodnight, glorious leader."

CHAPTER 5

Silence filled the ward, broken only by the beeps and whirrs of the machines monitoring the children. Each IV-line and plaster on their little bodies cried a reproach. Leaning back as she sat on the floor, metal cabinet cold against her shirt, Addie let the darkness of the room envelop her. She didn't mind the hospital so much when it was dark. With no bright lights reflecting off white walls, the echo of pain quieted, becoming easier to ignore. She shook her hair back and focused on now. If Matt and Lily woke while she was here, she might be able to calm them better than Anahera or any of the interns.

Drawing her legs up to her chest, she wrapped her arms around her knees. Her head rested back on the cabinet, eyes never leaving the boy lying so frail and small on the large metal bed.

Mia's face flashed through her mind. *Blank-eyed with grief, her hands clutching Matt's teddy bear, rocking slowly on her sofa as Eva offered her tea.* Leaving Mia tore at her heart, but someone should be here too.

The door creaked open, a sliver of light gleaming off steel legs and the glass of the monitors. Addie glanced over. The tall shape in the shadows wasn't Anahera. Ice wound around her spine at the sight of the unexpected figure, and her feet shifted to find a better grip on the lino floor. She ran her hand down her leg into the top of her boot. The carved bone hilt of the knife Ryder gave her when she was fifteen slipped into her hand with comforting familiarity.

The shadow in the doorway stumbled into the room. Her hand jolted off the knife. *What is Tama doing in here?* He moved past her in the darkness, and she stayed motionless, her heart racing as he crept closer to the two younger children. He stood at the foot of Lily's bed, shoulders shaking and hands fidgeting. His lips pressed together, and his eyes glinted in the glow from the monitors. Deep lines of pain etched his cheeks. Her heart rate slowed as a cold ache filled her chest. She wore that expression in her nightmares. Opening her mouth to talk to him, she caught her breath as words tumbled shaking from his lips.

"I'm sorry. I'm so sorry. I didn't want them to hurt you. I'll do it now. I promised you, and I will. I'll do it. I'll find what he wants and take it to him in the Valley of the Kings. I'll get it, and then no-one will hurt you anymore." He patted clumsily at Lily's blanket-covered foot, his black hair flopping over his face. "I'm so sorry, but I'll make sure you'll be okay."

Tama wheeled around and strode out, shoulders back like a burden had lifted. She curled her legs under and wound herself to her feet. *What in the world was that about?* Her gaze went to the two children, and her brows drew together. The monitors. The lights and beeps had changed. She lunged over the bench and slammed her hand on the buzzer.

Doc rushed in, pulling her sweater over her head and getting an arm stuck in her haste. Addie pocketed the item Tama had tucked by Lily's feet, leaving no evidence of his visit.

Anahera glared at the machines and pulled out her bag of instruments, checking the children thoroughly. Her stomach roiling, Addie focused on the floor, counting lino dots again. Silence spun around her, humming with expectation. Footsteps broke into her thoughts. She raised her eyes to Doc's and shrugged.

"This is impossible." Anahera said, her voice rough and rasping.

Her fingers curled into her palms. "It happened, therefore it's possible."

"Don't be annoying Adelia, you know what I mean. Catatonic children don't suddenly regain normal brain patterns and functioning for no reason. What happened?"

"I don't know. I saw the monitors change, so I buzzed you. I have no idea what made this happen." All true, but so much unsaid. Lying to Doc sent flickers of guilt waving through her, although to be fair, she didn't know what caused the change. She fingered the small pounamu pendant in her pocket. *Tama never takes it off. Why would he leave it?*

"Shall I fetch Ryder?" She needed to leave. Find Tama.

Anahera frowned at her then down at the beds.

"No. Let's leave him be. He always finds it hard when children are hurting, and there's not a lot we can tell him now. It would be adding another burden when he has too many of those already."

Addie couldn't meet Doc's eyes. She didn't want to burden Ryder. She also didn't want him noticing too much. Nothing could be explained anyway until she spoke to Tama.

"Okay, you know best, Doc. I'll head home, see if I can grab some sleep."

Doc eyed her but let her go. Addie was at the door when a cry rang out. Racing out of the ward, she struggled into her jacket, pushing through the swinging door into a chilled evening breeze. Lights reflected off Dust clouds by the west gate, illuminating the path, and she trotted over. Ryder's tall figure was a silhouette by the gate. The smaller shadow by him had to be Tama.

She slowed as she approached them. Ryder's voice had a stern deepness to it, dredging up remembered teenage misdemeanours. Without meaning to, she straightened her shoulders before she scowled and slouched deliberately.

The tone didn't appear to work on Tama. Clearly torn between his desire to listen to a man he idolised, and the intensity driving him, he shuffled from foot to foot, and his arms waved wildly.

"You don't understand! This is important. I have to go."

Ryder's tall frame blocked the way to the gate, and his sheer presence acted as an even greater obstacle.

"No."

Her mouth twisted. The flat implacability of the word squashed Tama where an argument wouldn't have.

"No-one goes out in the Dust. End of story. You need to turn your arse back around and go to bed."

"Addie does. She goes out in the Dust all the time. And you let her." He didn't sound sulky. Just resigned. Ryder met her gaze over Tama's shoulder, and she shrugged. She didn't try to be a bad role model. She simply forgot. His eyes, more grim than usual, slid past her as Doc ran up panting.

"Anahera," he said, "Good timing. Can you come take Tama? He needs looking after."

Tama turned and shambled past, not meeting her eye. Tightness spread over her chest, and she pulled back a hand that reached for him. The disconsolate look on his face would bring out the nurturer in Anahera. He'd be okay.

She, on the other hand...

Her eyes flicked up to Ryder, who stood with his arms crossed, no smile on his face. They stared at each other for a moment, and she pushed her feet into the ground so she wouldn't shuffle them in the dirt, keeping her chin lifted. In the end, he sighed and turned away to follow up with the guards on gate duty.

Addie cradled her elbow in her hand, lip tucked between her teeth.

"He'll try again." She forced the words out against her better judgement. "He'll keep trying, Ryder." The muscles in his back shifted and tensed at her words, but he didn't turn around. She pushed on. "If he gets out I'll go after him. I'll bring him back. You know I'm the only one who can."

His shoulders moved as if he was about to turn, but he stopped himself. When it was clear he had nothing to say, she shrugged again and wandered back to her room, her mind a turmoil of memory.

CHAPTER 6

Resting her chin on her hands, Addie gazed out over the squat buildings. Grey swirls eddied around spindly trees surrounding the boundary—the Dust fell thicker outside the walls they'd been confined to. In the deadlands, the sun struggled to penetrate the heavy clouds, dropping fine powder in an endless kind of rain.

The boundary trees beyond the compound walls served as a breaker of sorts, and the rising sun leaked through brown branches, weak and pale. She sighed as she remembered tall thin trunks with vibrantly waving tufts, silky sky stark behind them in a blue that turned purple at the end of day. Dust fell in heavy clumps at the edge of the broken trees, and she squinched her eyes shut, trying to hang on to the trees and sky of her past.

Soft boot steps scuffed the ground behind her, and she opened her eyes with a grimace. A happy place wasn't a happy place once it got invaded.

Ryder dropped down next to her. She huffed as she slid away from under his elbow. He grinned at her, wide mouth and big teeth flashing.

"So, this is where the Lark goes to hide? A ledge of a

broken window overlooking the compound. Like a starling's nest." He nudged her as if she hadn't already got his stupid joke. "Wrong bird, Lark."

She shuffled aside again but stopped when he smirked.

"What do you want, Ryder?"

He rubbed the stubble on his chin, his eyes drifting down to the compound. She stifled a smile. The way he never ceased monitoring, patrolling, protecting, drove her crazy as a teenager, but it always made her feel safe. Now when she saw him doing it, her heart swelled in a way she wished it wouldn't.

"I want you to tell me why I shouldn't stop you going out in the Dust if Tama leaves." His eyes met hers, and she had to fight not to look away.

"Well, that's easy. First, you have no say in what I do. Try stopping me and see where it gets you. Second—I'm right. If Tama goes, I'm the only one who can bring him back." Her heart sped under his steady gaze, and she turned her head away.

He took her chin and tugged her face around, forcing her eyes to meet his. Rough fingers held her in a gentle grip.

"So tell me what happened. Give me a way to help Tama."

She pulled away. "Nothing here can help him. If he goes, he'll either survive on his own, or he won't. If I go after him, we both know he has a better chance."

Ryder's hand dropped, and his eyes shifted to the dead trees on the horizon, a muscle jumping in his jaw. "The Dust is worse outside the boundary. A person can only hack it so long."

She chewed her lip and glanced at him sidelong.

Shouts and laughter wafted up from somewhere below, and he turned back to face her. "Unless that person's you, right, Lark? You never told me how you survived out there. You were too traumatised when you stumbled into our compound, a half-starved skinny little girl with enormous eyes." He leaned back, resting his head on the frame of the window. "And after a while it just seemed unimportant how you survived before you got here and more important how to keep you out of trouble now that you were."

Her fingers ran over the knife in her boot. There had certainly been trouble. "I never thanked you," she said, keeping her eyes focused on the brown trees with their crowns of Dust. "For helping me. I know I wasn't always easy."

He laughed, and she ignored the way her stomach fluttered when he did.

"Understatement. Hellion teen is more accurate I think. You grew up alright though." He leaned over, nudged her shoulder with his, and she bit down on a smile.

"And yet here I am, causing you more trouble."

"Not why I want to stop you."

She risked meeting his eyes. "So why?"

"We're losing Tama, we're most likely going to lose Matt and Lily, you say the Testing could affect us all, and I don't want to lose you too—" he cleared his throat, "to the Dust as well. That isn't how I run things round here."

She reached out to him but stopped, picking up a stick and flicking it away instead. His eyes followed her hand, and she fought the heat in her cheeks. "You can't save everyone, Ryder. I can take care of myself. Let me go after Tama if he gets past the watch you've set. You've got enough on your plate."

He eyed her, his mouth turning up slightly. "I thought you didn't need my permission."

She rolled her eyes. "I don't. I was being polite. If you're going to be annoying about it I won't bother."

"So much for the politeness," he murmured.

"You only get so much, Ryder. There's a quota."

"Clearly." His smile faded. "I know I can't stop you. And you're right, you *are* the one with the best chance at helping Tama." He shifted to lean back on the frame again. "That's the bit I don't like. He's my responsibility. I should be the one to help him."

She looked at him, his strong jaw clenched and his sharp eyes raking over the compound. Like a hawk. But protector rather than predator. Her own jaw softened.

"You can't do it all alone, Ryder. We're a community, or so you say. Communities take care of their own. Let me do what no one else can do. Let me do what no-one else should *have* to do."

His frown carved lines on his forehead she wished she could ease.

"Ryder. If you hadn't saved me when I came here, protected me, taught me, I wouldn't be able to help him now. Let me save Tama when he leaves. It's the same as you doing it."

He raised his brows. "You sound awfully sure he's going to leave."

She sighed and pushed herself off the wall, casting one last glance towards the trees.

"You forget. This isn't the first time."

CHAPTER 7

*A*ddie traced the stuck together casing of the newly repaired mask with a grimy finger. Broken scraps from the old filter lay scattered on the table top in a haphazard puzzle. A secret smile spread over her face—being useful always gave her a warm glow in her chest, especially when it was Ryder she could help.

Leaning back with a sigh, she rubbed a hand over her forehead, her eyes drifting to the open door. Weak sunlight made little patterns in lingering traces of Dust on the porch. The crater, around which the smaller units like hers clustered, dragged at her mind. She focused on the sunlight.

When the sirens sounded, the sensation of stiff wire threading her shoulders disappeared, and she sighed, even as her heart rate sped up. She'd expected Tama to leave long before this, had almost started to doubt he would. The chair scraped the floor as she stood, the noise grating down her nerves. Each step to the door was a step towards a decision she wouldn't regret, but her fingers clenched on clammy palms.

Sparse dirt and stone littered the crater. Ryder stood close to the centre, arms crossed and head cocked, listening to one of the gate guards. Her hand tightened on the door frame, rough metal scratching her fingers. Almost as if he heard the drumming of her heart, his head snapped to the side, and his eyes found her. Breath catching in her throat, she held his gaze. A deep line scored the centre of his brows, but he shrugged and gave her a quick nod before taking the guard by the shoulder, striding towards the admin block.

Her eyes closed, shutting out the crater. She needed to get some things together. Borrow some better binocs. Drop off Ryder's mask. Turning back to her room, her hand went to her pocket where Tama's pendant was nestled. *Okay. Talk to Anahera about the pendant first. Then everything else.*

Doc RAN her fingers over the blunt edges of the greenstone pendant, the dark whorl of black shimmering through the deep green as the light caught it. "You mean you lied to me, Adelia. You told me nothing happened."

She shifted, truth prickling its way up her spine. "Um, yeah I guess. I didn't want Tama to be in trouble. I meant to talk to him, but now he's gone." Her eyes went to the ward beyond them. "Do you know why he would have left this with Lily?"

Shaking her head, Anahera placed the pendant on the bench next to her. "I've never seen him without it. Ever since he was old enough not to try and take it off." She leaned back, shoving her hands in her coat pockets, and smiled sadly at Addie. "It must have been from his parents, or at least someone who loved him. A precious taonga like this one is usually handed down through families. They would have been gifting him protection, a connection to his whānau, his family. He knows this, we've talked about it." Doc's gaze turned to the ward where the children lay, silent. "Maybe that's why. He wants to protect them."

Addie ran her hand through her hair. "Do we put the pendant back? Or do I take it with me to give to him?"

Her lips pursed, Anahera frowned for a second before straightening abruptly and scooping the pendant off the bench. "We honour his wishes. We leave it with Lily."

ADDIE PULLED ON HER JACKET, slipping into its long heaviness like a second skin. She wound her scarf around her neck, leaving enough fabric to pull over her mouth. The leather clip that tightened the scarf into a makeshift Dust mask slid without friction when she tested it, eased from lingering stiffness by the oil Jasper left out for her. She wiped a finger of residual oil on the scarf, adding to the stains and grime already marking the dull crimson. Her pouches and knife holster hung loosely on her hips. She grimaced as she tightened the belt a notch. *Must remember to eat.*

She picked up her pack, eyes running over the barren little room. The charm necklace tucked inside her shirt lay heavy on her skin. It was the only object she always carried, the only thing fully hers. If she never came back, a new occupant could take her place easily. Her lips twisted. Once they'd cleared out cupboards full of her scavengings, that is. Not a task she envied anyone.

Her gaze fell on the neat package lying forgotten on her bed, and her stomach sank. *Take them or not?* Mia's insistence when she placed them in her hands had sent a flicker of guilt through her. If only the ridiculous goggles didn't obscure her vision more often than they protected her eyes, they might be worth taking. Her finger traced the careful wrapping, and a sigh escaped her. *If I don't take them, she'll find out.* The thought of Mia's crumpled face, hurt piled on hurt, decided her. She picked up the package and shoved it in the bottom of her pack.

Silence hit her as she stepped out into the compound, her door snicking shut at her back. People lined the wide path to the outside gate. She paused, her hand tight on the door handle, chewing her lip. No-one said a thing, but they all met her eyes. *Why have they all come?* Taking a breath, she released the door handle and walked slowly down the pathway, conscious of every step. Towards the front of the line she spied Doc, who smiled at her and mouthed, 'Take care,' as she passed. Metal screeched as the guards dragged open the gate as she came closer.

Ryder strode into the middle of the path, and she stopped. Her eyes flicked over his pack, long coat, and the goggles perched on his wound scarf. A small crossbow dangled from his hip, and a knife holster sat on the other leg. The mask she'd shoved at him in passing hung clipped to his backpack. Her heart stuttered. *Nope. Not happening.*

She stepped closer to him, keeping her voice low. "And what, oh great and glorious leader, do you think you're doing?"

"Coming with you. Not very smart today, are you?"

His eyes glinted fiercely in the morning light, and she lifted her chin. "I don't need you to protect me."

The air grew heavier as he leaned in so he was a hands-width from her face. "What makes you think I'm doing this for you?"

Heat sparked on her cheekbones. "I'm going to be moving fast. Think you can keep up?"

His lips curled, and he quirked an eyebrow. "If I can't, will you leave me behind?"

"Don't be ridiculous. But don't hold me back, either."

He stepped aside and bowed her forward. Hoisting her pack tighter on her shoulders, she walked past him, out the gate. He fell into step beside her, adjusting his longer strides to hers, and she squashed the flickering thought that it was nice to not be going alone. *But alone with Ryder is probably worse than alone by myself.* She darted a glance up at his square jaw and noticed, despite herself, the way the weak morning sun lit up the copper in his hair. *Yes. Worse and, in some ways, more dangerous.*

Tama's trail stretched out before her, easy to see in the dense Dust. Few people came out this far beyond the walls of the compound, and the trek through the shattered city passed quietly. Having Ryder at her side made her see the ruins differently. This had been his home. For her, it had always been scavenge, take, ignore. She bit the inside of her cheek as she snuck a glance up at his face. Shadows haunted his eyes. Grey powder floated by her knees, kicked up by her feet as she stomped a little harder than necessary.

The old column rose out of the Dust ahead of her, and she caught herself looking for useful pieces of debris. They passed the bus she hid under two weeks ago, and she ran her fingers along the beaten sidings, her thoughts with Mia. Glancing to her left, she realised Ryder was no longer behind her. She spun and saw him staring at what appeared to be the remains of a school. The clock tower still stood, although it leaned dangerously, its hands long bent by the weight of the Dust.

Her feet dragged as she walked to stand beside him.

"This was my school."

Her eyes darted to his face, jaw clenched and eyes like stone, before sliding back to the ruined building in front of her. Hard to imagine children ran here, played, laughed. Heavy powder smothered what might have been a basketball court in front of a long wing of shattered windows and broken brick. Ryder took a couple of steps forward and knelt, reaching out a hand to brush Dust off something in front of him.

His voice was steady, but his hand trembled as he pulled up a child's school bag. "I taught these kids. Most of them died in the first attacks. Others died from the Dust."

Oh god. Please don't let him open the bag. He doesn't need to know who it belonged to.

Her hand fluttered out to his shoulder and away. "There wasn't anything you could have done, Ryder. And what you could do, you did."

He placed the bag gently back on the ground, mercifully unopened.

"I know."

Standing, he took a breath and looked at her. Her heart constricted at the tears in his eyes.

"It's just been a long time since I've been this far out." He blinked and walked away. "Come on, we should keep going."

He didn't glance back, but she did. The schoolbag sat there, a silent reminder of what they faced. Wheeling back, she scooped it up, grey powder falling in clumps to the ground.

Frail books filled the once purple bag, the Dust eating away at them. She found a name. Alexa Wong. She shoved a book in her pack, keeping the name close to her as she trotted to catch up to Ryder. Alexa wouldn't be forgotten.

Ryder's eyes were fixed on the path ahead, but as she reached his shoulder, he glanced briefly down at her.

"Thank you, Lark."

She shrugged, pulling the scarf over her face to hide her twisting smile. She hadn't done it for him, but she tucked his words away in the place where she kept everything special.

CHAPTER 8

They wrangled the faded nylon and collapsible wooden poles of the tent up before the worst of the Dust started falling. The pegs ended up hidden beneath a shifting grey blanket on the ground. Ryder pitched the tent with the ease of someone who used to camp every summer, but his eyes scanned the sky frequently. She moved faster, trying to erase the line of concern between his brows.

Two thin bed rolls filled the cramped and narrow space inside the tent. Ryder tugged down the zip. Flickering heat ran over her chest. Alone with him, lying next to him, was not something she'd ever prepared for. The soft light dimmed fast as Dust fell steadily, muffling all sound from outside. *Not that much remained out there to make noise anymore.* Hard blue rubber met her back, lumps and rocks normally flattened by Dust still managed to dig into aching muscles. Her buckles pulled, scraping on the bed roll as she shuffled into a more comfortable spot. Faded light filtered through the nylon, enough to let her see Ryder pull off his jacket and ball it into a pillow. Shutting her eyes resolutely, she let exhaustion take hold. An odd half-dream like state where reality seemed to forget itself slipped over her.

She came to with a violent start, gasping and shaking, her heart racing. Silent darkness pressed down on her. A hand landed on her shoulder, and she bucked. But Ryder's rough voice rumbled through the gloom, and his hand gripped harder.

"Lark, stop. You're okay, there's nothing here, you're safe. It's only me."

Her heart continued to race, but she stopped struggling. Heat rushed to her cheeks. Of all people for this to happen in front of, it had to be Ryder. His hand slid off her, and in the dim light she saw him sit back and stare at her.

"You okay now?"

Shivers ran over her skin, and she pulled her jacket closer around her like armour. "Yes. Thanks." His gaze sat heavy on her, and she found herself trying to explain. "This happens sometimes. I must be tired."

Silence filled the tent, and she wished she could see his eyes. Thoughts of the past clawed at her mind, and she bit her lip. Probably a good thing darkness hid his expression. She turned her face away and lay down. "I'm going back to sleep now."

"'Night." Steady and strong, his voice gave nothing away.

Pressing her lips together, she closed her eyes, the skin on her face pulling taut. Manners won, and she mumbled, 'goodnight,' as she turned her shoulder to him and breathed out. Aching body drum tight, she focused on relaxing each part of her, starting with her toes, slowly slipping into black silence.

This time when she jerked awake, she cried out before biting the sound off, her teeth bruising her lip. Her shoulders hunched. She blinked a tear down her cheek. No way was she going to wipe it off.

A heavy sigh came from the darkness.

"If this is what you're like when you're tired then I vote we take it easier tomorrow. Do you ever just sleep?"

"Sometimes. I don't normally have company." *Damn. That came out wrong.*

Her whole body clenched as he stretched, his arm brushing her back. "I can tell. You're jumpy as a cat."

Rustling sounds filled the tent as he shifted to a more comfortable spot, grunting as he encountered the same rock that had attacked her back earlier. Her heart beat sped up. She hoped he couldn't tell.

His voice rumbled close to her ear, and heat flushed her cheeks. "When my son was about four, he used to have night terrors. No reason why that we could figure—this was before the Fae came. The times when he couldn't sleep for his fears, the only way to calm him was to hold him."

Her body stilled, and her breath stuck in her throat. She'd known he'd lost a son, but he never talked about him.

"Will you let me hold you, Addie?"

Ryder never called her Addie. Not since she was young. She bit her lip. It was only being held. Animals curled up together all the time. Her chest tightened. Likely he still thought of her as a child. Silence filled the tent, heavy with her most secret hopes and threaded with his quiet patience. *Broken buildings. Buried bags. Lost children.* She blinked. Maybe he needed this too. She jerked her head in a nod then realised the darkness might swallow it. "Okay."

Thoughts swirled through her mind—she should say something else, warn him not to get any ideas, but she was half certain she wanted him to have ideas and half terrified that he wouldn't. Most of her didn't want to mess up the comfort being offered.

He didn't seem to mind her brusqueness, simply slid closer, one arm snaking under her neck and the other lying heavily over her waist. The warmth and weight of him was unexpected, and her pulse made a leap for freedom. Moment by moment her heart slowed, her eyes grew heavy, and with a sigh, she let out the anxiety holding her rigid, softening into his arms. The tension passed through him for a second, his arm tightening momentarily over her waist before relaxing.

The Fae came for her as they did every night in her dreams, her skin on fire with remembered pain. But tonight, a solid warmth sheltered her back, strong arms encircled her, and behind her shut eyes the Fae shouted in retreat.

She awoke to dim sunlight, warm breath on her temple, and crushing embarrassment. At some point in the night, she had turned to face Ryder, and now they lay cocooned together, his arms tight around her. Her heart pounded against her ribs. She tried to turn away, but her face ended up pressed against his chest. Ryder shifted. Every muscle in her body tensed. She fought not to leap away, but when she stiffened, he rolled back, prying himself free. The loss of his warmth sent shivers of cold over her skin, even as her face burned.

Ryder's matter of fact demeanour made things easier. He grunted, "morning," at her and got up to get ready, giving her space to gather some dignity around her. When he ducked out of the tent, she let out a shaky sigh, her heartbeat finally slowing down. The scent of him hung in the air. She took a moment to breathe it in, to memorise it, to stow it away with the budding hope that confused her.

Light powdery swirls in a grey sky moved at her feet when she emerged from the tent. A parcel of dried nuts and chewy roots nearly hit her in the head. She dodged and snatched it out of the air. "Eat something," Ryder said, voice thick around his own breakfast. "I'll sort out the tent." Ignoring the heat flushing her cheeks, she diligently chomped down a handful of the nuts and tried not to stare at the muscles in his back as he pulled the pegs out of the ground.

Fresh Dust fall covered Tama's tracks with a film of grey. Her gaze drifted over the dead ground fading off into a dull sky. Ryder joined her, pack on his back and holding hers out to her, his eyebrows raised. When she set off, he didn't question how she knew which way to go. Her stomach clenched, and she pulled the scarf higher over her face. Trudging through the sparse scrubby landscape, she thought of how the path pulled her, the same unfamiliar mental tug that guided her as a child in the deadlands. Not something she could explain to Ryder, even if she wanted to. Tama had been here, though, and she simply followed the path her gut told her to.

The fine grains falling from the sky drifted lightly in whorls that mostly dissipated by the time they reached the air above where they walked. *Thank god, the Dust isn't as heavy as yesterday.* Ryder walked behind her, and the thought of him covered in a slow, burning grey film sent ice flooding her veins. The path ended at the bottom of a slope which was covered in scree-like stones and little else. She sighed. *Why did he have to take the hard route?* She paused at the bottom of the slope. Ryder cast a glance upwards then quirked a brow at her.

"Really?"

"'Fraid so. Don't blame me, blame Tama."

Under his dubious gaze, she settled her pack more firmly on her back and plodded up the slope. She angled her feet like a duck's to stop sliding down the ground which slid and skittered with every step.

They were nearing the top when a jagged line spiked down her core. All her senses snapped, pulling tight for the space of a heartbeat. She threw herself forward on the scree, grabbing at Ryder's arm, trying to drag him down. The man was like rock and just as immovable.

"Down!' She hissed. He crouched down and eyed her.

"I don't see anything."

"You won't see anything. That's the point. Get down!"

He raised his eyebrows and grimaced but lay down next to her, pulling his crossbow up to his shoulders.

"Going to tell me what's going on?" he asked.

"Fae tracker. They'll be looking for Tama, but they prey on anyone out in the dead lands."

"Tracker."

She nodded and pulled her scarf over her mouth. This close to the Dust covered earth, it was hard to not breathe in the fine grains. She jerked her head forward and began moving up the slope at a slow crawl. Ryder grunted behind her, but he kept up. He could be as sceptical as he liked, so long as he didn't make them into a target. He might believe her if she told him why she knew the Faery was there, but that was never going to happen. He'd never trust her again.

The scree slope was hard going. Sweat beaded on her back from the effort. Pebbles shifted under her fingers, her knees causing mini landslides with each inch forwards. Ryder's breath was ragged behind her.

At the top of the slope, she held her hand out behind her. He moved up to join her and stopped, panting harshly. "If you made me do that for no reason, Lark, I swear to god I'll skin you."

She frowned at him and directed his eyes with a jerk of her head. The slope ended in a small plateau. Dead skeletons of trees stood in a semicircle that tugged at a half-forgotten memory. Dust smothered the ground, a dense grey blanket, undisturbed for a very long time.

"A picnic spot." Ryder said. "The view must have been great once."

She turned her head to him then looked back to the plateau. He was right. That was what the clearing reminded her of. Instead of dead greyness, her mind showed her a little blue hatchback parked under a dark green tree. Her brother running, chasing the pigeons, and sparrows trying to steal their chips. Her mother laughing behind a camera, recording their trip. She blinked. Somewhere under that Dust would be the remains of picnic tables, choked and destroyed just like the happy picnic of her past.

Her eyes caught darkness shifting amongst the grey. Her heart raced, and her fingers itched to grab her knife.

"Can you see it?" She kept her voice quiet and barely breathed.

"See what?"

"Look towards the last tree on the right. Find the spot where your eyes want to slide past, then keep staring at it."

The moment Ryder saw the tracker, he went completely still beside her. Her own body lay rigid against the scree. Pulse racing. Lungs screaming for deep breaths.

Long draping black clung to the Faery's form. Silky silver wings shimmered behind it. Feathery strands swirled around its head like a halo in the windless air. Addie's stomach turned over, and she inched her hand down to grip her knife.

The Tracker stood motionless at the edge of the trees. Listening. Its head darted to the side, gaze passing over where they lay. Addie tried to control her racing heart. Tension radiated from Ryder. Her hand tightened on the hilt of her blade. Silver wings spread. The Dust at the Faery's feet swirled as the tracker rose steadily into the air, wheeling around to head out over the deadlands to the east.

She closed her eyes to the Fae's beauty, hating the yearning still pulling at her heart, her arms burning in remembered pain.

Working into a sitting position, she tugged down her scarf, gulping breaths catching in her throat.

Ryder sat up more slowly, his eyes thoughtful as they rested on her.

"I'm going to go ahead and assume that isn't the first one of those you've seen."

She shook her head, dragging her water bottle from the pack. The purifier wasn't looking good, but it would still work. She swooshed the canteen through the air, trying to make enough for a decent sip.

"You spend much time in the deadlands, you're bound to run across a tracker at least once. If you're lucky, they don't run across you."

"Just how long were you in the deadlands before you arrived on our doorstep, Lark? You never said."

She unscrewed the lid and drank down the small amount of water she'd managed to catch. It was silty on her tongue, but it wet her dry throat. She didn't want to change the purifier yet—there was a long way to go. Unable to put it off anymore, she turned her eyes to Ryder.

"Two years."

His eyebrows went up, and his mouth twisted. "Damn. Two years? That's a long time for an adult, and you're saying you did it as a, what, a thirteen-year-old?"

"Yes."

He stared at her, his hand stroking the stubble on his chin. She turned away from his open face, too aware that her own was so closed.

"I was frightened when the Dust first fell. Then I realised it didn't matter, it didn't hurt me. After that, I ran and didn't stop." She traced her finger in the Dust. "The trackers aren't the worst things out here Ryder. There are bigger things that go bump in the night. And when darkness falls, and Dust lands in clumps, and you wake up covered in a choking blanket of grey, you wonder if you're actually dead and walking through hell." Her shoulders creaked as she rolled the tension out. "More people lived in the deadlands back then. Small groups of travellers trying to get to a better place. Most of them were kind. Some weren't." And some things were best left buried. "I didn't stay long with anyone, and I don't think they minded not having an extra mouth to feed."

"How did you find water?"

"There are springs. They're not easy to find, and sometimes it would be days, but they're there, hidden deep beneath the crust. And in towns it was easier to find—you track the water fountains until you reach the reservoir. You just have to get used to seeing dead bodies and destroyed lives."

"Jesus, Lark. You were only a kid."

She shrugged and put the bottle away, pushing herself up and hauling her bag on her shoulder.

"Yep. Sucks, right?"

"And the trackers. Did they ever find you?"

She paused. "Once. I was more careful the next time."

Turning her back on him, she walked around the edge of the little plateau. The tracker would be following Tama, which meant they needed to go in the direction it went.

Ryder caught up, and she noticed again how he moderated his stride to fit hers.

"Now I understand why you scream at night."

After two days with no sign of the Fae, she wondered if the sense of Tama pulling her onwards led in the wrong direction. Calling a halt in a small grove, she fought off a crawling sensation of doubt. Scrappy trees poked at the grey sky above them. Rolling barren hillocks of Dust lay ahead.

A soft whisper cut through the shifting air as a Fae tracker flew over where they stood hidden, black gown flaring behind. Deadly and silent, its silvery wings shimmered in the sunlight. She grabbed at Ryder's shoulder, holding him still. His hand clenched on his knife hilt, and she fixed her eyes on the Fae until it disappeared. Rubbing her hand over her racing heart, she dropped her pack on the ground. *Okay. Doubts gone.*

Later that evening, they huddled in the small tent as Dust fell with soft patters around them. Torchlight cast strange shadows on the nylon, battling with the dead trees outside for what could be creepiest. Squashing a shudder, she rested her elbows on her crossed legs, her head nearly brushing the roof. Ryder stretched out, taking up more than his half of the tiny space, but she didn't mind. Every evening he made sure to take the spot in front of the flap, and she pretended not to notice. His hair burned copper in the torchlight, and the break from a razor showed in his scruffy beard. It suited him.

Ryder smiled at her absently, and she took a breath. Every night, he held her to stop the nightmares from coming. Every day, he followed her, trusting without question. The weight of her secrets twisted lead through her heart. If the tracker had found them, he could have died. He deserved more than her silence.

"The tracker. It was too close today. We need to be more careful." Blood rushed in her ears, and her fingers wound together. "I can't let them take me again."

He pushed up from where he leaned on one elbow, turning the full light of his eyes on her.

"I'm sorry, what did you say? Did you say 'again'?"

Words stuck in her throat. Licking her lips, she swallowed the dryness and forced out the truth.

"I was one of the first. I was twelve when they ripped me from my mother. She held on so tightly, her nails raked my arms as they pulled me into the sky." She rolled up her sleeve, fumbling as her hand shook. The scars were faint now but still visible, all that remained of the last time she held her mother. They still burned sometimes. When she remembered.

Ryder reached out, and she tried not to flinch when his fingers brushed over the silvery mark, his touch gentle and warm.

"Your mother must have loved you very much."

Ice crept through her heart. She yanked her sleeve down over her hand, brushing off his fingers.

"Of course she did, I was her only remaining child. My brother, Beckett, died in one of the first attacks." His chubby smiling face came to her sometimes in her dreams. Those were good dreams.

"Is that why you avoid crossing our crater?"

She shrugged, the compassion in his voice making her eyes burn with unshed tears. "One of the reasons."

Ryder nodded slowly. "I get that." His eyes didn't leave her face, and she tried not to fidget. "What happened when you were Taken?"

Tension shot through her body, and screams built behind the door in her mind. "I don't remember." His face closed down, and she rushed her words. "I'm telling the truth. I remember pain, I remember fear. I remember white lights and beds like hospital rooms, and the Fae, but nothing else. When I try to think about it, I start shaking and my vision blurs." She stared at her twisted hands. "I don't like to try."

Silence filled the tent, broken by rustles as he shifted to sit up. "So how come you ended up in the Dust?"

"I was returned. The testing came, and I ran."

His hand curled where it rested on the floor. and her heart pounded. "You were the one in your story, the one like Tama. No wonder you wanted to go after him."

The roof of the tent pressed on her head as she raised it quickly. "That's not the only reason."

"So why?"

"Mia."

Comprehension lit his eyes. Mia had befriended the scrawny starving teenager, even though, at twenty, she had been five years and a world apart from Addie. Mia had been her protector and her family since then.

"You really think Tama knows how to save Matt and Lily?"

"Yes. I do." She forced the words out. "I haven't hoped so hard for something for a long time."

Torchlight flickered on his face, and her gaze dropped from his eyes to the strong planes of his jaw.

"I understand," He said, "Tama needs us to bring him home. Well, he needs you."

"You too. He'll need you if I'm right."

Ryder's head cocked, and he regarded her intently. "Did you ever need me, Lark? Or anyone?"

Heat rushed through her, and her muscles locked, words whirling in her mind with no way out. When withdrawal darkened his eyes, she cursed herself. "I did," she muttered. Meeting his eyes briefly, she made herself say it. "I still do."

"Were you ever Tested?"

She bit her lip and stared up at the ceiling of the tent, heavy with Dust. Her eyes prickled, but it was a long-ago shame. She could bear it. "No. I was frightened. The compound council didn't trust me when I was returned because I was the only one to come back awake. They blamed me for the screaming madness of the others. So I ran away."

"Lark, you were twelve. No-one can blame you for running."

A smile twisted on her face, and her eyes burned. "When the Fae came to do the Testing, the council brought out the others. They told them I was gone. The Fae sent a tracker after me. It found me later, but I was stronger then. They tested Sanjeet and Ella. Whatever they discovered pleased them. They took them again and tested everyone else. I came back afterwards. I wish I hadn't. Some things can't be unseen."

She fell silent. The shame might be old, but it was strong. He reached out a hand and took hers. "Hey. I meant it, don't blame yourself. The Fae did this, not you. If you'd been there, you simply would have been tested with all the rest."

He'd seen her far too vulnerable in the last few days. Withdrawing her hand from his, she sat up straighter.

"Not everyone survived. A few were taken away with Sanjeet and Ella. Some lived but wished they hadn't when pain and madness followed. My mother," she took a breath, "my mother was one of the mad ones. When I returned, those who survived the testing relatively unhurt blamed me for what happened to their loved ones. They drove me out."

She risked a glance up as his silence filled the tent. His jaw clenched, and she tensed against his anger. When he spoke, his voice was like a whip, but she breathed again when she realised he wasn't lashing out at her.

"You were twelve, and they drove you out into the Dust. I've never heard of such a despicable act. I feel no sympathy for them. They can go fuck themselves. Whatever it is that made you different, it made you special. And even if you weren't, throwing you out made them monsters." He leaned back on his elbows but kept his eyes on hers. "And I don't like monsters."

Heavy lead lifted from her heart. Perhaps she should have told him before. Things she'd still left unsaid rolled out in her mind, and she shied away from telling him. Maybe he wouldn't think she was a monster, but she still wasn't sure on that count herself. Her face twisted before she could stop it. He raised an eyebrow, and she tried to think of something to say so he wouldn't notice.

"My memories aren't always nice," she said. "Sometimes it's easier to pretend they aren't there. And I don't like putting my loss on others. We've all lost people. I'm no different."

He cocked his head, and she fixed her gaze on her hands, still clutching her sleeves. Sometimes he saw too much. She heard him sigh and watched his chest rising and falling out of the corner of her eyes.

"You might have noticed I don't go to the field outside the southern gate if I can help it." His voice was quiet, warm.

The edge of her sleeve crumpled under her clenching fingers. "I have wondered." She made herself meet his eyes. They shone bright in the torchlight.

"That's where Sammie died." he said.

Her heart stopped for a second, then thudded into a pounding rhythm. Sammie. His wife. She'd heard all about his wife from Mia. She died about two months before Addie turned up at the compound.

Words didn't come. She ended up murmuring what she hoped was a sympathetic noise. She was terrible at this stuff. He flicked her a glance from under his eyelids. A blush crept up her neck. Of course he knew just how awkward she felt. His lips quirked, and he drew up his legs, resting his wrists on his knees.

"Sammie was a bit out of it by then. She didn't cope as well as I did with losing Cole, and I didn't cope well at all. Losing a child—well, it's the worst possible thing you can ever imagine. Your entire soul is ripped out and shredded in front of you. You walk around like an empty shell. Everyone says kind things, and you want to hit them. It's a special kind of hell."

She nodded. It was like that when Beckett died.

"But I coped. I had to. I didn't just have my wife to take care of, the whole compound looked to me. But Sammie, she had nothing. Nothing but an empty bed and memories that hurt."

It was hard to speak round the lump in her throat, but she couldn't help it. Ryder's pain showed in the taut skin around his eyes and the white grip of his hands. She didn't want him to hurt. "That's not true, she had you."

His smile didn't reach his eyes. "I don't think I was enough. She struggled to get out of bed until one day she got up, got dressed, and walked out the south gate into a Dust storm. I saw her face before it swallowed her. She looked so peaceful, but the Dust was merciless. Within six months, I lost my child and my wife. I was twenty-seven and my life was over."

She'd never wanted to hold someone so much before, but she just hugged her own knees tight and gazed at him.

He turned to face her, a flickering smile warming his eyes.

"And then a scrawny starving teenager turned up, and I had a purpose again."

Heat burned her cheeks, but she didn't look away.

"You thanked me the other day Lark, but I should thank you too. If you hadn't turned up when you did I might have ended up following Sammie into the Dust."

She found her voice again. "Is that why you get angry when people stay in the deadlands too long?"

He raised his eyebrows at her. "People meaning you? In a way. We lost too many to the Dust over the years. But with you it's different. You came to us out of the Dust. The only thing it's ever given back. I always thought there must be a reason."

Her heart sank a little. "Is that why you were kind to me? Because I was different?"

He let out a laugh and nudged her foot. "No. I was kind to you because it broke my heart, seeing how strong you tried to be when your pain was clear to anyone who bothered to pay attention. And later on, when the pain seemed to go away, well, I don't think I've always been easy on you, but I always tried to be fair when you broke the rules. And since you grew up, you've always been the only one I could count on to tell me to pull my head in or challenge me on decisions. Even Anahera doesn't do it that much. Says she wants me to make my own mistakes."

She couldn't help it, she snorted. His eyes twinkled back at her before softening as he leaned forward.

"You're right, we've all suffered. The Fae took so much from us. No-one likes to talk about it, Addie, but perhaps we should. Maybe if we did, we wouldn't feel so alone."

She bit back a smile, her heart swelling. *If it wasn't for the taking, I never would have met him.* She pushed down the thought, her arms burning.

When she lay down to sleep, she held herself a little rigidly, unsure if Ryder would want to put distance between himself and one of the Taken. He turned off the torch and slid his long body behind hers. Her head pillowed on his arm, after only a few days, felt as if it belonged there. His arm around her waist was warm, and she breathed in the feeling of safety. She stiffened as his hand stroked her hair off her face. "I'm sorry for what they did to you, Lark. You need to know that whatever happens, I will never kick you out. I promise."

Her eyes prickled again, but a smile spread on her face, easy in the darkness and hidden from his eyes.

CHAPTER 11

Deep in the deadlands, Dust fell heavily with no respite. Depression came easily, surrounded by an endless monotone of grey. Powdery grains coated everything, and clouds never left the sky. Sunlight struggled to fall weakly and with no joy on the parched landscape below.

Grime deadened each footfall, and despite being out in the open, claustrophobia kicked in as the fine powder whipped around them. Addie stopped and turned to check on Ryder's progress. His face, hidden under the mask, scarf, and goggles, was set in grim lines. Fine grains clung to the stubble on his cheeks. He stalked over to her, Dust kicking up with his strides.

"Goddamn it Lark, put your goggles on!" His voice came out muffled.

"I don't need them."

"The Dust is swirling everywhere. If you don't want to end up blind put the damn goggles on."

Ashen mist whipped past her face as she tried to stare him down. His whole body tensed, muscles rigid, his hand gripping the strap of his bag. She rolled her eyes, swinging her pack off her shoulder. Digging through to the bottom, she hunted for the goggles by feel. Wearing them was pointless—she didn't need them—but if it would help him relax then what was the harm?

They fit around her eyes, but the straps were set for someone bigger. She tugged, trying to tighten them. *Stupid things, more trouble than they're worth.* Mia's face flashed into her mind, and she squished the guilt. Ryder stepped over, and she dropped her hands as he pulled the straps tight. She made googly fish eyes at him through the lenses.

A smile warmed his voice. "I know you hate them, but I'm glad you put them on. Thank you."

She cocked her head, and her mouth twisted in a half smile.

"The Dust must be doing something to you Ryder, first time you've ever thanked me for doing what I'm told."

Powder fell from his scarf as his cheeks dislodged it in a grin under his mask. "That's because you never do what you're told."

"Touché. Okay, glorious leader, you take point for a bit while I get used to this aquarium on my face."

Ryder patted her shoulder and took the lead, pebbles kicking up with each step. He was doing better out here than she'd expected.

The goggles distorted her vision, warping everything and making distances hard to judge. Perhaps she could take them off? Her gaze went to Ryder, his strong back and long legs plodding on through dense drifts. No. Best he didn't start thinking about how she could see through the powdery haze. Best he thought she was too reckless.

The path narrowed. The slope fell away on one side, and the cliff rose high above them on the other. At least the Dust was cut off from one direction. She frowned. Ryder drifted too close to the slope.

"Watch out!" she called, the words caught and muffled in her scarf. He turned, head tipped and hand up to his ear. She pulled her scarf down and strode towards him, waving her hand at him to move back. "Too close, Ryder. You're too close to the edge."

Her foot slid out from under her, sending her tumbling down the hill, a storm of rocks and Dust cascading after her. Stones flew past, and she struggled to cover her face with her arms. A chunk of rock thunked into the goggles and bounced off. *That was lucky, who knew I'd be grateful for these eye prisons?*

"Lark!" Ryder's muffled shout cut off, and she twisted to see him caught in the edges of the landslide.

The short hill ended in a flat section dotted with large rocks, no doubt former victims of a landslide. She rolled to a stop and lay stunned for a few moments until Ryder groaned and sat up. *No point worrying him.* It hurt, a lot, but she clenched her jaw and pushed herself to her feet, wobbling as she caught her balance. She wiped Dust off her goggles and checked herself out. No blood. Well, no dripping blood. Plenty of grazes. Her coat sported a few more tatters, but the thick fabric had protected her. Ryder wiped a sticky red line off his cheek, leaving a smear, and pulled off the cracked and now useless mask. A frown showed above the rim of the goggles.

"So, tell me again who was too close to the edge?"

She raised her eyebrows at him. "Seriously? This is not my fault. Blame the goggles. If I hadn't been wearing them I wouldn't have made that mistake."

He held her eyes and shrugged slightly. Maybe that was an admission, but she doubted it.

"How do we get back up?" he asked, his eyes raking the slip in front of them as he brushed Dust and stones out of his hair.

She followed his gaze. Dust stirred by the landslide floated down to settle on the scree, making the slope slippery and difficult to climb.

Biting her lip, she remembered her early days out in the Dust. She cocked her head to one side and tried to *listen* to the strands of the world. Closing her eyes, a tug pulled at her, leading off to the left. She opened her eyes, her cheeks warming at Ryder's quizzical frown.

"I don't think we need to. The path will end up down here anyway. We just found ourselves a quicker way down."

His eyes stayed on her face, and she tried not to fidget. He shrugged, raising a brow at her.

"Okay. Whatever. After you, and don't fall down again."

She nodded, her lip between her teeth. He reached out and eased hair off her face, touching lightly around the graze on her forehead. His eyes were resigned, but a smile softened his voice.

"Don't sweat it, Lark. I trust you. You'll tell me when you're ready."

Her heart skipped, and she stepped back.

"Nothing to tell. Come on, let's keep going before the Dust comes down."

SOMETHING TUGGED AT HER, like a finger plucking a bowstring. She motioned Ryder to a halt. He followed her gaze up to the falling Dust, drifting from the sky and getting heavier as they watched. Not too heavy yet, but they needed to move faster.

"I think he's over there." Her voice whispered out. And she wasn't sure why, or how she knew with everything in her that not only was Tama over the rise, but one of the Fae was also. Her stomach flipped, and bile rose to the back of her throat. Definitely a Fae.

The hill rose gently but relentlessly. They crept up, crouching lower into a crawl as they neared the top.

Tama hunched on the ground, his hands and feet bound in silvery webbing and his eyes fixed on the Fae. The wonder and admiration settling on his face reached into hidden remembrances and prodded long forgotten secrets.

Ryder's voice whispered on her cheek. "So, how do we rescue him?"

"We have to catch it off guard. Take its wings. Do you think you can sneak around behind it?"

He looked at her.

"No." He said flatly. "You're not going to confront a Fae by yourself."

"I won't be by myself. You'll be coming to the rescue."

His jaw tightened on words he was probably dying to say. She touched his arm, his muscles tense under her fingers.

"Ryder. I think we can do this. You need to take its wings, I'm not strong enough. I can distract it though. You said you trusted me, so trust me on this. Please."

His eyes softened, and he moved his arm to grasp her hand briefly, the light touch sending shivers up her arm. "Only because you asked nicely."

He pulled out his knife. His eyes flickered over her mouth, and her pulse leaped. But he just gripped her shoulder in a little shake.

"Be safe, Lark. Don't do anything foolish."

"Would I ever?"

He smiled, giving her a salute as he crept away, silent footsteps in the deep Dust.

She tightened her trembling grip on the crossbow and walked out into the clearing. The Fae turned towards her. Her stomach twisted. This was a moment she had avoided since she escaped the first time. And here she was walking into the situation she most feared. If only she felt more heroic.

CHAPTER 12

Tama's eyes widened as she strode into the clearing. He stiffened where he sat, bound in silver webbing. She tried to smile, but her face didn't stay under her control, not with the Faery so close.

The Fae looked nothing like the one they'd seen before. This one wore red pantaloons, the colour a vibrant contrast to the endless grey around them. Dusky blue wings stretched their full span, and its hair stood high in tall crimson spikes bound with gold wire. She blew her own hair out of her eyes, keeping her gaze fixed on the Fae.

The Fae turned its head, something too cruel to be a smile flickering over the sharp golden planes of its face.

"Is this a rescue? Many years have passed since anyone dared try to steal what is rightfully ours." Its voice rasped on her nerves, ripping her ears apart with the thrum of violence in the rising notes.

Ignoring the nausea sparked by its shimmering eyes and dark melody, she gripped the crossbow, thinking of Ryder.

She wasn't alone.

She wasn't twelve anymore.

She coughed to get her voice to work. "He's not yours to take."

Its laugh sounded like nails on a chalkboard, and she couldn't restrain a shudder. *Let's hope it doesn't do that again. It's creepy enough as it is.*

The Fae grabbed Tama by the hair, pulling his head back. She had to stop herself darting forward. It paused, sniffing the air, then turned to stare directly at her. Its eyes were like the ocean, blue and green and shifting like the tide. She couldn't control her heartbeat. It raced as her hand, slippery on the crossbow, drew back the string.

"You," it said, its voice a melody slicing at her mind. "There's something about you. Something familiar."

Its long arm reached out. The hand at the end shifted into a claw. Its smile drew back to reveal sharpened teeth.

Lifting the crossbow to sight along the barrel was the hardest thing she'd ever done. It cocked its head, eyeing the weapon. "You are foolish, little human, if you hope to stop me with that toy."

Ryder rose up behind the Fae, knife out. With one strong arm, he hauled the wings towards him. His eyes widened as the touch of them burned his skin. He hacked while the Faery screamed and twisted, glamour fading to show the thin angular beast beneath.

She took aim with a much steadier hand and fired. The bolt heated to a red-hot glow as it neared its target. It slammed into the Faery's skull with a thwack, sounding much more solid than the small arrow had a right to be.

The tracker's angry cries cut off, and it buckled at the knees, falling to the ground, the Dust rising up into small eddies above it. Her eyes dragged from the body of the fallen Fae to Ryder, standing with his knife still raised and the wings cast on the ground, dusky blue marked with black blood. Burn marks travelled up his sleeve in the shape of scales. His eyes widened, and he stared at her with a suspicion that turned her heart into a burning stone in her chest.

She released the crossbow, letting the weapon fall against her hip from its strap. Turning her head away, she pulled the scarf over her mouth so he couldn't see her lips trembling.

"We have to hide the body," she said.

His voice was gravelly, and she tried not to read distrust into his tone. "We'll do that. But how about, as we do, you tell me what just happened."

"I don't know. I didn't do anything."

"Bullshit," he said, "I saw your eyes change. They swam like the Faeries' eyes do, and then the bolt burned red."

She glanced over to him and blinked at the knife he still held in the air. Her heart sank.

"I didn't do anything. I wished the bolt would kill the Fae, that's all I did. And it did. Don't Faeries grant wishes?"

His face froze, carved from stone. Harsh and immobile. This wasn't the Ryder who held her in the night, keeping the screams at bay, never once mentioning it in the daytime. This was the Ryder who led thousands of people, who kept them safe and dealt with threats. She squared her shoulders, turning to face him front on.

"Maybe now you don't trust me. You don't have to. This isn't about me. This is about Tama, and helping Matt and Lily. Whether my eyes looked different in the sunlight is hardly going to change that. I'll go on with or without you, so feel free to make your choice, but right now I'm going to start hauling this Fae carcass, and I'd appreciate a hand."

She didn't wait for his answer but bent down to pick up the Fae under its arms. This close to the body, she began to shake. She breathed through her mouth, so its scent didn't enter her to waken thoughts she couldn't deal with now.

Ryder stood for a moment then swore, sheathing his knife. He came up and pushed her away, taking the shoulders himself.

"Grab its feet. They're further away from the mess. You won't feel so ill."

She did what he asked. What did it matter if he thought she was squeamish at the hole in its head? Better that than the truth.

CHAPTER 13

The roof of the tent pressed down on the back of Addie's head, and she shifted, trying to hide the claustrophobia closing in on her. Tama must have grown in the short time he'd been away, or maybe he had always been bigger than she thought. His long legs took up most of the room in the small two-person tent. Dust filtered through the dead trees above them, and soft flumps broke the silence as larger clumps dislodged from spindly branches.

She squeezed her shoulder blades together and stretched her neck. Ryder sat cross legged, and his knee pushed against her leg. She liked his closeness, but found herself trying to give Tama more space. His eyes reminded her too much of what she used to see in the mirror.

Ryder sighed, pushing his hand through his hair and shaking out flakes of Dust. "Tama, we just want to help. Can you remember anything about this Valley you talked about back at the compound? Valley of Kings? Who are the kings?"

Tama's shoulders rounded and shadows played over his face as he caved even more into himself, but his eyes didn't leave Ryder. His hands twisted together, and a sudden rush of memory left Addie breathless. She deliberately untwisted her own hands, setting them on the floor next to her legs.

"I don't know anything about a valley, or about any kings." His voice was the soft tenor of the young man he was turning into, but his eyes were that of a frightened child.

She pushed back at the tug in her mind. "What about what you said in the ward?"

Tama glanced at her side long, "I don't know what you're talking about."

The lie rang against something deep within her, and she bit her lip, glancing at Ryder. He craned his neck, trying to see into Tama's face.

"Are you sure, buddy? It's really important you tell us if you remember anything."

The boy smiled at him, warm affection almost hiding the tension in his jaw. "I get it. And if I had any idea, I'd tell you. But I don't."

She poked Ryder in the leg, trying to hide it from Tama. He brushed her off.

"I believe you."

Addie had to look away so no one would notice how far her eyes rolled. Tama's lie was so obvious.

"Tomorrow we'll take you back, Tama. Home. You're safe now."

Tama stared up at Ryder, and the pain in his eyes cut at her. "Newhaven isn't my home."

Ryder leaned across and gripped his arm "It *is* your home, Tama. What are you talking about?"

The boy shook his head and muttered into his chest. "Nothing."

Addie knew what he meant. They had found him as a baby, crying, left outside the compound gates after dawn beside his parents' bodies. No-one else cared that he was a foundling. None of them were living where they'd been before the Fae came, and there had been many orphans. But it didn't always feel like home to her either.

She stifled a yawn, her jaw clicking. Ryder met her eyes, and she shrugged. She didn't have any answers for him. But she'd heard Tama in the ward, and he definitely mentioned kings.

Ryder shifted, and the pressure on her leg increased. She caught herself before she leaned into him. "Tama, you have to understand that it's over. We're going back tomorrow."

The boy's face twisted like his hands. "No, I have to go on."

"Why?" she said, her voice cold and sharp.

Ryder glared at her, and she stared back. Okay, so she was a bit blunt, but she was tired. Weren't they all? And it was the only question that mattered.

"There's something in the next city, not far from here." Tama mumbled, and he wouldn't meet her eyes. "It'll help the others."

She and Ryder exchanged a glance. "Do you mean Old Hamilton?"

Tama's eyes remained focused on his feet, but he shrugged. "Dunno. There's something over there that calls me, and if I can find it, I can help the others."

Addie tensed. Something didn't feel right. Intense energy radiated from him back in the ward. Here he was drained.

Ryder stroked his jaw, his hand catching on the new stubble. He shifted again in an attempt to stretch out his legs. She didn't want to give up the contact but moved over to give him more room.

"The thing is, Tama, it isn't only you anymore, or even Lily and Matt. The longer we stay away, the more the whole compound is at risk."

Tama's eyes flicked up to Ryder's face and down again. Clearly, he hadn't thought it through.

"I might be the only one who doesn't understand all this,"

Ryder continued, "but I'm still in charge. I'm going to sleep on it and then in the morning we'll decide if we go on, or go back. Deal?"

The thought of Matt filled her mind. Mia's quiet desperation. If Tama was right, and there was something they could use to help the children, then surely they owed it to them to try?

Sneaking a glance at Ryder's profile, she didn't bother to argue. She recognised the set of his jaw. She could always go on while Ryder took Tama back. He met her eyes, and she blinked. Well. She could be wrong, but it looked like he figured out what she was thinking. And agreed.

She almost missed Tama's quiet, "Deal."

The small space of the tent pressed down on her. It was unlikely they would, any of them, get any sleep. She lay by the side of the tent, Ryder lay by the door and Tama curled himself in the centre, his feet by the adults' heads. Addie steeled herself for the return of the nightmares. Even if the lanky teenager wasn't squashed between them, Ryder could hardly hold her in front of Tama; he wouldn't understand. The light from the glow-stick dimmed, and shadows from the branches faded into the roof of the tent.

She startled as Ryder slipped his hand into hers where it lay alongside her head. Opening her eyes, she saw him smile at her across Tama's boots before he closed his own eyes. Happiness flared, dying into embers of worry. There didn't seem to be any easy solution for the problems tomorrow would bring. A long time passed before she slept, but no nightmares filled her head.

CHAPTER 14

Something teased at her mind, and her eyes snapped open. Ryder still slept, his face showing the worries wakefulness hid. A wave of tenderness hit her. She stretched out a cautious hand to brush his hair off his face. Empty space between them. Her hand snatched back.

Tama had gone.

"Ryder! Wake up!"

She didn't bother shaking him awake, just pushed him hard and scrambled past him out of the tent. Hopes that Tama had been relieving himself disappeared with the clear tracks left in the fresh Dust.

The tracks went in the direction of Old Hamilton. Well. Guess that made that decision.

Ryder cursed as he stumbled out of the tent, flaps and ropes snaring him. She turned back to help.

"We need to pack fast," she said. "He's got a decent start."

"Did you know he would do this?"

She bit her lip for an instant then decided on honesty. "Not for certain. I thought he might, he's definitely hiding something."

He grunted at her. Turning, he swept Dust off the tent, pulling at the poles.

A deep line between his eyebrows darkened into something else. She grabbed his chin and turned his face to hers. Burns. Not bad, not yet, but the Dust was taking its toll. Dread coiled in her blood. He was exhausted as well. No wonder he hadn't noticed Tama sneaking past him. *I didn't wake up either,* she thought guiltily.

He smiled and shrugged.

"We knew this might happen, Lark. Don't worry. I'm tough."

She frowned and pushed him lightly away from the tent.

"Go, sort yourself out, I'll pack this up."

They moved faster than Tama, and if Ryder stumbled occasionally, well, the ground was uneven. That was all. Dust sickness would take longer than this. Surely.

Luck favoured them, and they caught up with Tama on the outskirts of the city. The old river bed wound below them, long dried up and choked with drifts of grey powder. Tama saw them coming and waited. His hands clenched and released. His boyish chin jutted out. She met his gaze, and he turned his head.

She stood back, letting Ryder pass her. Tama's shoulders curled in as he jammed his hands in his pockets, half turning from Ryder as he got closer. A tug deep inside, visions of the past surfacing, standing in school-rooms surrounded by people, none of whom understood her, none of whom liked her, all of whom avoided her. Odd that she should think of that now. She frowned, chewing her lip, letting pain push back worse thoughts.

Looking at his feet, Tama said "You won't understand. I had to come. It isn't far now." He turned to walk away, but Ryder grabbed him by the arm.

"Hey, buddy." His voice rang warm, but firm. "We don't run off like that. You know this. It isn't safe."

He cringed at Ryder's words, eyes darting up. Breath caught in Addie's throat. She remembered that face, the tension around the brow, the stubborn mouth. When you disappointed the person you most admired, but you knew you would do it again. Too familiar. She hoisted her pack and turned away from the flaring pain in Tama's eyes, focusing on the mutilated ruins around them. Easier to stay in the now, and refuse the past entry.

"Tell you what, Tama." Ryder said, "Let's make a deal."

Squashing a smile, she listened to a spiel she'd heard so many times the pattern of it resonated in her bones.

"I understand you don't want to come back yet, but I have responsibilities to you, *and* to Newhaven. So, let's find a middle ground."

Tama scuffed his feet, grimy powder flying up in the periphery of her vision. "It's not that I don't want to go back. I *can't.*"

"I get that. Here's the deal. We come with you to find whatever it is you're looking for, but you get two days, and two days only. Then we go home. Deal?"

Raising her eyes, she stared at Tama. Ryder didn't get it. The deal was always taken, always meant, but when stronger things rode your soul, you did what needed to be done. Even if it broke everything.

A flash of the old Tama flickered in the boy's smile, impish and relieved. He put out his hand to shake on the deal, and his gaze met hers. His smile fading, he stared back, shaking Ryder's hand firmly.

Moving up the slope away from the deep chasm of the river bed, they found themselves on a road lined by the crumbled ruins of buildings, a solemn funeral guard of broken concrete and rust. Cars lay scattered like children's toys. As they got closer to what must have been the centre of the city, the office blocks towering over them were mostly intact.

Ryder stopped, his eyes taking it all in. "I went to university here."

She never even had a chance to go to high school.

Meeting her eyes, he gestured at the ruins. "The crater must've been further out to leave these buildings like this."

Broken windows gaped like jagged teeth. At least any bodies would be long gone.

Turning a shoulder on the devastation, she poked Tama in the arm. "Alright, where are we going?"

He shifted, eyes flicking to her face and away. "That way." He pointed to the left and shrugged, not meeting her gaze. "That's all I know."

A sound sliced through the silence, filling the Dust with the terror of her childhood. The deep baying cut into her mind, splitting open the wall she had built over the worst parts of her past. She froze. "Oh no."

Ryder darted a glance at her. "What is it?"

"The Hounds."

"Hounds?"

She pushed them forwards, increasing the pace. "Fae trackers bring them in when they want to hunt in packs. The hounds help them find and corner their prey."

Great black beasts surged through her mind, visions of their teeth ripping into the flesh of the woman who had taken her in so long ago.

"We have to run. Now!"

They raced downhill, leaping over ruins of buildings and dodging around carcasses of cars. Dust continued to fall heavily. The baying of the hounds drew closer. Tama fell behind, and she dropped back to grab his arm. "Run. You have to run, Tama. The hounds won't stop." Hauling him beside her, she followed Ryder as he sprinted down an old main street. Grey heaviness deadened most sounds, but from their left a deep howl echoed as large black shapes ran sleekly in the distance. An answering call sounded from their right. She didn't bother looking.

She yanked down her scarf so her voice wouldn't be muffled. "Ryder! they're herding us. We need to get off this path, now!"

He didn't acknowledge with so much as a nod, but immediately veered off towards a broken and shattered building. She dragged Tama along their new path, legs catching the churned-up Dust and heart pounding against her ribs.

The hounds veered too, but Ryder swung round the other way. A fallen telephone kiosk blocked the cluttered remains of an alleyway in between toppled buildings. Ryder leaped over the obstacle, his hand sliding in the Dust coating it. She pushed Tama ahead, cursing as he scrambled awkwardly over the telephone booth. Once he was safe on the other side, she pulled herself up with her arms and swung her legs over.

Ryder better know what he's doing.

He stood at the other end of the alleyway, waiting for them, one hand gripping a metal fire escape.

"Are you mad?" she hissed. "No way is that ladder safe. The metal is corroded."

"Only one way to find out. You know as well as I do if we stay on the ground we don't stand a chance against those things. Now climb, I'll send the boy after you."

She debated arguing with him, insisting she be the last one to climb the ladder, but the Hounds' cry echoed through the air. She gripped the metal with both hands and climbed. She was the lightest—if it didn't hold her it wouldn't hold him.

Years of Dust coated the metal, and her grip slipped more than once. She tried not to rush too much, but once Tama clambered up behind her, she sped up to avoid him pushing at her feet. His fear was almost tangible. She spared a glance down and saw Ryder still waiting at the bottom. Her gut clenched. Foolishly noble as always. Bet he was waiting to make sure they got up in case his extra weight tipped the balance and the metal broke. She climbed faster.

Her arms burned when she reached the top of the building. She hauled herself over with shaking limbs. Tama fell down beside her. She leaned over to watch as Ryder raced up the ladder. The hounds' call rang out, and she let her chin fall on her arm. Beasts couldn't climb, but even up here, the three of them were effectively cornered. Prickles of pain tingled down her scars. The hounds weren't the only ones out there. Hounds had masters.

Ryder's chest heaved with dragging breaths as he jumped over the ledge. He didn't stop. Sprinting diagonally across the roof, he motioned at them to follow.

"Oi!" She hissed, trying not to be too loud. "Where are you going?"

"This. Way." He panted. "Throw them. Throw them off."

She pulled Tama to his feet and lurched after Ryder, her stomach twisting as she skirted holes and weak spots beneath her feet. When they reached the opposite edge of the roof, Ryder turned to face them, and the grin on his face held a manic edge.

She shook her head.

"No. Not happening. No. Find another way."

"Come on Lark, you're always reckless, think you can fly like your namesake?"

"Fly?" Tama's voice shook. She frowned at Ryder and put a hand on the boy's shoulder.

"No, Tama, we aren't going to fly."

"You're right, we're going to leap," Ryder said.

She closed her eyes. He was serious. She opened them again to see him pacing, measuring what could only be a run up.

"Ryder, no jokes, have you gone completely nuts?"

He smiled at her but continued to measure the steps. "You worry too much, Lark."

She put her head in her hands and pulled her palms down her face. He came to a stop in front of her.

"Okay, no jokes. It might look impossible, but it isn't. You have to trust me. I used to do parkour."

"That ninja running thing?" she asked.

"Yeah. I did stuff like this all the time."

"Great, but Tama and I haven't done this before, and I'm really not sure I want to start."

A hound called out, answered by a deeper howl from further away. *Blood. Hiding. Helplessness.* A shiver went down her spine, and she swallowed bile.

His hand gripped her arm, firm and warm through the heavy coat. "I wouldn't ask you to do this if I didn't believe you could. You have to have a little faith. Tama," his gaze flashed to the wide-eyed boy. "You can do this—I've seen you at the compound."

Tama nodded, and her eyebrows shot up. *What the heck?* Ryder's eyes came back to hers, and they held such understanding.

"Will you trust me, Lark?"

Well that was a foolish question.

"Of course," she muttered. "But if I fall and die a horrible death, you need to promise to feel bad about it."

A grin spread on his face. "Promise. I'll go first, then Tama, and then you come. We'll be ready to catch you." Warmth lit his eyes. "I promise you that too."

Acid churned as her stomach flipped over. What the hell had she just agreed to do?

His hand dropped from her arm, and he quirked a brow at her. "Here goes."

He started sprinting, and before she could call him back he soared through the air, coat flying out behind him like wings. He landed, rolled, and sprang to his feet. Elation shone in his eyes, visible even from here. He motioned quickly, and she turned to Tama.

"Your turn. You sure about this?"

The boy cocked his head, a small smile touching his eyes. "He says I can do it. Means I can."

He backed up to where a forlorn pipe jutted from the roof before taking off at a run. He too went sailing, landing a bit more clumsily. Rolling on his knees, he grinned at Ryder, who ruffled his hair then pointed at her.

Shit. I don't think I can do this. Okay. Tighten pack. Walk up to the pipe. She turned, wiping her palms down her pants. One deep breath, and she started running, her heart pounding, muscles springing beneath her. She skidded to a stop with her toes a bare centimetre from the edge.

Shit shit shit! This isn't possible. I can't throw myself off the edge.

She stared across the gap at Ryder, his palms pressed together in front of his lips. He nodded. Okay. Fine. She just needed to believe. Fairy tale stuff. How appropriate.

She jogged back to the pipe then wheeled around, sprinting, arms pumping at her sides. She didn't stop this time but threw herself off the edge, legs working, coat unfurling. She only just made the lip of the opposite edge, wavering backwards until Ryder's strong arm grabbed her. Tama pulled her forward.

The hounds' baying could still be heard around the other building. The three of them kicked up heavy Dust as they ran, dislodging decade-old scum.

This building was closer to the next, and the jump came easier this time. Guess it was like everything else in life—it seemed impossible until you'd done it.

Tama stood straighter. The lost look dropped from his face, and a familiar sparkle lit his grey eyes.

When they got to the edge of the third building, Ryder paused, waiting for her to reach him. She had let him take the lead, and she noticed he seemed to like being in charge again. It was good her scarf hid her smile, because she couldn't hold it in.

"So," he said, "the way I see it, if we keep jumping, eventually a Fae will turn up and find us from above. We need to find a way down and somewhere to hide."

Her smile faded, the adrenaline well and truly spent from her body, unable to fuel her sense of safety anymore. She hadn't thought much about what they'd do, simply followed Ryder, as happy as him that he'd taken charge.

"We can't hide," she said. "They'll track us down. The only option is to keep moving."

"Won't they just track us anyway?"

She shrugged. "Most likely yes, but at least we'll be out in the open with somewhere to run. If we hide, we're cornered. We don't want to be cornered."

His face set, jaw tightening. "No. I guess we don't." He gazed down into the swirling Dust and sighed. Then his face lit, and he held up a hand. "Right. This is the plan: we head down through the inside of the building. Hopefully the stairs are still intact, if not we go through the floors. There will be a basement access. We need to find our way underground."

"Underground?"

"Yes! Underground. There used to be access tunnels between buildings in the central cities to allow for city maintenance. If they're still standing, that's our way out."

The likelihood was so small, but in the light of his enthusiasm and Tama's hopeful face, she settled for nodding.

Ryder wasn't fooled. Seeing Tama looking over the edge into the Dust, he leaned closer to her. "Yeah. It's a slim chance. Thanks for not arguing about it. I'm all out of options."

"No worries," she managed.

"Right, let's look for an access point. The Dust will make it hard, but there should be a sign or something."

The frustrated baying of the hounds added urgency to their search. Tama tripped and stumbled, falling to his knees. She stretched her hand out to help him up, pulling it back when she realised he had found something. Scrambling back to a small metal hatch sticking out of the roof, he curled his fingertips around the edges of the entryway.

They pushed and strained, all three working together until they managed to force the lever that shifted the hatch.

Climbing through the access hatch, they ended up in what must have been an elevator shaft. The cables holding up the lift had broken. Ladders missing some rungs ran down the sides. She quirked an eyebrow at Ryder.

"This time, I go first," was all he said.

CHAPTER 15

The lift shaft stretched into endless darkness. Her vision narrowed to each rung in front of her aching hands, barely aware of the fading light of the glow stick on Ryder's pack below her. Her legs were exhausted jelly by the time they reached the bottom. The crack of another snapped glow stick echoed in the small basement, the faint luminescence brightening and bouncing off concrete walls.

Shaking out the wobbles, she brushed grime from a faded sign on a white metal door. She resolutely ignored the murky graffiti full of wings and pain. Her fingers traced the chipped outline of the climbing stick figure. Shivering, she wandered over to where the others crouched on the floor. "That exit goes to the stairs."

Ryder nodded, his eyes fixed on another access hatch sunk into the ground. Muscles strained as he tugged the handle. Metal graunched but didn't move. Shaking his hands, he stood and kicked at the handle until it twisted open. Tama pushed hair off his face and grabbed the edge of the hatch, helping Ryder pull it up. Dense darkness pooled in the opening. Damp air redolent with musty disuse and mould snaked out to curl around them.

She peered into the hole, her nose scrunching up. "Do you think the air will be okay?"

Ryder shrugged. "Honestly, no idea. Possibly not. This is our best chance so we might just have to risk it."

Blackness clutched at her as he dropped down onto the floor of the tunnel below, the green of the glow stick lighting his face in odd shadows. Tama shuffled to the edge of the hatch and tumbled down, Ryder steadying him as he landed. She looked down at Ryder who cocked his head to one side, holding up his hands in an offer to catch her. Screwing up her face, she jumped down, landing slightly too close to him.

The pale green glow didn't light very far. Walking down a tunnel into the dark depths reminded her of amusement park haunted mansions. But spookier. She tried not to think about the pile of masonry above their heads, not all of it stable. Trudging through the blackness, a niggle grew in her mind. *What if the glow stick dies before we find a door?* They had more, but wasting them all down here was not part of the plan. A new thought struck her.

Leaning over to Ryder as they walked, she said quietly, so Tama wouldn't overhear, "Have you thought about what we do if the doors out of this don't open?"

His eyebrows flicked upwards in acknowledgement, and he half shrugged, the glow stick dancing as his pack shifted with the movement. "I guess then we go back. Let's cross that bridge when we get there, alright?"

They padded along in silence, their footsteps slapping against the damp floor. She kept an eye on the glow, counting how many paces from them the light stretched, trying to work out if the circle was shrinking.

Tama strode next to her, calm in a way he hadn't been on the surface. She shivered, her shoulders rolling in when she thought of the destruction lying on top of them. *How can he be so peaceful?* Watching him sidelong, she noticed him reaching out at intervals, touching the walls. Her eyes widened, and she glanced away. The iron. He could sense the iron in the walls, the way it blocked the Fae magic. There was a reason the first survivors huddled in underground places. Ripping teeth and blood filled her mind. A shame the iron didn't affect the hounds.

When a door loomed up on the side of the tunnel, the yellow and black tape glowing oddly in the soft luminescence of the glow stick, she was so inured to the trek in the darkness that she didn't notice until Tama pointed it out. Relief flooded her.

Ryder grasped the handle and glanced at her. When the door opened, a weight lifted off her chest. The short flight of stairs outside led up to a car park basement, empty and forlorn.

Shoving the dying glow stick in the side pocket of his pack, Ryder waved them on.

Out of the iron embrace of the tunnel, Tama's fidgets became more pronounced. His eyes strayed to the skies at frequent intervals, and his hands clenched and unclenched at his sides as the trio left another block of shattered buildings behind them. Dust swirled in gentle eddies around their feet, and no eldritch baying disturbed the air.

Tama's head shifted as he glanced between her and Ryder, as if trying to decide who would be more likely to listen. Ryder cracked before she did.

"What is it, Tama?"

"The thing that's calling me. It's over there."

She closed her eyes. Of course it was. Of course the thing he wanted to get sat in the middle of the bloody impact crater.

Opening her eyes, she met Ryder's thoughtful gaze. She didn't bother forcing a smile. He knew she hated craters.

"Okay." His voice held that same authority she'd always bucked against, but now she could admit it reassured her. "Tama and I will go in. Lark, you stay here on guard. Let us know if you see or hear any of those dogs again."

"Hounds"

He gave her a look.

"They're called hounds. Not dogs. Different." Flakes of grey, piled in layer upon layer, skifted around her ankles as she kicked her feet through the Dust. No-one had disturbed this area in a long time. Perhaps nobody should. "The crater is open. Very open." A small shudder rippled through her, and she shifted her stance. Hopefully, they couldn't tell. "You'll have to be quick."

Tama jerked his head, and Ryder stepped close to her. He bent to meet her eyes.

"Hey. Hey, look at me. We'll be fine. But if we're not, and I mean this, Lark, you get yourself out of here. Understand?"

This time she did smile. They both knew that would never happen.

"You know I always do what you say, boss."

"Well, I tried. Come on, Tama. Lead the way."

Like an open wound, the shallow crater sprawled where tall buildings once stood. Rubble and twisted metal clustered around the exposed surface. Crumbled pavement slid under Addie's feet as she shifted, her eyes fixed on the two men walking into the dead earth of the crater. Crawling tingles covered her skin. Her teeth bit down on the inside of her cheek, pain to remind her where she was. She wasn't from Hamilton. This wasn't her impact crater. *Beckett's blood isn't in that soil.*

Tama tripped, Ryder's hand catching him under the elbow. She shook away the sudden vision of her brother falling, blood where his leg should have been. Tugging down her scarf, she inhaled, blinking away wetness. The crushing feeling in her chest would go away. She just needed to breathe. *Come on, this is ridiculous. You've got a job to do, Lark. Do it.*

She tightened her grip on the crossbow and glanced away from the crater, scanning the surrounding area. Grey, ruined buildings met her eyes. She remembered colour, occasionally.

It was deeply unfair that only the Fae lived with the bright colours of her childhood. Like rubbing salt into a wound. She wondered what Hamilton had been like, before, when it was the '*Garden City*'. Her eyes wandered. Those long flat buildings, shops maybe. Reds and yellows and blues would have competed for attention on store fronts. That big circular thing, a tub? She squinted and tried to imagine dark green leaves and colourful flowers. The university. A swirl of bright clothes and green lawns and green roofed buildings. Ryder had gone to university here. She wondered, suddenly, what he had been like as a young man. What it had been like to be an adult who could have dreams and hopes and normality. A family.

Pulling her thoughts back, she squinted at the crater before forcing her eyes all the way open.

Ryder stood over Tama in the centre, his attention outwards but his gaze darting down to the boy in intervals. Tama scrabbled in the Dust, and she hoped he'd remembered his gloves. *Hang on. He's probably like me. He doesn't need gloves.* She focused on him. Odd to think of someone else like her. A breeze wafted past, lifting strands of hair from her forehead. She jerked her head up, crossbow at the ready, but the skies were empty.

When she looked over towards the crater again, Ryder and Tama were coming back. Tama cradled something in his hands. Terror, not satisfaction, marked his face. Resolve shot through her. *No way are they taking this boy. No way will he suffer what I suffered.*

She didn't wait to see what he held, but ushered them away from the crater, where she could breathe and where they were less exposed.

They stopped in the relative shelter of a leaning overhang so Ryder could fish out a bag for Tama. She got her first glimpse at what he carried. Her breath stopped, and her eyes snapped to Ryder's. Unusual grimness lined his face, but he said nothing and passed the bag to Tama.

"Is that—"

"Yeah. At least, I think so."

Ice filled her veins. She watched Tama place a skull in the bag. Pain jolted through her head as a voice from the past pushed free of the barriers she kept it behind.

We will find it. We will find the weakness, and you will help us destroy it.

Ryder's hand slid under her elbow, and she smiled off his concern.

The skull fit neatly in the woven pack, and when Tama walked, it nestled against his side like it belonged there.

CHAPTER 16

Grey softness spread out in front of them in a depressing blanket, concealing the true shape of the land. Chilled wind blew Dust in soft eddies around them, the fine grains gritty as they clung to her lashes. She wiped her face, fingers smearing grime through the sweat on her forehead.

Ryder coughed, the sound muffled by the scarf wound tightly around his face. She flicked a glance at him sidelong. The cough started last night, and his hands shook a little as he divided up the rations. One look at his face, and she bit back her concern. *He's an adult. He knows what he's doing. At least, I hope he does.* Goggles, like the ones she'd given up on, the ones he'd not mentioned again, protected his eyes as he trudged through the endless drifts.

At fairly frequent interludes, tall poles reached up to the sky. An old highway. They'd left the ruins of the city behind them, but the occasional wreck of a house still broke the monotony.

Crumbling brick walls listed to the side, slow falls of Dust sliding off in a tiny cascade. Hoisting her pack, she veered off the road, ignoring Ryder's mumbled surprise. She pushed through the splintered door, stepping through piles of grey creeping over the step. Light filtered in through holes in the roof. A quick scan revealed little left by other scavengers, but there was more than food to be found in houses if you knew what to search for. Her fingers curled around a shattered picture frame.

She came out of the house to see Ryder waiting in the front garden while Tama paced back and forth on the road. A heavy frown sat above Ryder's goggles, and his scarf hid his mouth. She met his gaze with a defiant stare. With a small shrug, he turned back to the highway.

He joined her in the third house but spent more time staring at the smothered detritus of people's lives than being helpful. He would learn. You closed your eyes to the shattered emptiness so you could protect your heart. And you never missed an opportunity to search for something which might mean survival.

Tama got twitchier the further they got from the city, his hands moving and shoulders jerking. She stumped closer to him. "Which way now?"

He startled, his eyes like a deer in headlights before they veiled. With a jerk, he inclined his head towards what she dimly thought might be a westerly direction.

"There."

Ryder's face was unreadable under the protective gear, but his shoulders hunched, betraying his tension.

"Any point in asking you how you know?' His voice was muffled, gruff. A rush of warmth tinged with sadness flooded her. She missed being just the two of them. *Ridiculous*. Shifting her weight, she turned her gaze away from Ryder, towards Tama who kicked at the Dust, his head shaking.

She chewed her lip. Whatever pulled Tama tugged at her as well. A discordant note inside her head, winding around her thoughts. It made her want to run the opposite direction. "Is this the way to the Valley of the Kings you talked about?"

He shot her a venomous glance. "Like I'd ramble on about old kings or whatever. I never talked about that. You're lying."

She met Ryder's eyes through his goggles and shrugged. It didn't make any difference. They were committed to this now, and they didn't have any choice.

THE TREK down the highway was easier than walking through the city. Only the occasional car, abandoned, crashed, half covered by grey heaps, stood in their way. A lorry lay on its side, as if it had overturned and skidded a long way. The truck carriage rose out of the Dust at an angle. Something on the top of it moved in the heavy breeze. A plastic star hung on a cord. She gently lifted the spiky little thing, dislodging silty grains that skifted over her fingers. The line shook, and a dozen stars danced along its length. Ryder reached out, his light touch making the line shimmer.

"Fairy lights," he said.

A long forgotten moment shot into her head, driving down the motorway with her mother. She and her brother transfixed by the big trucks with their cabs all festooned with lights of different colours.

"Like a moving Christmas." She only realised she spoke out loud when Ryder's hand gripped her shoulder.

The urge to linger by the lorry dragged at her feet as they moved back along the too open highway. Ryder's voice broke into her thoughts. "Lark, it's getting darker, we need to find somewhere to camp."

Tama's head jolted up. "No! We've got to keep going!"

Ryder stopped, a muffled sigh escaping under his scarf. "Sorry, buddy. I call the shots, and we need shelter before the Dust comes down." His eyes darted between the two of them. "Well, I do at any rate."

Her chest constricted. She thought he had stumbled on a

rock before, but now she looked at him, exhaustion clearly drew tracks in his face.

"Tama, I know you want to keep going. I really do. I feel the same. But Ryder's right, we need to stop. We need to rest."

She scanned the horizon. About a kilometre away a grey mound loomed against the falling darkness. "There. It might be another house."

As they neared the heap, the broken remains of a gas station became visible. A decade of Dust coated the heavy roller door. She and Ryder heaved and pulled at the rusted metal.

Tama stared out into the darkening landscape, burning grey grains beginning to fall. One arm wrapped around his torso while he bit the nails of his other hand. No point asking him to help.

She gave one more push, muscles straining. Ryder needed to get inside. The tent was too small and he needed stronger shelter. The door shot up with a shriek. Tama jumped. She turned to smile at him, but the fear twisting his face stopped her.

"They're here," he whispered.

A great howl echoed through the still air, the call of the hounds freezing her heart. Tama stood, trembling, eyes wide and jaw clenched tight. She grabbed him, forcing him behind her. Ryder pressed against her shoulder. She glanced up at him. He focused on her, not on Tama, and her pulse jumped. The foolish man wanted to protect her. Guilt sent sick tendrils through her stomach. Her first impulse had been to run. He stared up at the sky, and she bit her lip. That wasn't true. She wanted to protect him too.

"Inside or out?" he asked, his voice calm, resigned.

She raised her chin and slid out her knife. "Out. Inside, we're trapped, and there's nothing to keep them from coming in."

"Not even the door?"

She shook her head, eyes scanning the horizon. "Not enough iron, and iron wouldn't stop the hounds anyway."

Two Fae appeared in the sky, and her stomach flipped. They floated to the ground, draperies fluttering regardless of the breeze. One had broader shoulders and shorter hair, with dark red wings dipped with black. The soft baby blue of the second one stood at odds with black claws and a flash of sharp teeth. Unhooking the small crossbow from her hip with one hand, she tightened her grip on her knife. *Never fought off two before. First time for everything, I guess.*

Tama muttered words she couldn't understand, and she hissed at him over her shoulder. "Quiet. Stay in the doorway, as out of sight as you can." She shifted her stance. "If it looks like we're failing, you need to run. Don't stop."

Ignoring the twisting in her gut, she stepped away from the doorway, hoping to draw their attention from Tama. It worked. They zeroed in on her. Their eyes, shimmering and shifting, caught in her thoughts. Closing her mind to them, she thought of Ryder, his hand in hers, and she pushed the Fae out of her head. They blinked.

The hounds attacked without warning, just a dark blur of movement. The baying was deafening. Ryder shouted as he fought off the beasts. *Don't look at him. He's tough. Don't look.*

The Fae split them apart. She stood alone between them and Tama. Swinging her knife, Addie drew their focus while she raised her crossbow in her other hand. The relaxed way the one in blue lifted its arm sparked fire in her. *How dare it ignore me.* Sparks flew from its fingers, and she didn't quite duck in time. A searing heat shot across her shoulder blade. Biting down on her lip, she smothered a cry.

No.

She had given them enough of her pain.

She pushed her shoulders back, standing tall. Harsh cries came from where Ryder battled the hounds. Each hiss and grunt of pain was a stab in her heart. She fought to ignore them, to ignore the rip of fabric and his swearing. Canine yelps filled the air too. Ryder would give as good as he got. She focused on the Fae, the sparks dancing on their fingers.

Steel raced down her spine. Right now, it didn't matter if Ryder saw what she could do, or if Tama saw—no way would she let the Fae take the boy without doing everything she could to stop them. When the red Fae lifted both arms, night tipped wings fanning out, she shot the crossbow at the blue one, wishing the bolt to burn. Flames flickered over the dart as it flew towards her target. Focusing on her knife, she imagined a shield. Sparks of Fae magic surrounded her, and she beat them back with the strokes of her blade.

"What the—? How are you doing that?" Tama's voice was loud behind her, and she cursed.

The Fae shared a glance. The blue one pulled out the burning bolt from its leg and quenched the small flames. It spread its wings, raising up its arms, a harsh chant curling through the air. Licking her lips, Addie tried to work out who was the bigger risk. The red one's mouth curled, showing pointed teeth. "We will take the boy. You interest us, but we can come back. You won't be going anywhere."

The two Fae stepped back as Dust swirled around them, thick and choking. Blinking rapidly, her vision dimmed as billowing clouds blocked the sun. Tama shouted once, then his cries cut off. The dark shapes of the hounds vanished. The world became a maelstrom, pushing her down. Shifting whispers turned into a booming rustle of whirling grains screeching against the metal roof of the station. She stumbled towards where she had last seen Ryder, managing only a few steps before the weight of grey powder forced her to her knees. Still she crept forward, feeling with her hands as Dust tore and bit at her clothes. Finally, she touched a hand, slick with blood and grime. She crawled on top of Ryder, shielding him from the worst of the storm. He would survive. He had to.

CHAPTER 17

Dust lay over her like a weighted blanket. For a moment, she wanted nothing more than to lie there. Getting up meant pain. *I could just close my eyes. Let it all go.* Her fingers pressed on Ryder's chest beneath her, still and cold. Fear gripped her heart like a vice. *I have to get him out of here.*

She arched her back, stilling when Dust slid off her and onto Ryder in a rustling stream. *Oh god. What if I suffocate him by moving?* She gritted her teeth. *Well he'd be dead either way.* She pushed up hard and fast, dragging him with her as greyness fell away from them.

Gasping in a lungful of air, powdery motes still clinging to her tongue, she tried to open her crusted eyes. They stung as she wiped her scarf over them. She knelt by Ryder. Dust covered his face, ashen under the grey powder. Deep cuts and rips on his arms bled bright red against his torn shirt. Her soul shrivelled. With a shaking hand, she pulled down his scarf, exposing his neck.

His pulse was weak, but there. Sobs shook her body. She patted at his face, wiping blood and grime from his eyes. Freshly fallen Dust replaced every bit she cleaned away.

It was evening.

The Dust wouldn't stop now.

Shelter.

She had to get him inside.

Fresh mounds of grey blocked the door of the gas station. She kicked her way through the dense powder. Holding Ryder around his chest, she tried to pull him up, muscles straining. She blinked away tears and laid him back down. *I'm too weak.* Dragging him over the threshold and across the floor, wincing at every bump, she glanced over her shoulder at the room.

Gloom filled the station, cold and quiet. An office tucked away at the back caught her eye. The glass from one window lay shattered on the floor, the pane in the door an empty space surrounded by jagged teeth. Looters most likely. She lifted Ryder's shoulders off the ground and dragged him as gently as possible through the debris. The office door could still shut, and she closed the venetian blinds to keep out the Dust. Not much, but it would have to do.

Digging into her pack, she pulled out the water bottle. The filter was dangerously close to its use by date, but a reassuring slosh eased her heart. Ryder's bag lay trapped beneath him. The clasps around his chest were tight and awkward to undo, and she cursed as she fought the buckles to get it off without hurting him. Pulling Ryder's bottle out, her hand brushed past the tent, and she bit her lip. *If his bag had been on more loosely we would have lost it and the tent as well.* He had more water in his bottle than she did. He was always more organised. She dribbled the water into his mouth, holding his lips closed so none would escape. Her hand trembled on his jaw. He was supposed to be the strong one. Foolish man. Her face crumpled. Why had he insisted on coming with her? He would die, and it would be her fault.

She rubbed her eyes and stared around the office for something to clean his wounds. Yellowed papers, glass and twisted aluminium, a broken stapler. Nothing useful. Her glance caught on a cupboard against the wall. The lock appeared battered, as if people had already tried to break through. Dents peppered the metal doors. She eyed her knife then looked back at Ryder. *Worth a try.*

Holding the knife above the lock she wished.

Nothing happened.

Rolling her shoulders back, she clenched her jaw. *I can do this.*

This time she closed her eyes, thought of Ryder, of how much she wanted to save him, and she wished. The heat coming off the knife startled her. She almost dropped it. Just before the heat died, she sliced through the lock.

There wasn't much in the cupboard. A pile of what had once been someone's lunch, now so desiccated it didn't even smell. Papers and a couple of hand drawn pictures labelled 'To Daddy, from Misha' stuck on the back wall. Crumpled in the corner were a white sports jacket, black t-shirt and shorts, balled up socks, and ridiculously orange shoes. Clearly Misha's daddy had kept a change of clothes in the office for when he went for a run or to the gym. Her eyes went to the pictures again, a big stick figure with a beard and a smile that escaped the borders of his face. A house with a happy stick family and a dog outside. She always wanted a dog, but mum always said no. Her finger traced the words. Misha. Another name to keep. To remember. To honour.

She pulled the clothes out, and another neat little box met her eye. Red. Still red. With a white cross on it. Her hands shook as she placed the clothes down and opened the box.

A full first aid kit. Her eyes welled.

Actual medicine.

Gauze.

Tape.

Scooting to Ryder she spread her treasures out next to her. She had to tug hard to wrench off his coat. The cuts on his arm were bad, but not as bad as they should be. Peering closer, she saw that the Dust, with its burning cloying nature, had sealed the wounds shut. He lost blood, but the Dust had probably saved his life.

At least, she hoped it could be saved.

Time slowed, seconds turning to hours. She winced each time she turned him on his side or back to dress a wound. His slackened face was pale in the dim light, eyes half open, lacking their usual warm flicker. The bandages wouldn't do anything, but she felt better wrapping something around his poor arms.

Finally, she had to admit there was nothing else she could do. She sat in the dark, her knees pulled up to her chest, eyes fixed on him, watching him breathe.

His moaning woke her. She scrambled to his side, worry battling with delighted relief that he was awake. Red blotches marred the greying skin of his face. Heat bloomed from his arms. She didn't need to check under the bandages. She had seen this before. Dust poisoning. He blinked at her, and she smiled back with trembling lips, tears blurring her vision.

"Hey," she said "It's okay. I got you. You're okay."

His lips, normally so firm and smooth, cracked and bled as he tried to speak.

"What? No, actually, don't say anything. Save your strength. You're okay. We're safe."

A word escaped his mouth, and she ducked down to hear.

He tried again. "Liar."

A sound, half a laugh, half a sob, leaped out of her, and her mouth twisted in a smile.

"I don't lie to you. Okay. Sometimes I do, but this is not that time."

His eyes, still so hazel beneath the bloodshot whites, smiled at her through what must be incredible pain.

She placed her hand near his cheek, not wanting to touch the damaged skin, before moving it to his chest. "Alright. You're in bad shape. But you're alive, and I swear, Ryder, I'm going to keep you that way."

He nodded and closed his eyes, wincing.

Shit. She didn't know what to do. What if she'd spent more time with Doc? Her fear of the lab and tests suddenly seemed so insignificant next to the fear that Ryder might die. Nausea swam through her. *What if what I am is something that could help him?*

Brushing her hair out of her eyes, trembling fingers snagging in the strands, her eyes were caught by faint movement at her knee. Ryder's fingers curled. Reaching out, she held his hand. He settled, sighed.

She blinked rapidly. There must be something. Some way. She grabbed the first aid kit with her free hand, scrabbling through the box. Her eyes lit on a scalpel, and a wild thought hit her. A couple of years ago she cut herself on a piece of scrap metal out scavenging, Jasper was with her and held her bleeding leg closed until help came. Her blood covered his hand, old and weathered and Dust burned. She tried to apologise later, but the words stuck in her throat at the sight of his hand, strong new skin without the wither of Dustblight. He said nothing, and she followed his lead, trying hard to forget something she couldn't explain.

She gazed down at Ryder. *Am I seriously considering this? It's a bit...icky.* Her fingers closed around the handle of the scalpel. Well. You never know until you try.

Shoving up the sleeve on her left arm, she gripped the scalpel in her right hand. Her arm trembled in front of her, and she froze. *I have no idea where to cut.* Aiming for where she half-remembered getting blood tests from when she was small, she slid the blade under her skin, into the vein. Just a tiny nick, the merest tingle of pain. The blood came out faster than she was expecting. She threw the blade into the kit and scooped up a cup. It was anyone's guess if this would work, or if so, how much was needed. She didn't want to lose too much, so she tied a tight bandage around her elbow, staunching the flow. Her face screwed up as she held the cup over Ryder. Taking a swab, she dipped the cotton in her blood. Dabbing it on his skin, she heaved a little but kept going. *All out of other options now.*

Sticky blood clung beneath her fingernails, tacky threads joining the swab to his skin as she finished. Her stomach turned over. She considered wiping out the cup but just tossed it to one side. Unlikely they would be using it.

Night dragged on, darkness closing in. She cracked a glow stick, shaking the fluid until a greenish tinge cast strange shadows on the floor. Her eyes burned with exhaustion. She kept them fixed on Ryder, trying to ignore the tingle in her arms and the eerie sense of music in her mind. By the time pale grey light filtered through the blinds, she was ready to wipe off the stench of blood. Using some of the sterile wash in the kit, she wiped his face clean. She inhaled sharply. Clear skin showed, fresh and new under the smeared blood. Not perfect, but better. His arms too, once she cleaned the gashes, were healing.

She expected elation, but instead cold fear clutched at her heart.

What in hell's name am I?

When Ryder shifted slightly, waking, she held her breath. He moved his head and blinked at her.

His voice was rough but ten times stronger than the night before. "I feel better."

She gave him a tight smile, but inside, she panicked. What if he asked her? He could never find out. He didn't like monsters. "I guess you were right when you said you were tough."

His eyes met hers, and she couldn't look away. She wondered if he knew she could read every emotion passing through his eyes, even though his face didn't change. Confusion, fear, relief, acceptance.

He spoke again. "Whatever it was that helped me, whatever you did—thank you Addie."

Her chin lifted as she breathed back quick tears.

"You're welcome."

CHAPTER 18

"I never wanted it you know. To be leader."

Ryder's voice snapped her out of her reflections as she leaned on the frame of the gas station door, watching the faint morning light turn Dust motes into glitter. She raised her head to gaze at him. New beard growth picked up copper tints from the weak sunshine, not quite concealing the tightness of his jaw underneath.

"So why did you take charge?"

He half shrugged and looked past her, at the Dust falling outside the door. For a moment, pain darkened his eyes before they shuttered, hiding his thoughts from view. He huffed out a sigh and ran a hand over his face. A burning weight lay on her chest. She rolled her shoulders to ease it, the straps of her pack rubbing at her neck. His eyes met hers, his mouth quirking in a half smile.

"Someone had to."

She nodded slowly, her gaze dropping down to her hands, the knife he'd given her playing between her fingers. She tried to think who else could have taken charge, but there was only one Ryder. Only one man who could have taken a group of such different and conflicting personalities and turned it into the most well-run compound she'd seen. Of course he stepped up. A smile flickered in her eyes. Ryder couldn't stop himself when he saw someone needed help. Too noble for his own good.

She cleared her throat, pushing past the swell of emotion. "Back in my old compound, we didn't have a leader. We were survivors clustering together. A couple of cops took charge, formed a council, but it was more about rations and rules than true community. We didn't get much of a chance to make it better before, well...before it all turned to crap."

His hand rested on hers for a moment. "It wasn't your fault, Lark, you know that."

She made herself smile, hoping he wouldn't notice it didn't reach her eyes.

"I know. It was the Fae. They put us in the position in the first place, taking away all possibility of making it work." She thrust her knife into its sheath. "I hate them."

The venom in her voice surprised her. It surprised Ryder too. He leaned back and eyed her.

"Is that why you want to go on? Because you hate them?"

Her braid tumbled over her shoulder as she shook her head. "No. I want to run away because I hate them." She ignored his snort. He thought she was so gung-ho even though the nightmares should have told him differently.

"I can't leave Tama out there, alone with the Fae."

His smile lit up his face, and he shouldered his pack, moving through the broken door frame. "And you wonder why I see you as a lieutenant. You're the same as me, Lark. Neither of us can say no to those who need us. Someone has to do it, and it looks like it's us."

Dust sat in heaped drifts, as if the fight with the Fae sparked an avalanche. Blowing in eddies around the tops of dead trees, it mimicked foggy days of her childhood when she and Beckett scared each other with stories of ghosts lurking in the mist. Shadows shifted, and she tensed, thinking she saw in the dark branches the swirling robe of a Fae tracker. A movement and a sigh, and the Dust blew in circles around an empty forest floor. Suppressing a shudder, she followed Ryder into the graveyard of trees. She would rather have the ghosts.

The day's trek dragged at aching leg muscles, her pack tugging her shoulders out of alignment. They trudged through endless piles of Dust, all the while the tug at her mind pulled her towards where the Fae must have taken Tama. Every time Ryder stumbled or took a breath too quickly her eyes darted to him, ready to call a halt. Finally, he stopped, pulling down the scarf and pushing up the goggles.

"For fuck's sake, Lark. I'm fine."

She shrugged, her eyes running over his arms. No blood. Good. "You nearly died, Ryder. Excuse me for being cautious."

"Yeah, but I didn't. You're as bad as my grandma."

His grandmother? Wow. Way to stroke a girl's ego.

She brushed past him, listening to the pull in her mind. "The Dust is deeper and falling faster than it did yesterday. If you're fine with that, great—because we've got a long way to go."

After only a few steps, she faltered. As though someone flipped a switch—as though someone cut the tie between her and Tama—he was gone. An empty hole in her mind remained where his presence had been seconds ago. She spun, scanning the trees, hoping to find the way dangling before her.

Night closed in. Light greyness turned to a sepia toned dirty glow as the sun went down behind the Dust. Dead branches reached like claws into the encroaching dark.

"I can't find it."

"What?"

She bit her lip, glancing sidelong at Ryder and trying to control her heart.

"Tracks," she settled for.

His sigh made her grimace. "Lark, you haven't been

following tracks since we left the compound. I don't care how you've been finding the way, but what I'm taking from this is that you can't see it anymore?"

She nodded tightly.

He stared at her for a second. "Fuck."

"Sorry."

He kicked at the ground, his hands on his head, shaking loose the Dust. Stopping, he crossed his arms and took a breath. "No. Don't be sorry. We're lucky we ever got this far."

Her heart started beating again. Reaching out, she brushed flakes of grey out of his beard, new and scruffy and somehow looking as if he'd always had one. He froze, his eyes meeting hers. She didn't quite snatch her hand away, but she backed up a step.

Looking anywhere but at his face, she stilled. Light. Through the branches.

Ryder stepped closer. "What the hell is that?"

Warm light, not the cold brightness of the Fae, filtered through the trees like a beacon. One she recognised. Ryder's arm was close against her shoulder, and she shifted slightly, pulling away from his touch.

"They're petrels."

He raised his eyebrows. "Petrels?"

"Yes. Wanderers who don't belong to any of the compounds. They travel through the deadlands and live in carts." Echoes of old pain slated into her mind. "Some are nice. Some aren't."

His brows drew in sharply, and his jaw jutted out, eyes darkening in anger. But she didn't think it was for her. "Are these some of the people you hung out with after you left?"

"After the Testing. After I ran. Yes. They have their own code, as we all do." She shifted, pulling her shoulders back against the tension threading her muscles like burning wire. "Like I said, mostly they were kind to children."

He chewed on his lip, and she found her eyes drawn to his fingers on his jaw. He spoke to her, and she blinked. "What?"

"I said, what do you reckon? Go in or stay out?"

She pulled her bag up on her shoulder and bent her head toward his pack. "We need shelter. The tent needs repairs, and they're likely to have thread and patches. And the trees will take most of the Dust. But we'll need something to trade. Plus they might not be friendly."

He rolled his eyes. "That's not a decision, just more things to think about."

"As you always like to remind me, you're the boss, Ryder. You make the decision."

He quirked his eyebrows at the snark, and she scrunched her face at him, hoping to keep his eyes up so he wouldn't see the way her hand clenched around her knife. When his eyes softened and he reached out to grip her shoulder, she knew he saw. Of course he did. He always noticed what she didn't want him to.

Memories scuttled through the back of her mind, hidden in shadows she tried not to look in. Pain didn't get better when you looked at it.

Whatever had been pulling her towards Tama was gone now. They needed directions to the Valley of Kings he rambled about, if such a place even existed.

"We go in."

Ryder pulled out his knife. "Best be prepared then."

He smiled, and her lips curled upwards in response. Within a breath, the smile disappeared as he stepped closer, awkwardly tucking a stray strand of hair behind her ear and sliding his hand down to cup the back of her head. Butterflies invaded her chest, making her heart race. She nodded, both hating and breathing in relief when his hand dropped.

He turned to face the trees, light flickering through steadily falling Dust. Pulling the scarf over his face, he wiped the goggles with the fabric before sliding them over his eyes.

She rubbed a powdery film off her own face. Maybe she should put goggles on as well, the petrels might get too close to the truth otherwise. Ryder spoke over his shoulder, his voice muffled.

"Don't worry Lark. This time you're not twelve, and you're not alone."

CHAPTER 19

The flickering light turned into the steady glow of a small fire. Thin trees opened to a clearing ringed by covered carts standing guard against the outside world. The quiet hum of people, all too aware of the threat of black tipped wings in the dark, grew louder with every step. Addie edged closer to Ryder, her sweaty palm slipping on her knife handle. Flames threw shifting shadows over the Dust, sending shivers crawling over her skin.

The carts loomed on either side of them as they walked a pathway into the centre, whispers trickling out from frayed canvas covers. A warm glow danced over the people gathered around the fire. Their eyes fixed on the newcomers. Rigged cloth stretched high over the flames to catch the Dust, allowing the fire to smoulder without suffocating under grey powder. No children played, no old people talked. The clearing filled with an expectant hush.

A man stood slowly, short hair falling in a blunt fringe across his forehead. Puckered red skin ridged his brows, milky white blindness staring fixedly from one eye. The petrels lived in the Dust, and the bleak grey life took its toll, leaving their skin mottled and melted in patches. She met his stare, aiming for confidence rather than threat. Twelve-year-old Adelia whimpered behind her eyes, and she fought off a frown. Their skin inspired curious compassion now, not fear. But the thought of her blood curing Ryder's Dustblight made her chest tighten.

She and Ryder stopped just inside the ring of carts, leaving space between them and the leader of the caravan. Ryder shifted a step in front of her, his broad shoulder blocking her from view. Her brows snapped together. Gripping her knife firmly, she took a deliberate step sideways to stand next to him, her shoulder nudging his arm. Tension flickered across his face. His arm shifted, as if he'd reached to push her back and stopped himself. She lifted her chin. *Strength matters here. Weakness makes you a target.*

The leader sauntered over to them, pausing long enough to send one of the younger men trotting over to a large cart closer to the fire. She tried to keep an eye on both of them.

"We don't often get people in from the Dust. What brings you here?"

His voice rang strong and clear, completely at odds with her expectations.

"My name is Ryder and this is Lark. We're looking for someone who was taken from us." Ryder's words carried across the clearing. Fabric rustled as the people around the fire shifted, their faces twisting into scowls. More than one picked up wooden staves, carved and deadly.

The leader spat, his puckered face shiny in the glow of the fire. "We didn't take anyone. We don't steal people, whatever you've heard. We leave that to the Fae."

Her tongue stuck to the roof of her too-dry mouth. She let Ryder speak.

"We didn't think you had. We hope you can offer us shelter for the night. Our tent needs repairs, and we're not as used to the Dust as you."

The man eyed their weapons and raised his brows at

Ryder, who smiled and shrugged. "Would you walk into unknown territory without a weapon at your side?"

A grin tugged at the petrel's scars. "Ha! No, I wouldn't."

He still didn't move or gesture for them to come around the fire. Images floated behind her eyes, other fires, other men, other rules. She cleared her throat. "What about the code?"

The crackling of the fire snapped through the silence. The petrel's eyes fixed on her, milky white and pale blue. "Code?"

She bit back the sarcasm writhing on her tongue. "Yes, the code. I lived with petrels once. Many years before. I know you all have a code."

Murmurs spread around the fire, and he waved a hand, quenching them. His head cocked, and he rubbed at his chin.

"Perhaps we do, but what's it to you?"

"Guesting laws. Shelter from the Dust. We can trade."

Ryder shifted next to her, but she didn't look at him. Trade was important. Perhaps she should have mentioned it.

The leader glanced to where the younger man had gone. A curtain twitched in the side of the largest cart. He turned back to them, a tight smile battling his clenched jaw. "One night. We'll help with the tent. Then you're on your way."

A sigh fluttered out of her before she could catch it. "Thank you, it is appreciated."

He looked to the cart again, his fingers playing round a medallion in his fist. "First though, you need to talk to Kidist."

DARKNESS FILLED THE CART, leavened by the flickering warm glow of the fire outside. Gloom lifted as her eyes adjusted. Rickety shelves leaning in from either side of the walls closed in on her. She took a shaky breath of musty air and stepped away from the threatening tumble of ornaments and oddments.

The scent of an unwashed body overlaid by sweet incense

crowded the space. She blinked at the shrivelled woman enthroned on a chair draped in torn brocade. A presence of iron strength emanated from the burned and twisted form. Her eyes shone through her ruined face.

"Sit down, dear."

The chair rocked a little when Addie sat. It steadied after a moment, and she relaxed.

Her eyes met the gaze of the old woman, and she pressed her back into the seat so she wouldn't fidget. The old petrel's eyes, dark brown flecked with grey, held the expression of someone used to dealing with pain and who rose through it. She knew that look. She saw it in the mirror. Her bum shifted in the chair, and she flexed her fingers, letting her eyes drop. Her gaze ran over the mottled Dustblighted arm resting on dusty brocade, catching and fixing on rough puckered scars ringing the woman's wrists.

"I am Kidist."

She dragged her eyes away from the scars, a small smile pushing at her cheeks while she bit the inside of her lip. "Adelia."

The woman cocked her head. "Yet, the man with you, he called you something else? He called you Lark."

"My last name. I don't know why he always calls me that."

Kidist smiled, her chapped lips lifting to reveal stained teeth. Her smile spread over her face, reflecting beauty in her eyes. Addie's cheeks tugged upwards in reply. The old woman leaned forward, placing a ruined hand on hers. "The Lark sings at daybreak, heralding in a new dawn. There are worse things to be called."

"I guess." Sings at dawn. New light. She never knew.

Her eyes went back to Kidist's wrists, ragged scars puckered grey against dark skin. "Those must have hurt."

Kidist inclined her head, her hand tracing up Addie's arm. "You bear scars too, though yours aren't so visible to the world." Tension like threaded wire prickled at the silvery marks on her skin, and she held her breath. Kidist's gentle touch settled on her wrist, warm and not unpleasant. "My scars are an old pain, from an old time. I try not to think of it too much. I will just say that Jonathan and his people have looked after me, and I try to do the same for them."

"Have they..." The words stuck in her throat, but she burned with the need to know. "Have they ever hurt children?"

Kidist gripped her wrist tightly for a second before releasing her and sitting back. "No. Not these ones. There are those who hurt children, and we do not suffer them to live when we find them."

Her breath shuddered in her throat.

"Good." She whispered out past the pain.

Warmth radiated from the other woman. Little by little it calmed her, helped her breathe without the constriction of remembered fear.

Her shoulders relaxed for the first time since they'd walked into the camp. "Thank you, Kidist."

The old woman reached stiffly to the table at the side of her chair where a pot of water sat, still steaming from the hot stones it nestled in. Picking up the hot pan, she gestured with her other hand. Addie turned to see a tiny shelf with small glasses on it.

She picked up a glass cut like crystal. Another glass with Mickey Mouse on it caught her eye, and she bit back a smile. Faded and chipped and kind of creepy with his eyes rubbed off, but still definitely Mickey Mouse. She passed them over to Kidist, who had waited with a smile while she examined them.

"I haven't seen glass like that for a while." Addie said. "Certainly not out in the Deadlands. Where did you get them?"

"We trade. There are skills we have which others need."

Probably best not to ask what. Kidist took some finely ground leaves from a small wooden box, releasing a strong scent reminding her of incense and herbs and the potpourri her mother used to keep in a big bowl in the hall. Flakes settled in the steaming water. The aroma grew stronger, filling her senses and relaxing her muscles even more.

"Is that where you get your food? The tea as well?"

"Partly. The food, yes. The tea we gather ourselves."

Her mind darted to the small crops they wrangled from the choking Dust, the precious water that they used to coax the shoots to survive. "Does it grow out here?"

Kidist's smile closed her out and held back secrets.

"Here, drink and put the past behind you. You are stronger than those who hurt you. You will rise, and they will turn to Dust."

"That's something I can drink to."

All the sweetness of the tea emptied out into the steam. The bitter sting cleansed her mind, wiping away a shadow. She closed her eyes. Kidist was right. Her fingers curled thinking of Dust under her fingernails as she scrabbled away from the men looming over her with their heavy sticks and hands. Iron set in her spine, and she pushed them from her mind. In their place rose images from a movie she saw when she was ten. The heroes took a broken sword and made it whole, made it strong, made it powerful.

Her eyelids fluttered open. Really? A broken sword? She eyed the tea and set the glass down, taking care not to rub over Mickey's face too much.

Kidist cocked her head. "The others will want to talk to you now, do the trade. Jonathan lets me speak first, but I don't do the business side of the deal." A grin sparked. "That stuff's a bit boring."

She smiled her thanks and stood, careful not to knock the table with the glasses. She hesitated, then when Kidist made a little gesture with her hand, she asked, "Why do you live like this? With the petrels?"

The old lady rubbed her wrists, "We are all petrels, even

you. This land was ripped from us, changed and ruined and desecrated. We are all strangers in it now."

Her eyes drifted over the shelves full of gathered treasure. "Maybe, but why don't you settle? Join a compound or start your own? There are plenty of abandoned places in the cities."

"Freedom." Kidist's voice rang hard in her ears, and she turned back to face her. "There is no freedom in your compounds where you live only at the mercy of the Fae, herded like cattle waiting to be picked off."

Harsh words but truth. The walls of the compound rose high. Their concrete and stone bulk meant safety, but also made them a target. The dead ground of the impact crater was a daily reminder why they lived surrounded by walls and struggling for food.

Her lip tucked between her teeth, and her shoulders tightened. "You think your way is better?"

"Our way, we don't live as long, but we live free."

A sigh escaped her. "I guess I understand that."

Kidist smiled again. "You will find your way, little Lark. Maybe one day you will sing freedom in the dawn."

CHAPTER 20

Crackling wood on the fire sent curls of acrid smoke wafting around them. Her binocs sat nestled at Jonathan's feet, the price for materials and tools to repair the tent. She stretched her legs out to the warmth, her eyes on Ryder. He worked steadily, flicking small grains of powder off the material at regular intervals as Dust filtered through the branches above. Neat stitches closed the tears ripped by hounds' teeth. His deft hands showing no mark from those same rending jaws.

A sigh floated from her mouth. He glanced up, smiling into her eyes. Lips turning up without thought, she held her breath as her heart fluttered.

A soft bag sloshed in front of her face, and she turned away from Ryder to shoot a questioning look at Jonathan. He grinned, waving the water-skin under her nose. *Well. Rude not to.* The liquid slid down her throat, thick and syrupy, the bitterness catching on her tongue.

"Good, isn't it?" Jonathan waved towards a young man who appeared from the dark and threw himself on the ground next to her. "Put hairs on your chest, won't it, Israel?"

The young man laughed, holding out a hand. Wiping her

mouth, she passed the bag along. The petrels travelled every-where. Maybe they would know.

"Ever heard of a place called the Valley of the Kings?"

Jonathan crossed himself, and the sight tugged at a memory of Paolo in the ward, holding Xiyu and praying for the children. Faces tumbled behind her eyes. Mia. Matt. Lily. So much rode on them finding Tama.

"Going there would be suicide," the petrel said. "You should forget about the boy and go back to your people. Saving him won't make a difference in the long run."

But it did. One child made all the difference in the world. Her back tightened and darker thoughts flickered into the light. *No-one came for me.* Saving Tama wasn't about the long run. It was about making sure another child didn't end up with scars on his mind and screams in the night.

"We can't go back without him." Ryder's voice rang firm, but his eyes remained fixed on his task.

"He's right," she said. "We won't abandon him."

Jonathan rolled his eyes and threw another dead stick on the fire. Sparks flew as Dust coating the twig lit, and she wrinkled her nose at the smell.

Israel leaned forward. "The Valley's not too far from here, over by where Raglan used to be."

She shifted back on her elbow. "Raglan?"

"Yeah, my parents took me there once. For summer." Fire-light danced on his dark face, highlighting his tight jaw and the tension around his eyes. "We hired a beach house and everything."

"Surfing. Raglan's great for surfing. Or was." Ryder's voice sounded far away, he'd stopped stitching, staring unseeing at the fabric in his hands.

Closing her eyes, she savoured the warmth of the fire touching her face like sunshine. Flashes of bright sun in a blue sky crowded her mind. The scent of the sea and toasty sand beneath her feet. Beach air whirled laughter around like seagulls diving over waves. Beckett. Familiar bands tightened around her heart, but she refused to stop remembering her brother running down the beach, hands covered in sand as he flicked salty grains at her, brown hair twisted into watery tight curls. She wrapped the vision around her heart fiercely. When she opened her eyes to grey darkness and the soft and incessant fall of Dust, she tried to keep the image close behind her eyes.

Ryder shook his head, and she could almost see the past falling from him, fading into the smoke of the fire. He placed the tent at his feet and faced Israel. "Why's it called a Valley? Raglan is a peninsula, it doesn't have a valley."

"I didn't name it. How would I know?"

Jonathan snorted. "Keep your sass in your pants, mate." He fixed his eye on Ryder. "The Fae named it. I've never seen the place, but I've talked to someone who has." His gaze darted to Kidist's cart. "The home of the Fae doesn't resemble anything from before, nothing like anything else in the country. A valley sits there now, surrounded by mountains. They moved them."

She drew her legs up to her chest, feet dragging at the dirt. "Moved mountains? Is that even possible?"

Jonathan shrugged and spat in the fire. "You're talking about the Fae. Pretty much anything is possible."

"So, what, they pulled them out of the earth?"

"No, you didn't listen. They moved them. They picked them up from the centre of the North Island and shoved them around their valley."

"Jesus."

Jonathan frowned at Ryder's blasphemy. Addie considered him as she chewed on a rough piece of bread. *How, after everything that happened, could he still believe in a god?*

"I knew they were powerful," Ryder said. "But fuck. Mountains?"

She swallowed. *Mountain tops peeking through clouds, suddenly hidden by purple cloth.* The image flashed into her mind, and she blinked it away.

"Mountains or not, we need to get there," she said. "Can you tell us the way?"

The young man eyed her. "Is he really that important, this boy?"

"Yes."

"Why?"

She stared at him. What a ridiculous question. "Because he's a child. Because he's alone and about to be harmed. Because he's ours."

The words dropped into his face like rain, his puckered skin easing and his mouth turning up. "Then I will show you the way."

Jonathan put out a hand. "Wait. That's not your decision, Israel."

The young man stretched back, his long legs reaching towards the banked fire and his curly hair falling around his shoulders. "Jono, you're going to give them the information, so why not let me show them the way? I'm going to help them, regardless."

The two of them stared at each other, and something about the way they did made her twitch back a smile and glance at Ryder. The twinkle in his eye made her bite the inside of her cheek. This must be what the two of them looked like to everybody else back home.

"Fine. But you know the rules. Two out, two home. Who do you wanna take?"

Israel glanced towards the carts, where two young women stood. One with long black hair looped in braids around her head raised a staff in a salute when she saw them looking.

"Pritika. I'll take Pritika. She's strong and tough. We'll make it back, Jono. A day's journey, easy."

"You better, boy."

Jonathan turned to frown at Addie, and she stared back.

What was she supposed to say? She could say she'd make sure they returned, but, considering Israel's confidence, that would be a bit rude.

She put out her hand. "Thanks."

SLEEPING in the open tempted her, but she compromised by setting up the tent with the flap facing towards the fire. The petrels didn't need to see how comfortable she was in the Dust. Plus, she wanted to keep her eye on Ryder.

The clean canvas pulled taut, straining against the new patch, but the stitches held tight. Her finger traced the neat row of threads. *Was there anything Ryder couldn't do?* It shouldn't have surprised her he could sew. He had to learn to do everything in their community. They all had. Ducking her head, she pulled the flap and scrambled inside. The scent of him washed over her, and she breathed in deeply. His voice rumbled as he said goodnight to Jonathan. Then he filled the opening and filled her senses. Deep lines showed around his eyes, crinkling into dark circles. She curled her legs under her and sat, waiting.

Throwing himself onto the bedroll, he groaned. "I'm too old for this sleeping on the ground thing."

"You're not old!"

He smiled, and her pulse leaped. "I'm getting older, Lark, every year. It's a bugger."

She arched a brow. "Yeah but you've got a few years left yet Ryder, not quite in your dotage. Even if you act like it sometimes."

A laugh broke out of him, and she beamed inside. He pushed himself up on his elbow, and his eyes fixed on hers, his smile fading.

"What if I don't, Lark. What if this is it? What happens to them?"

Mia's face flashed into her mind.

"They'll be ok," she said. "They'll follow someone else." Not that just anyone could replace Ryder.

A deep line appeared between his brows, and the shadows under his eyes darkened. *Looks like he knows that.* Heaviness pulled at her heart, and she forced herself to smile. "You'll just have to make it back then, won't you?"

His eyes lit up, and he reached out and tapped her knee.

"You too, Lark."

Mountains. A huge palace. A white room. Pain.

Her smile died. "Yeah. Me too." She watched him as he lay back down, grimacing as his back met the ground. "Do you think this is foolish, Ryder? Going to the Valley, I mean. Suicide, like Jonathan said?"

He opened his eyes, looking up at the patched canvas. His jaw clenched, and she wished she could stroke the tension away.

"Foolish or not, doesn't matter. We're doing it regardless. I'm not coming this far to turn back." He turned his head, meeting her eyes. "But yeah, I'm not ashamed to say it scares the crap out of me. There's a difference between patrolling the line between the monsters and your people, and willingly entering the monster's den."

Her hands trembled. She held them tightly in front of her, willing them to stop.

"It'll be okay, Addie. You don't have to do it alone."

She kept her eyes on her hands, aware of his stillness in the flickering light of the fire.

"We better get some sleep," he said. "We've got a long walk tomorrow."

Her lips twitched upwards. "It's a long walk every day."

A sigh huffed out of him. "That it is. Come on, Lark. Sleep."

She lay down, and he rolled over, pulling her close to him. His presence might not be enough to stave off the nightmares this near to the Valley, but she breathed out and willed herself to relax. His leg caught over her calf, and his arm lay heavily over her waist. Her heart thudded. His hand fumbled, closing on her wrist before he threaded his fingers through hers.

"Don't worry, Addie," he said, his voice a sleepy mumble against the back of her head. "I won't let them hurt you."

CHAPTER 21

After so long being just the two of them, travelling with other people should have been more jarring than it turned out to be. Pritika and Israel joked, moving through drifts and sudden eddies with practiced grace and a confidence born of familiarity. Their laughter was infectious, wafting through grey air like sunshine. She walked on the edges of their banter, hoarding smiles inside. Her eyes strayed to Ryder. Strength flowed from him. He threw in his own jokes more than once.

Gusting wind blew Dust off the ground towards them. The two petrels strode through the wall of grey, hoods down and faces bare, oblivious to the burning grains. Ryder put his scarf over his mouth and nose and frowned at hers knotted around her neck. She shrugged and scrunched up her face in a mock growl. He shook his head at her, but his features softened.

The walk took as long as she had feared. At least this time they had a decent meal in their bellies. The petrels had a weird paste they put on their sour bread, which made all the difference in helping it go down.

Pritika slowed to let her catch up, pointing ahead. "The mountains are over there, you'll see them more clearly soon."

She followed Pritika's arm with her eyes. In the distance, the Dust on the horizon loomed darker, denser. Like a wall. Mountains it was then.

The way had been mostly flat with some tough climbs, and they'd skirted most of the remaining towns. Made sense. Petrels didn't like going to towns if they could help it, dead ones or living ones.

Her eyes went to the woman beside her, her youth and energy shining out against the greyness.

"If you don't mind me asking, when did you join the petrels?"

Pritika smiled. Her skin was not as puckered or burned as Israel's, but they both shared the same bright eyes. Maybe Kidist was right. There was a certain freedom here not seen in the Newhaven children.

"I was two when my parents joined. My sister and I were part of the package."

"What about you, Israel?"

A cloud passed over his face, and Pritika touched the back of his hand lightly.

"I was eight. My parents died. I was alone, and the people at my compound either didn't care or were too caught up in their own troubles to care. I ran away."

"Into the Dust?"

He laughed, a free and easy sound she couldn't help but smile in response to. "I know, foolish, right? Anyway, I didn't get far before I sat down and waited. Jonathan's crew found me shortly afterwards. Kidist said she heard me crying and knew where to send them, but I hadn't cried. Not once. She's special, our Kidist."

"I can tell."

She could still see those eyes, brown flecked with grey, the pain in their depths tempered with steel. Whatever lent her the ability to hear a lost child, to survive whatever hell shaped her, special was an understatement. The thought of the scars on Kidist's wrists made her frown, and she pulled at her sleeve, covering her own scars.

As they moved closer, the mountains took on a more definite shape - a range of high peaks, disappearing into a swirling cloud bank of grey Dust. Their guides stopped, their eyes meeting.

"We could avoid it, go 'round the side."

"That would take another four hours. We won't get back before dark if we go that way."

"You sure?"

"It'll be okay. It's a dead one."

Dead one. Dead town.

Ryder walked up to the two petrels. "Is there a problem with the route?"

Israel shrugged. "We don't like towns much, but this should be alright."

The town reminded her of others she'd passed through before. A high road, a few stores lining it, crumpled and shattered and sad. She wandered up to the glassless windows of a Four Square, peering into the dim room. Nothing on the shelves. Cleared out years ago. Looking back to the road, she saw Pritika and Israel walking close together, eyes forward, refusing to look at the buildings. Interesting how much it affected them. Ryder stooped over a strange clump in the ground, and she wandered over to him.

"What is it?"

"A sign I think."

He pulled out his knife and used the blade to scrape the years of Dust off the twisted, rusted metal beneath. The words were hard to read, the yellow letters faded and chipped.

"Welcome to Waitetuna."

Something in his voice made her examine him more closely, seeing the tightness around his eyes.

"Did you know this town?"

"Not well. A mate I knew in Raglan, his gran lived here. We came out once, a group of us. Built a fence for her." He stood abruptly, shaking the Dust off his knife. "Fat lot of good that would have done her."

Her arms lifted, wanting to hold him, make him feel better. She pulled her pack higher on her shoulder and fidgeted with the straps.

"I guess, at the time, it made a difference."

His face loosened a little, and the side of his mouth turned up as his eyes met hers.

"Yeah. Yeah it did." He chuckled, and the vice around her heart eased. "She made us ginger slice. We would've built two fences for that slice."

Israel shouted, waving them on. Here in the dead town, his face lost its vibrant light and his lips fixed in a harsh line.

They left Waitetuna behind. The Main Street made way for shattered houses scattered behind sticks of trees that must once have been beautiful hedges. The petrels shook off the gloom hanging over the detritus of people's lives. Their laughter and banter filtered back through the muffled air.

They trekked on for another four hours. The further they got, the more she worried about their guides making it home in time. When she raised that with Pritika, the girl just waved off her concern. Israel butted in, his curly hair falling over his face as he shook his head.

"We'll be fine," he said. "We do it all the time."

"Not all the time, Izzy, but yeah, don't worry Adelia. We know what we're doing."

The mountains were larger now, filling the sky ahead. No slope led up to them. The ground lay flat and undisturbed until it hit a rearing wall of rock, like fortress walls. Her heart thudded against her ribs, and she breathed out the fear curdling her insides. It was as intimidating as the Fae probably intended.

"WE'RE HERE. This is as far as we take you. This is the way into the Valley."

The side of the mountain sheared off, like someone had sliced it roughly. Stone and earth formed intricate patterns, making her think of cross sections of geodes in primary school. Clouds of Dust covered the top of the mountain, swirling back into itself and not dropping.

She patted the mountain. No secret door. "Doesn't look like a way in."

Israel grinned and pushed her head so her gaze moved to her left. A ladder snaked its way up the side of the cliff, made from bits of old buildings—some metal piping, some wooden beams.

"Oh. Yes. That's lots better."

The ladder went straight up, disappearing in the eddies of Dust above. Small stone piles dotted the base of the cliff, with tall thin carved figures perched on top.

"Cairns."

She turned to Ryder. "What?"

"Cairns. Like shrines. Looks like someone's trying to ward people away—or worship the Fae."

A cold burning shot through her. Worship the Fae. They couldn't. Surely not. The thought made her stomach churn.

Pritika's voice softened, as if this close to the Valley she worried about the Fae noticing. "Some people visit the valley. They don't often make it back out. I believe they build the cairns to remember those who have gone and warn those about to go in."

"Like us."

The other woman shrugged a little. "Yes, like you."

Israel moved into her line of sight, tall and lanky. "For what it's worth, I think you're doing the right thing. Someone has to give a shit about lost kids, right?"

She saw him then as a frightened and abandoned eight-year-old, Dust covered and lost. She remembered nights crying in the deadlands, wondering if she would die alone in the Dust. "Yes. And we do."

Ryder came up by her shoulder. "Thank you both for bringing us here. You sure you're going to be fine getting back?"

They shared a glance and Israel nodded. "Worst comes to worst, there's always the trees. They tend to leave you alone when you're high up in the trees. Remember that." His grin burst out, pulling at the mottled skin. "But we'll be good. You go rescue your boy."

Pritika put her hand out, and after a second, she reached out and clasped it.

"Take care of yourselves, Adelia."

"You too."

The words ripped away to float meaningless and swamped by Dust as Pritika and Israel walked away from them into the barren deadlands.

She meant to watch until they were gone but realised she didn't want to see them swallowed up by the greyness. Turning, she eyed the ladder dubiously.

Ryder gave it a bit of shake. The haphazard rungs made from pieces of broken wood and metal stayed attached to the cliff, which was more than she expected.

"Do we go up?" he asked.

Her eyes darted to where the rungs disappeared into grey gloom, then back to him.

"I think so."

He raised a brow, and she shrugged. "I don't want to go up any more than you do, but you heard Israel. If the Valley of the Kings exists, then we'll find it up there. We don't have any choice."

She swung her pack higher on her shoulders and tightened

the clasps around her chest. Taking a hold of the broken beams, she took a breath.

"Whoa. Hang on, Lark. Who said you're going first?"

"Pretty sure I did."

He frowned at her. "We have no idea if it's safe up in those clouds or if this piece of junk will even hold. You're not going first."

Her lips tugged up a little. "Yes, I am, because it makes sense, and you know it does. I'm lighter, so it's safer for me to be above you if your weight breaks the ladder. And the Dust doesn't bother me in the same way. You know this, Ryder."

Tension tightened his eyes, and a muscle twitched in his jaw. His eyes shifted between her and the ladder. He stood back, his arms crossed.

She put a foot on and pulled herself up. The rungs shook slightly, and Ryder moved quickly to stand below her, hand at her back. She rolled her eyes at him. If all those people had gone up, it wasn't likely to break.

Even though the hodge podge of beams and metal palings nestled firmly on the cliff, each pull upwards strained at her shoulders. Her legs shook with fatigue the closer they came to the swirling maelstrom of grey Dust above them.

Going into the Dust, knowing that Ryder had nearly died under ashen piles not so long ago, made every step harder. The choking powdery weight had her hands gripping the rungs so tightly her shoulders started cramping. But it was more than that. If the stories were true, then beyond the Dust lay the home of the Fae. The nest. Had she been there before? She must have. *Why am I doing this?* Her foot slipped, and she clung to the rails before stomping on upwards.

Tama, bound and helpless, frightened and alone. *I'm doing it because he shouldn't have to go through what I went through.* Her jaw clenched, and she hauled herself upwards with renewed vigour. *None of them should.*

CHAPTER 22

*A*ir met her hand as she reached for the next rung. No more ladder, no more cliff. With a sigh of relief, she hauled herself over the edge and stumbled a little on legs of jelly. She rubbed at burning biceps and stretched out the ache in her shoulders. A small plateau ran out into clouds. Dense grey fog nearly obscured a winding path.

Scrabbling noises brought her back around to the edge, but Ryder shook off her offer of help and heaved himself up. Her eyes ran over him, checking for fatigue, hoping he wouldn't notice. Strength showed in his stance. His arms didn't fumble as he rearranged his pack. A smile crept over his face, and he cocked his head, mimicking her, looking her up and down. She bit her lip and shrugged a little, ignoring the flutter in her stomach as his gaze roved over her. So she didn't want him to get sick. He could deal with it. Patting her on the shoulder, he pushed her on, into the mist.

Pebbles scattered the path, rolling underfoot and sending jarring pain through burning legs. Something in the air pulled her onwards, tugging at the hidden door in her mind. Part of her wanted to turn and run. The urge was so strong, she half swivelled before catching herself. Her fists clenched. Tama was here somewhere, so she would keep going. *No-one came for me. This time I can change it.*

Dust lay more lightly on the ground, and white mist took over from grey. The air looked cleaner, and she pulled down her scarf to take a deep breath. Clouds banked up ahead. With a glance at Ryder, who gestured her on, she plunged into soft whiteness. Dampness caressed her skin like the touch of heaven. She rubbed droplets into her arms, sticking out her tongue to catch the moisture. Ryder came up beside her, pushing up his goggles and rubbing his hand over his face. His eyes lingered on her mouth, and she closed it, licking the last drops of wetness off her lips. Ignoring the skip in her heartbeat, she quickened her pace, striding ahead of him.

Without warning, they broke through the cloud. She stumbled to a stop, Ryder crashing into her back. The sight ahead of her left her breathless, words fleeing her brain.

They stood on a mountain, white fog behind them, nothing but clear blue sky in front of them. Blue. Like in the story books, like from her childhood. Tears sprang to her eyes, and she blinked them away. She wanted to see.

Mountains rose in a ring around a lake valley, spreading for kilometres into the distance. Clouds crowned the tops of the peaks opposite, and dark grey ringed the base of the horizon. She pulled off her scarf with shaking hands and shrugged off her jacket. She wanted to feel light, wanted to feel clean air on her skin. Lush green fields and parks surrounding the clear water of the lake below made her heart stutter. Her face crumpled. The peaceful storybook land faded as shadows filled her head. How did they have so much when her people had nothing?

"Lark, the city, do you see it?"

She followed his pointing finger. A large city lay nestled at the shore of the lake.

"There's no wall around it."

"I guess they think the mountains will keep everyone away. But look in the centre."

The sun shone much brighter with no Dust to dull it, and she squinted against the glare. Ryder passed her his binocs. The focusing dial shifted stiffly, and the glasses wavered a little before she found the building in the middle of the City. Colour filled her vision. People swirled in a busy hustle around white buildings, adorned in bright rainbow hues that spun in her mind like a kaleidoscope. Dragging her eyes away, she focused the lenses on the castle. High and airy turrets rose pristine and shining against blue sky. A storybook palace. Filled with Faeries. Their tall draped and shimmering figures flitted around the walls, their wings catching the sunlight. A hot ache spread through her chest. Her fingers clenched on the metal case. They had no right to be so beautiful, to have such a glorious city. She panned out over the vista again, her breath hitching. "But the people, they're human. Why are they living with the Fae?"

Ryder's voice rumbled harshly by her ear. "I don't know."

She lowered the binocs and drank in the soul lifting beauty of the valley, her stomach twisting. Ryder's gaze fixed on the city, his hand resting on the hilt of his knife.

"You know," he said, "this sounds weird, but I was expecting a queen. In the stories, it's always the Queen of the Faeries who draws in young travellers or a changeling child. I always pictured something like a Queen bee in a hive. Didn't expect Kings."

A thought tried to attract her attention, but it lay so far buried in her brain, it merely stuttered like a warning light in the periphery. Too far off to do anything about it.

Taking a step closer to the edge, she glanced down the path. "Do we head down or not?"

Ryder scanned the clearing, drawing in a deep breath of fresh air. Her eyes caught on the rise and fall of his chest, but she flicked her gaze away before he looked back at her.

"I say we camp up here for the night," he said. "I doubt anyone will know we're here, and sleeping with no Dust falling, well, that's something I want to do."

Knowing she didn't have to walk into the city yet released a coiled spring of tension in her back. She smiled in agreement.

While Ryder took charge of cleaning the tent and setting it up, hiding it from view with leaves and twigs from the bright green trees around them, she changed the purifiers in the water bottles, filling them up with water from the clean air.

Rustling branches caught her attention. She glanced over at Ryder clambering up a gnarled and knotted tree. The purifier sat in her hand, forgotten, as she drank in the sight of his muscles rippling under his shirt and his long legs leaping from branch to branch. Leaves dipped to cover him, and he disappeared into the canopy. Her fingers pressed into the foam disc, and with a start she remembered what she was doing. Heat rushing to her cheeks, she shoved the purifier back in the bottle, screwing the lid on with more force than necessary. Ryder's voice rang out in a shout. She leaped up, heart pounding. He pushed his head out from the leaves, grinned, and jumped down to the ground. She shut her eyes until she heard him land, then opened them to see him trotting up to her with a wide smile.

"Fancy a wash? A water hole and a stream are right down there. Let's check it out."

CRYSTAL CLEAR WATER lapped at the rocks edging the pool. Her fingers trailed through it, icy cold shivers spreading goosebumps up her arm. A waterfall cascaded from an opening in the cliff, and spray misted over them, covering her face with freshness. She shot a glance at Ryder and grinned.

"Last one in's a rotten egg!"

He grinned back, and they both stripped off their Dust soaked clothes. She was naked and in the water with a splash. Ryder dived in alongside her, splashing her again, and she squealed. Icy water slid over her parched skin in a shimmer of sensation. Chill tingles gave way to a burning awareness of Ryder, naked in the water near her. Her eyes darted to him, his chest, the hairs on his arms, golden in the sunlight. *Get a grip, Addie.* She dipped her head back and waved her hair in the water, hoping the cold would knock some sense into her. Silence made her glance up. Ryder was staring at her. At her chest. Breath left her body. She ducked below the water, heat rising on her cheeks. To be fair, she had to fight from staring at him too, at the taut muscles ridging his abdomen, the iron sinews of his shoulders. Guess they were even.

"Sorry," he said, his voice ragged.

"No, don't be. I mean, it's okay, it's normal."

He looked away, tension twitching in his jaw.

Her heart raced, and she wiped water from her face. She should know what to do, what to say.

"Do you want to hold me?" She bit her lip, wanting nothing more than to sink beneath the water. That wasn't what she meant to say. His eyes widened, and his muscles jumped. But he shook his head firmly. Her heart froze. The butterflies in her stomach died.

"Not a good idea, Lark."

A painful lump constricted her throat, but her words tumbled past it. "No, of course not. I understand. I don't know why I said it. I'll leave you to wash."

She ducked under the water before she could hear him be kind to her, arrowing herself through the pool to break the surface on the other side by the waterfall. Ryder turned his back. She watched him out of the side of her eyes. He reached out to scoop up water, and the muscles in his back shifted. Her stomach tightened, and she caught her breath. Droplets beaded on his skin, shining in the sunlight, and her eyes tracked one as it made its way down to his hips. *No. He's made it clear it isn't an option.* Resolutely turning her eyes away from him, she tried her best to clean herself, ignoring the splashes from behind her and the images they threw into her mind. She waited until she heard him get out then counted to thirty before she turned around.

THAT NIGHT, he stayed on the other side of the tent. She decided to stay awake so she wouldn't cry out and make him feel bad for not holding her. Lying very still, she missed the warmth of his arm around her. Every time he shifted position or his breathing caught, she froze, body rigid beneath her. Ears straining for the sound of his movement, muscles coiled beneath her, she waited, only letting out the air trapped in her lungs when everything around her went quiet.

No soft flumps of Dust punctuated the night. The silence was unsettling. Without a blanket of grey powder, the nylon of the tent was almost translucent.

Lights.

Shining in the sky.

She sat up quickly. "Ryder! Stars!"

He rolled over, and she felt vindicated that he'd been awake too. Excitement took over and pushed all else from her mind. She scrambled over him to reach the zip of the flap, and he caught her around her waist. His touch was electric, and she stilled.

"Wait. Stop clambering over me like an elephant and let me up. I want to see them too."

"Okay but hurry up." She tried to sit back, but his hand still gripped her waist, holding her still. After a second, his fingers slowly unclamped. She sat back, pulse thumping.

Ryder rolled to his knees and unzipped the tent flap. Fresh

and clear air breezed in, the scent of pine filling the small space.

"After you." He waved her out.

She didn't wait, scooting through the flap and standing to stare out above the valley.

Stars scattered the sky like someone spilled diamonds on a black cloak then set a fire nearby to make them shine. She craned her neck backwards trying to see them all. Ryder came to stand next to her. Without thinking, she reached out her hand. After a second, he took it.

"I haven't seen stars since I was a child," she said, "since before the Fae. I used to spend most evenings outside with my mother, watching for shooting stars. But we never saw anything like this."

"No electric lights. No pollution. Reminds me of camping trips in University."

The chill air sent shivers over her skin, but she ignored her chattering teeth and the pain in her neck. She wanted to draw the stars in through her eyes so they would never leave her again.

Ryder's hand gently released hers, and he moved away from her side. Stars filled the absence. He was only gone a moment then warmth draped around her shoulders. She smiled gratefully as she shrugged on her jacket.

"Here," he said. "You're going to break your neck. Lie back on the slope."

She scrambled after him, lying on the ground, her neck supported on her arm. It was like staring into infinity. He lay next to her. Suddenly, his pointing arm came into view. "Look! Shooting star!"

The point of light streaked through the night and was gone. *Much like humanity. No, don't spoil this, just think of the stars.*

It was a long time before she fell asleep. This time she didn't wake to the fear of the Faeries.

CHAPTER 23

*W*aking the next morning, her opening eyes gazed on a horizon streaked with gold and pink as the sun rose. She tried to take in the intensity of colour around her. No grey clouds obscured the sky. No Dust clung to her body. Crisp, fresh air filled her lungs as she breathed deeply, relishing the unfamiliar sensation. Wetness mottled her back from sleeping on the grass. She patted clumsily at the rolled-up wad of fabric under her head. At some point, Ryder put his coat there as a pillow.

Ryder.

She sat up and searched for him, pushing away the tickle of yesterday's humiliation. It was just another emotion to squash and stuff in an overcrowded room in her head.

He stood at the edge of the cliff, looking out over the Valley at the sunrise. Golden light bathed him in warmth, the copper in his hair like fire in the early morning rays. She blinked at him. He looked like a king. She frowned, batting away wetness from the corner of her eye with the back of her hand. She must be tired, or allergic to something in this weird fresh air. Not crying. What was there to cry about?

She pushed to her feet and stood irresolute for a second.

With a mental shake, she walked towards him, stopping just behind his shoulder. Her breath caught in her chest as she followed his gaze. A vast sunrise painted the sky more vividly from here. The sun itself shone large, hot and burning. Everyone knew you weren't supposed to gaze at the sun, but after seventeen years of only seeing it as a dull grey glow, it was hard not to. The horizon burned bright red puffing out in streaks and grades of orange and gold and pink. The colours reflected in the lake below, where they took on new life, rippling and melding amongst the sparkles of the sunlight itself.

"It's like the sky fell into the water." Ryder's voice rumbled next to her.

The stars had embraced her heart like a warm blanket, but this took her heart and squeezed. So much light. All the colours of the world. Her fingers curled against her palms. Years of grey dullness filled her head. She didn't want to forget, but she let the sunrise burn out some of it for a while.

Ryder's face was calm, peaceful, but lines etched tight around his eyes. His shoulders betrayed his tension. She should probably say something. "So beautiful."

"And it sure as hell isn't Raglan. The Fae made all of this, Lark. There's nothing down there that used to be here."

Behind his words she heard what chilled her own blood—the power that it must have taken, the mind-blowing idea that the natural world could be moved and shaped at whim. What chance did they possibly have?

Ryder dragged his face away from the sunrise and turned to her. A small smile tugged at his lips, but his eyes remained fierce. "They might be powerful, but we'll do it anyway, right Lark? Let's go get that boy and get out of here."

Entering the city felt like walking into one of the fairy hills from stories she'd read as a child, filled with lost humans and time standing still. Vibrant hues shone and danced gaily in the wind, stealing her breath away. The sky glowed so blue it hurt her eyes, but she couldn't help sneaking constant glances.

It took a while to notice the lack of brightness in the people they passed. Colour adorned their surroundings while they wore brown, black, and navy. Attractive clothes, but all so similar—long flowing trousers, short tunics with wrap around ties, and arm band ribbons.

"Have you noticed?" Ryder said in a quiet voice.

"Yes, they're all dressed the same."

He poked her and shook his head. "No. Actually look at them, not just their clothes."

Frowning slightly, she let her eyes rove over their faces. What did he mean? There were people from everywhere, just like in their compound. Then it hit her.

"They're not paying any attention to us."

"Yeah." Ryder's hand rested on his knife hilt and tension ran up his arm. "Two complete strangers, and we may as well not even be here. And look at their eyes."

Face after face passed them, blank and slack, all light gone from their eyes.

Glazed.

Enchanted.

The valley really was a fairy hill.

A woman walked past them. Unlike the others, she glanced at them. Her features froze in shock for a second, before the mask came down again.

Addie pushed at Ryder's elbow. "That one. She's the only one who's different. Let's follow her."

Very unobtrusively, the woman sped up. *Interesting*. Other people barely acknowledged their existence.

They followed her through a wide winding lane lined with small trees in beautiful pots. Broad steps ahead led down to a small square pond and a patio. The people they passed simply moved out of their way without breaking a step.

The woman glanced over her shoulder, seeing them still behind her. She slowed down and stopped beside a tall statue of flowing white marble. Shadow covered her averted face. but as they neared, she spoke in a soft but urgent undertone.

"Please. Stop following me. It will be safer for all of us."

She appeared to be about Ryder's age, although it was hard to tell. Maybe older. Dust aged people in a way this woman in her green and blue paradise wouldn't know. Addie shut down the spurt of anger with a feeling of surprise. *Not like this woman had anything to do with it.*

Ryder moved to where the woman couldn't help but see him, crossing his arms and lifting his strong jaw. Ah. His take-no-prisoners 'I ain't taking any shit' stance. She remembered that well. Hopefully it worked better against this woman than it ever had against a teenage Adelia.

"How's about no," he said. "We need information, and you're the only non-zombie around."

The woman winced at the word zombie, and Addie took in the people passing them by, ignoring them. Not even seeing them.

In the stories, the Fairy Queen trapped humans to be her servants. Chills ran up her spine as her eyes tracked the people walking purposefully but without intent. Worker bees. Her gaze returned to the woman in front of her.

"Are you enslaved?"

The other woman's hands twisted the hem of her tunic, and for a second, Addie thought she might run. But then her shoulders slumped, and her face relaxed. "I can't talk to you here. They'll see. You better come with me."

CHAPTER 24

Drawn curtains of thin brown fabric dimmed the light filtering into the small room. Addie tapped her fingers on her leg, trying to pin down the nagging sense of something missing. On the way to her home, the woman introduced herself as Sera but closed her lips tightly to all other questions.

Nothing sat out of place in her neat and serviceable little house. No photos, no books, no ornaments decorated the walls. A round table with one chair sat awkwardly against the back wall. Sera glanced between the single chair and her guests, as if wondering who to offer it to. In the end, she stood by the table.

Waiting.

She tugged at the curtain, and a stray ray of sun caught her blonde hair, turning it to gold. Addie drew in a breath. Sunlight but no dancing motes of Dust. The nagging pull at her mind eased, then twisted into something darker, angrier. Every surface, rough or smooth, lay smugly clean of grey powder. Her nails scratched her palms. She breathed out, straightening her fingers despite the tension firing through them. She fixed her eyes on Sera, ignoring the rest of the room.

The woman fidgeted with her sleeve, and her eyes darted from Addie's face to Ryder's and back.

"Who are you?" Sera asked. "You're not Fae, and you're not like the others."

"We've come to find someone," Addie said. "Someone they stole."

Sera's hand crept to the edge of the table, fiddling with the edge, and her eyes flicked everywhere but towards Addie.

"They steal a lot of people. I don't know who they stole or why you came after them, but you won't get them back. Where did you come from?"

Addie swapped glances with Ryder, leaning up against the wall with his arms crossed. He jerked a nod, and she turned back to Sera.

"No. You first," she said. "What's with all the zombie people? Are you all enslaved or what?"

Sera's hand dropped, and her shoulders hunched forward. "They're not zombies."

"Looks like a zombie, acts like a zombie, I'm calling them zombies. They didn't even see us!"

Small lines appeared at the corners of Sera's eyes, and she turned her face, blond hair falling over her eyes like a curtain. "The Faeries have us in thrall. They enchanted us at the beginning, brought us to the Valley, made us work for them."

Addie ignored a rising heat in her chest and the rapid pace of her heart. She forced the question past the sensation of her throat closing. "What sort of work?"

"The Fae need to eat. They need their castle cleaned and their horses cared for." Sera's mouth twisted. "They need entertainment."

Her stomach turned, and bile hit the back of her throat.

Ryder spoke up. "You're clearly not enchanted. Why are you still here?"

"The thrall doesn't work on everyone. We keep up the pretence."

Addie stared at her, every part of her body wishing it was out of the valley, back in the Dust, with the petrels, anywhere but here. "Why would you do that?"

Sera's hands twisted together. "You don't understand. Living like this is hell, but it *is* living. My mother is in thrall, and so are my brothers. If I walk out of turn, I can't guarantee that my family will be left alone. This is the only way I can protect them." Tears glistened in her eyes, and her hand twitched towards the curtain. "Being here with you is a terrible risk. For you as well as for me. If anyone figures out you shouldn't be here, than the safest way for me to deal with that is to turn you in."

Ryder shifted, readiness showing in taut muscles pushing from the wall, his hand drifting to his knife. Addie's lips smiled tight reassurance while behind her eyes screams echoed. *White room. Blood Red Eyes. Silver and Pain.* The knot of anger in her chest crumbled. Fear drove both her and Sera. Fear of the Fae, of the pain, of intruders bringing death and Dust in their wake. She curled trembling fingers against her side. Sera's fear chained her here, but her mother lived. Dark tendrils of shame wound through Addie's mind. Terror had driven her to run. To abandon her mother to madness.

Ryder's gaze met hers. He settled back, but his hand didn't leave his knife. Sunlight played on the floor, and her eyes dropped from his to follow the beams as they danced. Counting the cracks on the floor tiles helped slow her racing heart.

Ryder's voice rumbled, slicing through her thoughts. "Have you thought about taking your family and leaving?"

She glanced up as Sera shrugged, a small tight movement, her mouth turning down. "Where would I go? I wouldn't survive in the Dust." The woman's eyes widened as she glanced between her and Ryder. "They say there are creatures as big as a house prowling the borders of our land. I hear them sometimes, wailing in the night. And the communes of survivors in the deadlands? We've heard the stories of those too, of how there is no law, no morals, people are killed and beaten and women are raped." Sera's chin trembled as she lifted it "I would rather be enslaved than live a life of torture."

Addie's arms prickled, and she clenched her jaw on rising bile, her stomach churning. *No. If I had to do it again, I would choose the same.* Her mother's face smiled sadly behind her eyes, and she blinked the image away. *Freedom has a cost.*

Ryder leaned back against the wall, eyes on Sera, hand no longer on his knife but curled into a tight fist. Venom laced his voice. "The Fae enslave you but teach you to fear other humans. We're little more than bugs to them, useful animals. They don't give a shit how many of us die if they end up with what they want. Why would you believe anything they tell you?"

Sunlight glinting off clean benches caught her eye. *He's right.* The Fae set them against each other so easily that her anger at the lush green valley angled its way to the people living here rather than the Fae who made it so. Ryder's eyes flashed flecks of gold in the sun, and she read his hatred for the Fae in the harsh lines around his temple. Her fingers twitched. *No. I'm not like them. It's different.* But ice flooded her veins.

Sera glanced between the two of them. Her mouth tightened, and she flopped down in the chair.

"Your friend will be at the palace. That's where they take all those they steal, and where they do all the tests."

"Do you know how to get into the palace?" Ryder asked.

"No." Sera shook her head quickly, leaning back in her seat. "I don't go anywhere near it."

Ryder's eyes narrowed, and his hand rubbed at the scruff on his jaw. Addie followed the movement of his hand with her gaze. She didn't blame Sera. She wouldn't go anywhere near the palace if she could help it either.

"So," Ryder said, his voice quiet and calm, "you don't, but do you know anyone else who does?"

Sera's eyelids twitched, and a little shoot of hope raised its head. If she knew someone who could guide them, help them, they might be able to find a way in. Exactly what they were supposed to do once they got in was unclear. Any plan boiled down to two things: get Tama, get out.

Easy.

Ryder pushed off the wall to stand a little closer, a little taller. He must have noticed Sera's tell too. She frowned at him. No need to intimidate the poor woman. An image of Tama shot into her head, frightened and by himself. Flickers of long repressed pain shuddered through Addie. *Okay, perhaps intimidation is justified.*

Sera leaned back into the wall. "You need to realise the danger we would be in, were we to help."

Addie bit her tongue. Best to let Ryder do this bit.

He settled back slightly, still tall but not so looming. "I'm aware you'd be in danger, and I'm sorry. But a child is also in danger, and we might be able to help him. We're not asking you to come with us, to fight with us, just help us find the way. For a boy."

Sera's face crumpled.

Addie rubbed absently at her chest under her collarbone, trying to release the tension burning under her skin. No-one had come for her. No rescue party begged people for help for the twelve-year-old girl curled up alone in a dark room. Ever since she stepped into the Valley, the past she had locked behind the door in her mind knocked harder, trying to escape. She shook her head, pushing the thoughts away, and focused on Sera's voice.

"Look, even if I can somehow convince someone to take you into the palace, you don't know what's happening to your boy, where he'd be. None of us have been inside. None of us can help you. You'll go in blind and bad things will happen."

Addie's voice stuck in her throat, but she coughed and pushed it out. "I've been inside."

They stared at her, and she wished she hadn't said anything.

Ryder's lips compressed, and he eyed her but didn't speak. Sera, on the other hand, gaped at her. "What do you mean you've been inside the palace? How is that even possible?"

"I was taken, years ago." The words were hard to force out, but somehow easier to tell this stranger she didn't like very much than to tell those at the compound. It didn't matter what Sera thought of her.

Sera's whole body stilled, standing so motionless that the fluttering of her pulse as it sped up showed against her pale skin. The woman's voice, when she spoke, rasped out in a harsh whisper. "Impossible."

Addie made a face. "It isn't, because it happened. They take children all the time."

"But they don't escape."

That was true. She'd never heard of another Taken child getting out. And here she was trying to go back in. Lead sat heavily inside her.

"Well, I did."

Sera's gaze pinned her to the spot. She shuffled, glancing at Ryder, who took the hint. He placed a hand gently on Sera's arm, bringing her eyes round to him.

"Lark was a kid. She was taken. Then she managed to escape the testing. We want to help Tama, our friend, escape too. If she can find her way round the palace on the inside, we might have a chance. Will you help us?"

She watched as emotions tangled on Sera's face. Finally, the other woman took a shuddering breath and stepped closer, her eyes wide.

"I'll do it. If you could escape, maybe more can. If we told people, if they knew, then perhaps this—" She waved her arms to the outside. "—could end."

Addie stepped back, the wall of the tiny unit meeting her back. "Whoa, hold on there. I'm only here for Tama. This isn't a revolution. This is a rescue." Trying to steal back a child from mountain-moving Fae was crazy enough. There was no way they'd be able to fight off the Fae forever. They were here to stay.

Ryder's brows lowered, and he stared at the floor. *What? Surely he wasn't the revolutionary type.*

"Maybe. But it gives me hope anyway." Sera picked up her shawl as she spoke, "I will see what I can do, but the person I'm thinking of will want to meet you."

"Can he or she take us to the palace?" Ryder asked.

"Yes, but remember it's only to the palace, the two of you have to do the rest."

Addie coughed, waiting until they turned back to her. "That all sounds great. There's just one problem."

Ryder sighed. "Of course there is. Out with it."

"I have been inside the palace, but I don't remember anything." She spread her arms out in a shrug, her treacherous mind knocking at the door in her head. "All I see are flashes of unpleasant things, the same things I see in my nightmares, but nothing else."

Sera frowned, disbelief dripping from her voice. "What, nothing?"

Her heart raced, and the scars on her arms burned as tightness spread in a hot wire up the back of her neck. She pressed her lips together to hide the trembling and glared at the other woman.

Sera stared back. "Do you think you could if you tried?"

Holding her breath, chest aching, she counted to ten in her head. *It isn't Sera's fault. She probably didn't mean it like that. Just let it slide.*

Pain built up behind her lips, and her words tumbled out in a snarl. "If I *tried*? I spent my whole life trying to forget."

Ryder's hand gripped her arm, a light touch that sent sparks dancing up and down her skin. His mouth was a tight line and his jaw could have broken concrete. "If we're going to have a real shot at rescuing Tama, we need an idea of what we'll be up against when we get inside." His hand drifted down her arm to wrap around hers. "I'm so sorry, Lark. I wish you could keep those memories where they're hidden. God knows I have some I don't want to prod, but I need you to remember."

Her arms crept up to wrap around her torso, and she pushed them back down again. God, she was sick of looking weak in front of him. She lifted her chin. The hammering on the door inside her mind became a clamour.

"I'll try. No idea if it will work, but I'll try."

His face softened, and he reached out and pushed a lock of hair off her face. "You're the bravest person I know, Adelia Lark. Don't forget that."

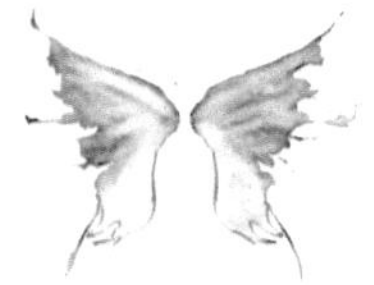

CHAPTER 25

She didn't feel brave as she sat down, cross-legged and alone in the small room, and tried to concentrate. She hadn't lied when she told Ryder she couldn't remember. Every time she tried to think about it, her mind faltered. So many walls and barriers in her mind, built over so many years. She didn't want to let out the darkness and pain lurking behind them.

Closing her eyes, she forced herself to think back to a time before she locked the door in her mind. She remembered the taking, being pulled from her mother. What happened next? Clouds filled her mind, covering the door. Breathing deeply through trembling lips, hands curling against the hard stone floor, she willed the clouds aside and opened the lock. The past flooded out. Pain shuddered through her but she blinked it away.

Pulled upwards through swirling Dust, held by a Fae, her arms bleeding from her mother's desperation. Screams filled the air. The people below, the compound, shuttered out of existence. Disappeared. She turned, small child that she was, seeking to cling to the only thing close, the Fae who had stolen her.

Purple robes swaddled her. The Fae's shining wings spread out bright against grey clouds, and on its bony sternum lay a gold brooch, intricately worked, with a small dragon's face.

She remembered those yellow eyes and glinting scales.

The dragon came to her often in times of sadness when she needed comfort.

Cold realisation of where that fondly held image came from had her shooting up from the floor. She paced across the small room, heart pounding. Her eyes stretched wide, and she tried to control her breathing as nausea rose.

This isn't going to help.

Pulling her hands down her face, she walked back to the small mat. *Try again. You owe it to Tama. You need to remember what's going to happen.*

She sat down again. Breathing slowly, trying to unclench her hands out of the rigid claws sitting on her lap, she closed her eyes. She let her past snake out.

Flying. She remembered flying, the treacherous exhilaration of swooping through the sky. They landed, but young Addie's eyes were locked on the brooch. When she was set on her feet she turned, her gaze meeting a rioting swirl of colour. Tall Fae and their human slaves surrounded her and the other children, Sanjeet and Ella. Bright robes and garish wings clashed with jewellery adorning elaborate multi-hued hair-styles. More Fae appeared with more children. Silence rose from the small faces around her. Fear and horror caught the tears before they fell. She took some strength from the pres-ence of others, knowing that whatever she faced she wouldn't be alone.

Alone. The hard stone floor of Sera's house chilled her through her clothes. She brushed at the tears she didn't cry as a child and pushed past the fog of memory, through the bricks of the wall in her head. Vast palace chambers rose above her, filled with a breath-taking rainbow maelstrom of Fae and gold. Shining doors, glittering wings, and rich tapestries confused her vision. She clutched tightly to the purple robe next to her. The swirl picked her up and rushed her along until she stumbled to a halt in front of a dais at the end of a large hall.

The man on the dais wore a robe of many hues, billowing drapery spreading over a massive gilded throne. On his elaborate coiffured hair sat a tall slender crown made of gold and winking with jewels. Children crouched at his feet.

They wore chains.

Her eyes flew open, and she drew a ragged breath as remembered fear pulsed through her. She stared up at the splintered beams of the small room, trying to convince her heart rate to slow. The walls in her mind began to rise again, but she remembered Tama and forced her brain to go on.

The King reached forward as they were pushed closer to the dais, long thin fingers with claw-like nails grabbed at little Ella's chin, surveying her face. After a long moment, he said 'Yes,' the harsh voice a melody scraping raw the nerves in her body.

Her friend was taken away.

A hard hand shoved at her, and she shuffled forward, shudders running up her arms. Cold fingers pinched at her jaw, digging into her skin. The King pulled her closer to him and gazed into her eyes with an awful shimmering gleam that made nausea twist her stomach and bile creep into the back of her throat.

Cruel lips moved. "Yes."

A sharp yank on her arm, and her captor dragged her away.

She tried to turn back to see what would happen to Sanjeet and the other children, but tall Fae bodies obscured her vision. Another 'yes' rang out, then a 'no,' followed by a harsh and terrifying scream. She swung her head around and kept her eyes on the floor after that.

They took her to a white and bare room, like an operating

theatre in a hospital. Long white counters squatted in the middle of the windowless room. She clutched at the hand of the Fae escorting her, and the purple robes shimmered as it froze. Its long claw like fingers returned a slight pressure before abruptly detaching from her grip. A wave of its arm in front of her face, and she collapsed.

Her mind skittered away from the recollection. She clenched her fists on her knees and pushed it back.

Shivers wracked her body as she lay on a bench of icy white marble. The straps holding her down weren't tight, but her body refused to shift an inch. There didn't seem to be any IV-lines or anything; she was simply paralysed. Her eyes snapped back and forth as waves of panic flooded her.

Another Fae came, tall, white, flowing. Beautiful until you looked closely. She found she could turn her head again, but when she moved it, her eyes met a tray of silver and bone instruments. The Fae picked up a long thin needle and moved it closer to her eyes.

Her lungs heaved. Screams filled her head, but no sound came from her throat. Her lips didn't part. She couldn't scream even though she desperately tried to. Her pain remained trapped inside her.

The fae swept a hand over her face and her eyes froze in place. Agony took over all thought. Sharp bone slid into her eyeball, spiking pain deep into her soul. All the time the needle was seeking, scraping through flesh, so too were flickering trails of energy shooting through her brain, reading her, raking through her. The Fae instrument rattled and searched every part of her being and stripped her down to the core. A blinding burst of pain slammed the door in her mind shut again.

Addie sat up in Sera's house, heart racing, and turned her head to vomit. Heaving sobs wracked her body, and she couldn't stop retching. The fear she had shoved down, denied, ignored for fourteen years cascaded through her in waves that left her shuddering. Swirling memories of agony and terror, the sensations of their claws on her skin. The door in her mind had cracked. The darkness had escaped.

She'd been so afraid. That poor little girl. She had been so afraid.

Trembling hands went to her eyes. Oh god. The remembered pain of those evil needles shot through her, leaving her breathless.

And then, above it all, she remembered Ryder saying, '*I saw your eyes change. They swam like the Faeries' eyes do*." She remembered his look of distrust. "*I don't like monsters*."

He could never know.

By the time Ryder came back with their host, and more food, she had taken control of herself. Fear of Ryder looking at her with distrust again effectively quenched the terror of the Faeries. She glanced at him then at the food he held out to her. "Bread," he said through a mouthful of it. "Fresh bread. from real flour. Do you remember it, Lark?"

Soft and white with a golden crust, so different from the hard, solid, grey looking rolls they had at home. You softened those in soups before you ate them. She tore off a piece and popped it in her mouth. The taste brought back a wave of images, happier ones this time. Sitting with her mother and Beckett at a park, the one Beckett called 'the birdie park' because of all the swans and geese. They would have a picnic, fresh bread and toppings, some dip if mum was feeling fancy. Then Beckett would convince mum to let him feed the ducks. He always tried to make sure the smallest duck got some. Addie closed her eyes and let thoughts of her little brother push back the newly uncovered pain.

For some time, they ate in silence, relishing tastes and textures long forgotten. Once she caught Ryder putting a piece of melon down, half eaten, tears in his eyes. She looked away. Memories hurt, even if they were good.

When the meal was finished and they sat staring at the crumbs, Ryder cleared his throat and met her eyes.

She only froze for a second. "I remembered some things. Not all of it. I know where they took him. I think I could even find the way, but I have no idea what they'll do to him." Not technically a lie. She didn't know if they wanted him for the same reason. Her stomach churned. He'd been taken. He'd already gone through what she went through. *So had Lily and Matt.* Her stomach churned and she took a sip of water, hoping to keep the food down. God. She hadn't thought of that before. She had been so focused on stopping them from getting Tama *this* time. And what if they'd gone back to fetch the other two children now that they had Tama? What if they were all being tortured as she sat here eating bread?

"You okay?" His hand reached out to hers. She looked at it a fraction too long, and when she made to take it, he'd withdrawn it.

"Yeah. Yeah I'm fine." She took another sip of water. The images of the white room had escaped, and now they danced in her mind, taunting her. "Fine."

CHAPTER 26

*S*era didn't know much and clearly didn't want to be involved in any way. Despite this, she provided them with clothes and identity disks in the shape of brooches to allow them access to the palace. Addie glanced up from the heavy pewter brooch at Ryder, reading in his face the same wariness she felt. This was a lot of trust to put in the actions of a stranger. His eyes met hers, and he gave a scarcely perceptible shrug. What other choice did they have?

The way to the palace stretched out ahead of them, both smaller and larger than she remembered. The first time she had seen the path. she focused only on those around her. Now she took in not only the swirling colours but the broad sweeping promenade covered in people and Fae, lined by statues and gardens. She tugged at the unfamiliar tunic, missing her coat and boots, Dust stained and stinky as they were. A hard poke in the ribs from Ryder made her roll her eyes, but she let her fingers drop.

Her heart raced as the palace got closer and the number of Fae clustered around them increased. For over a decade she had hidden from her past, and here she was about to walk brazenly into the one place above all others she never wanted to see again.

The only thing keeping each foot moving, one after another, was the thought of Tama, locked in a cell, or strapped to a bench in the White Room, or chained to the base of the king's throne. Images of him mixed with thoughts of Matt and Lily and a young Addie. *No child should have to bear that pain.* A Fae glanced over at them. She fought down rising panic. *They won't know who I am. They can't.*

She tried to relax her face. Let her eyes glaze. The gilded doors of the palace rose before them, ornate and oppressive. Massive carven masterpieces, a series of panels divided each door. Each panel appeared to tell a story. Her heart pounded so hard she thought it must surely be audible to anyone who stood close enough. The doors hadn't registered to the small terrified child rushed through the crowd of Fae and stolen children. To the adult, they symbolised a point of no return.

As they joined the line for admittance, she examined the beautifully carved oak. Those were the Fae, their wings and draperies making them easy to identify. And there was the first battle. The first impacts that ripped into the earth, leaving desolate craters behind. The next one showed the Dust, and she frowned. Typical. They'd ignored the one all humans hung on to. The second battle, where it appeared the Fae could be turned around, that the iron and firepower of the world's armies could defeat them. Which was, of course, why they brought the Dust to choke the earth and destroy electronics and render their weapons useless. She glanced at Ryder, and it was her turn to poke him. He barely suppressed the rigid rage and contempt on his face, and they were close to the front of the line.

"Zombie time, remember?" she breathed at him.

Within a second, his face was expressionless. It was unnerving how much control he had.

The group ahead of them moved away, and they stepped

forward. It seemed impossible the clerks on the desk wouldn't hear the pounding of her heart, but seeing they were human helped her to breathe more freely. In the end, it wasn't as difficult as anticipated. The clerks checked the identity disks, marked them off on a piece of paper, and sent them on their way.

Her fingers curled into the side of her tunic, and her breath shook in her chest. Walking through a Faery palace to try and rescue a stolen boy sounded noble, but all she wanted to do was run. *What am I doing here? I am no hero.* Biting the inside of her cheek, she inhaled deeply through her nose and forced her legs onwards.

Trying to act like they belonged, they headed down a long passageway filled with fluttering bright wings. Fae drifted past, their glamor different here, more shifting. One brushed through them, claws and teeth shivering under translucent sliding skin. She blinked, her stomach twisting, and tried not to recoil as porcelain flesh took the place of the monster below. Gauzy draperies of a multitude of colours floated through the air. Some of the Fae had tight braided bands and severe, warrior-like clothing. The others had twisting floating aureoles of hair dancing over shimmery clothes.

Her hands clenched as the urge to run nearly overrode all rational thought. But Ryder strode next to her, and he bumped her shoulder with the side of his arm. The brief touch sent tingles over her skin. Warmth flooded her heart, driving away the icy fear.

They turned down a quiet hall, no Fae to be seen and only the occasional human. Slowing their steps, but not daring to stop completely, Ryder glanced casually around before bending his head closer to hers.

"So now what?"

She bit her lip then consciously cleared the frown from her brow. Who knew if eyes still watched them.

"I think it's down here. The rooms are anyway. I

remember that lion thing." Ryder turned to look where she gestured, but she kept her eyes in the other direction. Heavy brooding gold, the fierce face twisted into a roar, the lion had terrified twelve-year-old Addie each time she'd been dragged to the white room. Thoughts of the past tangled with the fear sending spikes through her mind. She fixed her eyes on Ryder's chest, watching his steady breathing, letting it calm her own. "I'm not certain if Tama will be here or if he's been taken somewhere else, but this is as good a place as any to start looking."

The hall shone with spotless cleanliness. Even with the best intentions, nothing at home ever escaped a grimy coating of Dust. Anger furled within her. They lived like scavengers on the refuse left to them while the Fae and their pet humans lived like this. She took a breath and banked the embers of rage. Fear flickered around the edges of her fury, and she tried to push it aside. None of that would help now.

Heavy oak doors lined the hall. Following the tug inside her, she closed her ears to the muffled sobs of a child coming from behind the walls. She pushed Ryder forward, hating the lines around his eyes, the twist of his mouth. *We can't save everyone.*

At the fourth door, she stopped. "He's in here."

Ryder glanced between her and the heavy oak panels. Something passed across his face before he shook it off. "Let me guess, you just know, right?"

She stared back, her chin lifting slightly. "That's right."

He sighed, grasping the handle and turning it gently. She went to stop him but checked herself. They would face whatever lay beyond regardless. He eyed her and pushed the door open.

"Well," he said in an undertone. "I wasn't expecting that."

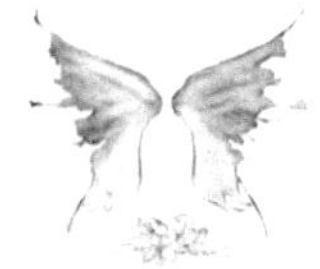

CHAPTER 27

Addie froze, her eyes fixed on Tama sitting on a chair in the middle of the room. Golden robes draped his body, and two humans combed his hair and attached ornaments to his tunic. She nearly missed the two Fae moving towards her until they filled her vision. Her breath caught in her throat, and her heart lurched.

The one in purple appeared almost human. Almost handsome. He stared at her, his eyes shimmering oceans which captivated rather than repelled. Strong fingers stretched towards her. "You. I remember you. You were a child last time you were here."

His voice rang in a melody that tugged at something inside her. She closed her eyes against its beauty, her hands clenching. He was a Fae.

Ryder stepped in front of her, his broad shoulders a shield, and the tug towards the Fae lessened.

The other Fae spoke with a harsh jarring hiss. "Impossible. She cannot have been. All those who were taken are accounted for."

"Not all." The purple Fae smiled at her, and her body froze. "This is the one who got away."

Tremors started in her fingers and spread through her limbs, her knees wobbling.

"Tama." Ryder's voice was low, cutting through her fear. "Tama we need you to come with us."

She stared at the boy. The expression carved into his face hit her in her heart. The feeling it betrayed was one she knew deep in her bones, that of a person torn between worlds.

His mouth twisted, and he shook his head. "No."

The one word carried a weight like no other. She pulled at Ryder's arm. They had to grab Tama and leave. Now. This was a disaster.

Ryder took a step closer to the small group, shaking off her grip, his hand sliding towards his knife. "Tama, this isn't a discussion, mate. You have to come home, now."

A flash of sadness stirred in Tama's eyes, and her heart sank. His lip curled. "I don't have a home. I never did. The Fae say I'm important. I mean something here."

Ryder drew a sharp breath, and she fought the urge to reach out to him. As a leader, he tried so hard to make Newhaven a home, but when you were a foundling or a lost child sometimes it was never enough. Home was a place she'd lost a long time ago. Guilt stirred in her gut as tears glistened in the corners of Tama's eyes. *I was never the only one. I should have remembered.*

The doors snicked shut behind them, and Ryder's jaw clenched, his shoulders tensing as his hand gripped his knife.

He will die. He will die, and it will be my fault.

She reached within herself, tapped into the strangeness she tried so hard to pretend didn't exist, and wished. Human servants screamed as the crystal table next to them shattered, fine shards punching through the air. The Fae whipped round. She grabbed Ryder's hand, raced for the window. She didn't stop to think but jumped straight out, trusting him to follow. Almost without volition, her head turned as she fell. She saw the purple Fae staring at her, thrusting out his arm to stop the hissing one leaping after her. The last thing she saw before she hit the ground below was a dragon brooch, delicately wrought in gold.

She pushed herself up, the wind knocked out of her and muscles spasming with the pain and shock of the landing. Thank god they landed on grass not stone. Ryder grabbed her arm and yanked her to her feet. He ran, long legs eating up the path, and she stumbled after him, refusing to look up at the window above. The Fae would either chase or track them. It was unlikely she would escape, but she wouldn't give them the satisfaction of going down without a fight.

"Down here." Ryder pulled her arm, and they raced into a lane covered with brightly coloured awnings. A market of some sort. He slowed.

She tugged at him. "Why are you stopping? We have to keep going!"

"Not in a run. Too suspicious. Just follow me."

Falling in behind him, she kept her focus on his broad shoulders as he made his way calmly through the crowd. She refused to think about the purple gown, the brooch, and a Fae who let them go.

The markets embraced them in a tumult of aromas. Long forgotten spices and the scent of grilled fish assailed her. She gritted her teeth, tugging at the ridiculous tunic again. *I am stronger than this.* She forced her hands to relax and timed her breaths with her steps until her heart beat returned to normal. When Ryder turned to her, she met his eyes with the appearance of equanimity.

"You alright?"

Okay. Maybe she didn't look as calm as she hoped.

"Yeah. I'm fine. What's the plan?"

"I'm thinking about whether we go back to Sera's. Whether that's safe. They're bound to question the guys at the gate—if they figure out how we got in, they might be able to trace us back to her."

She nodded, scanning the stalls closest to them. Pots and pans and trinket boxes met her eyes. She wondered if Ryder had deliberately avoided stopping near the food stalls. The smells of the food probably had the same impact on him as it did on her. Oddly, the thought calmed her in a way her self-talk hadn't.

"I think you're right, we don't want to put her in danger. But we do need to go back for our gear."

Ryder stroked his jaw, looking at her, and she crossed her arms.

"Oh no, Ryder Hendrix, you are not going to do that. That is a nope."

"It makes sense. We find somewhere for you to hole up, I go and get the stuff—only putting one person in danger makes for better odds."

She glared at him, but it just bounced off his stubborn chin. "In which case, I should be the one going into danger, not you."

He smiled. "See now, we're going to have to agree to disagree. I'm still technically in charge, and I say I go. Anyway," he put his hand on her shoulder and steered her to a dark looking lane wending off the main market road. "I'm the oldest."

A snort of laughter escaped her, and she made up for it by scowling extra hard. It made sense, but everything in her rebelled against letting him go into danger. *Especially since I almost lost him not so long ago.*

The lane led to a number of small houses crammed together. Rickety steps and broken shutters perched forlornly against walls of peeling paint. Shabby even for Dust standards and very out of place in this city of plenty. One of the doors opened, and they shifted into the shadows of an overhanging shutter. A woman came out. Her hair was bound in a messy knot, and a small tattered basket was clutched in a hand marred by burns. A jagged scar marked her face from her right eye down to her jaw, red and puck-ered with age.

Ryder's words were little more than a rumble in his chest, but she still felt his anger. "So not everything in this place is shiny."

The woman's gaze cut to them as she walked past them. Meeting those eyes, all the air left Addie at once, and she stepped forward through Ryder's restraining grip.

"Ella? Ella, oh my god, is that you?"

The woman jerked away from Addie's outstretched hand with a fierce stare, dark blue eyes shadowed by dark circles and old scars.

"Ella, it's Addie. It's Adelia Lark." Her hand trembled, and she took a slow step forward. "Do you remember me?"

At her name, the other woman stilled before her shoulders slumped, and she sighed. "So, you didn't get away. You're here. But not like the others." Her voice was rough, and Addie remembered all those nights screaming. Perhaps Ella had never stopped. A heavy weight of guilt swept over her in a suffocating wave. She had run away, and Ella had been taken again.

"I did escape." She stepped closer. Ella didn't move. "I'm so sorry, Ella. I'm so sorry they took you, that they hurt you."

The other woman's face crumpled, and at once she looked like the little lost girl standing next to Addie in the Fae throne room. "You promised, Addie. You promised you would help us. But you left, and you never came back."

The words ripped out her heart. Ryder's voice rumbled beside her, reminding her of his presence. "She was twelve. It was the Fae's fault, not hers."

His faith in her, his defence of her, flooded her with warmth, but she waved a hand to shush him.

"I'm so sorry, Ella. When I came back, everyone had been taken, and the others drove me out. There wasn't anything I could do." *I could have stayed in the first place.* Guilt curled through her and left a sour taste in her mouth. "But I wish I'd taken you with me." She glanced back towards the house Ella came from. Had she lived here all this time? "Did Sanjeet come with you? Is he here?"

Ella shook her head. "He did better with the experiments than me. They believed they broke me, but he continued to stay strong. I still see him. He brings me food when he can."

A crash of falling pans followed by angry murmurs at the end of the lane cut through the silence, shooting tension through her shoulders. Ryder stepped forwards. "Can we take this reunion off the street? I need to go and get our stuff. Lark, do you think you'd be alright here with your friend?"

They had never really been friends. Ella attended a different school from Addie before the Fae came, and afterwards they were grouped together as the few remaining children in the compound. They had been allies, but never anything closer. There'd been too much pain.

She glanced at Ella, who nodded then glanced down at her empty basket, fingers clenched tightly over the broken reeds. Addie caught Ryder's eye, and he smiled reassurance. Somehow, he'd bring back food.

CHAPTER 28

*E*mbers glowing in a small fireplace cast a dim light over rickety walls and an empty floor. A thin pallet covered in worn blankets lay forlornly at one edge of Ella's small room. A counter in the corner for food preparation was clean but not as sparkling as the one in Sera's house. The tiny cupboard tucked beneath it had no door. Addie sank down on the hearth, crossing her legs, careful not to bump Ella who stretched out her legs by the dying warmth.

Silence filled the bare room, and she stretched out a prickle at the base of her neck. She bit her lip as she tugged at her sleeves. How did you talk about something like what they experienced as children? How could you ask someone what they'd gone through when you only had to glance around to see it was hell?

How do I ask her if she's still mostly human?

Ella spoke first, her voice flat and dull. "You look well."

Addie hoped the sting in her heart came from her own guilt and not from her old friend's hidden anger. "I was lucky."

Such a pathetic answer, and yet the only true one she could give. Her gaze drifted over splintered floorboards. For all the rage at the world that consumed her, she had it a lot better than some.

"Are there many of you like this?"

Ella shifted, her eyes fixed on Addie. "The ones they deem 'broken'? There are some. We were strong enough not to die, but we didn't meet their requirements. We live here so they don't have to see us, but if you make it out of the White Room, they don't kill you. They send someone to inspect us every few months or so—make sure we haven't grown wings yet."

Addie's knees stopped jiggling. "Wings?"

"Figure of speech. I doubt we'd grow wings, but those who are stronger usually get some of their gifts."

Gifts. Curses more like.

She shuffled her feet. Guilt gnawing at her stomach. "I am sorry, that they...broke you."

Ella moved her hand sharply. "No. Don't be sorry. They didn't break me. I would rather live here than be forced to serve them. Sanjeet burns with hatred for them and has to live every day surrounded by reminders of what they did to him. Yes, the Fae ruined my vision and my arm, damaged my hip so it hurts to walk very far. But those are the marks of a survivor, and I'm proud of them." A fierce light lit her one good eye. "I fought them, Adelia, and in the end, I won. It might not look like it, but I am freer than most who live here."

Addie rubbed away the prickles in her eyes, releasing her breath in a huff. "We came to rescue one of our boys. Tama. He ran, and we followed. But they took him." Her gaze avoided Ella's. "I failed Tama, too. But I'm not leaving without him."

A light rap sounded on the door, and Addie leaped up to open it without hesitation. Ryder always knocked the same way.

He pushed past her without looking and went straight to Ella, handing her a parcel. Her eyes widened, and a small smile creeped across her lips. Taking the food, she went to the small bench, laying it out like treasure.

Ryder's hands rested on his hips, and his back moved in a deep breath before he spoke to her over his shoulder.

"Sera is safe. So far. I told her to lay low. But she did tell me some surprising news."

Her skin tingled. "Yeah? What is it?"

He turned, crossing his arms over his chest. Her heart stopped at the lack of expression on his face.

"The Fae put out a message—they're willing to let Tama go, let me go, not punish those who helped us, if we give them *you*."

Her blood turned to ice.

Ryder's brows drew in, and his mouth turned down. He didn't appear angry, but the sternness in his face made her stomach flip. "Why would they want you, Lark, instead of Tama? Why now, after all this time, would they want to get their hands on *you*?"

Tight bands constricted her heart. "I don't know"

"No!" He flinched from his own fury and pressed his lips together. "Not good enough. Tell me. Why you?"

Anger flared, burning away the ice in her veins. "You have no right to talk to me that way. I told you, I don't know. Maybe Tama told them something, and they believed him."

His lip curled. "Blaming a boy? Nice, Lark. And as for right, I have every right. I'm leader of the compound you chose to live in. That makes me responsible for you and for Tama, and in case you've forgotten, every member of that compound who might be tested if we don't fix this mess before then." He stared at her, his eyes cold. "I never pushed you, never questioned you, because I don't want to hurt you. But we're way past that. I deserve the truth, Lark."

It was ridiculous how much a heart could hurt. She'd always known it was dangerous to let herself have feelings for someone, especially someone who clearly showed how little he was interested. But his scorn cut deep. Memories of how he listened to her at the compound, asked her advice, brought her tea, shattered under the stark image of his turned back in the water of the lake.

Hands steepled against her forehead, she took a breath. "I don't blame Tama. He's a kid. But I'm not lying when I say I have no idea why they want me." Her voice cracked a little, and she coughed, raising her chin. 'You might not like it Ryder, but I *really* don't like it."

His shoulders dropped, and he moved towards her before shifting position and clasping his hands behind his back.

Defiance fled her with a deep sigh. Ryder was right. *He always is, damn him.* So many years and so many half-truths between them. He deserved the truth, but when she told him, trust would disappear. She frowned down at her boots. No other choice remained. The spectre of the Fae loomed over her, but they still had to save Tama. She needed Ryder.

"I remembered."

He said nothing but quirked an eyebrow, his lips still tightly pressed together.

She cleared her throat and tried again.

"I remembered what happened when they took me. I told you I remembered medical equipment. Well it wasn't like any equipment I've seen before or since. It hurt. A lot. Burning pain like nothing I'd ever felt. Sometimes agony suffocated everything that I used to be, drowning it in fear and fire, until I was a consciousness made only of screaming hurt." He gazed at her steadily, his jaw clenched and eyes bright. Turning from his pity, she paced to the doorway and pulled the cloth curtain a little aside, staring at the road. "They were so beautiful. After a while, I started to only think of the beauty, not of the pain. That was when they stopped. I was put in a room with walls like glass, only sticky to touch. I lay in the middle and dreamed of beautiful Faeries."

She let the cloth fall but didn't turn around. In the corner,

Ella stifled a sob. They had all learned to hide their pain, even Ryder.

"When they returned me, I was like Tama. I couldn't think of anything but the sadness I felt at being apart from the Fae. Then the others woke up. They screamed and screamed, and the pain came back.

"I've told you the rest. The testing. The running. I hate them Ryder, more than you can possibly imagine. I don't want to go back to them. But you have to believe me that if I genuinely thought by giving myself up, the Fae would leave Tama alone, I would do it in an instant." Her voice hurt her throat with the anger she choked back.

He looked at her, and tears stung the corners of her eyes at the realisation he was weighing up her words with the thought that to save many she might need to go. "Even now, you'd consider it? Give me up to them? What happened to the 'I don't like monsters' crap?"

Anger twisted his face, and he lunged toward her, gripping her arm. "Don't be ridiculous, Lark, I'm not giving you up. I told you I would *never* kick you out, and I'm not going to start now." His voice shook, and he blinked rapidly. "How could you even think I would?"

Because everyone I love leaves me. The words stayed locked in her head, and she glared back.

He held her gaze, a fierce light in his own eyes, then released her arm. Shuddering, he stepped back, sighed and rubbed his hands down his face.

"The best way for us to rescue Tama, to somehow beat them, is for us to have as much knowledge as possible. I know they hurt you." His voice broke, and he coughed. "I know you don't want Tama to be hurt. Just, help me out here, Lark. What is it about you they want so much?"

She wrapped her arms around herself and tried to stop her voice from shaking. "I have no idea. That's the honest truth. And not knowing is worse than if I did. You know about my nightmares. Can you imagine wondering why it happened? Being terrified every time you see a Fae that what they did to you will happen again?"

His face gave nothing away except for a twitch of a jaw muscle. Heat rimmed her eyes, that dry burn when there were no tears to shed. For a moment, she thought he might understand, but the cold wall rising in front of him sent splinters through her heart.

Ella spoke into the brittle silence. "They will want you because in all their time on earth you are the only child who escaped. The only one who grew to adulthood with no more tests, experiments, shaping. You aren't supposed to exist. You weren't supposed to be able to survive." Ella walked towards them as she spoke, stopping in front of Addie and staring down Ryder. "They will want her to test. To dissect. To rip apart. If she goes to them, she will die. And I won't allow anyone to take her."

His hands flew up in surrender, but a heavy frown settled on his forehead. "No argument here. I'm not going to let anyone take her either." His gaze flicked past Ella to meet hers. Shock flared in his eyes, the gold flecks in the hazel like ice battling with fire. Tendons stood out on his neck, and he stepped closer, his voice shaking. "Tell me you really think I would give you up to die."

The tightness around his eyes matched that around her heart. She wanted to look away but made herself shake her head. Realisation hit her like a punch in the gut. Hurt. He was hurt, not angry. Her own pain filtered away, replaced with lead in her stomach. She stretched out her hand towards him, past Ella, her brain no longer in the way, just a desire to stop him from hurting.

His eyes dropped to her hand, and he lowered his arms, taking her fingers in his and squeezing them slightly before letting go. The warmth of his touch faded as her hand tucked back around her side.

"I know you won't give me up to the Fae."

A sigh left him, and he rubbed his head with his hands, leaving his hair sticking up at funny angles. "And I believe you. It still doesn't solve the problem. We're in a town full of Fae who've decided you're their biggest prize, and we still don't have Tama."

Thinking of the boy's face, full of awe looking up at the Fae, sent fresh shivers down her spine.

Ryder slumped against the wall. Ella raised her eyebrows at Addie. "We could talk to Sanjeet. He's still working in the palace. He might be able to help you find your boy."

Hope stuttered and died. "Then he would be in danger too." Her gaze switched between Ryder and Ella. "I'm not sure we're willing to do that."

Ella's lip curled. "He's in danger every day. He's careful to toe the line between being interesting enough for them to keep around and not such a threat that they fear him."

Ryder spoke, and although he seemed to be avoiding her eyes, he lifted his head. "It would be worth trying, Addie. We can't give up now. You can't go back to the palace but maybe I can."

The tight bands clenched around her heart again. "Sorry, I must've missed the discussion where we decided that I wouldn't go back to the palace. Of course I'm going back! If you're going, I'm going."

He smiled, his eyes warming, and he stood straighter. "Not this time, Lark. I'm pulling rank. You'll be staying as far away from the Fae as possible. Hear me? If we can convince this Sanjeet friend of yours to help we probably won't even need you."

A smothering hush rolled in from outside, sending tingles up her spine. The Dust breathed silence, but the City carried a hum of busyness and movement. The blanketing quiet sent her hand to her knife. Ryder already had his out, moving to cover Ella.

Her eyes flicked around the house, the empty barrenness of her friend's life. Addie couldn't let this be taken from her as well. She would die first.

The wall disappeared in a crumbling mess of shattered wood. Her heart jolted.

Fae filled the gaping hole in a swarm of draperies and clawed hands. Wings beat against each other in the small opening. No colours lit their swirling robes, just deep black laced with silver, blocking the light. Pounding blasts of energy knocked Ryder off his feet. He hit the ground and tried to stand, but the magic was too strong. The Fae didn't appear to be trying to hurt him, more pushing him away so they could focus on her. They didn't seem to want to hurt her either. Fire raged through her blood, and her eyes narrowed. She desperately wanted to hurt them, to rain down agonies on their flesh.

The sound of their wings beat in time with her pounding heartbeat, deafening in the small enclosure of Ella's room. Blasts of white crackling energy shot toward her. She heard the bolts as they hit her, quick bursts of dissipating melody ringing a discordant hum in her head.

Pushing into the blasts of light, clenching her fist around her knife, she tried to move forward. Her body trembled, her knees threatening to give way. She couldn't last much longer. Ryder leaped in front of her, white energy crackling up his skin. A Fae knocked Ryder away, sending him spinning to the ground. It snatched at her. She pulled back, straining against its grip until claws raked her arm, slashing over the faded scars left by her mother's nails. Bright blood welled and dripped slowly to the floor. Pressure from her hand wasn't enough to stop redness from oozing out. She gritted her teeth against the pain. Ryder struggled to his feet again and wrapped his scarf around her arm once before he was thrown back by the bolts of magic.

The glow surrounding Ryder grew darker in colour, turning from the blue-white that crackled through the air to a deep red shot with streaks of black. His back arched against the dirt floor, magic coursing through him.

"No!"

She reached for him, only to be pulled back. Ella brushed past to stand in front of her, arms raised. "Go Adelia," she said over her shoulder. "Find Sanjeet, save your boy, get out of here."

A glow surrounded Ella's arms, and blue light burst from her, knocking back the Fae.

Addie stared, mouth dropping as a dark realisation hit her. Ryder pushed himself off the floor, stumbling as he grabbed her in one hand and their packs in the other. He ran, dragging her behind him. The flimsy wall at the back of the room gave way as he kicked at it.

Another blue light burst out, and more Fae went tumbling. Addie couldn't drag her eyes away. One Fae stepped forward, iron grey and gold. It raised an arm and sent a burgundy bolt straight at Ella's heart. She convulsed. Addie lunged, Ryder's grip on her shoulder tightening.

"No, Lark, there's nothing you can do!"

She pulled herself out from his grasp and stumbled back to her childhood friend.

Ella shoved herself up and raised trembling arms, sending another wave of blue. The Fae shot a bolt of dark magic that smacked into Ella's light. The collision flashed outwards, breaking the air with a sound like shattering glass, knocking over the Fae and Ella and shooting straight into Addie. Flames licked through her mind, burning her from the inside out. She took a breath to scream. Black night took her.

CHAPTER 29

Coming to in pitch black would have been frightening, but warm fingers held her hand tightly. Ryder. Lead filled her body. Moving her eyes sent pain cascading through her skull. She squeezed his hand and managed to breathe out, "Thank you," before the darkness took her again.

The next time she opened her eyes, a pale green glow lit the small space, reflecting off bare stone walls. She tried to move her head and let out a breath when it didn't explode in pain. Ryder sat hunched near her feet. His elbows rested on his drawn up knees, his hands covering his face. She let herself watch him for a moment. He was always so strong. She wished he knew he didn't have to be strong for her.

Her voice cracked but came out as more than a whisper. A win to be able to speak at all. "How long have I been out?"

His hands dropped, and he smiled, making her heart catch. Shuffling closer to her, he brushed her forehead with the back of his hand. Warm fingers slid along her wrist, settling on her racing pulse.

"Best part of a day, most of a night."

She grimaced. Sitting back, he looked at her and reached out a hand to tuck stray hair behind her ear.

"Ella? Did she make it?"

His expression told her the answer before he spoke. Stinging tears sprang to her eyes, and she squeezed them shut.

"I'm sorry, Addie."

She shook her head and gulped a breath. "So much of me hurts that she's gone. That I didn't save her. But she was so brave, Ryder. She fought them every day." She looked up at his face, his mouth tender and an unfamiliar warm light in his eyes. "It's just so unfair."

Gentle fingers warmed her cheeks as he wiped away her tears. "It *is* unfair. The Fae are monsters, and we're going to do what we can to get out alive and back home."

"I can't let her sacrifice mean nothing. We need to find Sanjeet, ask him to help us rescue Tama."

He sat back, his hands twisting together and his eyes not meeting hers.

"I'm taking you home."

Cold disbelief shivered down her skin. She struggled to sit up. "You'd leave without Tama?"

He sighed, his brows drawn close together and his jaw tight. "I don't want to leave him here, but he made his choice. If we try to rescue him, they will find you. I can't let them take you." His voice shook, and she blinked at him. "I thought you died, Addie."

Bright worried eyes melted her heart. "I don't remember anything after they blasted me, after Ella was hit." Her lips trembled, and she inhaled tears. "How did you get us away?"

"The Fae were knocked over by the blast as well. I was out of it over by the wall, and you took most of the brunt of it anyway." His hand snuck out and brushed over her arm for a moment as if to reassure himself she was really there. "I grabbed you out of the ruins of the house and ran. I thought you were dead. but I hoped I was wrong." His smile wobbled, and his hands twisted tight together. "Turns out I was wrong."

She bit her lip. The question burned at the back of her

throat, but her heart shied away from asking. He noticed. Of course. "What is it Addie?"

"Ella. Do you… do you think you might be wrong about her too?"

His eyes shut for a second and a burning ache filled her chest.

"No. I'm sorry Addie. I saw her body. She's gone."

Tears poured in earnest then, sliding down her cheeks in a flood. Ryder said nothing but scooted closer and lifted her shoulders, turning her around to pull her close and hold her while she wept.

She cried for the children they had been, lost and frightened and alone. Cried for the damage they both lived with. Cried for the bravery of a friend from her past.

Tears drained her, leaving her husky and sore. She leaned into Ryder and breathed him in. His chest rumbled under her cheek.

"I do wonder," he said, "how she did it. Those blue waves she pushed at them. She was human. Where did they come from?"

Her stomach clenched, and she hoped she didn't pause too long before answering. She pulled back. "Living here with the Fae, she must've picked up some tricks. I don't know how she did it. Flash powder maybe."

His eyes were on her again, but he didn't push.

"I don't want to leave the boy, but I'm not letting you anywhere near the Fae."

Guilt, hope, and fear tangled inside her, shredding her heart into ribbons. Leaving Tama should never be an option, but the boy had said he didn't want to leave. *Neither did you.* The voice in her mind sounded from nowhere, and she shook her head slightly, trying to dislodge it. Ryder's hands clenched so tight she could see white where the blood flow cut off. The man lived to protect children. Why on earth was he giving up?

I thought you died.

She bit the inside of her cheek. For her. He was doing it for her. The strange green light reflected in his warm eyes, and in a flash, all she wanted was home and him.

But he would never forgive himself if he left Tama to the Fae.

"How about a deal, Ryder."

The rush of tension out of his shoulders told her he'd been ready for an argument.

"What's the deal?"

"We can't leave Tama. You know we can't. But you're right. I'm putting you in danger. I didn't want to involve Sanjeet, but we might have to. I'll lay low, I promise, and you sneak back down and find Sera, convince her to help us find Sanjeet."

The thought of him entering the vipers' nest alone, without her, cut her up inside. But she'd feel worse if she ended up being the reason he got hurt because she drew Fae eyes to them.

His gaze fixed on her face. "I'll take the deal, but with one change."

"What's that?"

He took her hand. "I'll take you up to the clearing, close by the ladder. If I don't come back in a day, two at most, you head down that ladder and leave."

Darkness clawed at the edges of her mind. "I won't leave you here."

"If you don't promise me that, there's no deal and I leave with you."

A ragged breath tore at her throat. She didn't want to lie to him. But hell would cover the earth before she left him. "I promise."

CHAPTER 30

*A*ddie paused at the start of the lane leading up the hill. Turning, she let her eyes linger on the colours rippling through the valley. The Fae weren't going to give up Tama, and he wanted to stay.

So did you.

She pulled the strap higher on her backpack, noting the lack of Dust puffing out from her cleaned coat.

"Come on, Lark. Let's get you to that clearing."

Her gaze turned back to Ryder. Sunlight suited him. Her heart dropped; going back into the Dust was going to be incredibly difficult. She tried to soak him in, the glints of light in his coppery hair, the edges of his scarf fluttering in the breeze. Fresh air. Soon there would be none. She breathed deeply as she walked away from the city and towards Ryder.

A rustling wind played at her back, raising the hairs on her neck. Ryder's eyes widened, and he stretched out his arm, pushing her away. "Lark! Run!"

Knowing it was foolish, she flashed a glance behind her. Fae filled the sky, painting the blue with many hued draperies and the stark susurration of their wings. Her heart stopped then thudded a crescendo against her ribs. She stumbled backwards. They wouldn't escape, but she needed to get to Ryder.

The Fae were faster.

Between one breath and the next the Fae landed, surrounding Ryder. They disarmed him, drawing his arms behind his back with disconcerting speed.

Tendrils of horror wrapped around her limbs, rooting her to the ground.

A Fae claw sliced Ryder's cheek and fiery rage filled her, battling the brittle ice of fear. They would kill him. She had no doubts. He was nothing to them.

The Fae held its hand up to its face, watching as Ryder's blood dripped into the grass below, taking her heart beat with every drop.

"The human bleeds easily." Another clawed finger dug into the skin of Ryder's neck. He winced but didn't pull back. "We know he is dear to you. The boy told us."

Lead filled her chest. Betrayal had never crossed her mind. The enchantment on Tama must have been stronger than she thought.

"You will come with us, or he will die. Choose fast."

Her eyes fixed on Ryder, and he shook his head, straining against the arms binding him, burning him. "No. Don't do it Lark. Don't you *dare* do it."

She didn't want the Fae to see just how much they hurt her, but she couldn't stop her mouth twisting, tears springing to her eyes.

Ryder knew she would never give up someone else to save her own skin. The knowledge shone in the brittle glistening of his eyes, the tendons in his jaw standing out as he worked against his rage.

The Fae watched, expressionless, their extended wings ruffling gently in the breeze. How could things so beautiful be so lifeless?

She threw her knife on the ground, followed by her crossbow. Ryder sagged between wiry Fae arms. Despair darkened his eyes. She shook her head wordlessly. Without him she would suffocate, no matter how much air she still breathed. Giving him up would never be an option.

"A wise choice." The Fae slashed out at Ryder, stopping just shy of his artery. A delicate cut bloomed bright crimson as swimming golden eyes stared over his head into her eyes. Hauling Ryder to his feet, they took to the sky in a jarring rustle, carrying him with them. She gazed after them until Fae surrounded her, blocking her vision. They lifted her into the air, flying in great bounds towards the city.

Hidden in a cocoon of wings, she let burning tears fall.

THEY TOUCHED down in the courtyard in front of the palace, the Fae dropping her unceremoniously to the ground. Carved flagstone cut into her knees when she stumbled and fell. She pushed to her feet and turned to find Ryder. Crimson blood dripped down pale skin, but he stood tall, glaring at the Fae taking his pack and weapons. She shrugged off her own bag, hardly noticing as they snatched it away.

Sunlight shone off the walls of the palace, drawing her gaze. Human servants ringed the courtyard, pushed out to the edges. Standing with heads bowed and hands clasped, they reminded her of a surreal sort of honour guard.

A rough hand shoved her in the back. She stumbled forward. They passed the massive panelled doors and marched down a broad passageway, footsteps clattering on the marble floor. Fae crowded every corner of the hall. Her breathing became shallower as clawing panic cut at her mind. It would be better if they whispered, talked, or did anything other than stand silently. Staring. Waiting.

Golden doors loomed at the end of the passageway, swinging open with a whisper as they approached. Noise spilled from the room beyond—music and chatter and bright bell-like laughter. The sounds died as they entered, Ryder's blood staining his neck and shoulders, and she feeling very naked without her knife. Their guards spread out either side of them, creating a distance between the shining rainbow splendour of the inner court and the two humans.

A marble dais topped by an ornate throne sat at the end of the hall. The King appeared exactly the same. Even his robes were the same riot of colours. His face rooted her to the floor. He, of all the Fae, did not look expressionless. He looked interested, genial, watchful.

Ryder swore, lunging forward against his restraints at the same time as she saw the children. They cowered, broken, at the end of chains running from their necks to the base of the throne. Ice ran through her veins, followed by a dark burning fire. The King made a leisurely gesture with one hand, and a guard stepped forward and whacked a long spear pole into Ryder's stomach. He doubled over, winded.

Something in her recognised the King at a deep bone level, more than just his face. A melody drifted into her head and settled. Panic rose, a sick, heart-pounding fear gripped her, and she shook her head, trying to get the twisting harmonies out.

A tall Fae edged forward to stand at the right-hand side of the King. Dressed in purple, golden wings laced with fire, it was the same one she saw in Tama's room. Her eyes dragged down to his chest where the dragon brooch lay nestled in silken folds. The Fae gestured, a quick sharp movement. The melody in her head stopped, as if cut off, and she staggered.

Her breath caught. This Fae's eyes shimmered golden green, but the usual nausea didn't bring bile to her throat. The King shifted on his throne, and she dragged her gaze back to him. He didn't frown but looked like he wanted to, his shoulders set in a rigid line and his fingers curled tightly over the edge of the chair's arms.

"So. The one for whom we searched for so long has returned to us." His voice echoed the melody so recently winding through her head, and a shudder wracked her body.

She lifted her chin and stared at him, avoiding his eyes which glistened and glowed with a shifting intensity that cut the ground from under her feet.

The King's head moved slowly from her to Ryder, kneeling on the mosaic floor, kept there by a Fae hand on each shoulder, crusted blood cracking on his skin.

"I don't think we need this one anymore."

The Fae with the dragon brooch gestured again, and the guards flanking Ryder stepped back a pace, although their hands remained on his shoulders.

This time the King did frown, if only for a fraction of a second, before he gazed lazily up at the tall Fae whose indigo robes floated even though no breeze entered the hall.

"You would interfere on this? Your mother's influence only carries so far."

The other Fae bowed slightly. "Only a suggestion, my Lord, but the man runs a compound, he may have useful information. Plus, he is important to the girl, and she will be more compliant if we are holding him."

The King's fingers stroked down the chains binding the children to his throne. "Very well. Take them to the cells to wait. Get the White Room prepared."

Ryder remained silent as they dragged him to his feet. Two more guards yanked at her arms and hauled her off behind him. She glanced back at the dais, at the King sprawled in his throne, his hand on one of the captive children's heads, and the tall Fae stared after her, hand on the dragon brooch which haunted her dreams.

CHAPTER 31

Rough hands shoved her, and she stumbled into the cell. A dungeon. An actual dungeon. Like from the stories. Hope fled as the door slammed behind her and she let her eyes close too. No way to escape. No leaping out a window from this room; the only light came from a narrow barred slit high up by the ceiling. There was no way out of this.

Ryder's voice cut through the dark thoughts whirling through her mind. "I guess we should be grateful there are pallets and we don't have to sleep on the floor. I'm too old for that crap."

Opening her eyes, she looked over at Ryder. He was in here because of her. Everything was because of her. She tried to speak through the nausea.

"Because sleeping on the ground for the last week is different how?"

He sat gingerly on the pallet, as if the thin pine might break under his weight. "Because, Lark, I was trying to make a joke."

"Well you suck at it."

He leaned back on the stone wall, and her jaw clenched at the dark red marks on his face and arms where they'd beaten him. Her throat tightened, and she tugged violently at her scarf to loosen it.

"Whoa," he said, raising his hands in surrender. "Hold off on the anger. I'm not the one who put us in here."

"No, that was me."

The words escaped, flying from her mouth before she had time to pull them back. Their eyes met for a second then her gaze slid away, shame firing heat in her cheeks. *I haven't saved him at all. He'll die in here.*

"That isn't true, Addie."

Why did he always call her that when she was weakest? Shrugging, she pulled the scarf off and turned to gesture at the cell, her words cutting her throat as they forced their way out.

"It is, though. All this, the dungeon, the King, Tama caught up in some Fae fantasy, is because of me." *And you, in pain, in danger.*

"You actually believe that, don't you?"

Crossing her arms, she stared down at him, dirt on his face mixed with fresh blood. He appeared so relaxed, but muscles coiled beneath his clothes, a wired spring ready to leap into action should the door open. Nausea roiled in her stomach. Ryder was everything to her, and she couldn't save him.

Burning pain rimmed dry eyes where tears refused to fall. She kept her gaze on his face as she nodded, not trusting her voice.

"Oh sweetheart, this isn't because of you."

Sweetheart? Her heart skipped. He looked unsure, like the word just slipped out, but he smiled at her. Heat flooded her chest as her pulse started racing.

He pushed to his feet and walked over to her, carefully, as if she were an animal about to flee. Fair enough, she felt like running.

Stopping barely a hands width from her, he gazed down at her. He really was tall. Her eyes fixed on his neck, at the smears of blood and sweat on olive skin. She watched his throat work as he swallowed, and she bit her lip. *Maybe he's nervous too.*

"The Fae did this, Addie. You need to know that. All you do is try your damnedest to help everyone. It isn't your fault we didn't succeed."

He sounded as if he meant it. She took a big breath, her chest tight.

"But you're hurt."

He reached out, cutting her off. "I'll live."

"What if you don't?"

The glint in his eyes warmed her heart and weakened her knees.

"Well, if I don't then at least it will be because I fought for something. Not because I gave up." He shrugged, a crooked grin lighting up his face. "Not much consolation, but it sounds better."

A smile pulled at her lips. "You're the only one who makes me laugh when I'm sad, Ryder Hendrix."

He stepped closer. "And you're the only one who makes my heart beat, Adelia Lark."

Time slowed, stopped, the words floating around her head before sinking into her heart. Rushing back to life, the world swayed under her feet, melting warmth filling her chest.

"Why now?"

Her voice whispered out of her. Scratchy and fragile. She focused on the collar of his shirt, noticing the grime covering faded grey and sweat tracks on his skin. Avoiding his eyes and with a quick breath, ignoring the clenched feeling in her gut, fingers twisting in her scarf, she asked him again.

"Why here? I thought after the time in the pool—" the heat rushed to her cheeks, and she frowned "I mean, anyway, I thought you didn't. and then now you say this, and I just wonder why now? When there's no time?"

She rolled her eyes at her tongue-tied mumbles. His jaw

tilted, his eyes trying to meet hers, but she had seen rejection in his face once and couldn't bear to look again. His fingers under her chin firmly dealt with her hesitation. Radiance glowed from hazel depths, and she blinked rapidly.

He was smiling at her. Not that devil may care grin he flashed so readily. This smile took her heart and wrapped gentle hands around it.

"I guess that's why," he said, warmth from his fingers on her face sending tingles over her skin. "When there's no time, well, then you have to use it for the things that matter. And it matters to me you know I care." She flinched away from his openness, and he gripped her jaw tighter.

"No, you don't get to run, Lark. Not this time. How do you manage to be such a stubborn ass about so many things but such a coward about us?"

She scowled at him, and his fingers grew more gentle, stroking tenderly as his smile grew, sending delicious shivers down her spine.

"I'm not sure when it happened, but I'm crazy about you," he said. She ventured a smile up at him, and he grinned, imps dancing in his eyes. "Literally crazy. You've driven me mad."

She jabbed under his rib, and he winced, his grin slipping. He wrapped his other arm around her shoulders, rigid with her withheld breaths. Fire raced through her blood, and the scarf dropped as her fingers slid from his ribs to his waist. Leaning his forehead to touch hers, he cupped her face in his palm. He smelled of sweat and musky grime and Ryder. The tough knot in her stomach melted, spreading sparkly warmth through her veins.

"I think it was when I thought you died. Carrying you to safety. Watching over you as you lay unconscious." His voice was almost a whisper of breath against her skin, and her hand rose hesitantly to touch his where it rested on her shoulder.

"That wasn't the moment I fell for you. That was a couple years ago after the storm ripped off Jasper's roof, and by the time I got there, you were perched on top of his house in a howling gale fixing tiles like a demon." His fingers curled under hers. "But when I thought I lost you, I realised how much I love you."

She couldn't say it. It sat there, filling her heart and her whole soul, but she couldn't say it.

She had to say something. She cleared her throat.

"I don't know if I love you Ryder, but I don't want to be without you, and that's kind of the same thing, I guess."

His mouth twisted. "Kind of."

Addie's heart hurt at the expression on his face, but she still couldn't say the words. Her hands went up to his cheeks. "You take that part of me that's shattered, and you piece it back together. And when another piece shatters, you put that back too. I've never met anyone quite like you. You make me so mad, and I swear most of the time I don't know if you even like me. But you take care of me, and no-one's done that for a very long time."

He smiled, and within a breath, he snatched her into his arms and against the hardness of his chest. When their lips met, her insides lit up, tingles shooting through her body. His hand tangled in her hair, and she didn't even care that her braid was matted and filthy. Tendrils of desperation and fear still swirled at the back of her mind, but she pushed them away. Time was too short to worry about when the clock would run out.

Ryder's hand on her waist slid lower, and the heat of his body warmed her, as did the memory of him in the pool. She smiled against his cheek as he kissed down her jaw.

"What are you smiling at?" His voice was muffled against her throat, and she felt his lips smile back.

"You."

His hands tightened on her, and he lifted his head to

murmur into her ear, "Guess that's fair, I smile when I think about you, too."

This had to be a dream. No way Ryder Hendrix was saying everything she'd ever wanted to hear, no way her hands were running over his chest, his shoulders. He nipped her ear lobe, and she couldn't stop her smile from taking over her face. She wasn't waking up. "Guess this is real." The whispered words fluttered out by accident, and she bit her lip.

He pulled back and gazed at her, his eyes roving over her face, her mouth.

"I think you're amazing, Lark. You're not like anyone else. You're so strong, so brave," his voice deepened, and he stroked his thumb over her lips. "So beautiful."

Echoes of the past flickered in her mind. *Stumbling through the compound doors for the first time. Surprised suspicious eyes. Ryder, cutting through the noise. A calm kindness despite the fresh grief on his face. Ryder protecting her. Ryder giving her a knife. Ryder teaching her to protect herself. Treating her like a second in command. Respecting her opinion. Looking after her in the night.* There'd never been one moment where she hadn't loved him.

"Right back atcha."

He laughed, squeezing her to him. "You really aren't good at words, are you?"

Bubbles of happiness floated through her. He didn't mind. She was inarticulate and awkward and scowled more than she smiled, and he didn't care.

Sliding her hand through his hair, she tugged his head to hers. She fastened her lips to his, the firm softness so biteable. When he gently slipped his tongue into her mouth, she stopped thinking. There was nothing in the world but the taste and feel of him.

The bolt of the door slamming back shot through her euphoria, and she stepped away from Ryder. He slid his hand down to hold hers, and her shoulders straightened.

Light flooded in with the Fae who entered. She tried not to squint too much. Dressed all in white, its eyes were a swimming vortex of black and starlight. Spiking pain sent fire over her scars, and her hand went limp in Ryder's grasp.

"This is the subject." She realised the Fae was speaking to another one, a smaller Faery whose sombre maroon robes complemented its subdued demeanour.

"You will measure her so we can prepare. She is different from the younglings, make sure you take that into account in your notes."

The smaller one bowed. "Yes, Ministrator"

The Ministrator's eyes burned into hers. She squeezed Ryder's hand tightly and stood her ground, her heart thudding against her ribs.

"You will not fight, or he will die. This is how it will be."

Rage sparked flames in her mind. She lunged forward. The Ministrator's wings flashed out, white speared through with gold filling her vision. Her breathing tore raggedly through her chest, and she wanted to spit at the Fae for threatening Ryder, for existing. Ryder grabbed her arm and yanked her backwards. He stroked her neck, moving so he was at her shoulder, face close to hers.

"It's okay, Lark. Back down."

Her breath shuddered through her as she took his hand and stepped back. The Fae would kill Ryder eventually, the knowledge carved through her heart like a razor. But every second gained was a win.

Satisfied she would comply, the Ministrator folded its wings and nodded at the smaller Fae.

"You may proceed, Makellan. If she gives you trouble, you know what to do."

Makellan bowed, and the Ministrator left.

Breathing came easier once the white Fae with his expressionless face had gone. The smaller Fae almost smiled at her as it approached, but she recoiled from the long fingers reaching out. Clawed hands gripped her arm like a vice, prying Ryder away from her, but its voice was surprisingly humanlike, the melodic cadences of other Fae muted to a soft hum.

"Sit, over there. This won't take long."

She couldn't look at Ryder.

If I look at him, I will cry. Look at the Fae instead. No. Not a good idea. Look at the wall.

The measurements were gentle, but her stomach swirled with nausea at being prodded and poked like a hunk of meat. The Fae didn't appear to write anything down. But a slate tablet edged with silver hung around its neck, and white lines of curly text appeared and disappeared at various points in the process.

"Your heart beat is not as fast as the younglings. Is this normal?"

Ryder jerked forward. "For fuck's sake!"

This time it was her hand that stopped him. Her eyes calmed him despite the anger surging through her at the remark.

She cocked her head, glaring at the Fae. More expression marked its face than most others. It waited for her reply with quirked eyebrows and pursed lips.

"Maybe I'm just not as afraid of you as they are."

"I see."

More lines appeared on the tablet.

After minutes that passed like hours, the little Fae stepped back, tucking its measuring probes back into a silk pouch at its waist. It checked the tablet, nodded, and walked to the door.

"Aren't you going to say goodbye?" *Jesus, why am I so mouthy?*

It turned, wings fluttering. "There is no need. We shall prepare, and you will be brought up to the White Room soon." It peered at her as if waiting for a reply, but no words remained. The White Room filled her head. Sterile, cold, terrifying.

The Fae regarded her for a moment before leaving. The door closed with a quiet thud that echoed in her ears.

Ryder stood in front of her, his arms on her shoulders.

"Oh sweetheart, you're shaking."

Tremors, uncontrollable shivers, wracked her body. Standing upright was a battle she was not sure she would win.

His arms wrapped around her, holding her tight so she wouldn't break.

"Addie, you don't have to be strong now. It's just me."

Her breath came in gasping shudders, and she snatched at the collars of his shirt. "They'll break me, Ryder. I can't do this. I can't do it again."

He stroked the back of her head, holding her to him. "They won't break you, Addie. They'll try, but they won't succeed. Nothing has broken you yet. You're the strongest person I know."

She wanted to believe him. God, how she wanted to believe. But she remembered what happened in the White Room now. Knowing what was coming was worse than the fear of the unknown. Cold hard benches and pain that wracked her whole being.

Ryder's voice rumbled against her hair. "I just wish I knew what they wanted you for."

Knowledge of what she could do flooded through her. *Changeling.* She finally let herself think the word. Her hand tightened on his shirt. She couldn't tell him. He hated the Fae, hated monsters. To see his face turn to hate so soon after seeing it in affection would break her more surely than any Fae lab.

Her face turned into his chest, and she focused on breathing. He didn't say anything else, and her heart eased a little. They both knew no words could fix this. She would be taken and would either break or survive. That was all there was to it.

CHAPTER 32

When the Fae came for her, she turned to Ryder and kissed him, desperately trying to let him know through her touch how much he meant to her. He kissed her back, fire and despair. She tried to tuck the moment away somewhere safe inside. Clawed hands dragged her away from his outstretched arms, and she drank him in with her eyes. If she never saw him again, she wanted to remember every little thing. His skin on hers, the fierce light in his eyes, the strength of his embrace, the curve of his lips.

The boom of the closing door sent her spiralling back to when she was twelve. Once more, footsteps echoing down long corridors lined in black lacquered panels. Once more, the churning in her gut as they passed the lion statue. Heavy oak doors strapped with brass drew in all the shadows of the hall, a well of darkness guarding the White Room.

With one touch, the door opened to beaming light reflecting off sparse white walls. Shining air surrounded marble benches covered in restraints.

It was the same.

Her stomach heaved. Forcing steel into shaking knees, she

refused to let her head drop. These monsters had no right to her misery.

"Strip her."

She tried to stop the long claws and cold hands, but shudders wracked her body. Trembling weakened her hands. They took off her clothes. She hunched over, vulnerable and shivering, staring at the Fae crowded along the edges of the room. The bright purple of the tallest one stood out against more muted hues, and she averted her eyes from the jaunty dragon brooch with its confusing associations.

Vice like hands dug into her limbs and lifted her onto the bench. Bare skin touched the marble she remembered from nightmares. Her body jerked, trying to escape. Chest heaving with the effort of breathing through a blanket of panic, she fought against restraining arms, bucking and twisting. Heavy metal and leather straps crossed her body, holding her down. She bit back a cry.

A voice laced with lush melodies cut through the rush of her pulse in her ears.

"Is this really necessary?"

She blinked. A restraint slipped over her brow, holding her head still. Breathing faster and swallowing the bitter taste in her mouth, she gritted her teeth. She focused her energy into the fight to stay whole, to not break.

The purple Fae approached and leaned over her, dark hair curling over his forehead. Their expressions were always inscrutable, but lines carved around this one's mouth, a glint of puzzlement in the shimmering eyes. He stretched out a hand, and she froze. He stroked her cheek, his fingers soft on her skin, his head on one side. "I remember this one."

Another Fae came into her line of sight. Stark white and silver robes oddly medical in appearance, coppery tresses bound firmly into two winding horns.

"Lord Aesthetius, you should not be here. You are too close to the subject. Your judgement is impaired."

Aesthetius. Was that his name? A bell chimed in her mind. *I know this name.* A memory surfaced—*her hands twisting, trying to rub off the silvery stuff they'd put all over her, trying not to cry, and a purple draped arm coming into view, wiping away her tears.* She stared, and the Fae gazed back before the two-horned one gestured and Aesthetius stepped back.

"Of course, Ministrator. I will go."

But he didn't leave. He unhooked the dragon brooch in one long fingered hand, and when the Ministrator turned away to address another white clothed Fae, he slipped it into her hand, just out of sight.

She fixed her gaze on the ceiling, seeing Aesthetius leaving from the corners of her eyes. *What the hell was that about?* Her fingers curled around the dragon brooch, another echoed thought flashing into her mind from its hiding place—*small twelve-year-old hands exploring the golden jewellery as the Fae sat with her. Watching.*

The image of the dragon had always been a talisman for her, and she hadn't known why. Maybe it could be a talisman now. Her mind recoiled. How could something from the Fae be a protection? But her fingers clutched tighter, the jewelled eyes digging into her palm.

The Ministrator turned back and smeared silver stuff over her body, suffocating her skin, freezing her limbs. She squeezed her eyes shut, but long claws dragged them open again.

"We require you to be aware for the procedure."

"Why?" Her voice ripped out of her, trembling and raw. "Why are you doing this?"

The Fae stepped back, as if surprised, cocking its head on one side in a disturbingly human pose. A long silver needle dangled carelessly from its hand. "Because you survived. Out there, without our guidance. You not only survived, but you are strong. The magic is strong. We need your resistance to iron, and we need the magic in your blood. We need to know how you work."

With a small shrug, it lifted the sharp spike closer to her face.

Pain burned like fire from inside her skull, her skin shrivelling under the silver webbing binding her body. Cascading waves of agony more terrifying than her nightmares. She fell into blackness, her vision dying. Streaks of colour lit up the darkness, throbbing with an intensity matching the paroxysms of torment. Red, gold, silver, green, and finally a purple which calmed her until the next spasm. She clenched her hand around the brooch as her body jerked, wracked with pain.

Memories burst through the walls she'd constructed—secret shameful fears, her brother's face as she told him she hated him. His face stayed with her, tear drenched and reproachful, as the burning needle dug deeper and deeper into her mind. Her feelings for Ryder were ripped apart, her most treasured moments cast out into a maelstrom of colour and darkness. A part of her remembered she didn't want them to see her cry. It fled under the tearing and mutilation of her mind.

Then the hidden door.

The one she refused to ever open.

The one she denied existed.

Torment knocked at it now, feeling round the edges, seeking a way in. She fought then, knowing deep within her what lay behind the door was not something she wanted anyone to see.

Agony whipped through her, snapping the locks she'd placed on the door, tearing it open. There, inside, was a dragon. A little dragon, blinking gold eyes, daring them to enter.

The pain vanished, and the sudden release left her shaking and struggling to breathe.

She lay on the bench, the surface warm now and

comforting on her shredded skin. She blinked red wetness from her eyes, seeing in her mind a door closing, a dragon returning to sleep.

The restraint on her head felt heavy, but she could move her eyes. It hurt, but just a little. Blinking again, she looked to find the Fae. The Ministrator clustered with three others, one in black the rest in white. Their wings half uncurled, fluttering with an anxiety they didn't show on their faces. Words came to her through a fog, and she strained to hear.

"But the power is there. You are certain?"

"Of course I am certain. You saw the same as I, did you not? The power is strong. Too strong."

"Are you saying the human is a threat?"

She nearly laughed. She could barely move her fingers. What sort of threat was she?

"You saw the dragon. She shouldn't be able to do that."

Her fingers curled tighter around the brooch.

"It wasn't just the dragon. I saw wings."

She blinked again. *Dragons had wings. What were they talking about?*

The Ministrator's voice rang harshly against her ears. "We can't let this one live. We have the other changeling, the boy, and more will come. This one is too dangerous. Her spirit is too strong."

Her body wracked and ruined, her mind in splinters, she stared at the ceiling. *So they want to kill me. I thought that's what they were already doing.* She closed her eyes. Caring was difficult. With death would come an end to pain.

"What about the other one? The man?"

Her eyes snapped open, her whole body tensing. *Ryder.*

"He is of no more use. Dispose of him."

No. She couldn't let that happen.

Deep within her, a dragon unfurled its wings and began to fly.

CHAPTER 33

The sensation of spreading wings flooded through her, dark and deep but somehow comforting. Familiar. Part of her. A sparkling tide washed out the tendrils of the Fae magic poisoning her body, replacing it with strength.

The dragon awoke, stalking out of the locked room in her mind. In its wake, she found the knowledge she had always possessed, always hidden.

Changeling.

Not a half aware being like the humans they kept to play on. Not a survivor like Ella. A true changeling. Human, but now Fae also. Every cell sparked with it.

Dust didn't hurt her because it was part of her.

They were right.

She *was* a threat.

Focusing her foggy mind on the restraints, she burned them off with a thought, a wish. She sat up, blinking more red from her eyes, and inspected her arms. The Fae fell deathly silent. Wings outstretched, hands to the ready, they spread around the room, circling her. Silver webbing clung to her, tacky with blood. She wiped it off. *Clothes. I need clothes.* They lay in a crumpled heap on the other side of the room, and she frowned at them.

The dragon inside pushed her on. *Fire*, it whispered, *show them fire*. She stared under her lashes at the Ministrator. Light flickered as his hand flew up. Raising her arms, she let rage fill her. Her eyes shimmered, sharpening her vision. She didn't want to hurt the other Fae. But she wanted the Ministrator to burn.

Flames swirled in her mind, burning hot and bright gold. They danced up her arms and flashed through the room, surrounding the Fae, who all disappeared in a flare of blue light.

Disappointment filled her. She had wanted to watch the Ministrator's face melt.

Ryder.

They would hurt him.

She squeezed her eyes shut and breathed deeply, willing away the last foggy remnants of Fae presence in her mind. When her eyes opened, it was as if cobwebs fled from her. The room shone with a diamond brilliance, and a clarity she'd not felt in years washed over her.

She knew who she was.

The acceptance of it seeped into her soul. *Changeling*. The thought of it was a grief, yet when the dragon filled her mind, she found she didn't have the heart to hate it.

Pushing off the bench, she landed on legs that wobbled only once before she willed iron into them.

Iron.

She would be iron from blood to bone to will, and they would not be able to touch her again.

Her clothes were gone, eaten by the flames. A small pang passed through her. Lifting her chin, she scanned the room. There was a folded pile of clothing inside a cupboard, worn and tattered, but human. She hesitated then snatched them up. Humans needed to stick together. They would be happy, surely, some good had come from their pain. She hoped so.

The waist on the baggy jeans slid low on her hips, and she threaded a scarf through as a bulky makeshift belt. The unicorn t-shirt hugged her ribs and barely fit her shoulders. Cold fury flooded her, and she wondered what young teen had worn it, how long they'd screamed before pain destroyed their mind.

She threw back the door, defying the shifting shadows in the hall outside. The Fae would no doubt be back. Fire sparked on her fingers, twining up her arm. *Let them come.*

Her bare feet made little noise as she ran along the hallway. *If they hurt Ryder before I reach him, I will burn it all down.*

Guards flanked the door to the cell. Human. Her fire died out. She didn't want to kill any humans.

The guard on the left lowered his spear. "Stand down."

He sounded so young.

"No. I need you to leave. I don't want to hurt you."

The young guard looked at his companion, who blinked. That was her only warning before they jumped her.

She leaped up and didn't come back down again.

The shock on their faces was nothing compared to what filled her. Her back twitched, and she glanced over her shoulder, half expecting to see something snatching her out of the air.

They spread behind her, filling her vision. Gauzy and pale, as if made from pure light, they pulsed in time with her heartbeat, strong strokes keeping her aloft.

Bloody hell.

Wings.

They closed suddenly as the shock hit her, and she tumbled to the ground.

She lay for a second, breathless and stunned.

Wings. Holy crow. Wings.

The guards gaped at her.

Guards. Ryder. She rolled to her feet, feeling the drag of the gauzy wings at her back. She tried to twitch her shoulders, and they popped out again. They weren't as solid or as real as the wings of the Fae, but shimmered and flowed with a light that brightened her eyes.

The guards shuffled under the weight of her stare.

"Like I said, I don't want to hurt you. I will, but I don't want to. Please just leave."

One guard looked like he might make a break for it, but the other one took a step forward.

"What are you?"

She considered.

"Changeling. Human. Angry."

A moment longer, then he pulled back his spear, motioning for his companion to put down his sword.

"I won't stop you. But I won't open the door."

She smiled, a silvery shimmer passing over her vision. "Won't be a problem."

They held their ground for a moment, and then the smaller guard left, stumbling backwards a step before turning tail and running away. The other guard watched him go then stepped quickly towards her. "Before you leave, you should seek out a man called Sanjeet."

Sanjeet. The name took her back to the last time she'd seen him, shuffling away from the King with a tall Fae at his side.

She wanted to get to Ryder and get the hell out. "What do you know about Sanjeet?"

The guard shouldered his spear. "He has been waiting for you."

He strode away, and the cell door filled her vision and her thoughts. Heavy and solid stone. As she touched the silver lock, a sizzle sparked up her fingers. Fae magic. She didn't have time for some open sesame crap. She had to get to Ryder.

Placing her hands on the door, she sent the fire through it, wishing as she did so. Nothing happened. *Maybe it needs more than wishes.* Her eyebrows drew together. She summoned her rage, her pain, and let the dragon out. A pulse of light burst from her, and the lock exploded. Shoving the door open, she rushed in, blinking in the dim light.

"Lark?"

She turned to Ryder's voice, his silhouette solidifying as he took a hasty step towards her. A smile split her face, and she moved towards him, arms outstretched. He was safe.

A bright glow at her back deepened as her wings extended with her arms.

Shock twisted his smile. He recoiled, his arm shielding his face. Shuddering, he lowered his arm and backed away from her. Her heart stopped, a lead weight in her chest that shattered, sending fragments bleeding through her.

The wings sagged too, as if connected to her emotions. His face shut down, eyes turning to ice and lips curling into a snarl. Cold anger radiated from him. Shivers scattered over her skin, setting her limbs to trembling. She tugged down the too small t-shirt as if that would help.

His voice rasped out, cutting the silence. "Tell me you didn't know about this. Tell me you didn't know you were one of them. I want to hear you say it."

She shook her head numbly, her lips pressed together.

"Tell me!"

She shut her eyes at the shouted words. His ragged breathing filled her ears.

"What are you?"

Her eyes snapped open. "Human! How can you even ask?"

He gestured to the wings, static now and scarcely visible.

Voice choked with unshed tears, her fingers curling into fists, she tried not to plead. "I'm still human. I'm just a changeling. It isn't my fault. They did this to me."

He crossed his arms, tension showing in the rigid lines of

his shoulders. "And you knew, didn't you? That's why you survived the Dust, how come you could track Tama, and save me, and all those things. Because you *knew* you were one of *them*."

He was right. She had always known. She just hadn't wanted to.

All the justifications, the pleas, the defence, all dropped away. The only thing left was acceptance.

"Yes."

His face fell, and it hurt her that he wanted to hear a denial.

"Christ, Adelia. All that time you said you didn't remember, you still knew you were this, this changeling?"

"Yes."

He turned away from her with his hands over his eyes, and she stepped towards him, despite her best intentions to stay cold and noble. "But I really couldn't remember."

His lip curled. "You still lied."

She thought she had been prepared for hatred, but this despairing contempt was a knife shredding her from the inside out.

She didn't mean to lie.

Guess it didn't matter now.

Trying to breathe through the ache in her chest, she held her hand out towards him. "We better go. They'll be coming soon."

He stared her down. "We don't leave without Tama. Whatever it is they did to you, they will do to him. Or don't you care about that now you're like *them*?"

She took the bitter words but couldn't meet his eyes, dark now and cold with anger. Foolish of her to think this could ever have been different.

No-one loved a monster.

Her hand gripped tight on the shattered frame of the door, splinters driving into her skin.

"You know something, Ryder? I've tried my whole life to fit in, to be what people wanted me to be. To hide what I am from others. To hide it from myself. But know what I always needed?" Her fingers played over the dragon brooch, warm from more than the fire. "To just be myself."

She shifted her shoulders, flicking the translucent wings open, and with a wish called up a ball of energy in her hand. Glancing over at him, she saw the pain he'd tried to hide written large on his face. She smiled through her own hurt.

"I might be a monster, Ryder, but I'm your monster. And we have a boy to rescue."

CHAPTER 34

Silence lay heavy between them as they headed towards the part of the palace where they last left Tama. Anger radiated off Ryder like heat. She tried to focus on the corridor ahead, but she kept stealing glances at him. He stalked next to her, jaw clenched and eyes hard as flint as he stared anywhere but at her.

He paused at the archway of the passage leading to Tama's room. "This is too easy."

She stopped, arms wrapping around her. "Define easy."

"There are no Fae. Where are they? Where are the guards? You've escaped, broken me out, and now they've all decided to what? Take a nap? It's a trap."

"Yes, probably."

His brows drew together. "You don't sound worried about it."

How could she say that she had no room for worry about the Fae when the devastating chill of his disgust filled every thought?

"No point being worried. We're not leaving without him, and we don't have any other way to do this. If it's a trap, what do you want to do?"

His face twisted in a scowl, and she wished she had softer words to show him she understood. The weight of his anger choked her, and her voice came out clipped by a pain she refused to let him see.

"We go in, and we do what we can." She let fire spark along her fingers. "Turns out I can do quite a lot."

She held his eyes in a challenge, and his gaze slid away.

"Fine," he said. "But I go first."

The fire sputtered out, and she shook her head. "That doesn't make sense—the front is where the danger will be."

He glanced back at her, and her breath caught at the expression in his eyes. "You said it yourself, Lark. You might be a monster, but you're *my* monster. I go first."

Words tumbled behind her tongue as hope and relief tangled inside her. She moved toward him, but he flinched. She stumbled back, hope dying. As he passed her, he paused. Fresh lines marked his face, and he refused to meet her eyes. "I promised you I would never kick you out, Lark, and that's a promise I mean to keep. But I gave you my heart, and you lied to me. This discussion isn't over."

She didn't reply. There was nothing she could say.

No guards stood outside Tama's room, but the presence of Fae filtered out like a weight pressing on her mind. She put out a hand to tap Ryder on the shoulder, to let him know, but her fingers curled back, fearful of another recoil. Clenching her jaw, she stretched them out, jabbing him with more force than she intended. When he turned to scowl at her, she gestured at the room and held up three fingers. Tension rippled through his shoulders, and he jerked his head, then opened the door in a rush.

The sight of Aesthetius brought her up short. He stood in the centre of the room. His mouth curled up at one corner, an odd light in his shimmering eyes. The expression reminded her a bit of her mother's face watching her cross the line first in a race as a child. *Pride? No. Ridiculous.*

Ryder flexed his arms, his hand drifting to his knife. She scanned the room. A sullen and fearful Tama sat next to a man about her age, dark black hair curling over a long face with a sharp nose. But it was his eyes that she remembered.

"Sanjeet?" Her voice, barely more than a whisper, scratched out of a throat swollen with hope and guilt.

Ryder lunged toward the Fae, and she threw an arm out to stop him. He glared at her, the suspicion in his eyes sending a spike into her heart.

Sanjeet stood and walked to stand next to Aesthetius, leaving Tama staring after him with wide eyes. "Adelia. It's been a long time."

Her eyes flicked between him and the Fae. "Too long and not long enough," she said.

Aesthetius smiled, and she and Ryder both took a step back. As she did, the gauzy wings at her back sprang out, making her jump and Tama swear. The Fae's smile froze then widened in a grin so unlike a Fae her breath caught. No sharp teeth, no scorn, no contempt. An actual smile. Her fingers stole to the brooch in her pocket.

"You survived." His voice rang a melody in her mind, a singing hum even as she heard the words in her ears.

"Was that because of you?" she asked.

Ryder jerked next to her, and she cursed inwardly. She still had to know.

"No. It was all you. I merely tried to show you the way."

The marble floor shifted under her feet, and a haze filled the room until all she saw was Aesthetius.

Light from the window danced around his dark hair, turning it into a shimmering curling mess of shining black. She met his gaze, and for the first time, the shifting colours of Fae eyes did not make her ill.

So many questions and really only one that mattered. "Why?"

Aesthetius moved towards her, and she became aware of Ryder stepping closer and just in front of her.

"Don't touch her." The fierce rumble snapped her back into the moment.

Her hands twitched into position, ready to defend Ryder, sparks flickering on her fingertips. Aesthetius stopped, glancing from her to Ryder. His smile faded, but he didn't blast Ryder away. She relaxed, the flames dying. Something tugged at her mind, and her gaze dragged to Tama, his eyes fixed on her fingers and his mouth twisting. She dropped her hands to her side and turned away from his disconcerting stare.

Aesthetius surveyed Ryder, and she tried not to bristle. They were so different. The Fae was taller, lean and strong, his hands those of someone who never had to work hard. Power radiated from him, mesmerising and frightening. Princely. Ryder's whole body was whipcord tough, his clothes stained with blood and grime. But her gaze traced the line of his jaw, the defiance in his eyes, and the heart and iron will of him filled her world.

He would die to protect her. As much as he hated her right now, he would do that for her. The knowledge settled into her heart and started patching up the cracks.

She laid a hand on his shoulder, feeling the tension of muscles ready to leap. "Please, Ryder. I need to know."

He stayed frozen for a second then nodded slowly, but he didn't move away. She turned and leaned her forehead on his shoulder, breathing him in. If only he knew how much he meant to her. He might think she was a monster, but he wasn't running. She sighed against his back and raised her head, stepping to his side.

"Tell me, Aesthetius. Tell me why you tried to help me."

"You don't remember everything, do you?"

Her certainty wavered, and the wings shivered behind her,

sending tingles down her spine. *More secrets. Would they never be done?*

"The first time you came here, you were different from all the rest. You turned to me like no other human had in hundreds of years."

Ryder stifled an exclamation, and Tama sat up straighter behind the Fae. Her hand flew up to stop Aesthetius.

"Hang on, hundreds of years? It's only been fifteen."

The Fae shook his head, and Sanjeet, returning to stand next to Tama, raised his voice. "Turns out we were wrong about that, Adelia. The Fae have been taking humans, children and adults, since time began." His mouth screwed up, and his eyes held a world of remembered pain. "The stories were all true."

She gazed back at Aesthetius, who slightly inclined his head, his eyes fixed on her wings.

"You changed me," he said. "Just as we changed you."

More images flickered to life. *Sitting in his chambers, telling him a story, his face reflecting intense focus and interest. The door opening, and a shutter coming down on his expression as he stood, moving away from her as other Fae entered. Him taking her to the White Room and standing too long outside the door before his hand gently stroked her head. A sigh shaking him before he finally surrendered her up.*

Her hands trembled, and she curled them into fists. "How did you change me? And why didn't it change him?" She jerked her head to Sanjeet.

Aesthetius glanced between them.

"Because he didn't already carry the magic inside him. You did."

"Impossible." Her voice was flat, but underneath it lay a searing knowledge.

"This is why we have been searching. For the ones like you. Like the boy. Changeling blood is rare, only one or two each generation. Imagine their shock at the strength of yours."

"Jesus." Ryder stood listening with his arms crossed. Clearly, he accepted the Fae weren't an immediate threat. "Are you saying that she's always been, what, half Faery?"

Aesthetius shrugged, a fluid movement that sent his wings fluttering outwards. Her own wings lowered. *Her own wings.*

"She is what she is, a changeling child."

The tightness in Ryder's face, the bleakness of it, was too painful. She turned her gaze on Tama. He hunched forward in his seat, quiet and coiled in around himself. He darted a glance up at her then stared back at the floor again. *Like when I count the dots in the lino in the ward.*

"What about Tama? Is he the same?"

Sanjeet rested a hand on the boy's shoulder. "He is a changeling, yes. Not as strong, but he has not been fully tested. They will want him if you are gone."

Tama's hands twisted together, and a muscle jumped in his jaw.

"Tough, because they won't have him." Ryder strode towards Tama as he spoke, stopping in front of the boy and crouching down so he was at eye level. "Hey buddy. Time to go home."

Tama avoided his eyes, casting a glance up at Aesthetius. When the Fae inclined his head, the teen heaved a sigh and wavered a smile at Ryder.

A frown gathered on Ryder's face, his hand tightening on the arm of the boy's chair. Her heart ached for him, but she saw the confusion on Tama's face. The same pull towards the Fae tugged at her mind.

"Sanjeet, will you come with us?"

Those familiar eyes brightened. "I certainly hoped to. I have information that might be helpful."

Warmth spread through her. She hadn't been able to save Ella, but Sanjeet would finally go home. Well, back to humanity anyway. Her brows contracted. Humanity. That might mean she didn't have a home anymore.

Aesthetius' voice, melodious and soft, broke into the darkness behind her eyes.

"I have packs here for you, and food." He looked at Ryder. "A new coat if you will have it."

She bit her lip. Who would've ever thought she'd be worried about a Faery. "But what about you? Won't they punish you if you let us go?"

He passed Tama the leather bag where the skull still bulged. "I think you should hold on to this Tama. Keep it for me." Turning to face her, he smiled. "I am not without influence here. I will remain unharmed."

An image of him stopping the actions of the king with the wave of a hand crept into her mind. Influence. Hell of an influence to be able to challenge a king. Just what kind of Fae was he? Not that she'd have to care once they'd got out of this hellish city.

CHAPTER 35

They ran through the city, only slowing when they hit the mountain rise blocking the way home. Cliffs rose above them, grey and dark, shrouded at the top with Dust. Scrubby trees at the bottom made way to rich, green forest and the pool where they had washed. She rubbed her chest at the ache in her heart, turning her gaze back to the path in front of her. Just ahead, Sanjeet walked at Tama's side, helping him up the steep rocks.

Ryder's voice cut into her thoughts. "Do you trust him?"

She regarded the man who was once her classmate.

"Do you know what I remember about Sanjeet? He was a pain at school. Like, really annoying. But one day I was crying behind the bike shed because it was my birthday the next day and dad rang mum to say he wasn't coming. Sanjeet must've heard me. He came and sat down on the grass next to me. Didn't say anything, but he sat and let me cry until I was done." She turned to face Ryder. "Ella thought he was okay, and the guard told me to talk to Sanjeet. I want to trust him. I would trust the boy with my life, but I don't know the man."

Ryder looked like he was going to say something, but then he rubbed his hand over his mouth, pulling at his lip.

Hoisting her pack up on her shoulder, she gazed ahead towards Sanjeet and Tama. "But I'm not leaving him here. Not again."

"Fair enough."

Her foot skidded on the gravel, and his hand slipped under her arm, the warmth of his grasp burning through the layers of fabric. She willed the wings not to appear. He snatched his hand away and strode on ahead. Her fingers snuck to her elbow as if she could still feel his touch.

The top of the rise led into the Dust. The ground turned dry and dead as green grass sloped away into grey dense clouds. From here the blue sky just stopped, like someone had drawn a line. Sanjeet halted. His eyes were wide when she turned to him.

"You okay?"

He nodded, a quick abrupt movement that showed more than anything how far from okay he was.

"I'm fine. Just..." Rolling his shoulders back, he fidgeted with the scarf, Mia's goggles sitting atop his black hair. "I haven't been in the Dust since I was Taken."

Tama moved closer to Sanjeet and stretched out a hand to the man who had once been a boy lost and alone. "Don't worry mate, you'll be all good. Come on, take my hand. I'll help you."

Ryder strode past them both. "I'll go ahead. Lark, you take the back."

She bit back the words to argue with him. Any threat they had was likely to come from behind them anyway.

One by one, the others disappeared into the Dust. She took a moment, looking behind her. The blue of the sky and the green of the fields still called her, but the Valley of Kings was an abomination. Her wings shifted at her back, catching in the breeze.

Changeling child.

No matter whether the magic had been in her all along,

the fact she had wings, could blast open doors, was all because of the Fae. Because of the pain they inflicted.

Clouds of Dust lay ahead of her, dense and comforting in a funny way, like being wrapped in a blanket after too long in the cold. Her vision shimmered, and she realised she could see through the swirling grey now. Not as if the Dust didn't exist, but if she concentrated, it became translucent in patches. Suddenly, she missed the goggles.

A step forward, and the grey surrounded her. The others waited just ahead, and she jogged a few paces to catch up.

Sanjeet trembled, but Tama had a strong grip on his hand. The boy met her eyes, and his own shimmered back at her, gold and grey. A sensation swam up from the ground through her feet and into her heart. If the Fae had never come, never taken her, she wouldn't have this. She would be plain old Adelia Lark. Would she swap it? Get rid of the wings that, despite herself, she actually liked?

Her arms prickled where her mother's nails had raked her skin. She knew that to stay with her she would have given up everything else. Her eyes lit on Ryder, goggles and scarf concealing his face, head down against the Dust, pushing on towards the ladder and hopefully less of a storm.

If I hadn't been Taken, I never would have met Ryder. She would keep the pain to be able to keep him.

The grief on his face burned in her mind. So much loss. So much hurt. She didn't think Ryder would keep his pain to keep her.

Leaving seemed to take longer than coming in, and she was on the verge of asking Ryder if they'd gone the wrong way when two wooden poles loomed up out of the clouds. She scooted past Sanjeet and Tama to stand next to Ryder, looking down into the swirling maelstrom below.

"It looks worse from here," she said.

"A lot of things look worse now," Ryder replied.

She couldn't see his eyes through the goggles very clearly. *Thank goodness for small mercies.* "You still want to take point?"

In answer, he slipped his knife into the sheath on his back and took hold of the ladder, swinging himself down to disappear into the twisting Dust storm below.

"I guess that's a yes."

The others were at her side now, and she turned to them. "Sanjeet. It will be tough. Tama will be ahead of you, and I will be right behind you. Look up and you'll see my foot." She cast a glance over the side of the cliff. "Best to not look down."

He lifted his chin, and she saw his courage gathering behind his eyes.

Tama met her gaze, a flicker in his expression betraying his anxiety. His hands clenched, but his shoulders went back, exactly like when Ryder asked him to leap off a building in the deadlands. Slipping over the side, he waited for Sanjeet to put his feet on the ladder before he moved downwards.

She took a last glance behind her, not that the Dust left much visible. Beyond the ashen clouds, she saw in her mind a valley of abundance and fear. She was happy to be going home, whatever welcome she might receive.

The journey down the side of the cliff took forever, but at least travelling down was easier than climbing up had been. Sanjeet's laboured breathing filtered through the air. She began to hum a tune. Tama picked it up, and the two of them strung together a melody. The Dust lightened, and she frowned. Strange, but surely not related. Coincidence.

They passed through the storm. Underneath the swirling cloud, the world stretched out below, grey and barren and lifeless.

The trek back would be long.

RYDER STOMPED the last peg into the hard ground. Small and worn, the tent wouldn't fit four of them. Addie fingered the brooch where it lay in her pocket.

Changeling child.

She cleared her throat. "I'll stand watch."

Ryder crossed his arms, and she smiled wearily at him.

"It's the sensible thing to do."

He didn't say anything, but he turned, staring at Sanjeet and Tama until they mumbled and shuffled inside the tent. Taking a step forward, his muscles pulled against his shirt with the tension he held in.

"Being out in the Dust all night is not sensible, Lark. It's foolish."

Chilled stone sat in her chest, surrounding her heart. "Not for me."

"No," his mouth twisted. "I guess not."

They stood staring at each other, and she wrapped her arms around herself to keep the emotions inside, where they belonged.

Golden irises glinted in the grey light, and she blinked away prickles at the corners of her eyelids.

He rubbed his hands over his face and through his hair, ending with his hands clasped behind his head.

"Fuck, Addie. Why didn't you tell me?"

Because you'd hate me. Because you'd leave. Because I was scared.

She looked up at the Dust, falling more heavily. "You best get inside too, Ryder."

He moved, but not to the tent. She gazed at him, barely a hand's breadth away.

Her scarf was wound around his neck. She'd offered hers to Sanjeet, but instead Ryder had given him his and taken hers. *Doesn't mean anything.*

"You owe me this, Lark." In the end neither his harsh voice nor the demand pulled her closer. The pain in his eyes did.

"I lied." Her voice was husky to her own ears, and she swallowed.

"You lied about a lot of things, Lark, which particular lie are you referring to?"

His face was so forbidding. The urge to turn tail and run was strong, but she fought it down. Whatever he decided to do, he deserved the truth. "When I said I didn't know if I loved you. I lied."

He still looked fierce and blank, but his eyes twitched. Hope stirred deep inside her.

She swallowed past the emotions in her throat.

"I've known I loved you for about six years. Since you danced with me at my twenty-first celebration. I'd actually had a kind of crush on you for ages. When you took my hand to present me to the compound as an adult and the band began playing, in that moment, it didn't matter that Dust still fell and I still had nightmares every day. For the first time since I was a child, I felt like I belonged, and it was you and your smile and your kindness that made me feel that way. And halfway round the dance floor, when you smiled and pulled me closer, I fell for you completely."

His eyes were fixed on the ground, but he turned slightly to face her. When he spoke, his voice lost the harsh gravel that made him into a stranger.

"You never said anything."

Her mouth twisted, and she shrugged one shoulder. "When have I ever been articulate about feelings? Besides, not long afterwards you started seeing Marianne, and I knew you still thought of me as a kid. I shoved it away with all the other uncomfortable feelings and got on with things."

He sighed. "What about when I told you how I felt? Why did you lie then?"

She pressed her lips together then blurted out, "Because I was scared. I'm always scared. People who I love go away—

they die or they get hurt and they leave. It was easier to say I didn't know."

His eyes glittered, and his jaw twitched—she ached to stroke the tightness away.

"This doesn't change anything, Lark."

Her heart burned inside her. "I understand. But I wanted to tell you. I didn't want any more lies, any half-truths, between us."

His eyes went to her mouth, and she held her breath. When he nodded briefly and turned to go into the tent, she pushed away the hurt and rejection.

The dusky crimson of her scarf stood out against the grey of the canvas as he ducked inside. For a moment, she remembered the touch of his lips on hers.

CHAPTER 36

The night stretched out, minutes into hours. Dust fell thick and dense, wrapping around her like a cocoon. She held her hand out and let grey powder catch on her fingertips. Silky grains shimmered on her skin, and she stared for a moment before wiping the residue off on her trousers. She sat cross legged in front of the tent flap, burningly aware of Ryder lying scant inches from her on the other side.

Sitting in the muffled silence of the grey world, she opened the door inside her and let the past out. She had been terrified her first time in the Dust at night without shelter. Too scared to approach the caravan she glimpsed in the dark, she sat in the swirling clouds ten feet away and waited. It had been almost more frightening when she hadn't suffocated. She shifted now and let out a sigh, tensing when she felt, rather than heard, Ryder suddenly stilling behind her in the tent.

Morning came, dreary and dull, but for the first time, she saw the sun glinting through the Dust. Rays of white light reflected off motes of grey in a silvery shimmer that tugged at her heart. She wondered if this was her new eyes or just that she never noticed before.

The zip sounded behind her, and she pushed herself up,

shaking her legs to get rid of the pins and needles. Ryder unfolded himself from the flaps. She bit back a smile at the endearing mess of his hair. He grunted at her as he left to relieve himself. She began the task of getting the others out, sending them off to do their business and packing down the tent.

Somewhere near mid-morning, a shadow caught her eyes. Black against the grey sky. Her muscles tensed, and her voice hissed out. "Ryder, tracker!"

He turned, his eyes following where she pointed. Sanjeet swore, and Tama went completely still.

Ryder cocked his head. "Looks far away. Do you think they've seen us?"

She bit her lip and glanced at Sanjeet, who shrugged. "It's hard to tell," he said. "We shouldn't be able to see the Fae at all. I think it wants to be seen."

Tama spoke up, and his voice came out in a raspy whisper, his face twisting. "They do. They call to me."

She scanned the horizon. There was nowhere to hide on the flat desolate plains. Not even an abandoned truck stood out against the endless Dust. "What do you think?"

Ryder's jaw twitched as he gritted his teeth. "Why ask me? You're the expert on Faeries."

Her eyes lighted on her scarf, carefully knotted and tucked into his shirt, and her chin lifted. "Oh, my mistake. I thought you were the leader here but guess you're going for teenage boy instead."

They glared at each other, and she ignored Tama's muttered, "Whatever, not all of us act like that."

The tightness in Ryder's face softened, and he raised his eyebrows at her. "Really? That's the best you've got?"

"To be fair, yours was a bit rubbish too."

Sanjeet waved an arm at them.

"Kind of in the middle of a crisis here. Bit of focus please. If they're out so openly, then they want us to see them, but the fact they're not attacking worries me more. We need to get away."

Tama opened his mouth, glanced to Ryder and pressed his lips shut firmly. She frowned. "What is it, Tama?"

He shook his head then blurted out— "Can't you hide us? With the magic?"

She regarded him with her head tilted.

Beside her, Ryder said, "Absolutely not."

"But she could."

"Just because you can do something doesn't mean you should."

Ryder didn't appear angry or disgusted. He had a look of his old self back. He was slipping into the mentor role with Tama again.

"It might be a good idea." Sanjeet's voice sounded soft, as if uncertain of the mood of the room.

"No," Ryder said. "It would be a bad idea."

She turned fully to face him. "Why?" She wasn't angry, only curious at his tone. There was no bitterness, simply an authority she'd missed.

"Because I think they can't see us. I think maybe that thing Aesthetius gave you is covering us." Her fingers strayed to the brooch in her pocket as her eyes widened. She forgot how much he noticed.

"I think that if you use the magic," his voice stumbled over the word, and his mouth twisted. But his eyes held none of the same hurt that had dwelled there for the last two days. "If you use it, they will notice us. I think they're trying to make you do precisely that."

Sanjeet snorted. "And you base this assumption on what, exactly?"

Ryder shrugged. "Gut instinct."

A smile tugged at her lips as a decade of recollections of Ryder knowing what was best flashed in her head. "I've always trusted you, and I can't think of a reason to stop now. I think you're right. If they knew where we were, they would be right in front of us. They're trying to flush us out."

He smiled, and for the first time in what felt like forever, a sparkling glint reflected in his eyes. "So, we go on," he said.

"We go on."

CHAPTER 37

They trudged through endless grey fields, and she tried not to think of the lush green valley behind them, or of watching stars with Ryder at her side. Her eyes kept straying to her dusty crimson scarf wrapped around his neck, and shards of stone fell away from her heart.

That night, they found a small grove of dead and dying sticks of trees. A patchy clearing sat in the middle, and they pitched the tent. Not much food remained. Dry bread filled the gap in their stomachs. She leaned back on a scratchy trunk, resting her arms on her knees, and darted a glance at Ryder. When Tama and Sanjeet went to finish the nightly wash-up, she sighed and spoke the fear that had coiled in her stomach all day.

"They haven't found us, but they know where we're from. What if they attack the compound?"

He met her eyes, and she didn't bother trying to hide the horror of what she'd seen when she was twelve. It was Ryder, and he'd know how she felt whether she tried to conceal it or not. The same anxiety carved lines in his brow.

"You said they tested everyone, but they want you and Tama. Would they still test everyone else?"

The water canteen rolled between her hands, and she shrugged. "With two of us in the same place, they might wonder if they should investigate everyone. Not that either Tama or I are from there originally."

His face showed everything he was thinking. At least, to her it did. He met her eyes, and in them lurked a world of frustration and anger.

"How many days away do you think we are?"

She put the canteen down and clasped her hands in front of her, trying to stop the trembling. "Too many. Two or three perhaps?"

He swore and pushed himself up, kicking at the Dust as he paced.

Gaze dropping to her twisting hands, she tried not to think about Anahera and Mia going through a testing. She glanced up when Ryder stopped in front of her, standing with one hand on his hip and the other stroking at his beard. A shutter closed off his face, hiding his thoughts.

"Could you do something to get us home faster?"

Her brows contracted, and she leaned back a little. The bark of the trunk scraped against her coat. "Um, like what, running?"

He shook his head, his gaze sliding away in exasperation. A little tremor ran through her. "Hang on. Exactly what do you mean, Ryder? Are you asking if I can, what, magic us there?"

He stared at her, eyes dark and hooded. "Can you?"

She pushed herself up to face him. He was still so much taller than her, but she needed to be close, to see his eyes. Her heart pounded against her ribs.

"I don't know. I could try. I could ask Sanjeet. He might have some ideas."

He jerked his head, and she wet her lip.

"You're okay with us using magic?"

"If we got home faster, we could try to stop whatever is

going to happen, or at least be there, not abandon them." His voice came out in a rough rasp, fear filling his tone with gravel. "For that, I'd do whatever it took."

Her hand reached out to him, and he backed away. She snapped it back to her side like she had been burned, her other arm snaking around her waist. He bit his lip and stepped forward again, his mouth opening. Before he said anything, Sanjeet and Tama came back into view. A muscle jumped in his jaw, and he turned away. She faced the ground. Dust curled around her feet in little tendrils. Grey powder sat still and heavy around his boots. Letting out a sigh, she raised her head as the others joined them. Shadows darkened Tama's eyes as he took in the anger carved into Ryder's face. She ignored his worry, hers was too consuming.

"Sanjeet," she said, "is there a way we could reach the compound more quickly using magic?"

The word was a small one but so difficult for her to say. Magic belonged to stories, to legends, to Fae. Not to humans.

He glanced between her and Ryder, and Tama stood frozen, a little intake of breath the only sign that he'd heard.

"I'm not sure if you'll be able to do it, but the Fae can shift between places. They fly as well."

She flexed her wings, and they spread out, soft and gossamer-fine energy at her back. "I don't think that flying is an option. I can't carry all three of you." Her eyes sparked, and she bit back a laugh at the image. Ryder raised his eyebrows at her, but his face lost some of its granite look.

"So how does she do that other thing," Ryder asked. "The shifting?"

Sanjeet shrugged at Ryder. "Sorry, that was never really a topic of conversation. Who knows how Fae magic works?"

Tama spoke, and she had to strain to hear him, his voice swallowed by uncertainty. "You reach inside and light the fire. That's what Aesthetius told me." He stared at her with eyes that were too old for his fifteen-year-old face. "It isn't just wishing. I wish as hard as I can, and nothing happens. You need the fire as well."

Her breath stopped, and she remembered the dragon curling inside her mind, sending little tendrils of fire out with each one of its breaths.

Ryder's arms flexed where they crossed his chest, and he frowned down at the ground. Sanjeet gave her a lopsided smile. "So, Adelia, want to try and light the fire?"

"The inside one or a literal one?"

Sanjeet quirked a brow at her. "Well, probably no point in an actual fire—the Dust would choke it. But yeah, do you want to try something? See if you can figure out a way to wish us to your home?"

Everything inside her stilled at the same time as a fiery snake of magic curled its way through her limbs.

Dust kicked up where Tama shuffled at the edge of the conversation. His face twisted in a scowl. "What about the tracker? You all said she shouldn't use magic because they would notice."

Sanjeet shrugged. "I think we're alright when it isn't around—there must be a range the trackers can pick up."

"Okay." The word croaked out, and she coughed and tried again. "Okay. What should I try?"

Ryder raised his head to look at her, and she flicked her eyes over his face, scared of what she might see.

Taut muscles worked in his jaw, but warmth leaked back into his eyes. His voice was a soft rumble. "How about you start with something small, and we find out what you can do. Can you control the Dust?"

Images flashed into her mind—swirling Dust called from the sky, smothering Ryder, choking them. Hurt flickered through her. *Why would he ask me that?* But his gaze stayed steady on hers, and thought kicked in. *Something familiar. Something that has never hurt me. Something I can maybe help with.*

Crouching down, she stretched a hand over the ground.

She nudged the dragon inside and imagined fire lapping out. Her arm warmed, and her vision sharpened as the edges of the world shimmered. Lifting her hand, she ignored the bitten off exclamations and let herself smile at the Dust curling around her fingers, forming a whorl of tendrils around her arm.

Grey powder rose with her as she stood, playing around her leg and her arm but never touching skin. She risked a glance at Ryder. His face was a mix of distrust of Fae magic and something that might have been pride, might have been hope.

His eyes met hers, and she knew they had the same idea.

"Try it."

"Are you sure?"

"Only way to find out."

She stretched her other hand out to Ryder and tried to imagine him in a bubble, safe, and protected. Tapping that wish into her deepest longing came easily. A shimmer surrounded him, and when he stumbled back, dragging in a harsh breath, she stopped.

"No, keep going, Lark. It's fine. Weird, but fine."

Keeping her eyes on his, she lifted the other arm and sent the Dust away.

Powder swirled around Ryder, falling like gentle rain over the top of him. The motes of grey didn't touch him. They twined over the shimmer that shielded him, close to but never reaching him.

Butterflies of excitement battled with the heaviness of dread in her chest. His eyes widened, but he gave her an uncertain smile. Hope furled inside her. She let the shield and the Dust fall.

Tama kicked at powder on the ground, breaking the silence in the clearing. "Do you think you could shield them from other things?"

The beasts they narrowly avoided on the way sprang into her mind. She shrugged. "Not sure. Possibly?"

She didn't say it—she thought she would be able to protect Ryder, but the others weren't so closely linked to her desire for safety. She wanted to keep them safe, but protecting Ryder was the same as protecting herself, protecting her heart.

Sanjeet stepped closer to her, putting a hand on her shoulder and looking into her eyes, his own shining with a fervour that made her gut clench. "There was a reason we waited for you to come back, Adelia. You might be the only one who actually has a chance against the Fae."

She grimaced, trying not to pull away from his hand. She didn't want to upset him. "Yeah, I'm no chosen one. I can do a couple of tricks, and there's a whole heap of Fae with better ones. If we have a chance against the Fae, it will be because we do it together."

Ryder's voice cut through her discomfort. "Even if she can cover us all with this anti-Dust shield, we still have to walk home. The boy can't keep going through nights as well as days." A smile lurked in his eyes. "Neither can I. We need something to give us more speed. Any suggestions?"

Tama looked up at the sky. She let her own gaze float upwards, and, like Tama, wondered what it would be like to fly. The wings at her back shivered. She brought her eyes down to Tama's wingless shoulders and the droop of his neck as he turned back to face them.

"What about the Elfhame?" he said.

She stared at him. "The what?"

"Aesthetius talked about the Elfhame, the land of the Faeries, where they came from."

She screwed up her face. "And this helps us get home how?"

He scowled at her, and Ryder put a hand on her shoulder in passing as he walked closer to Tama. "It's okay, Tama, what were you suggesting?"

He turned pointedly away from her and spoke to Ryder. "Elfhame lies under our world. Alongside it. Time stands still when you go into it. He told me stories."

Ryder nodded "I remember those stories, my mother used to read them to me."

She closed her eyes and searched for her mother in her mind, Beckett curled up on her knee, reading stories about lost princesses in fairyland.

"He told me the stories are true. Time isn't the same there."

It clicked. "So, if we go there, you think we can zip home faster by, what, travelling through a land full of Fae instead of here?"

Ryder shot her an admonitory frown, and she shrugged slightly. She might sound harsh, but she couldn't quite figure how Tama's suggestion was a good idea.

Standing at Tama's shoulder, Ryder glanced at Sanjeet. *Here we go, bring everyone else on side. This is familiar.* "Sanjeet, have you heard about this? Would it work?"

Her childhood friend rubbed a hand over his cheek, grimacing. "I'm not sure. Perhaps, but even if we could find Elfhame, I have no idea how we would navigate our way through, how we would end up back where we want to go. I can tell you that the Fae go back and forth fairly regularly."

The three of them turned to her, and she raised her eyebrows.

"Really? I've just about figured out how to make a Dust shield, and I can make things explode if I try hard enough. But you want me to somehow take us into a whole other place, and figure out where to go, and then get us home? Because I don't think I'm up to that part in the handbook yet."

She shook her head at Ryder as he gazed steadily at her, waves of anxiety sweeping through her chest.

"No, you can't do this now, Ryder, the 'I'm the one in charge, and I know what I'm doing' thing never worked on me, even when I was a kid. It won't work now. I'm not being stubborn. I'm being realistic."

He flicked a glance at the others, and Sanjeet took Tama's arm. "Come on Tama, let's get the tent ready."

Tama hesitated, his eyes darting between her and Ryder, hands clenching. Sanjeet put his arm around the boy's shoulders and pulled him with him, casting a small smile her way as they circled around her. She realised her wings had spread out, stiff and vibrating with the pulses of her edginess. Breathing deeply, she tried to calm her heart rate.

Ryder rubbed his hand over the stubble on his jaw, his eyes going from her wings to her face, then stepped closer. "What is it?"

"What is what?'

"The real reason you're so antsy about this suggestion?"

A snake of fire coiled around her insides, and she blinked, trying to remove lightning from her eyes. His frown lifted, and his eyes softened. He stretched out a hand to grip her shoulder briefly.

"It's okay, Lark. You know you can tell me anything." Her eyes flashed, and he lifted one shoulder and grimaced. "And if you don't, you should."

Air rattled through her lungs as she fought down the sparking fire inside. Magic wasn't helpful if it burned you up because your emotions raced out of control. Her jaw clenched, and her voice came out tight and sharp like wire.

"What if I screw up? What if I get everyone killed with the magic?'

His brows flicked up in acknowledgement, and he rubbed the back of his neck. "Okay. So that's why you're so snarly." He glanced back to where Sanjeet and Tama were putting up the tent. "Walk with me a bit, Lark. Take some of that edge off."

Her legs moved stiffly, but after a short while pacing beside him, calm radiating from him in a way it hadn't for days, the fire receded. The lightning behind her eyes died down, and she could breathe without her chest hurting.

"The day I ended up in charge, when they voted me leader, I went home and threw up. I couldn't handle the thought that I was responsible for all those lives." A clump of Dust fell from a tree as they passed, puffing little tufts up from the ground, where they swirled around her ankles as she walked through it.

She bit her lip and looked sidelong at him. He cast her a smile.

"I realise you think I love being in charge. And yeah, I think now I'm pretty good at it, but I still want to throw up every time I remember that protecting the lives and wellbeing of several thousand people comes down to me and my decisions." He stopped, turning to face her. "What if I screw up? What if I get everyone killed with my idiocy?" Her arms tightened as they crossed in front of her, and she met his eyes, warm with understanding. "Being the one who can do something means you have to do it, even when you're shit scared."

A sigh escaped her. "But this is a bit different, Ryder. You're good at being in charge." A smile flitted like surprise over his face. "Shut up, you know you are. I might be some changeling thing, but I've only been doing this for a few days. I have no idea what I'm doing. I hate that."

He reached out a hand tentatively towards her wings, still extended but floating gently rather than the stiff warning of before. She couldn't sense his hand on them like she would if it had been on her arm, but his touch sent a pulse of energy deep into her. Her eyes widened as she watched his face, tight but open too.

"Lark, of everyone I know, you're the one I most trust to do the best with a crazy situation. You've got wings. This is the craziest situation I could've ever thought of. Hell, you can do magic. For what it's worth? I believe you can do this."

Her vision blurred, and she put a hand to her flushed cheek.

A smile spread over his face. Her heart skipped at his expression. "And we'll be there with you. I won't let you screw up too much."

Her cheeks spread upwards in an answering smile, but she didn't let it out. Best to not read into anything too much. Best not to let him see how much her heart beat for him.

<h1 style="text-align:center">CHAPTER 38</h1>

That night, Ryder stayed outside with her for a while, watching Dust fall through a shimmering protection she placed over him. The expression on his face was as magical as the energy she was using to keep up the shield.

He sat with his knees up, arms resting on his legs, eyes on the sky. She rested her own head on her hands and watched his profile, his strong jaw with the unkempt beard that suited him so well she hardly remembered him clean shaven. A sigh escaped him, and he turned to look at her. She risked a smile, and her heart sang when he smiled in return.

"Addie." He stopped, and her contentment faded as his expression turned sombre.

"Ryder."

A lift of his brows that reminded her of the old Ryder.

"I wanted to say sorry. For the anger. For making you do this—" He waved at the shimmer around him. "—even though I yelled at you for using magic in the first place."

She blinked rapidly, the prickles in her eyes nothing compared to her racing pulse and the butterflies taking off in her stomach.

"It's okay."

He shook his head slightly. "No, it's not."

"Yeah it is. I understand."

"No, I don't think you do, not really."

He grimaced and shifted, stretching one leg out and kneading the back of his neck to release tight muscles. "The Fae, they took everything from me. You know that. They did the same to you." Her eyes stayed fixed on him, and her mind saw a younger Ryder, whose wife and son were dead because of the Fae. Because of magic like hers.

His eyes drifted back to the heavens, shadows falling over his face. "They came from the sky. They destroyed everything, took everything." He turned to gaze at her, and this time he reached out his hand.

"But they gave me something too. They gave me you."

She stilled, her heartbeat the only thing moving in her body. He kept his hand out, steady, patient, waiting, and his eyes glowed warm through their sadness.

Creeping out her hand, she twined her fingers with his. His shoulders relaxed before he tugged her to him, wrapping her in his arms. Bubbles of happiness flooded her in a rush. He clasped the back of her head, holding her tight against his chest.

"I need you to know something, Addie. The only thing in this whole crazy mess that hasn't changed." The murmured words in her hair sent shivers down her spine. "I love you."

Her heart stopped then thudded through her chest. The heat of him bloomed under her cheek, and her hand clutched his tighter, wishing she could remember this feeling forever.

"The changeling thing, it'll take getting used to, but it kept you alive, kept me alive. And it's who you are. You were a changeling when I met you and every day since then as I liked you, respected you, and fell head over heels for you." He let her go to pull back a little, and she gazed up into his face, trying to not betray just how much her pulse was racing and hope blossoming. "*You* are my everything now, and I'm not going to let the Fae take that away from me again."

Her hand stole up to his cheek, and he leaned his face into her palm, turning to kiss it, his eyes on her the whole time. "Can you forgive me?"

Her eyes opened wide. "Forgive you? Can *you* forgive *me*?"

"There's nothing to forgive."

Her eyes strayed to his mouth, and he smiled, leaning his head down to gently place his lips on hers. For a moment, she worried she wouldn't be able to maintain the shield around him if she didn't concentrate. As soon as they kissed, the shield glowed a bright iridescent silver, spreading out to encase both of them in a cocoon of light.

The pressure on her lips lessened for a second as shimmers surrounded them. Then he took her mouth in a hard kiss, pressing her against him as if he could draw her into his very being. She knew a moment's resistance, as years of being hard, of building a tight shell to protect herself kicked in, then she surrendered, softening against his chest.

Heat blossomed as he kissed her fiercely. Her hands were on him, in his hair and sliding down to his cheek, running over his shoulders. His hand slid down her waist and down her leg, hooking it under her knee and pulling her closer onto him.

The bright cocoon shimmered with flickers of flame. His hand slid up along her ribs towards her breasts, then stopped. He pulled back from the kiss and took a ragged breath. "This probably isn't a good idea right now. Right here."

"You bet it isn't." The voice was muffled by the tent, but it was unmistakably choking back laughter.

Blood rushed to her cheeks, and she hid her head against Ryder's shoulder as he threw his head back in laughter. "Sorry, Sanjeet."

"All good mate, but I think it's best to keep it **PG**. Know what I mean?"

"Oh god." She wouldn't be able to look Tama in the face.

Ryder grinned into her hair, and she gazed up at him. His eyes were warm and tender, and he bent his head to kiss her lips lightly, in a promise.

His jaw flexed under her fingers, and she breathed in the scent of him. The flickers of flame in the shining dome around them died to a smoulder. She snuggled close to him, relishing his strength, his warmth.

In the morning, she woke with Ryder at her back. For the first time in a long time, peace flooded her mind.

CHAPTER 39

"*D*o you know what you're doing?"

Ryder's voice tickled her ear, and his hand rested lightly on the small of her back. She shrugged a smile. "Nope."

They stood at the edge of the clearing, dead trees casting no shadow, Tama on Ryder's other side and Sanjeet next to him.

"I guess we're winging it then."

"In more ways than one."

He laughed at her small joke and lightness settled around her heart. Eyeing him sidelong, she sent out a mental push, and her wings extended, popping into being.

"Are they always there?" Tama's voice was flat, but longing shone in his face, sending a pang through her heart. At first being changeling had been difficult to accept, but now the thought of magic sparked a rush of tingles through her blood. And not just because Ryder had accepted it. That helped, but something inside of her that had always been muffled had broken free, shouting from the rooftops in exhilaration. Tama must have it in him also. Seeing the magic but not being able to access it must be very difficult.

She tried to soften her face. Show him she understood. "Kind of. They're always there as in I can always sense them, but they aren't always visible unless I want them to be. I have no idea how they manage to get through my clothes." She shrugged, the wings rising and falling with the movement. "Magic is weird."

Ryder's hand fell from her back when her wings appeared, but he reached down now and took her hand, his thumb running over the pulse in her wrist.

"Are you ready?"

The smile he coaxed from her by his very existence spread across her face. "No, but let's break into fairyland anyway."

She stretched out her hand and took Sanjeet's. One by one, they formed a circle. Eyes closed, she listened to Sanjeet's voice, its calm monotone belying the tension radiating through his grip.

"When the Fae go between places they travel through another realm. The other world lies just under this one, like stepping through a veil. Look inside, look outwards, see where the veil can be ripped, and then step through."

She huffed out a breath. The discussions and advice from earlier filtered through her brain, and she pushed them all aside, focusing on the texture of the world, the muffled silence of the deadlands breaking under her thoughts into a twisting maelstrom of colour. The dragon inside crouched, ready to pounce, head focused forwards and sparks from his tail spreading through her. Her hand tightened on Ryder's, and he squeezed gently back. The world faded, and she opened her eyes to see a tall shimmering doorway, opaque and pearlescent, rising from the ground in front of her.

You won't know where the door goes, none of us will, but you can try to direct your thoughts to where you want it to take us. She walked forward. This was it. Either this was the best idea ever or they would die a deeply horrible death.

She slowed her steps as they approached the door, hearing

the energy resonate with a deep melody. She began humming, a tune from when she was small, a tune Aesthetius sang to her when she was staring out the window of her room wracked in pain, his hand stroking her head. A song she'd forgotten. Until now.

Ryder was at her shoulder. She dragged her eyes from the portal to glance at him. He stared at the door, jaw clenched and eyes wide. But he turned to her and lifted his brows, lips lifting slightly, then gestured forwards with a little bow. She tried to smile through her humming. Sanjeet squeezed her other hand, and she puffed out her cheeks. It was time. Each step from the Dust to the shimmering portal took a lifetime. Reaching the edge, she filled her lungs, closed her eyes, and stepped over the line. The song erupted into her ears in a cacophony of sound, as if the whole world was a melody. It quieted as she opened her eyes and pulled the others through behind her.

They stood on the threshold, still and uncertain. A world of colour and light spread out in front of them. Dark stone shot through with gold lay under their feet. She took another step forward, and as they did, the portal dimmed and closed behind them.

They were in Elfhame, and they didn't know what they were doing.

Tama was the first to recover, moving forward and lifting his face to a sky free from clouds of Dust. A golden pink colour lit the horizon, shifting hues if you looked too long. He brushed a hand across his cheek. "So beautiful." His voice trembled "Can you hear it singing to you, Addie?"

The song thrummed a beat next to her heart, fighting to fill her senses even as she tried to push it away.

Ryder's voice was in her ear. "If you squeeze any harder, Lark, I won't be able to use this hand again." Consciously trying to relax her shoulders, she let go of his hand. He flicked his fingers a couple of times as if to get the blood flow back.

"Okay, where to from here?" He walked closer to Tama as he spoke, but the question was directed at her.

Crap. As if she knew. "Sanjeet? Any ideas?"

He shrugged, and a grimace twisted his face. "Not really. Which way do you think we should go?"

She narrowed her gaze at him, and he spread his hands expansively. "Seriously Adelia, there's nothing else I can suggest. Can you feel the way or not?"

Biting the inside of her cheek, she let her eyes roam over the landscape in front of them. Fields of green streaked with what could be red tipped grasses stretched to the horizon. To her right lay a forest. Not a dark thick forest like in children's books or vaguely remembered from tramps with her dad when he was still around, but an airy golden woodland. Leaves fell in gentle eddies to the ground, catching the light and sending dappled ripples to the edges of the trees. To her left, a road stretched towards mountains, high and tipped with snow. She cast a glance behind them to where scrub and loam led to a cliff. She took a few steps towards the edge, seeing but not hearing the surf miles below.

The road felt wrong, so did the fields. The forest called to her, the golden light sending tendrils of song beckoning her in. It was either a trap or the magic giving her a huge sign.

A sigh fluttered out of her. Either way they had to go somewhere. A thought struck her. She eyed Tama, hands tight in his pockets and his shoulders hunched as Ryder paced the edges of the stone platform near him. "I'm not the only one who might know. Tama. Which way calls you?"

His eyes darted to hers, and they swam for a second in gold before the deep grey of his irises showed through. "Does it matter what I think?"

She walked towards him, her hands in her own pockets, mirroring him. "Yes. You're changeling too. You found the way to the Valley of the Kings back in the Dust, maybe you can find the way here"

Shooting a glance at her, he turned his face away, a muscle playing along his jaw.

"Back in the palace," Addie said, "you told me I never understood. Well, I'm trying to now. I'm not great at it, but you don't have to do this by yourself." Her eyes flicked to Ryder, who stood with his back to them, staring at the horizon, his attention fixed on the conversation behind him. "None of us do. So, come on. What does your gut tell you? You tell me yours, and I'll tell you mine."

Some of the tension seemed to go out of Tama's shoulders, and he put his head on one side as he turned to regard her. "The forest."

A smile teased at her lips. "Same."

Sanjeet coughed. "For what it's worth, I feel the same."

Ryder turned, and they all looked at him. He grimaced. "My gut still says to get the hell out of here the way we came. Unfortunately, that's not an option, so we should probably follow yours. Forest it is then."

CHAPTER 40

The forest closed around them, and she twitched her shoulders at the sensation of being wrapped in a warm blanket. Her wings longed to spread out, but she kept them hidden, tucked out of sight. The dappled light softened everything, and a part of her wished she could enjoy a stroll down the twisting lanes with Ryder, stop under a tree for a while.

Her eyes went to his back, the muscles of his shoulders moving under the backpack as he talked with Tama, his hands gesturing. As if he felt her gaze, he glanced over his shoulder and cast her a small smile. She tucked it away into her locked room, trusting the dragon to keep it safe.

Sanjeet walked quietly beside her, eyes taking everything in.

She nudged him with her shoulder. "Do you think magic is doing this?"

He startled, looking at her with raised brows. "Doing what?"

"Making us comfortable, happy with where we are. Is that a Faery tale thing?"

His lips pursed, and she could see him thinking. "Maybe.

Might be the Fae blood. Mine's not enough to make me a real changeling, but I have enough to pick up on certain things. And the sense of peace here is very strong."

She hoisted the pack up higher on her shoulders. Trying to figure out how to carry the bag around her wings had been awkward. In the end she'd given up, finding that the wings managed to slide out from under the bag wherever she put it. Every time she thought about them, vibrations shivered under her skin and wonder spread through her.

Ryder dropped back to check on them, and she kept her eyes on Tama, who stood below one of the giant trees, gazing up at the leafy sky. Staying focused on the teen was difficult though, Ryder drew her eyes like a clichéd moth to a flame. Sanjeet waggled his eyebrows at her and strode on, heading to Tama and coaxing him to carry on walking.

"So. Lark."

"Ryder."

He glanced ahead, and seeing the others moving on, he turned to pull her close, grinning at her before taking her lips in a kiss that melted her insides. Her arms wrapped around his neck, and she leaned into him, smiling into his embrace.

When he pulled away, he leaned his forehead on hers, stroking her hair behind her ear and lingering on the pounding pulse in her throat. A bright light shimmered at shoulder height. She turned her head to see her wings folded around them. They stepped away from each other at the same moment, arms dropping awkwardly.

She bit the inside of her cheek. "You know, I'm kinda beginning to like these things, but they can be a bit creepy too."

"No shit." He smiled, but tension sat heavily in his shoulders. He reached out his hand, and she clasped it, trying to tell the wings to get back in. But his touch set them fluttering, and she rolled her eyes.

"At least you don't look like a winged monkey."

She screwed her face up.

"Okay, now you look like a winged monkey."

She swung a punch at him. He grinned down at her as he dodged the hit. "Monkey punch."

Something in the forest was getting to Ryder too. His face was less lined with care, although his eyes still shone clear and focused. She pushed down a niggling sensation something wasn't right, tried to simply enjoy this moment, laughter and light under dappled green trees.

When they took a break after about an hour, she brought up the sensation of nagging unquiet again.

"There's such a feeling of peace in this place, even the melody of the trees is a lullaby. The Fae on the other hand, are hard and evil bastards."

Tama's voice was quiet but clear. "Aesthetius isn't."

She considered him. "No, I guess he isn't. Not to us, but who knows what he's done in his lifetime." She found that she didn't like to think of him being cruel. "Anyway, the point is, why do we feel so comfortable here? It can't be just the changeling thing because Ryder feels the same. Don't you?"

He lifted his head, clearly surprised. "I guess I do. I just thought, you know, there was another reason." His eyes met hers, and her cheeks burned.

Tama kicked his feet against the soft moss on the forest floor. His mouth opened, and then he glanced at her and closed it, shoving his hands in his pockets. She quirked a brow at Ryder, who swallowed a smile.

"What's the matter mate? Spit it out."

The boy's eyes darted between them. "I'm just wondering why they would have left here. To go there."

Images of deadlands smothered in Dust filled her head. The Valley of Kings had been a paradise to her eyes, but compared to Elfhame, it was nothing.

"They didn't all leave."

She turned to Sanjeet, a frown lowering on her brow when

he didn't continue. "Don't leave it there, Sanjeet. You spit it out too."

A tired smile full of old pain sent a pang through her heart. She bit back an urge to apologise but tried to smile back.

"They talk around us," he said, "as if we don't exist. Like we're furniture. Or well-trained dogs. Mostly, it doesn't matter because the thralls are practically pets." His shoulders moved as if to shake off bad thoughts. "But sometimes we hear things. The ones on Earth, they're an outpost. The Dust is temporary, until they learn how to counter the iron."

Images flashed into her mind, helping with the small stocks of iron they had, fashioning the small number of arrows and guns that they could provide. The iron never burned her like it burned the Fae. Ryder leaned back against the tree trunk and sighed.

"They want the changelings because they want part-human magic that's resistant to iron. Why? So they can lift the Dust and conquer the whole world?"

She fingered the knife in her belt, avoiding looking at the brooch she now wore on her shirt. "Like I said, evil bastards"

Ryder shook his head. "It has to be more than that. Tama's right—even without the Dust, why would they want to leave here?"

White Room. Harsh melodies. Pain. Dying. Iron. A swirl of words from the Fae speaking over her body on the white marble bench spun through her head. Her eyes fell on the bag Tama carried, the skull still nestled inside it. Bile burned her throat, and she had to swallow before she could speak.

"I think they're dying. They're dying, and they think changelings carry the secret to helping them live."

CHAPTER 41

Realising the Fae wanted the earth for more than just power stripped away the peace of the woodlands, tainting their steps with heavy dread. The edge of the forest looked well defined, as if for centuries it existed at this point. Creeping uncertainty of what they would find beyond played on her mind. Stepping from the forest, the golden rustle of trees gave way to the still quiet of flat fields and hedgerows. Her eyes narrowed. Hedgerows.

"Looks like there might be people around here," she said. "Fae. Fae people. You know what I mean."

The air hung around them, humid and still. Grass in the field waved like it was being ruffled by a breeze. Sunlight kissed her skin, not unpleasant but warm enough that Ryder took off his coat and threaded it through the straps at the base of his pack.

His arms showed no sign of the damage they'd taken from the hounds. She remembered the blood and the tearing, the smothering Dust. The sight of him striding through bright green fields seemed like an illusion.

She shook off lingering darkness and raised her eyes to the sky. The absence of Dust was a blessing, one she'd not thought to find again after leaving the Valley of the Kings. Her fingers grazed the top of the grasses as she passed by. *I want to go home, of course I do, but this isn't bad either.*

They were only a little way along the road when voices rang through the air and hoof-beats thundered closer. Ryder spun and gestured urgently at them. They scampered into the hedgerow.

The trees of the hedge were thick and closely set. They crouched at the base of them where the ground dipped low into a ditch and held their breath as the group came nearer.

The lively hunting party laughed and sang, bright bell-like voices dancing through the sky. Brightly coloured clothes garbed their lean bodies, and their hair flowed loosely around them, twisting itself into intricate designs then untwirling to float in the breeze.

They did not ride horses, rather massive beasts more like panther than steed, large fangs rubbing against the golden bridles that appeared to be more for show than anything else. The beasts responded to something other than reins to know where to turn.

Strange, seeing the Fae like this, unburdened by their roles in the king's palace, relaxed and nearly human in their joking companionship.

Then she saw their prey. A slight figure in dirty ragged jeans and t-shirt peered out from where he crouched, barely hidden by long grasses on the other side of the road. He stared fearfully at the Fae with human eyes.

Her blood froze, and she willed him with everything inside her to turn back, to go through the grasses that concealed him. She could feel the moment Ryder saw him too. His body stilled, and he stopped breathing. Terror and something very like resignation twisted the teen's face, and he ran, heading for the hedge.

The Fae let out a shout, spurring the beasts towards him. Their glamor shifted, and sharp teeth appeared. They cornered him faster than she thought possible. His screams rent the air, driving away the melody of the earth and sparking the fire inside her.

Hating herself, she grabbed at Ryder's arm, pulling him down, seeing Sanjeet on the other side doing the same. They could do nothing but be captured alongside the poor boy. As immoral, as sickening as it felt, they had their own child to protect and a community of thousands to safeguard.

Hiding while he screamed and struggled was the hardest thing she had ever done. Every cell in her body demanded she throw herself at the Fae, fight them off. But Tama shivered uncontrollably next to her. She couldn't allow him to be captured as well.

The moment stretched. It felt like an eternity before the teen's screams cut off. The Fae left, their voices joyful once more.

Their clothes were spattered with blood.

There was no boy with them.

She froze, her stomach churning on a sudden awful realisation. The sound of the beasts' hooves faded, and quiet fell, leaving only the hum of the grass and the sweet song of the birds.

"What was that?" Tama's voice shook, and she found she couldn't meet his eyes. They had hidden. Hidden while a child was murdered for sport by monsters. It didn't matter that she'd thought they were capturing him. She'd known what life she was condemning him to. Loathing filled her being. For herself, for the Fae.

Ryder spat on the ground next to him. Bile burned her throat too, and she swallowed, tears leaking, stinging her eyes. His face was set in stone, and he avoided Tama's eyes. "They killed that child. A fucking child. I hate them. I fucking hate them."

Sanjeet sat with his hands over his face, shuddering as he

tried to hold back sobs. "I always wondered where they took the other children, the ones they didn't want to keep."

Ryder pushed himself to his feet and stalked a few paces away. Her heart spasmed at the tension radiating from him. She rose more slowly, her stomach threatening to leave through her mouth. Sanjeet curled over his knees, reliving horrific times in his past if the shudders were anything to go by. She looked down at Tama, wide-eyed and uncertain. He was a child himself. He shouldn't have to do it. Ryder? She looked at him. His fight to hold in his tears tore her heart to pieces. No. Ryder did not need to bury another child.

She swallowed. *I can do this. I have to do this.*

Each step towards the tattered body took forever. The music of the earth that had returned with the departure of the Fae shifted to a darker melody the closer she got to the boy. Two steps away, she stopped, trying to breathe. In her head she saw Beckett and heard the screams of the child in the throne room so long ago.

Even though the images turned her stomach, they gave her strength too. She would do this. She would do it, and Ryder wouldn't have to. Wouldn't have to see his son's face on this shattered body.

She pulled out the knife, intending to dig, and then a thought made her lip curl in a sneer. Let their gift be useful for something. Transferring the blade to her left hand, she held out her right. Light swirled as the magic spun. As each stone dropped into a cairn over the teen's body, she let the tears fall.

For him, for Beckett, and for all the rest of them.

Lost children all.

The last stone settled, and her hand fell. She staggered back and collapsed. Putting her head between her knees, she drew deep breaths. A hand lightly brushed her shoulder. She peered up at Sanjeet, a small bunch of wildflowers in his hand.

"Thank you, Adelia."

Tama hovered behind him, eyes wide and mouth pinched. Hopefully Sanjeet had been sensible and only brought him up once the body was hidden by stones. Ryder stood a little distance away, tightening the strap on his back. As if he felt her gaze on him, he glanced up, meeting her eyes. After a moment he turned away, his face like stone. Tama knelt next to her as Sanjeet laid the flowers on the cairn.

"Will he hate you now? For being like them?"

The urgency in Tama's voice wasn't for her, but for himself. She smiled stiffly through the pain and shrugged.

"Ryder's smarter than that, kid."

His gaze flicked behind her, and he scootched away, scrambling to his feet. She didn't need his reaction to tell her Ryder was coming—she could sense him. He had a melody all his own, one that harmonised with hers if she let it.

She pushed upwards with her hand, awkwardly clambering, startling as he cupped her elbow, his strength holding her. Her eyes sought his, unsure of what they might see. There was no warmth, just a searing focus. His grip tightened on her arm. He pulled her towards him, taking her mouth in a fierce kiss. She tasted his pain, his fear, his grief. She took it all in and tried to give back comfort and the love she struggled to tell him was in her heart.

He pulled away, leaving behind a lingering taste of him on her lips. Holding her hips fast, he leaned his forehead on hers.

"It could've been you, Lark. If you hadn't been who you are, what you are. I could have lost you before I even knew you." He stroked her hair off her face, cupping her jaw in his hand. "You are nothing like the Fae. You'll never be one of them."

CHAPTER 42

Hedgerows and golden waving fields gave way to a rutted path winding between dark green hillocks. Ryder stayed close to her side, whether to reassure himself she was still here, or to seek comfort, she couldn't decide. She couldn't help looking around, seeing all the places someone could leap out at them, and breathed easier once they came out of the strange path into a rolling vista of green grass covered in blue flowers.

"The flippin' land of OZ." Ryder muttered.

She quirked her brow at him and turned to survey the fields. Okay, perhaps he was right. But the view was very pretty.

"Where do you think the story came from?" Sanjeet asked.

"You mean—"

"Yep, think about it. The Wizard came from earth to OZ. Dorothy, a child, is brought to OZ and tormented. Makes sense, right?"

She snorted. "If that's true, we'd have to meet a good Faery. Bit unlikely if you ask me."

As if on cue, horns blew in the distance. The hunting party. Hounds bayed, and Tama blanched. No hedgerows lined the path. Nowhere to hide. The horns sounded again, closer, and Ryder grabbed her arm and pushed Tama in front of him.

"Run!"

Thoughts of the beasts ripping the child apart flashed into her mind. She sprinted, chest heaving. Ryder gripped her wrist like a steel vice, dragging her onwards. Sanjeet raced at her side, breaths tearing out of him. She didn't notice the close eye he kept on Tama until he sped up a couple of steps and caught the boy as he stumbled.

"Come on mate. You can keep going. Just a bit longer."

A bit longer. They had no idea where they were going or what would keep them safe.

Trees lay ahead, a small copse, possibly not enough space to hide. It would have to do.

"There!" Ryder's hand pointed across her vision. She turned her head to see the small cottage nestled amongst the gnarled trunks. A frown twisted her brows. No cottage sat there the first time she looked.

"What if someone's in the house?" Tama's voice shook. He probably saw the same images whirling on repeat in her brain.

"Then we deal with one Fae in a shelter rather than twenty Fae in the open."

Ryder was right. They had no other option.

They raced across the last hundred metres.

Fifty metres.

Ten.

Ryder burst into the cottage, knife out, and they piled in behind. Sanjeet slammed the door shut. She shoved the bolt home as the baying of the hounds echoed through the open sky.

She leaned on the door, trying to get her breath under control and listening for indications the hunting party might have caught their scent.

"Sanjeet." Ryder's voice came out flat, even. She turned with Sanjeet, leaving her back on the door. Her eyes fell on the small cowering shape of an old woman. A Fae.

She had never seen an old one before, but deep lines scored the Fae's face. Her sturdy woollen clothes, olive green and sky blue in colour, were so different from the gauzy robes of the court. This was the first Fae she'd met whose hair remained settled at the back of her neck. Even Aesthetius' shaggy mop shifted and moved with his emotions and thoughts. If not for the small tattered wings fluttering woefully like a trapped butterfly, she would've thought her human.

Pushing off the door, Addie shifted closer, her jacket falling open and the dragon brooch glinting in the frail light filtering through the small window of the single room. The Fae's eyes were dragged to it like to a magnet, and her fingers crept up to cradle the dragon.

"Where did you get that?"

She wished the Fae wasn't old. It was so much harder to refuse things to old people.

"From a friend."

The Fae's eyes shimmered green and gold, and she drew her severe skirt tighter around her legs. "You possess friends in very high places."

Looking at each of them in turn, the Fae shied away from Ryder and his knife. He lowered the blade, far too chivalrous for his own good. The old woman's eyes fixed on Tama and the bag he carried.

"You bring death with you."

Her brow wrinkled, and the Fae gestured at Tama. *The skull.* The air hung closer, quieter, heavier next to it. For the first time, she wondered what impact carrying the skull had on Tama.

"Death is not common here." The Fae pulled back, its small wings curling slightly to the front like a kind of shield.

Tama cradled the satchel, his eyes dark. "It's pretty bloody common where we're from."

Okay. This wasn't going well.

Addie stepped forward, drawing the Fae's eyes away from Tama.

"Is that why the skull scares you? Because death isn't usual here?"

"It scares me because the Fae do not die unless by iron and magic and will."

Ryder spoke up, his voice gentler than she would have expected as he approached the small dainty Fae and its trembling wings.

"But they did die. The first time they came. We fought them off with iron, not with magic, and they retreated."

"Retreated, yes. Died, no."

Ryder's brows lowered in a frown. Addie reached out her fingers and brushed lightly over the leather satchel, feeling the desolation within. "Do you mean all the Fae what, just left? Recouped?"

The Fae's eyes fixed on the bag. "Not all, clearly."

"Lark and I killed one before, in the deadlands," said Ryder.

The Fae darted a glance between them. "Iron, and magic, and will."

The words burned in her mind like fire.

"But this death was much longer ago," the old Fae continued. "It has the feel of the ancients."

Sanjeet exclaimed, and the Fae shot a glance at him. "You have heard the tales, I see."

Addie put a hand on Tama's shoulder and tried to get him to sit. She needed the Fae to talk, and looming over her wouldn't help.

"Not all of us have," she said.

The Fae looked at the brooch again. "Lord Aesthetius sent you?"

Lord, huh. "Yes, he did. Kind of. Before we left, he told me to keep the dragon, that it would help me find the way. I guess he was right."

The Fae glanced up, and her eyes did not shimmer in the usual way. They shifted, as if her whole face became something else for a moment. Addie had to fight not to step away. Remarkable how easily you could forget what they were.

"He is one to whom I owe loyalty and service. Few of the High Fae care about or even know about ones such as I anymore. He has done much to protect me."

Addie raised her brows. "This means what for us?"

The Fae smiled, and some of her frail air fled, changing the dynamic in the room. "I will tell you what I can. Give you shelter. Do what I can for one afternoon to honour my commitment to the one whose brooch you wear."

She opened her mouth to say thank you, and Ryder put his hand up quickly. "No. I don't know if it's true, Addie, but I remember stories about the Fae. If you thank them, you owe them a favour."

Her lips pressed shut as the old Fae's shifting eyes twinkled at her. That had been close. "Right. Well, I'm pleased you are honouring your commitment." Her eyes flicked to Ryder, who nodded at her. Okay. "What can you tell us about these ancient ones?"

"The ancient ones left Elfhame to walk the earth. They spent time between here and there, learning about and guiding their human kin. They did not condone the takings, but they did not stop them either. The king or the queen would entice travellers and musicians and great knights and enchant them, keeping them in Elfhame as servants until they tired of them and sent them back, lost and wandering and always with the music of Elfhame in their veins. In those days, Fae rarely stole a human infant, as one of ours was always left in its place, and we did not want to spread Fae magic through the human population. But then we began to realise the virtues of human blood.

The age of iron came, and the ancients who walked the earth began to weaken. Their blood began to change. Those with both human and Fae blood did not weaken. They could withstand the earth's iron as well as the Dust of Faery."

She flicked a finger at the bag. "The death you carry with you is a reminder of the frailty of the Fae, also a reminder that they wandered your world for a long time."

Something else sat behind her words. Addie could see it in her face. They waited. Eventually, the Fae spoke up. "But I do not think the skull is Fae."

"Hang on, I'm confused. What do you think it is?"

"I think it is changeling."

CHAPTER 43

*A*ddie sipped at the tepid soup, flavoursome but not as filling as one would have thought. Guess Faery magic couldn't make everything perfectly. So very Fae-like to drop a bomb like the word 'changeling' then clam up. She mopped up the last bits of liquid with some dry sourdough.

Changeling.

If the skull was as old as the Fae had suggested, that meant at some point, a long time ago, there had been someone like her.

Someone like Tama.

"What I don't understand," she moved the bread around in her mouth to help the words come out, "is why the Fae wanted the skull in the first place. You still seem nervous around it. Why did they want it, and why did they send Tama to fetch it instead of getting it themselves?" She tossed the crust back in the bowl, as if five days before she hadn't wondered where the next meal would come from. "That's what I don't understand."

Ryder's quiet voice filled the room. "I've been thinking about that. We found the skull, the remains, under a reservoir lid of pure iron. Maybe they weren't able to retrieve it."

She drew patterns on the table top with one finger. "Then why didn't they send some of their pet humans to do the job?"

Sanjeet spoke up. "Because they wouldn't have survived in the Dust."

"This is true." She conceded his point with a salute. "So instead they stole children and sent them out into the Dust to die or to retrieve a bit of dead person. Fucking Fae." She glanced up. "Present company excluded I'm sure."

The Fae smiled at her. "Well, I had my moments, but they're all behind me now."

She was glad she'd already swallowed the bread. She might have choked otherwise.

Ryder, leaning on the wall behind the Fae, smiled grimly, and she noticed for the first time his hand still on his knife.

Tama shifted in his chair, a frown on his face. "So, if it's a changeling, do they want it for the same reason they take us now?"

The old Fae nodded. "I would say yes. Both King Valkor and the Queen of the Emerald Fields seek that which has been lost—the power of iron combined with Fae blood that lives in the changelings—this is power indeed. They hope to replicate it."

"By doing what, shoving great big needles in our eyes and ripping apart our minds? Shredding every cell so we wish we could die because the pain is endless." Her voice rasped out, and from the corner of her eye, she saw Ryder start towards her before settling back deliberately, muscles showing in his arms as he gripped the windowsill behind him.

The Fae stared at her unblinkingly. She forced herself to sit back, and her eyes flicked to Tama, sitting trembling and wide-eyed. *Crap.* Releasing a breath, she rubbed her hands over her face.

"Right. Okay. Replicating magic." She stood, locking eyes with Ryder. "Well they're not getting mine."

He smiled slowly at her, his eyes warm. Peace settled in her bones, chasing out the chill.

Sanjeet sighed. "That is only half the story, though. Is it true Aesthetius was banned from Elfhame? There have been rumours. They think we do not hear."

"You didn't think to tell us this before we came?"

Ryder's voice was calm but held a note she recognised. Clearly Sanjeet did too because he flushed and stood a little straighter, chin out.

"When we first left, I didn't think it was important, and when we decided to come to Elfhame, I was so focused on Adelia opening the portal, I simply didn't think about it at all."

She frowned. "What difference would it make either way?"

The old Fae leaned forward. Addie had to fight not to step back. "His mother assigned him to the court of King Valkor, whether as a spy or to remove his ideas from her own court no-one can decide."

"His ideas?"

A breeze blew in from the crack under the window. The light filtering in around Ryder changed subtly from golden to pink.

Sunset.

The Fae pulled her shawl around her. "Aesthetius believes the High Fae need to share their power. He was always like that, even as a small youngling, but his views have become more, strident shall we say, in the last fourteen years."

She didn't like the way the Fae stared at her when she said that. What was it to her if he was strident or not in his opinions?

"The sun is going down. We need to be gone first thing tomorrow, find where to make another portal and get out of here."

With her head quizzically on one side, the old Fae looked

like one of those animals dressed in human clothing that you used to see in children's books. "I will give you shelter for one night, in payment of my bond to Aesthetius. None shall harm you while you are here."

She was about to thank the Fae when she bit back the words, saying, "how nice of you," instead.

STONE FLAGSTONES PUSHED into her back. Hard, but no harder than the ground outside. The Fae lay asleep in the small bed in the corner. Thinking of Fae sleeping made them too human in a way. A lot easier to hate things that didn't sleep.

Delicate moonbeams broke the soft shadows of the darkness. So unlike the compound and the Dust deadened dark. She rolled on her side, trying not to disturb Tama as he lay with his back toward her. It reminded her of when she was small. She and Beckett had a 'camping trip' in the living room where slivers of moonlight twisted familiar walls and furniture into ghostly and magical shapes. Sleep probably wouldn't happen tonight. Her eyes lit on Ryder. He wasn't even lying down. He set himself up between her and the Fae, sitting with his back leaning on the leg of the table and his knife out on his lap. The Fae had twinkled at him, waggled her brows in a disturbingly human way, and taken herself off to bed.

Addie watched him in the silvery light. His eyes tracked the room, from the door to the Fae to the window and back. Like when he patrolled the compound. He always tried to keep them safe. She smiled, secret and satisfied, then shut her eyes and let herself sleep, secure in the knowledge he stood between her and the world.

CHAPTER 44

*P*ink light played at the edges of the horizon as the sun rose, rays spreading over the vast green fields of Elfhame. The cold, stone wall of the tiny cottage at her back was like an anchor, holding her steady in a world waiting to trap them at any moment. It shouldn't have been so hard to leave the home of a Fae. Stepping from cozy warmth into crisp chill air redolent with music sent shivers down her neck.

Ryder appeared at her shoulder. "Where to now?"

Closing her eyes, she focused on the ringing note tugging on her mind. *Towards the sunrise.* The pull stroked at her senses, coaxing. She flicked a glance at Tama, who stood with his face lifted to the sun, his eyes shut. *He feels it too.* The knowledge eased a tightness in her chest. She might be a changeling, but at least someone else like her existed.

Each step down the path through green fields and stretches of woodlands filled her with anticipation. *Soon. We will be leaving Elfhame soon.* Ryder called a rest break in a spinney of gold and red aspens. She fought back the urge driving her to keep going. She propped herself against a tree, and Tama threw himself to the ground, pulling his knees to his chest and clasping his hands around them. Her eyes shutting, she let the music of the forest surround her.

Sanjeet's voice cut into her thoughts. "You should talk to him, you know."

Opening her eyes, she sighed and screwed up her face. "But Tama doesn't want to talk to me. You've seen the way he looks at me. Surly teenagers are a thing."

A perfunctory smile flitted over Sanjeet's face, his gaze steady. "He's jealous. He can sense the magic but can't access it. That makes him angry."

She scrutinised him, seeing the lines near his eyes, the tension in the jaw. "He's not the only one, is he Sanjeet?"

He glanced away, shrugging. "Let's just say I understand how he feels."

She should've been shocked. Who would choose to be changeling? To be different and tainted? But she'd felt wings at her back, the warmth of fire flickering up her arms. She heard the call of the dragon deep inside. To hear the dragon but not be able to do anything would be impossibly hard.

"I'm sorry."

"Don't be." He turned back to face her and smiled, this time with his eyes too. "I've had a very long time to accept that however much fae ancestry is in my blood it isn't enough to make me a changeling."

He pushed up off the ground and stretched, his long limbs reaching to the sky.

"Talk to him, Adelia."

She saluted, and he rolled his eyes at her. He walked past Tama, bending to place a hand on the boy's shoulder and offer a smile before going to join Ryder at the edge of the spinney.

Pushing to her feet, she strolled over to Tama. *Give him time to think.* Or time to run so she wouldn't have to do this. *Let's hope those wings stay in.* She sent the strongest vibes she could to them.

"Hey. Tama. Whatcha doing?"

"Sitting down waiting until I'm told to go somewhere."

Great. Excellent start. Okay, talk to him. That should be simple. Ease into the magic thing gently. She flumped down next to him, making sure to avoid the creepy bag with the skull.

He stared at her, his eyes pools of shining grey. She hadn't noticed them much before. She tried not to meet people's eyes as a general rule; they could learn too much about you. But she remembered Ana saying how his grey eyes meant his family was likely from the East Coast. A long way from the compound in Auckland. Here in Elfhame, the grey glinted with silver.

"Cool. So, are you able to use any of your magic yet?"

"You really don't know how to talk to people do you? Ryder said you didn't, but I didn't believe him."

She smiled ruefully. "You should probably always believe Ryder."

His gaze went back to his feet where he scratched at the dirt, drawing. Not brilliant drawings—sticks weren't exactly oil paints—but as she watched, she recognised the compound, or maybe the palace. And people with wings who didn't look like Fae.

Chewing on the inside of her cheek she gazed at him, noticing the way the bones of adulthood were beginning to settle, leaving his face too big for his body. His arms were strong, but skinny, and his legs seemed to grow every day. Hard enough being a teenager, nevermind knowing you were different. Just not different enough for anyone to admire or fear you. She remembered that feeling.

Maybe she should've told him that.

"Do you remember, in the deadlands when we were running from the hounds, and we jumped the buildings?"

"Yup."

"Well, this is like that. You jumped then because you

trusted Ryder when he said you could. I need you to trust me now. I think I can help you find the magic, but I can't do this unless you trust me. Because the magic is locked inside you, and I'm not forcing it out."

He didn't look at her, but he stopped drawing.

"Do you want to touch my wings?"

A gorgon might have turned him to stone.

"Yes." His voice barely breathed out, deep longing thrumming through it.

Slowly, she extended her wings. They fluttered a little, pearly white and translucent and shot with silver. Catching the breeze, they rolled around her to bend towards Tama. His hand stretched out and stopped just before making contact. Glancing at her, he waited until she nodded, dipping her wing closer to him. Gentle fingers lightly stroked the edge, sending a tingle through her system.

Light flooded Tama's face, his grey eyes turning solid silver in a shimmery blink. She held her breath as a haze in the air above his shoulder blades took on, for a second, the shape of wings.

"Tama?"

He shuddered and pulled his hand back, cradling it as if to keep the sensation going. "I can sense magic inside me, but I can't make it work. You reckon you can help?"

"I think so, but if you take this step, you will be changeling forever."

"Even if I don't, I will still feel that way forever. I always felt different. I never wanted to, but I have." His eyes met hers, and she caught a flicker of her old self in his eyes, teenager and outsider and lost. "I'm just tired of pretending that I'm something other than I am. I want to be myself. Whatever that is."

Her heart swelled, and she tapped him on the arm.

"Good. Because I've been doing a lot of thinking since this all happened." She gestured over her shoulder at the wings, a solid reminder of her difference. "Despite every-thing, I'm glad that whatever was inside me can now be free."

She wished she had better words. How to describe the power, the strength that flooded her each time she took owner-ship of who she was? The sense of complete freedom at no longer hiding. The secret fierce happiness she took in Ryder's acceptance of who she was—*all* of who she was.

Tama dragged the stick in the dirt, scratching over his pictures. "At first, when I realised how angry Ryder was with you, I worried that if I became one too I wouldn't be able to go back home. That's kinda why I wanted to stay with the Fae. But then he seemed to be okay with it."

He smiled suddenly and turned his face to hers, his eyes light grey now and shy. "And I think the wings are kinda awesome."

She grinned at him, and for the first time, it didn't feel awkward. "If I'm totally honest, they're pretty cool. So, let's get started on this. Find the thing inside you. The door that keeps everything in."

Lines formed on his forehead. "I don't have a door, but I have, like, a box."

"Okay, a box is cool, can you open it?"

He shook his head, and his eyes scrunched tighter shut. "It's locked."

"Right. We need to find the key." Her fingers brushed the dragon brooch and a thought hit her. "Tama, you remember your pounamu? The one you left with Lily and Matt?"

Heat flushed his cheeks. "Yup."

"I know the pendant's important to you. This sounds odd, but is it like a talisman for you?"

He shrugged. "I don't know what a talisman is."

"Something that protects you. Or at least you kind of believe it will. Something you hold or think about when you're scared or lonely."

He stilled then nodded, his hand moving as if to hold the pendant that no longer sat at his throat.

"I want you to think about your pounamu. Think of how it makes you feel. You don't have to tell me, but just focus hard. Imagine yourself holding it next to that box."

A melody like a chant surrounded Tama's body, rising in a hum. Stretching out her hand, she laid it over his heart. The melody grew louder, spreading up her arm and into her head. Her mind shifted, and she saw Tama standing near a large metal box. The trunk was battered, old, worn, but the lock was strong. He stood next to it, his pounamu now around his neck, the dark green stone glowing with a soft light that high-lighted the jaw and cheekbones of the man he was becoming. He closed his eyes as light shot out from his hands in a beam that made the lock glow until it shattered in golden sparks. He opened his eyes and knelt in front of the box. His hands shook as he reached them towards the lid, closing tight on the edge and not moving. Although she wasn't there with him, some of her energy filtered out to mix with his. His head lifted, and he met her eyes. She smiled, easy and warm here where there were no barriers except what Tama made.

"It will be okay. The only things in that box are you, Tama. The good, the bad, the scary. Everything that makes you who you are. I'm not afraid of you, and you don't need to be either."

He smiled back, and she sighed at the beauty of his face with the mask of fear and anger taken away. Both of them struggled to connect to others, but here, they could be who they really were.

Tama strained as he lifted the lid. Blinding light spilled from the open box. Golden and green and dark earthy red leaped out, freed from its prison, surrounding him in a glorious glow. He laughed then stilled, tears springing. She sensed the loss of parents, the echoed remembrance of a mother placing the greenstone around his neck, her tears brushing his cheeks. Even as a baby he understood he was being left behind. The teenager recognised his mother's love, but anger at her death burned bright like a flame within the swirl of his thoughts.

Addie reached out a hand, incorporeal but heavy with the strength of her magic, and stroked his hair. He swallowed, taking the dark light, the bright gold, and the red flame into his hands and holding it tight.

"Take the magic. Make it yours. Find the shape it wants to take."

She pulled out of his mind as he wrapped the flame around his arm and smiled. When she saw the wings, this time they were grey and shimmered like Dust in moonlight.

CHAPTER 45

Summoning the portal to go home was a lot easier than creating the first one. Practising with Tama was making her stronger. Plus, she really wanted to leave Elfhame. A shimmering door appeared, a glistening rainbow path through an archway of singing light. She didn't glance behind her as she left, but Tama took one lingering look at green fields and blue sky before following her with a sigh.

The bell-like music filling the air cut off as soon as they stepped out from the portal. Unsettling silence rang in her ears. The Dust of the deadlands muffled all sounds. No birds sang. No melody wove through the broken sticks of trees. The city lay around them, wrecked and shattered, a stark reminder of what the Fae had done. Tension ran through her, tightening muscles and catching at her breath. The portal opened in a damn impact crater. The conflict in her heart resolved, sharpening into a deadly focus. She would not let them destroy her home. Not again.

Ryder flexed his shoulders. "I guess there's no way to know what day it is here, right?"

She shook her head, and Sanjeet replied. "No, but it should, according to the tales, be the same day we left."

Taking point, she led them as fast as possible out of the crater, pockmarked with twisted metal and burn marks that showed through the Dust. This area of the city was her patch. She'd spent many days scavenging the wrecks and the buildings, turning over the jumbled leftovers of a destroyed world. Each step she took, each piece of Dust-swallowed masonry she leaped over, she thought of green fields and golden sunrises and wondered how she had ever gotten so used to the desolation.

They passed the old bank and the bus she hid under the day of the taking, so long ago. Mia flashed into her mind, and instead of her friend's clean unit in the compound, she imagined Mia's body ruined and wrecked lying in the broken columns and rusted metal. Step by step. She could only get through it if she pushed the fears away. No dead Mia, no dead Ana, no dead Jasper. Just metal, just concrete, just Dust.

Newhaven loomed ahead of them, shadowy in the grey morning light. Ryder's strides grew longer as hers slowed. The compound appeared quiet, but it was often quieter in the mornings.

A shout rang out from the guards on the wall as they neared the compound. Her heart lifted. They were alive. She hadn't arrived too late.

Ryder's steps quickened, and a smile spread across his face as he glanced at her over his shoulder. "Home, Lark. We're home!"

She smiled back, but a sigh weighed her down. She wasn't sure what was home for her anymore, not with wings on her back and magic in her heart.

The gates swung open, and two of the younger guards came out to flank the entryway, their eyes like saucers. Jonas stalked through the gate and shook Ryder's hand, grinning from ear to ear.

Tama sighed next to her, and she put her arm around his shoulders. He jumped at the unexpected touch, and she smiled at him. "Don't worry kid. This time you've got me. And I've got you. And Sanjeet. We'll be the odd ones out together, okay?"

A small smile tugged at Tama's lips, and she squeezed his shoulders in a one-armed hug. Sanjeet puffed out his cheeks, tugging at the hem of his tunic. The siren sounded, once, harsh but not alarming in the still air, and a small crowd formed. Anahera was at the front of it all, running in her white coat, curly hair bouncing behind her and a huge smile on her face.

Stepping forward, her own smile growing, a whisper of movement twitched on her back. She stumbled as her wings extended and silvery translucence threaded with fire fluttered gently behind her.

Crap.

The silence was deafening.

Tama crept closer and took her hand. "I've got you," he whispered.

She blinked as tears threatened, putting up her chin. The two of them and Sanjeet stood a few feet from the gate as the people of Newhaven closed ranks and stared. She had never felt like so much of an outsider in her life. Tama took a breath, extended his hand, and squinted at his palm. A small flickering flame crept out and twined around his arm. She swallowed a proud smile and squeezed his other hand. "I got you, kid."

Ryder stepped away from Jonas, positioning himself between the compound and the three of them. A muscle worked in his jaw. She couldn't tell if he was angry at the Haveners for their caution or at himself for not planning for it.

Jasper shuffled through the lines, passing Ryder with a nod. He ruffled Tama's hair and winked at him. Meeting her eyes, he smiled. "The Lark has wings now. Welcome home, little bird."

Soft movement hushed at her back as her wings dipped towards him, and she smiled back, warmth flooding her chest.

"Thank you, Jasper."

The silence of the Haveners broke gradually. The voices might not have been angry, but they weren't exploding in welcome either.

Anahera took the arm of the medic next to her and pulled him towards their little group. She passed Ryder, and what she read in his face seemed to settle her shoulders a little. She smiled at Tama, although fear sat tensely in the corners of her eyes, then her mouth twisted as she regarded Addie.

She waved. "Hey, Doc."

"Did you know? All that time when you were dodging medicals and check-ups, did you know?"

She swallowed past the painful lump in her throat, shaking her head. "No. I knew I was different, but not like this. I swear. Neither did Tama. It was always there inside us, but the Fae woke it through pain and terror."

She gazed at the crowd beyond Anahera, singling out Paolo and Eva, wondering where Mia was, what Mia would think. Projecting her voice to carry, she held tight to Tama's hand.

"We didn't ask for this. We didn't seek it. But it's who we are. We came back because this is our home, and because we want to help protect you." She lowered her voice for Anahera's ears alone. "At the very least, take in the boy."

Doc scowled at her. "Don't be ridiculous, Adelia Lark. You're all coming back inside, even your new friend." Anahera's eyes flicked over Sanjeet in the same appraising way she regarded every new patient. "Newhaven is what it is because of its people. And you're one of us." Her scowl faded, and she quirked her eyebrows wryly. "Wings and flames and all."

CHAPTER 46

Shifting in her seat, Addie scanned the small council room and wished someone had thought to open a window. *Too many people, too many voices.* Ryder stood at the head of the oval table, hands on hips, head cocked as he listened. Dust covered and grimy, he held every eye.

One of the technicians, Sione, leaned forward. His dark eyes flashed, and he struck his hand on the table. "We don't stand a chance against the Fae. One is bad enough, but you say we need to expect an army of them?"

She bit her lip and scowled. He was right, but they didn't have a choice. Guilt stirred tendrils of acid in her stomach, and she pushed it down. No. Remember what Ryder said. If she accepted this was her fault, then logically she should think it was Tama's fault too, and she didn't think Tama should be blamed for what the Fae did to him. She rolled her eyes internally. Knowing something didn't make the guilt go away. She shoved it down for later.

Kira shifted at the other end of the table, her mouth closing on an unspoken thought. Addie watched the engineer as the others argued through their bravado that they would be fine or wearily repeated variations on Sione's statement. Kira had been her classmate when she first arrived out of the Dust. Neither of them had been particularly popular, and so they often ended up sitting together. Not exactly a friend, but an ally more than once. Now Kira worked on the generator, and they'd not had much to do with each other for a long time save the trade of various scavenged items. She was smart and a good judge of character. Catching Ryder's eye, Addie flicked her gaze at Kira then back to him. She wanted to stay out of this as much as possible. Her wings were hidden, and she'd asked Tama, sitting quietly next to her, not to bring the fire unless Ryder asked him to.

"Kira." Ryder didn't raise his voice, but all other discussions cut short. "What do you think?"

Kira raised her eyebrows at Ryder, ruffling her short spiky hair. "About?"

"About the Fae, the battle, our chances."

Kira chewed her lip, tugging at an earlobe full of rings. Her eyes met Addie's, and no fear shone in them, only a wry contemplation.

"Sione's right." Kira said. "Army of Fae come here, and we're gone. We've all seen the impact crater. We're all old enough to remember what made it. We've got some iron, some weapons, but not enough." Sitting up straight, Kira fixed her eyes on Addie and everyone else turned to stare. "But we've got something we never had last time—we've got a changeling." Her glance slid to Tama. "Maybe two."

Tama lifted his chin and glared at Kira.

"Nah, taihoa Tama, wait. I'm not saying it's a bad thing. But Craig said you made fire before, out at the gate. Was he telling the truth?"

Tama nodded, harsh and brief.

Kira smiled at him. "Ka pai e hoa, that's good. And Addie, you've got wings now."

"Get to the point, Kira." Ryder stepped in, as he always

did. Not that he needed to, Addie could see where Kira was going.

"The point is, that two changelings might turn the tide a bit. Who knows if we'll survive in the end, but it will give us a fighting chance at least."

Pressing her lips together, Addie put a hand on Tama's arm and darted a glance to the head of the table. Blimmin' Ryder would skite about this. *Don't offer to help. They'll say no. Let them come to that decision themselves. Let them ask you to help. Trust me, they will.*

She couldn't stay quiet. They needed to know what they were up against. "You realise fighting the Fae is a suicide mission."

Ryder's eyes met hers, and one corner of his mouth turned up. "Perhaps. Maybe not this time. Kira is right. Two changelings might just turn the tide. Regardless, at this point, if we don't fight, we either die now or submit and die more slowly later. I'm not okay with either."

Tama spoke up, his voice low but strong. "What about the kids?"

"This is what we made the bunker for." Ryder said. "Anyone who isn't willing or able to fight the Fae should be safe in there. Jasper and I have stocked it on and off for the last few years. The supplies should get them through whatever comes."

Visions of children coming out after the battle, of what they might find, tangled in her head with thoughts of the devastating aftermath of the first attacks. Buildings ripped apart, bodies strewn across the roads. Children with dull eyes and tight mouths. Her fingers tightened on the arm of the chair as her heart ached.

Sione scowled. "Death might be kinder."

Part of her agreed, but the other part thought of the life she lived now. Tattered and chaotic and threatened as it was—

she was still alive, and loved. Death was not kinder. Death was an end.

✦

THE MEETING BROKE APART, everyone going their separate ways, grim but determined. Ryder stood at the door, gripping arms with a couple of the younger men as they left. He caught her eye, waved at the last man and came over to them.

"So, Tama, you know what you're doing?"

"Why do I have to go with Doc?"

"It isn't for long. Addie will be coming to you soon. But Ana needs to check you over first."

The boy looked at her, and she nodded. "He's right. Go with Doctor Rongoa or she'll hound you forever."

She patted Tama on the shoulder and pushed him lightly off in Doc's direction. Her eyes turned back to Ryder, and her lips twitched upwards.

"What's so funny?"

"You."

He quirked his brows at her. "Me?"

"Yeah. Look at you slipping straight back into the leadership thing. Reluctant leader my ass. You love it."

He filled the space, comfortable in his boundaries, comfortable in his strength and competence. The Fae could gather outside the compound, but this was his turf. Her heart glowed watching him.

Warmth sparked in his eyes, and affection curled his mouth. "You're right. I do. Now I'm going to keep being leader and tell you that you have places to be. Get Tama ready."

Her brows contracted, and her lips twisted, her gaze sliding away from him. He moved closer, putting his hand under his chin and bringing her head back around to face him. "Lark? What is it?"

"Tama. He's a kid, Ryder. He should be in the bunker with the rest of the children, not out here fighting Fae."

His eyes softened even as his jaw tightened, his hand moving to cup her face. A part of her was blindingly aware of everyone else in the room, but his gaze drew her in.

"I know. I wish he didn't have to be, but he's the only other one with powers like yours, like theirs. He chose to fight. He told me he didn't want to be hiding when he thought he might be able to save someone."

Guilt and shame teased through her mind. Tama never ran. Everything he did was to help others. She had run, and kept running. An image of him confronting the Fae sent a shudder through her. He was just a child. He shouldn't have to think about how to save and protect other children from death. Hot fury spread through her, sparking the fire inside. The Fae had so much to answer for.

"Hey, Lark, it's okay. Cool it now."

Sparks danced around her hands. *Crap*. Taking a breath, she concentrated, coaxing the flames back deep down where they would come when called.

Ryder's arm slid around her shoulders, pulling her close, and she breathed him in as he kissed the top of her head. She flicked her eyes open at the drop in surrounding noise. *Oh no.* Heat flamed on her cheeks, and his arms tightened around her as she pushed him away. The last thing they needed was for everyone to see the commander with a changeling.

She backed away, and he snatched her hand. "Hey, no running, remember?"

"This is kind of the wrong place, Ryder."

He glanced around then back to her. "What? You think no-one was expecting this?"

Prickles of embarrassment spread over her skin, and her brain stuttered to a halt. "You think they were?"

A small but glorious smile lit his face. "Well, Paolo has already said 'about time' to me and so has Ana."

Her eyes flashed to Paolo at the other end of the room, and he gave a knowing look and winked.

"Oh."

He squeezed her hand before raising her fingers to his lips. "You better go. I'll see you later."

As she walked out of the briefing room, more than one of the people in there smiled at her, genuine smiles full of warmth. She tried her hardest to return them. It was difficult being awkward. She always worried people would think she was rude. But striding through those who were busy with last minute plans to save their compound because of her, because of Tama, because of the Fae, she realised no-one minded her awkwardness. They accepted her for who she was.

They always had.

CHAPTER 47

Night fell before Addie made her way to Mia's home. She tried to convince herself she'd been too busy with the 'situation room' and preparations for the upcoming battle. As her steps slowed and she stared at the dim glow coming from the windows of the square compartment, she knew it wasn't that. The Fae stole Mia's son. Her daughter died from Dustblight two years earlier. Addie was a changeling. *What if Mia doesn't want to speak to me?*

Her hands dug into her pockets, and she let her gaze slide away from the compartment, up towards the sky. A rare wind blew dark greyness into streaks across the horizon. Somewhere up there would be the moon, filtering a silky glow through endless clouds of Dust. A bright shimmer caught at the edge of her vision. Her heart stopped, and she fixed her eyes on the heavens.

There.

For a moment, the swirling darkness parted, and radiant white light shone, edging the Dust clouds with silver and striking awe deep into her heart.

A full moon.

Someone gasped in the silence, but she couldn't drag her

eyes away. All too soon the clouds spun fine gossamer threads over the moon's face, veiling it once again. Her eyes stayed fixed on the blurring dark, willing the moon to come back.

"Did you see that?"

Her gaze falling from charcoal clouds, she nodded her head at Kira. The engineer stood with her arm around the waist of another young woman who still stared at the sky, the pale light of the open door behind them glinting off the tear tracks on her cheeks.

Kira inclined her head at her, a smile tugging at her lips. "Guess we owe you some thanks, Adelia."

Her eyes widened. "What? No, that's nothing to do with me."

The other woman shrugged and pushed her girlfriend towards the open door. "Well, say what you like. But you come back with wings, and we get a moon for the first time in fifteen years. I was always pretty good at dot-to-dot."

The aluminium door closed behind them. Addie turned and scrunched up her face. It couldn't be put off any longer.

Summoning her courage, she knocked on Mia's door.

It opened to yellow light beaming from a small lantern in the corner of the room. No welcoming glow warmed Mia's eyes, and she didn't move back from the doorway. New lines carved around her eyes and mouth made her look much older than her years.

Swallowing away a choking sensation in her chest, Addie cleared her throat. "Hi. Can I come in?"

The silence stretched out, and her insides twisted, heat flaming on her cheeks. When Mia stepped back and let her in, relief flooded through her. Walking into rooms that had been like a second home for so long, she glanced at Mia's wan face and stumbled at the fear darkening her friend's eyes.

A pit of darkness and bile coiled in her stomach.

This was worse than Ryder's initial disgust. A part of her always expected Ryder to reject her or at least never expected him to fall for her. But Mia had been her friend and protector since she arrived as a traumatised teen. *She's my only family.*

Her tongue swelled into a lump in her mouth, blocking her words. She tried for a smile instead. Before, Mia had always been one of the three people her smiles came naturally for. Rubbing her chest as if somehow the pain would go away, she backed up a step, giving her friend more space. She hoped the wings would stay out of sight. They strained at her shoulders, a stab of hurt at the edges of them.

"I came to see how Matt was. How you were."

"You've seen."

She understood, really, she did. But she rubbed at her chest again as the pain turned to a slow burn.

"Sanjeet should come and talk to him. He's been through it too and he can help him." Her breath came out ragged, and she swallowed through a swollen throat. "It's okay, Mia. Matt won't turn out like me. He's safe now."

Mia's eyes flickered, and her expression softened for a moment. But fear etched into every line and curve of her face. "He isn't safe. They're coming again—they're coming for *you. You're* making him unsafe, and you promised you'd save him."

She could barely breathe through the crushing weight on her chest. "He should be okay in the bunker." Empty words. More empty promises. "I hoped I could visit him?"

"You were at the ward this morning. You saw him then."

"Please, Mia. Not for long. I'll leave straight afterwards." Memories of long evenings spent sipping tea and talking about everything and nothing withered in the light of Mia's fearful reluctance.

Xiyu appeared behind Mia, carrying mugs of hot water from the kitchenette. "It'll be okay. She won't hurt them. I think it will be good for them to see her."

Mia jerked her head and turned towards the small living area curtained off from the entrance, the faded red of the fabric a familiar sight.

Pulling the fabric aside, Addie stepped through to where Matt and Lily sat curled on a sofa.

A well of quiet surrounded the children. They awoke when she and Tama visited the ward straight after they arrived. Tama's pounamu hung back around his neck, but he made rough talismans for both of them out of the teeth of the changeling skull. They now wore the half-Faery teeth around their necks. Her eyes darted to Mia. *She can't have been happy about that. But I like it.*

The patched couch was big enough for them to have a large cushion each, but they chose to sit as close as possible to one another. She thought of Ella and Sanjeet, the tight bond arising from shared experience.

They stared at her wings. Longing twisted with fear shone from their faces, exactly as it had with Tama. Xiyu perched on the edge of the sofa. Mia stood in the doorway, her fear an almost tangible thing.

Matt's voice hushed out, raspy with disuse. "Did it hurt?"

Pain more intense than anything ever experienced before.

"Not too badly. The wings don't hurt at all."

"Will we get wings?" Lily's straight black fringe fell over her eyes like a shield.

She shook her head. "I don't think so."

"What's going to happen?"

Matt had never been this serious before. He had been a bit of a scamp, chatty and cheerful, smart and cheeky. This cold, quiet, and contained child reminded her too much of herself, and her heart sank to her boots. It was on the tip of her tongue to tell them not to worry: they would be safe in the bunker and the grown-ups would sort it all out. But then she remembered being dragged away from her screaming mother as grown-ups just watched. The pain and torture that she went through, that they went through. Matt and Lily were no longer just eleven-year-olds. They were warriors, and warriors deserved the truth.

"The Fae are coming. We're going to fight them. I don't know if we will win. We probably won't, but we're not going to just stand and take it anymore."

Mia moved into her line of sight. "Hardly reassuring, Addie!"

She nodded but kept her gaze on the children, Mia's anger a burning dagger over her shoulder. Their solemn eyes met hers, the flickering of remembered pain connecting them all together.

"They need to know. If we fail, then they will need to take the next steps. Learn, hide, run, protect. Can you do that?"

Their faces were so small, but strength emanated from them. Knowing you could make a difference was a shield against the darkness.

"Yes." Their voices came in unison, and the tiniest echo of melody sang behind them.

CHAPTER 48

*H*er unit closed in on her, somehow smaller than before she left despite the fact it was several times larger than the tent and a lot emptier. She towel-dried her hair and scrutinised the room as if she'd never been there before. Someone else wouldn't be able to tell who lived here or even that anyone did. Her eyes lit upon the clutter by the sink. Okay, well the dishes would tell you someone messy lived here. But there was nothing personal.

She flicked the still damp tresses behind her shoulder. Throwing the towel on the back of a chair, she dragged her pack up from the side of the cabinet. She had to dig around a little, but she pulled out Alexa's school book and the child's picture she'd taken from the old gas station. Pressing her lips together, she held them close to her chest as she scanned the room. Next to the small table was a side bench shoved full of stuff from scavenging ready to be fixed. *Perfect.* She made a little space and balanced the book against the wall, placing the picture carefully in front of it. *I should find something to pin it up with.* Her fingers traced the faded colours of the picture. Everything might be destroyed tomorrow when the Fae came, but for tonight these belonged here.

A sharp knock brought her head up. Pulling her tank top lower over the waistband of her trousers, she tried to hold back a smile. She slid open the door, and her heart danced. Ryder filled the doorway. He'd left the beard but trimmed it close. He smelled like soap and clean clothes. Warmth spread over her in a wave.

A light sparked in his eyes. "Don't often see you with your hair down, Lark. I like it."

The tresses weighed heavy on her back, and she flicked a stray strand off her face self-consciously. "You're here late."

He grinned. "Well, took me some time to shower. There was a lot of grime."

The thought of him naked under water filled her mind. Her cheeks flushed, and her stomach tightened.

"Are you going to ask me in, Addie?"

She nodded, her heart pounding in her ears, and stood aside.

His arm brushed against her chest as he walked past her through the small doorway. She gulped and fumbled the door shut. Trying to get some control back in her breathing, she took a moment before she turned.

"Can I offer you something? I don't have much, but I'm sure I can find a drink."

He shook his head, and the light in his eyes deepened to a smouldering warmth. He filled the space, his height and presence dominating her vision.

"I'm good, thanks. I didn't come for a drink."

Butterflies took off in her stomach.

"Oh?"

He smiled slowly, and she fought down the heat flooding her face.

"I figured we had some important things to do before tomorrow."

A sharp pang constricted her heart. Tomorrow. But as he smiled at her, with eyes that understood the pain and fear and held such tenderness, tension fled. Tomorrow could wait. Tonight was only him.

He waited, letting her make the first move. She had no doubt that if she asked him to, he would leave. But she didn't want him to. Taking a couple of steps towards him, she looked up into his face, putting out her hand to cup his cheek.

His breath hitched, and it emboldened her, knowing she had an effect on him. She stroked his face, her thumb moving to rub gently over his mouth. She bit her own lip and moved closer. Sliding her other hand over his chest, she pulled her head back slightly as he dipped lower to take her mouth.

"Ryder, there's something I want to tell you."

His breath warmed her face, and his body was hard under her hand. She couldn't stop her heart from racing. But this was important.

"You know you can tell me anything."

His eyes were an impossible hazel. Bright gold flecked with green, and right now they glinted at her.

She took a breath and let out the thing she had held onto for so many years, that had been her waking thought and her evening prayer.

"I love you, Ryder Hendrix. More than anything in the world." A smile lit his face like sunshine, and all at once the words were easy to say. "You're wonderful, and I love everything about you. I love you." She was smiling now too, giddy with the freedom of finally saying what lived in her heart.

He crushed her to him, and his lips took hers in a fierce kiss.

She opened her mouth to him, and his tongue played with hers, lighting her blood on fire. His hand slid lower over her bottom, pulling her leg up and tugging her against him. A gasp escaped her at the hardness of him, and he paused, kissing her softly and leaning back a little.

"Lark, not sure how to ask this—and feel free to tell me to fuck off—but is this your first time?"

Oh god, am I that out of practice? "No. That was a long time ago, with—"

"Nah! No, no. I don't need to hear who." He frowned, "As long as it wasn't that creep Keegan."

She bared her teeth in an awkward grimace, and he closed his eyes.

"Oh god. Lark, how could you?"

"Oh, like you never made mistakes when you were twenty."

He slid his arms around her and swayed her hips closer to his again. "I never make mistakes."

Heat curled inside her. She bit his lip, and he shuddered, his grip tightening around her as he devoured her mouth again.

His hands slid up to caress her breasts, and she breathed in sharply at the overload of sensation. Her wings sprang out, vibrant pearly white, shining with a luminescent glow. She froze. He pulled his head back and looked at the wings, then at her face, his lips swollen and his cheeks flushed.

"I'm sorry," she got out.

"Don't be sorry, baby. I'm getting used to them." He quirked an eyebrow at her then tugged her closer to him. She melted into his kiss then her eyes shot open, and she pushed him away, staring up at him with indignation.

"'Baby?' Really?"

Imps danced in his eyes. "Yeah. Baby. Would you prefer Princess?" A grin split his face. "My beautiful Fairy Princess."

She laughed and punched him, and he kissed her in her laughter.

His hands on her body lit a flame she had every intention of quenching. She fumbled at his buttons, and he ripped his shirt over his head and tossed it on the floor. He was beautiful. Hard muscles covered by olive skin. Her fingers explored him, and she traced over the tattooed words guarding his heart with her nails until he gasped. *Kia Kaha.* "This means 'be strong' doesn't it?"

He nodded. Her heart swelled until she thought it would burst from her chest.

Be strong.

That was everything he was.

She met his eyes, drowning in the warm depths, and stroked his jaw.

His eyes sparked, and he slid his hands under her tank top, pulling it off. Her pants were next until they both stood naked and vulnerable in the shadow of the gathering gloom.

They sought solace and affection and love in each other, and when he came inside her, she shattered in a blinding burst of shining silver that spread out to cocoon them both. He buried his face in her neck and sighed.

"I love you, Addie, all of you."

Afterwards she lay in his arms, relishing the closeness of him, the touch of his skin on hers. Darkness clouded her thoughts, and she bit her trembling lip. She tried not to let him notice, but tension snaked through her. His arm tightened around her, pulling her closer against him. He kissed her tenderly on the side of her head. "Don't worry about tomorrow, sweetheart. Right now is all that matters. Right now is good."

She turned in his arms, burying her face into his chest, breathing in the scent of him as he stroked her back. He was right. For tonight, this was enough.

CHAPTER 49

Day dawned, still smothered by the dank gloom of night. Charcoal clouds gathered in a seething vortex outside the compound.

One minute the sky beyond the walls was a wall of grey, light filtering through cracks in the cloud, and the next, the horizon burst with Fae. Swirling colors and sparkling bolts of magic stole her breath. A flicker of yearning cut through the adrenaline pumping in her system. The wings at her back snapped into life and pulsed in time with her heartbeat.

Uncurling her clenched fingers, she stood shoulder to shoulder with Tama at the door of her unit, watching the first waves roll through the sky.

The magic hit the outer buildings and the wall first, shattering them into rubble. Screams tore the air as people dove for cover.

The rolling wave of power slammed into the inner compound. Buildings shook, and windows smashed. Falling masonry drove the people outside, fish in a barrel to be picked off one by one. Bolts of energy rained down on them, but it didn't appear as if the Fae were trying to kill them yet. Screams echoed through the chaos. Dead or not, people were hurt. Helpless. She raced out, dragging Tama behind her, wishing he was safe in the bunker.

The Fae landed, Dust swirling around them as their robes billowed and shimmered. They spread into a line, marching slowly forward over the rubble.

Strike after strike pounded the compound, sending Dust and dirt exploding into the air. People staggered as the ground shook and buildings toppled. All the while, crimson hued magic swallowed the light.

The Fae were fast. Faster than the humans. Faster than her. She sprinted to the centre of the impact crater, Tama keeping pace beside her. Silver lightning spun around the two of them, protecting them from the chaos raining from the sky. Hope took wing inside her mind, images of a skull clutched in the hands of a changeling and a bright cleansing fire chasing away the darkness.

They worked together, their magic mixing and combining in a melody that sprang from her deepest core. Flames appeared, targeted and sharp, swirling like knives through Dust. Her magic sought out Fae, crashing into them with the strength of iron, blood, and will.

A hunter dressed in crimson ducked under her bolts of magic, stabbing its arm straight into the silver lightning surrounding them. The shield shook, shattered, and the Fae snatched at Tama, dragging him away. His eyes shimmered gold, and fire sparked from his hand. Pulling back, the Fae snarled. She shoved a burst of magic at him. The bolt pushed the Fae backwards, and he vanished.

"Damn!" She kicked at the ground. "Those things don't die."

She cast a quick glance around, her heart knowing exactly where he would be. Ryder clambered over the rubble, pulling people to freedom.

A familiar baying sound carried through the air, and chills ran up her spine.

Hounds. Oh crap.

She met Ryder's eyes across the compound, and he grinned at her, hoisting his knife, then turned to sprint towards the hounds flowing in a black swathe through the hole in the wall. Kira and Sione were at his side. She resolutely looked away from the snarling ripping beasts and the images they conjured up of blood on Ryder's arms and his still body in the Dust.

"D'you think we're holding them off?" Tama's voice shook a little, but his strength flowed from his heart in a golden melody that lifted her spirits.

"Perhaps." They'd forced many to vanish, but still more came.

A wave of red cleaved the air, and a dozen of the crimson guards appeared in the sky. They dropped to the ground, their robes flaring like floating blood.

The concerted attack overwhelmed her. As many times as she blocked blows, the screams of her people who were not so lucky ripped into her heart. She felt stretched out. Tama faltered at her side.

A flash of white caught the corner of her eye. Doc, rushing out to Paolo, his leg ripped off by the slicing magic of the crimson guard. Ice gripped her heart. The world slowed as a ripping bolt of energy slashed across Doc's chest, throwing her backwards to land heavily on the dirt. Red blood bloomed through her open lab coat.

"Ana!" Ryder's voice cut through the cacophony of falling buildings and screaming people.

No. God no. What was he doing?

Ryder raced toward Doc, hurling himself to the ground to escape the bolts. Addie's fire flickered out, and the shield faded. Each step forward was like wading through sand, her eyes fixed on Ryder as he hauled Doc up and into his arms, staggering to his feet. A Fae landed just behind him, crimson robes billowing out, hair whipping itself up into a vibrant halo of red. Addie raised her hand, but her fire had died. The Fae met her eyes, smiled, teeth sharp against the white of its skin, and sent a thin slicing fiery bolt right at Ryder.

The impact shuddered through her body, her breath escaping in a rush. Ryder's back arched. He dropped to his knees, his arms loosening for a second before tightening around Doc, trying to protect her even through the pain. They fell sideways to the ground. He carefully let her go then pushed himself up and around to face the Fae.

His back was blood.

Red dripped through his shredded jacket like overflowing water. She ran, the ground no longer sucking at her feet. The Fae grinned wider and wove both hands in the air, sending two bolts of energy to punch Ryder directly in the chest. He fell. Blood sprayed bright against the grey light.

The world stopped. Every second slowed. If she could just get there. If she could just catch him, he would be okay.

His head hit the ground hard, his eyes open but fixed, unseeing.

Her heart shattered.

Every feeling, every promise, every hidden stupid mistake, flooded out from the cracks. The dragon rose from the bloody ruins of her chest. It filled every cell of her, rage and grief giving it shape and purpose.

Her eyes flashed, the shimmering blue so intense that the world itself changed. She no longer saw the Fae hidden behind its glamor but a cruel creature, warped and twisted and evil. Her arms fell to her side, and her fingers spread. Fire crackled to life, twining around her arms, sending blue sparks into the ground as she stepped ever closer. Raising her palms, glowing with magic, she fixed her eyes on the Fae. She shoved the magic towards him, and this time she was faster.

He burned.

The shrill, inhuman scream of the dying Fae echoed through the compound. She took another step until she stood over Ryder. Tension threaded her arms, and blue flames sizzled in the sudden stillness.

"Anyone else touches him, and I kill them."

Another line of hunters rose behind the first.

A flash of purple appeared close to her. She jerked around, arms out to attack, and Aesthetius filled her vision. He gazed at the carnage, the dead, the dying, and the damaged. Compassion twisted his face into something human. With his glamor no longer hiding him from her eyes, she saw him as he was, tall and golden and strong. His eyes went from her to the hunters.

"If any touch her, I will kill them."

The line of hunters stilled, motionless for a second. Sudden flight and movement caught her eye, and she thrust her arm out, sending a wave of magic towards them. She knocked two out, and a purple bolt came ringing past her ear from behind, puncturing the sternum of the first, passing through him and bowling over the second.

She stood shoulder to shoulder with Aesthetius, Fae and changeling, protecting the compound.

Tama crouched where she'd left him. She could sense his melody, still twined with hers, still safe. He sent a fire, all he could manage, and she added her magic to swallow and shape it and cast it at the hunters, where it exploded.

One of the Fae snarled, leaping forward and shaping the double bolts that had killed Ryder. Aesthetius stepped in front of her, throwing his arm out to protect Tama as the boy ran forward. Tama's grief rang in the changing tune of the melody throbbing in her mind. Her eyes, still filtering the world through a strange blue clarity, raked over Tama. Wings of Dust followed in his wake. She blinked. They weren't real, not there, but beneath the glamor, she saw Dust floating beside him in the shape of great wings.

Aesthetius flicked a hand. The Fae stumbled backwards, teeth bared in an angry growl.

A hunter in black grabbed the red one, holding it back.

"No." Its voice hissed a jarring chord in her mind. "His mother would not be pleased." The red hunter's eyes swam, and its claws curled inwards.

"And what of the King?"

"It is for him to decide. Come."

With a swirl of Dust and magic, the Fae were gone.

The emptiness and silence they left in their wake was like rousing from a nightmare to a cold room.

Her eyes darted to Ryder, motionless at her feet. She fell onto her knees beside him, her hand reaching out, shaking, to feel for a pulse. His blood soaked into the dirt. Her trousers grew damp where she knelt in a rivulet of it.

Ryder's skin felt cold, but she didn't know if that was just because she was so warm. Her hand trembled so much she couldn't tell whether or not his heart beat. She swore, pushing away the tears sliding silently down her cheeks, and tried to keep her hand steady. Aesthetius crouched beside her and reached out, taking her hand away. She would have fought him, but he replaced her hand with his. She held her breath as he waited.

"There is a pulse. He lives, but he needs care now."

Care, a doctor.

Doc.

Oh god.

She spun around on her knees, fell forward onto her hands and crawled the few steps to where Doc lay. The blood from her chest no longer oozed, but her face was pale and drawn. She breathed though. Eva, helped by Edwin, one of the medics, lifted Paolo from the blood drenched ground. He was still alive, though perhaps for not much longer with the amount of blood he was losing. What was left of the medical team raced out with stretchers, and she sat back on her heels, her hand tight on Ryder's shoulder and her eyes watching the skies.

Aesthetius stood behind her, with wings of fire and gold. Power radiated from him. The medical team hesitated as they approached. She waved them closer.

"He's fine. He's with us. Didn't you see him slicing them?"

As had she. She killed one.

I killed a Fae.

She gazed up at Aesthetius, her eyes returned to normal and his golden glow gone.

"Why are you here?"

"I have come to make a deal."

CHAPTER 50

She leaned against the entrance into Ryder's ward. The ridges of the door frame pushed into her shoulder. Tension sparked under her skin, but exhaustion settled lead in her limbs. If she didn't lean, she would fall. The interns rushed around, doing what they could, but the stark expression on Edwin's face turned hope to a barren wasteland inside her.

Kira, Craig, and Sione had turned to her, straight after the interns brought him in. Asking for orders, asking for leadership. She didn't have the energy to tell them to leave her alone. Kira had noticed though and smiled wryly, eyes stiff and sad. "Tough titties, Addie. You've been his second in command for ages. We've all known it. Now you're in charge, and you're going to have to deal with it. What do we do now?"

She rubbed a hand over her face. The instructions she'd handed out were basic, and she hoped they would be enough. Hoped she could keep them safe.

"Why do you want to make a deal?"

Aesthetius stood on the opposite side of the doorway, his dark head nearly brushing the ceiling, and his hands clasped in front of him.

"You could call it guilt, or remorse, or something different, newer. I wish to protect you and yours."

A sigh shuddered out of her. Ryder lay broken in the room behind her. So much for her ability to protect anyone. Fatigue dragged at her eyes, and her arms trembled as she crossed them tighter.

"Why? Because of some weird connection when I was young? I don't quite buy that."

He shook his head, another human quirk.

"No. Not because of that, and yet, that was when I believe I started thinking this way. You know there are different kinds of Fae?"

She blinked, afraid if she nodded her head might fall off.

"I am of royal blood. My mother is Queen of Elfhame."

Figured. The golden sheen around him which she could see now if she tried had to come from somewhere.

He frowned, and her eyes narrowed. Fae didn't frown. "Being royal is usually something to smile about I would have thought."

His eyes shimmered, and she thought of Ryder, lying in a white bed with his chest ripped open.

"You know the Fae brought the Dust, that we can move and manipulate it. But there are only a few who can create the Dust. Those who can are in the royal line."

Her foggy brain struggled to join the dots. Her eyes didn't leave his, and her breath caught.

"It was my mother, my family, me, who created the Dust and destroyed your world. Now I wish to save it."

She stared at him, his face solemn and lined and human like, while in her head swam. Crashing, destroying bursts of magic that left craters. The choking Dust killing millions. Beckett.

Lead turned to flame in her body. She launched across the hall, slapping his too-human face and slamming him into the wall.

Pain choked her, whirling thoughts in her head, too many to get out. Her forearm dug into his neck. She dragged in air, her lips trying to form words but her throat closing on the image of her brother's little body ripped apart by magic.

She had almost forgotten Aesthetius was the enemy.

She had almost begun to like him.

He raised his arms to her shoulders, gently holding them but not pushing her away.

"I was always against the plan, but only because I thought it was too drastic. Not until I met a small human child who turned to me for comfort did I question what I believed to be true. I have always told you the truth, Adelia. We changed you, but you changed me as well."

His eyes shimmered in a face that showed emotion. He was right. He had become more human.

"I don't know if I can forgive you." The words bled out of her.

He smiled at her, and the sadness in his eyes brought angry tears to her own. He had no right to be sad.

"I don't need you to forgive me. I still want to protect you."

She stepped back, her legs like jelly, resenting the strength of his hand under her elbow.

"And this deal, it will protect us?"

"Yes. It is an old magic, and if you agree, this should keep your people safe."

Her head turned, her eyes flicking to Ryder in the room behind her. "It's too late for all of my people."

"No. It is not too late. He can be saved. The question is at what cost?"

"What do you mean?"

"Have you ever used the power to heal?"

Images of her blood caking Ryder's skin, peeling off the residue to see all the wounds had vanished.

"Once. It was a bit icky. But that was to cure his Dustblight, I don't think I can do that again."

Aesthetius walked closer, slowly and carefully. "You can. The immortality of the Fae runs in your veins. This is what healed him before."

Shock like ice spiked through the cloud in her mind. "Did you just say I'm immortal?"

"No, you are not, but your blood carries traces. This is why you can resist the Dust—your body is healing all the time. Now you control your magic. You should be able to heal him."

She straightened, hope like iron in her spine. "Tell me how!"

"Wait, you need to hear the cost first."

"Whatever it is, I'll pay it. I'll do it." Ryder, alive and well was worth anything she had to give. Her heart pounded at the thought.

"The deal I spoke of requires a bond between us, an agreement. Magic from both of us is needed to seal the bond and protect this place until King Valkor recognises the deal."

Her brows lowered. "Okay, I follow that, I think, but I thought we were talking about Ryder."

His hand brushed her shoulder. "You are already drained from the battle. If you use your magic to heal Ryder, there will be no more left in you to seal the bond. You will be saving his life and risking the lives of everyone else in this compound."

Hope bled out as her heart shrivelled inside her. Desperate thoughts whirled in her head. Her hands gripped each other tightly, her nails pressing into her skin.

"Are you sure there is no other way? Can you help him?"

He shook his head, his eyes glistening in sympathy. "On my own, I cannot. There are complications when a Fae tries to heal a human—I think he would not like the way it turned out. Plus, I need to save my energy for the bigger battle. As do you."

Numb grief sank like lead in her stomach. She couldn't do

it. She couldn't sacrifice thousands of people for one man, even if that man was Ryder. For a long moment, she imagined it, bringing him back, holding him. But she knew what he would say. What she would say to him if he did it to her. Kira had gripped her shoulder before leaving the ward, her last words had been: "I believe you can do this, Addie, I believe you can save us." She couldn't throw that faith under the bus just for one man.

Even if that man is Ryder.

Pain cracked her voice into a whisper. "But then he will die."

"No." Tama walked up to her out of the shadows, young face carved into grim lines. "He will not die. I will do it."

His eyes shifted in a hazy glow as he let his power move to the surface. He was definitely stronger than before, but whether he could do this was another matter.

"Tama, you fought alongside me. This might take more than you have."

"I don't care." His voice was fierce, and his eyes glowed. Once again she glimpsed a hint of wings made from Dust outlining his shoulders. "Ryder's my friend. He looked after me ever since I first came here. He'd do the same for me." He must have caught her uncertainty because he smiled, his fingers beating a rapid tattoo on his leg. "Don't worry Addie, I looked in the box, remember. I'm not afraid of who I am anymore. I can do this." Jerking forward, he gripped her arm. "Let me do this."

She was reminded of before the Fae appeared, the way he had been so adamant about wanting to protect those who went into the bunker and not join them. *If you had the ability to do something to help, you had to do it.* She knew that. Tama did too. Ryder taught them both.

"Okay."

Her eyes went to Aesthetius, and he nodded. "I will help Tama."

"What do we do if the Fae come back?"

"I think we will have some time yet—they need to consult with King Valkor and possibly my mother. They will not want to anger the Queen of the Emerald Fields. But, if you need me, call me, and I will come."

"I will." Her eyes went to Ryder in the hospital bed beyond. If the Fae came, she would call him. He would come, and Ryder would die.

CHAPTER 51

Addie stood at the foot of the metal bed where green sheets tucked over Ryder's long legs, his feet right at the end of the cot. The snap of the drip as Edwin hooked up a new IV line brought her eyes to the bag of fluid—so little left. A finger resting on Ryder's wrist, the intern took his pulse. Addie watched the machines. Red lines. Beeps. Green stutters. All meaningless while the man of her heart lay there with his eyes closed and a shadow of death in his face.

A sigh floated from Edwin's lips, and Addie gripped the metal bar at the foot of the bed, her fingers aching.

"I'm sorry, Addie. It's not looking good. If this Fae thing doesn't work, there's nothing else we can do. He's fading, and with Doc still out of it—" His voice broke, and she turned to him, the shadowed depths of his brown eyes sunken into hollow cheeks.

"I understand." Her voice came out flat, quiet, detached from the screaming void inside her. "Can you give me a moment?"

Edwin brushed a hand over his eyes and gathered his tray of useless syringes.

"Of course. I'll be around if you need me. You know where the buzzer is."

The door snicked shut behind him. Her knees shook, but she locked them tight and made herself look at Ryder's face. So pale. Dried blood still trailed the edges of his jaw. A burning ache filled her chest, squeezing her heart, trapping air in her lungs. She looked up at the ceiling, blinking rapidly and pressing her lips together.

Strong. She had to be strong.

I don't want to be strong.

Forcing iron into her shaking limbs, she walked around the bed until she stood next to his shattered torso. Magic simmered beneath her skin, begging to be let out, and it took every ounce of will she had not to try and fix him. She put her hands in her pockets so she wouldn't hold his, wouldn't feel his weak pulse, wouldn't forget what she'd promised.

"Hey. It's me. It's Lark."

Grief swallowed her voice, and she coughed and tried again. "I wanted to say I'm sorry. For, well. For everything. For getting you involved in this. For bringing the Fae here." Tears slid down her cheeks, and her mouth twisted. "For stuffing up so badly. For letting you get hurt."

Ragged breath tore at the painful lump in her throat. "But you know what, I'm trying really, really hard to not be sorry that I'm not helping you now. Because I know you wouldn't want me to. But if this doesn't work, if you don't make it, I'm going to hate myself forever."

Her shoulders caved in, and her head sunk to her chest, a gulping sob ripping out of her. She stood. Hands in pockets. Shoulders shaking. Grief flooding out of her in a torrent as she tried, and failed, to stifle her cries. Not once did she touch him.

After a long while, she heaved a shuddering breath and wiped her face. "I'm not going to say it, Ryder. Because I'll see you later. You better make it."

The void inside her spread numbing tendrils into her mind, freezing her heart.

"Right. Better go."

I love you.

"Lots of things to do."

Please, god, don't die.

"Catch you later, Ryder."

I hope you know how much I need you.

Spinning on her heel, she marched from the room. She stood in the doorway, fighting the urge to go back.

A sudden shrill beep from the machines filled the air. The flatline of a stopped heart. Not breathing, fighting the fear, she turned. The little green beeps on Ryder's machines lay still then shot up. Knees giving out, she clung to the door as people clattered down the hallway, pushing a defibrillator trolley, shoving past her into the next room.

Anahera's room.

Relief turned to guilt, turned to dread.

Time slowed as she followed the running interns. Air closed round her like molasses. Reality warped as Anahera's body jerked from the electricity jolting through her. Her beaming smile no longer curved a slack mouth filled with tubes. Ana's arm slipped off the bed, and Addie stared at the hand that had always offered affection, even to a stubborn and wary teenager. Bile rose at the back of her throat. The constant beep of the machines was too harsh a swan song for someone as vibrant as Ana.

Footsteps behind her warned her, but too late. Tama was taller than her, and there was no way she could block the sight.

"No!"

She tried to hold him back, but he pushed her aside and stumbled into the room.

"Do something!"

Edwin threw her a glance from red rimmed eyes. "Get him out of here!"

Tama's arm was rigid under her hand. She tugged him towards the door, her heart shrivelling at the pain in his face. "Come on. Come with me, Tama. There's nothing we can do here."

He jerked his head to face her, a fierce golden light in his shimmering eyes. "Wrong. I can help her. I know I can."

The ground shifted beneath her feet.

"Tama—"

"No. You don't understand, Addie. Doc is my family. You have Mia. I have Doc. I can't let her die. Not when I can save her."

But if you save her, Ryder will die. The words stuck in her throat. That was no burden to lay on fifteen-year-old shoulders.

Aesthetius walked into the room, wings cinched tightly at his back, a melody swirling through the air. He took Tama by the hand and coaxed him into the hallway. "Tama. The magic is limited. You can only save one of them."

Tama pulled away, and Addie averted her eyes from the fire in his.

"I can save both. I know I can."

"No." Aesthetius's voice was gentle, but implacable. "You can't. We will not tell you what you must do. The decision is yours."

The shrill whine of the machines faded as Addie's mind caved in on itself. She stood in the hallway between two rooms, each holding a part of her heart. Tama leaned his forehead on the wall, hands curling into fists against the glass.

Aesthetius's voice cut through the muffled silence pressing down on her. "However, neither of them has much time. You must choose."

Tama's hand went to the pounamu pendant around his neck as wings of Dust shimmered into being at his back.

Addie's hand flew toward him, but she pulled it back, crossing her arms.

"If Doc dies," Tama said, his voice breaking, "we still got the medics. But there's no one else to be Ryder."

Her heart thudded back into place, and she crossed the hallway in two quick strides. She pulled him into a hard embrace. His tears soaked her shoulder, and grief and hope battled inside her.

Aesthetius met her eyes over Tama's head. "Then we start now."

CHAPTER 52

*L*eaving the ward was like ripping out a part of her and hoping it would survive without her. Weak sunlight lit up motes of Dust and concrete floating through the air. Doc used to call days like this glitter days. She brushed at her eyes and swallowed the grief. There was work to do. Sione pounced on her as she left the shelter of the doorway to walk to the perimeter.

"We've shored up the outer wall," he said, "put extra height on. We marked the drop zones too, so everyone can avoid them."

"Great work."

He stroked his chin, clearly he had more to say. She raised her eyebrows at him.

"Yes? What else?"

"Do you really expect the wall to stop the Fae?"

"No. They'll fly right over it. Rebuilding the wall is for us —helps people feel like something's being done."

He puffed out air and stared at her. Maybe a bit too blunt. Oh well. She didn't like lying.

"So, what's the real plan then?"

Amazing, the assumption that she had a plan. Thoughts

of Ryder crossed her mind. To be fair, she always assumed he had a plan too. Maybe he'd always been just as clueless as her. Firmly shutting away her last image of him, in between Tama and Aesthetius and a glow of golden green light, she tried to look like she knew what she was doing. The suppressed sympathy on Sione's face told her she failed.

"The plan is that Aesthetius and I are going to come up with something to protect the compound."

"Sounds a little vague."

"Yeah well, magic, y'know."

Sione shoved his hands in his pockets, chewing at his bottom lip. "Do you trust this Fae?"

He brought the Dust. He stole me from my mother.

"Yes. Yes, I do." *When the hell had that happened?* But she did. She didn't know if she could forgive him, but trust him? Yes.

He regarded her out of large brown eyes. As she stared back, she noticed his lashes, how long and soft they were on someone so brawny. No wonder Mia used to flirt with him all the time.

Mia. Someone else to find time to see.

"Okay, Addie. If you trust him, I will too. Just try and do this vague magicky thing soon, alright? This wall won't reassure people for long."

She threw Sione a little salute and turned to where she had last seen Sanjeet. Despite being healthy and strong, the Dust played havoc with his lungs, and he wheezed as he helped with the clearing of the rubble. He paused, wiping his brow, then perched on a big block of masonry, his hands between his knees and his head hanging down. A little frown tightened her brow.

Avoiding the people who waved and stared at her wings, she made her way over to him. Scootching herself onto the block, she sat quietly, leaning into his shoulder. They stayed there for some time. She watched the people moving around the compound and thought of Ryder. Tried not to think of Doc. Sanjeet stared at his hands.

Finally, he let out a sigh, his shoulders slumping.

"Thank you, Adelia."

"For what?"

"For just being here."

She bumped his shoulder with hers. "No problem. That's what friends are for."

He nodded, and a sad little smile pulled at his lips.

"Although, friends are also good to talk to. What's the matter, Sanjeet?"

He screwed up his face and gestured at the compound.

"This. Everyone here seems to have a purpose, friends, loyalty. I was just wondering what it would have been like to grow up here. To have family."

He lost his parents too. The testing had taken them all. She wondered, for the first time, if he knew his parents were dead.

"I'm sorry."

He smiled back at her, twisted and small, but a smile. "I know."

Shouts rang out from across the crater, and a faint scream sounded. She leapt to her feet. On the other side of the compound, the air broke apart, and Fae poured through the gap in the clouds.

The world stilled. She was only half aware of Sanjeet rising to his feet next to her, of yells and running people. For a moment, all hung in the balance.

"Adelia!" Sanjeet's voice pulled her from the darkness in her head, and she turned to him. "We need Aesthetius. Where is he?"

Call and I will come.

Ryder would die.

She clenched her fists, her eyes narrowing at the small unit of red gowned Fae with their flaring wings descending to the compound. The dragon rose inside her.

"We don't need him. Not yet, anyway. We can do this."

Her wings spread behind her, and she ran. Sanjeet kept pace beside her, and Sione raced to join them. Screams echoed through the compound. Sparks flickered into life along her arms.

Feet pounding on the dirt, they rounded the edge of the main building. The walls of the old hospital gaped open, and they dodged falling bricks. Seven Fae soldiers hovered above, casting bolts at the people below.

Sanjeet bumped into her shoulder as she skidded to a halt. "I thought Aesthetius said they'd back off."

She raised her arms, winding flames glowing blue. "I don't think these guys got the memo."

"Addie," Sione grabbed her shoulder. "I don't know much about magic, but can you do this or do we need your Fae friend?"

Call and I will come.

"I got this."

With a wish, she stepped forwards and pushed the flames skyward. Blue fire engulfed two of the Fae. Their red wings shredded in the pulsing energy. Ripples of power pushed the remaining Fae into a tumbling mess.

Wings and robes tangled as they thumped to the ground. The perimeter guards raced to attack. A scream split the air, and Addie spun on her heel. Two Fae had landed and stood near the entry to the bunker, surrounded by broken masonry and anything else people could throw.

Leaving the stunned Fae to the wrath of the guards, she grabbed Sione and headed to the bunker. *If they touch those children, I will destroy them.*

She tried to not look at the faces of the three bodies they passed, fixing her eyes on the living protecting the bunker.

Keegan stood shoulder to shoulder with his friend Davy. No swagger left, just determination and blood.

Kira hefted a bar of iron in her hand, her eyes shining fierce through streaks of blood running from her hairline. The Fae hovered out of reach of the iron, flames curling around its clawed fingertips, and pointed teeth bared. A charred heap at Kira's feet shifted, and rage swam through Addie's blood as she recognised Eva, her pearls and cardigan melted onto her body.

The Fae raised a languid arm, and Addie hurled herself in front of Kira. Her wings covered the engineer, and she flung up a shield. A fraction too late. Crimson flames hit her in the chest. Sparks of pain radiated like a burning spider web. She battled to maintain the shield while her body struggled to repair itself.

Sione yelled and threw himself at the Fae, ducking the flames and barrelling into it. Claws scraped down his neck, blood welling bright against brown skin. Kira moved from cover, and Addie let her shield fall. A rush of magic flooded her body, knitting together burned flesh.

The Fae not struggling with Sione leaped into the air and spun, arms flying out. Addie reached for the magic, but the spark dimmed. *If I use this there will be no more to seal the bond.* Her fingers curled, and she reached for her knife. Crimson bolts shot towards her. Teeth clenched, she braced for the impact. It never came. Keegan shoved her out of the way. The bolts hit him in the chest and face, that charming smile torn from his flesh.

Her hand shook as she reached down. Picked up the iron bar he had carried. Swung it with all her fury and grief, smashing it into the face of the Fae. The bar glowed orange, and the Fae screamed, a high pitched inhuman squall. It fell backwards in a cindering heap.

The bar dropped from her trembling fingers, the clang as

it landed the only sound, bar the weeping from Kira, hunched over Eva's lifeless body.

So much death.

Her knees shook, and she stumbled. Sanjeet's arm slid round her waist, and she leaned on him. Her eyes fixed on Keegan's lifeless form, Davy kneeling beside him, blood covering his shoulder.

"Did I do this, Sanjeet? Did they do this because of me?"

His grip tightened, and his chest shifted under her cheek as he drew in a sharp breath. "No. Adelia, this is not your fault."

She forced iron into her knees, stood straighter, turned to face him. "Yes, Sanjeet. It is. I should have called Aesthetius. Keegan died to protect me because I didn't want to use up my magic. Eva—" Her voice faltered, and she thought of Paolo, of telling him his beloved wife was gone.

"Stop it."

She glanced away from the fire in his dark eyes.

"The Fae did this. Save your anger for them. We still have a fight ahead."

A commotion on the other side of the grounds brought her eyes up. Her heart stopped. Ryder was walking, actually walking, around the corner. Tall and strong and alive. He was alive. Her heart stuttered to life again, pounding in a rhythm that brought the fire of the dragon flickering to the surface. He returned the handshakes and one-armed embraces of the people he passed, but his eyes searched the grounds.

Without conscious thought, she pushed out of Sanjeet's grip, walking then breaking into a run. Ryder moved towards her, and she leapt into his arms, tears blinding her. Her wings wrapped them in a white cocoon, and she breathed him in.

"You're alive."

"Yes, I am, thanks to Tama and your Fae friend, and the kids."

She kissed him, her wet cheeks rubbing against his, and she felt his lips smile.

"Adelia Lark, are you crying over me?"

She hiccupped a laugh. "I'm probably allergic to something."

He pulled her closer and kissed her forehead. "It's ok, sweetheart. I love you too."

Here inside the shelter of her wings, she shuddered, the thought of losing him wracking her body with emotion she'd pushed down to be strong for everyone else. Her voice caught, and she clutched at him. "I thought you were dead. I thought I'd lost you. If you ever do that to me again I will be so mad."

"Trust me, I have no intention of dying. I need to live long enough to send the Fae to hell."

Images of Eva, of Keegan, of Doc raced through her head. Hell was too good for the Fae.

She leaned back to look in his face, letting her wings fall behind her. Her brows drew together. "You said the kids helped too? Which kids?"

Mia's voice rasped from the side. "Our kids."

Mia. She looked over at her friend, Xiyu Chang standing next to her, their children holding tight to their hands.

Flicking a glance between the adults and the children, she disentangled herself from Ryder, who held onto her fingers until she squatted down in front of Matt and Lily.

"You helped to save Ryder?"

Matt nodded, and Lily replied for the two of them. "Yes. We felt the magic happening, but it wasn't scary, like before. We heard the song, and we sang along."

"It was like golden light and sunshine." Matt's frail voice and his small hand reaching for hers made her blink back tears.

"Thank you," she whispered to the two of them. "You did a good thing."

Ryder scooped the kids up in a giant bear hug. She sat back on her heels.

Aesthetius appeared in the background, and her blood chilled.

Right. Vague magic plan time.

CHAPTER 53

"You can't seriously be considering this."

Fear sat in her blood like lead, but she shrugged in reply to Ryder and schooled her face to the mask she'd worn for so many years. She leaned on the small cabinet in her unit. "I don't think there's much of a choice."

"It isn't enough for you that you've got wings, magic, that you're half Fae already, you want to *bond* with him?"

She blinked at the disgust he was trying to hide. To be fair, the thought made her stomach curdle too.

"No. No, it's not like that, and you know it isn't. Stop being such a jerk."

He half turned from her with an explosive snort. "For crying out loud Lark, I'm trying to stop you from putting yourself in danger, and you think that's being a jerk?"

The cold tang of fear took the edge off her anger. "I won't be in danger."

He stalked up to her, standing almost face to face, the back of her legs pushing into the cabinet. "You're going to let some Fae bind you to him for eternity. I call that pretty big danger."

Every muscle tensed. The wings fought to spread out, but she refused. They would just make this worse.

"Aesthetius says the bond is a formality more than anything else, that the magic will protect us. He's not trying to harm us."

He stepped back, arms crossing in front of him.

"You trust him."

"I trust him."

"He stole you from your mother. He surrendered you to the Fae to torture. He's helped us now, sure, but to bind yourself to a Faery forever is stupid. And you know it. I won't let you do this."

Her brows rose. Fire flickered on one hand, but she crossed her arms and squashed the flames. "*Let me*? Ryder, you know you never let me do anything. I make my own decisions. You can't stop me making this one."

"Watch me."

"It isn't your right. I don't belong to you."

"You don't belong to him either!"

He'd never shouted at her before. Not since she was a teen and deserved it.

He took a shuddering breath and covered his face with trembling hands. She didn't step closer to him, wasn't quite ready to give up that ground, but she moved to the table and sat down. After a second, she uncrossed her arms, fidgeting with the edges of the chair.

"Ryder, it's going to be okay."

He stared down at her, eyes fierce and jaw clenched. "You don't know that."

"No. But I believe Aesthetius when he says that this blood bond thing is important to the Fae, a contract they won't break. Sanjeet said the same."

He sank down into the chair opposite her, forearms on the table, hands clenched together.

"What if this changes you, Addie? What if you don't come back to me?"

Her hand stretched across the table, and he clasped it tight.

"I will always come back to you. They've changed me once, Ryder, but I'm still me. I'm still Adelia."

A sigh wracked out of him, and his voice was rough. "Yes. But an Adelia who turns to a Fae for help when all I can do is sit on the side-lines and watch."

Jealous. Holy crap. Ryder is jealous of the Fae. Surely not. But as he looked away, not meeting her eyes, a certainty shook her. He actually was.

Getting up, she moved round the table to kneel next to him, holding his hand the whole time. He swivelled to face her.

"Ryder. I turn to him because he can help. And yes, he took me from my mother, and I hate him for it. But he cared for me too. I have changed him as much as he changed me. I don't want to be Fae. Sometimes I don't want to be changeling. I don't want to do this blood bond with Aesthetius. But what I want doesn't matter."

His eyes bored into hers, and she squeezed his hand.

"We have no other option. If this has the slightest chance of saving Newhaven and I don't do it, I would hate myself forever. Of course, forever would likely be very short because of the nasty big Fae army on our doorstep."

His grip on her tightened, and his mouth pressed into a thin line.

She stroked his face. "Would you really sacrifice all those people just to make sure I lived for a few hours longer?"

He stared at her for a moment then kissed her hand, pulling her up to sit on his lap. His arms wrapped around her tightly, and she rested her head on his.

"My heart says yes. But my brain says no."

"I know it's scary, Ryder, but as some wise man once told me—'being the one who can do something means you have to do it, even when you're shit scared.'"

A smile lurked in his eyes and lit her soul even as fear spread through her like ice.

"So you do listen to me."

She bit her lip and stroked the hair off his forehead. "Sometimes. When I feel like it."

CHAPTER 54

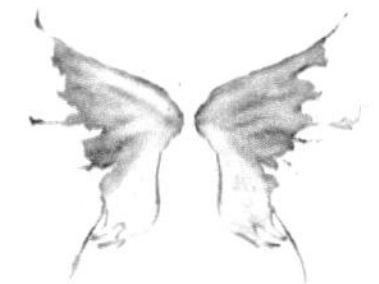

Aesthetius sliced the blade through her palm in one quick movement. Blood, red and bright, snaked down her wrist. He passed her the knife. The obsidian was cold under her fingers.

"Do it. Fast and sharp."

The blade cut through his skin like butter. Thick, silvery blood oozed out. He clasped her hand with his, the red mixing with the silver. He winced as the iron in her blood entered his system. Lightning shot up her arm, strong and vibrant, as their blood joined. His magic was heat and fire charging through her, twining with hers. He stilled. His eyes shimmered to bright blue then back to a pearlescent lilac. She sensed his heart beat, or whatever Fae had instead of hearts. His life pulsed within her, at once repelling and comforting. A melody sang through her blood now and would be with her until she died.

His grip on hers loosened. She unclenched her fingers, letting his wrist fall away.

Silence filled the space like a physical being in the room.

"So, I kinda assumed there'd be words to go with the magic. You know. Like a ceremony or something."

Aesthetius put his head on one side, and she could've sworn he was laughing at her. But his voice stayed crystal calm as ever.

"That *was* the ceremony. There is no need for words when the blood does all the work. But I will make you this promise, Adelia Lark. From this moment on, you are bound to me and I to you. My blood bond will protect you and yours until the day of my death. Should I ask you, you will come to my aid. The magic of the blood bond is older than many Fae still living. It is strong and will suffice."

"See, much better with words."

He raised a brow, and she smiled. He appeared more and more human every moment.

He brought the Dust. He took me from my mother.

She glanced down at her hands, at the already fading red line. Was this a betrayal? Her mother—what would she think? Standing, she brushed her hands on her trousers. She would be happy to know her daughter lived. That some lives, at least, would be spared.

"What do we do now?"

"Now we build a shield."

Her mouth twisted. "Yes, I thought it would be something obvious like that."

"I will show you, but you must do it. This is your home and requires your protection."

He led the way to the impact crater, and for the first time, she didn't hesitate to cross the dead soil. In the middle, he turned to face her. She had to crane her neck to look into his eyes.

"You are going to place a shield over the compound, Adelia. It will be strong and constructed of your magic and mine and will hold them off. At least for a while."

She didn't like the sound of the last bit, but any time without Fae was a good length of time.

"How?"

"Sing with me."

His music, a melody following him at all times, danced around her, through her. The new blood in her body sang and harmonised. Together, they slowly wove in the air what appeared at first to be a net, but as the music built, the strands tightened and multiplied. A shining barrier emerged from the strands. She instinctively pushed it upwards.

When the music stopped, she took a shuddering breath, willing her shaky knees to hold her. A shimmering dome covered the compound. Translucent and fragile and invisible to most. But she could see it. She could hear it. The shield sang a melody with notes of Aesthetius's song and new tones, sharper and harsher but strong.

Mine. That is my *melody.*

She blinked back a wetness in her eyes.

Outside the dome, the clouds darkened, a swirling mass of grey splitting down the middle, separating to show a golden glow for just a moment, spilling out color and movement.

The Fae gathered, a storm cloud of red outside the boundaries of her shield. Her heart raced in time with the pounding of their wings as they hovered above, testing the dome with flickers of crimson magic.

What if it didn't hold? Her stomach clenched. She checked for any cracks, but the music sang louder than ever. The shield held.

"What now?" Ryder's voice came from over her shoulder, and she leaned back into his solid presence, her wings folding gently away so they were a pressure at her back, nothing more. The weight of his hand on her hip calmed her heart beat, and she breathed a little easier.

Aesthetius spread his wings, broad strokes of lilac and gold against the grey concrete. "Now, I go and speak to them"

Her eyes widened. "Wait up. You're going out there? To that army? I'm not sure that's a great idea."

He smiled. "I must parley. Those are the rules."

He paused, his shimmering eyes scanning her face. She tried to smile back through her anxiety. What if he didn't come back? What would they do?

"You mustn't worry for me, little changeling. They do not dare attack me."

"Famous last words," she muttered as he took off into the sky, his wings taking him effortlessly towards the shield. She watched closely, but he simply went through. "Huh. Magic."

Ryder's hand slid round her waist, holding her closer. "I guess now we wait. How long is that shield of yours going to last?"

She craned her neck around to peer at him. "You can see it?"

"Kind of. More, I can sense it's there. It feels the same as when those wings of yours wrap around me. Like you're up there watching over all of us." He kissed the back of her head. "It's kinda nice."

Warmth flooded her, bubbles of happiness tangling with the guilt and fear. They might all die, but she had him. She snaked a hand down to clasp his.

"I don't know how long the dome will hold if things go wrong.'

"Let's hope they don't go wrong then."

WHATEVER HAPPENED at a parley seemed to involve a lot of bowing. She gripped Ryder's hand, anchoring herself as she watched the future being arranged.

Aesthetius bowed again and turned back to the shield, followed by a Fae dressed in white. The Ministrator. Her fingers sparked fire, and Ryder yelped and whipped his hand away.

"Oh god! Sorry!"

"No worries," he said, sucking his fingers. "Who's that guy?"

Her throat closed up, and she shook her hand to get the flames away. "The one who hurt me."

Anger pulsed through him, and his stance changed. "Do you think we'd break the rules of parley if we killed him?"

I want to watch him burn. "Yeah. I think we would."

"A damn shame."

The two Fae were waiting outside the dome. Pressure sank into her mind like lead weights, insistent and unrelenting. *Oh. I have to open the door.* Forcing herself to open the shield for the Fae who'd tortured her and so many others made nausea swim in her stomach.

A shimmer of light, and Aesthetius and the Ministrator slipped through. She shut it carefully afterwards and stared at the white Fae the whole way down.

Hatred pushed out through her skin in a visceral force. Ryder took her hand, and she squeezed until she breathed normally again.

Aesthetius eyed her as they came closer, and she was deeply conscious of the vulnerable humans ringing the yard. The Ministrator might only be one Fae, but she knew more than most just how lethal one Fae could be.

They bowed, and she stood straight, glaring at them. Aesthetius pushed his head at her, but she lifted her chin and refused to bow.

"You might have wings now, Changeling," said the Ministrator, "but your execrable manners betray your human nature."

"Probably the nicest thing anyone's said to me all day."

Ryder squeezed her hand in a gentle reprimand, but she heard him stifle a snort and wasn't fooled. She would talk to this Fae, but she'd be damned if she'd show any respect, not when fire burned in her like molten lead, ready to explode.

The Ministrator stared, eyes shimmering in a nauseating purple and black. She stared back. Yawned.

Aesthetius stepped forward. "I have informed the Ministrator of our blood bond. He requested to ascertain the truth of my statement."

"Well tell him we didn't lie then he can leave."

"I find it hard to believe you could have bonded with this animal, Aesthetius."

Ryder bristled, the tension in his arm shooting through his hand on hers, but she smiled. Animals were lovely. She'd be one over a Fae any day.

"Check the bond, Ministrator." Aesthetius sounded fed up too. She just wanted the Fae to go. Leave before she lost control and set the flames free.

The white robed Fae stretched out his arms, and her knees nearly buckled from a wave of panic. Ryder grabbed her waist and held her up until the dragon uncurled. *No, remember this, it cannot touch you now.*

The touch of the Ministrator's mind on hers, probing and prodding filled her with nausea, and she pushed him back behind her eyes. Aesthetius' melody swam in her head, a silver lifeline floating through the darkness. When the Fae pulled back, the taint in her mind dissipated, and she blinked back tears.

"The bond is real."

"No shit." She spat on the ground, something she hated. But the bile in her mouth was gagging her, and she would rather die than vomit in front of this monster.

Aesthetius bowed to the Ministrator. "Will you honour the bond?"

The white Fae stared at her for a long moment, and she tried not to show how much he shrivelled her insides.

"We will honour the bond. We can do no less. We will not pursue you, Adelia Lark, or the boy. Your home will not be touched by us. The blood bond is sacred and cannot be broken. Aesthetius stands guarantor of this."

The Fae's eyes shimmered into pure black, and his hair arranged itself into horns of white twined with black. "But, should you leave this compound, the bond will not protect you." He glanced between her and Aesthetius. "Sentiment and tradition will only get you so far."

Trade would be restricted, their supplies limited. To a large extent, they would be on their own. She gazed around at the compound, to the people who sheltered within its walls. They would manage this hardship.

The Ministrator spread his wings, white and edged with blood red. "This is not the last time we meet, Changeling."

She bared her teeth. "I certainly hope not, Ministrator." One day, she would burn them all down.

He flew into the sky, and she wondered what would happen if she let him crash into the shield. She opened the dome with a thought and let him out, like her mother had opened the door to let out a wasp.

With his departure, the tension in the yard ratcheted down a few notches. She let go of Ryder's hand and tried not to notice as he massaged feeling back into his fingers.

"And what will you do, Aesthetius? Will you go back to the King or stay here? Or to your mother?"

He smiled. "I am ambassador of the Queen of the Emerald Fields to King Valkor Below the Mountains. I will return to the king's court. I will do what I can there to change things."

"Will you free the other humans?"

Aesthetius shook his head, his brow clear but his eyes reflecting his sorrow. "This I cannot do. But I will do my best to protect them." His hand stretched out, and he lightly touched the dragon brooch pinned to her t-shirt. "Changeling child you were, and you will change us also." She put her own hand up to touch his arm, sliding it down his wrist to take his hand in hers.

Murderer, tyrant, saviour, friend.

"Thank you." The words seemed insufficient when she thought of the lives he had saved by his actions, the danger he put himself in. But she was never good with words.

He leaned down and placed his forehead on hers, and she closed her eyes, breathing in the inhuman scent of him, for once not minding. His voice echoed in her mind like music, and she thought she would always know him by his melody alone.

"Take care, little changeling."

CHAPTER 55

Kira held tight to her girlfriend's hand and suggested a party. Grief for their friends shadowed all of them, fear for those still in the ward an almost tangible emotion. It might have been slightly macabre, drinking and laughing so soon after such devastation, but the evening reminded Addie of her uncle's wake and her mother reassuring her that while you should mourn the dead, celebrating the fact that they had lived was also important.

As person after person came up to admire her wings and thank her for what she'd done, discomfort rose like a burning fever. Every smile reminded her of Doc and the choices she had made. Every young man who walked past was a reminder that Keegan no longer lived. She was thankful Paolo was still in the ward. His quiet, desperate grief still cut her inside. Gripping tight to the bottle, she edged further away from the centre of the yard and the light.

Ryder sat on a bench at a table with five other men. Laughter and the sound of clinking glasses rang into the air at frequent intervals. A smile spread through her eyes to her cheeks watching him. The darkness settled around her, and she wondered if she could slip away.

"Darkness and light, madness and blight, one leaves, one stays."

Warmth filled her eyes. "Hi, Jasper."

The old man smiled and patted her arm, tugging at her sleeve. He inclined his head away from the yard, towards the units, and she nodded with a lopsided smile.

She let him take her by the hand and lead her away from the celebrations, shamefully grateful that now she had someone to blame if anyone realised she had gone.

His shambling gait took them on an indirect path around the impact crater, and a smile crept onto her face. Bless his heart. He certainly never had a problem crossing it. Sometimes people shook you with the care they took of you. Her eyes went to the crater, fresh blood still caking the dirt. She still didn't like the area, but the horror had gone. Her wings fluttered. She could fight back now, and that made a difference.

Shelves lined Jasper's small tidy unit, covered in remnants from his life. He motioned her to sit down, and she perched on the little chair to wait. A photo on the sideboard caught her eye, and she stared at the beaming woman and the toddler with the ice-cream until he returned. He maneuvered a container through the doorway, pausing when he noticed where her eyes had fallen. A sad little smile crossed his face. "My wife and son," he said. His voice didn't twitch, and his words were clear.

The box covered the whole of the small table, and he stood back, gesturing for her to open it. She pulled off the heavy plastic lid peppered in holes, and all thought fled. Seedlings. Big seedlings. Green and strong. Growing in a bed of Dust. The box lid slid from her loose fingers, clattering to the floor.

She cleared her throat. "Are there others?"

"Others there are, and others there be, green leaves, green shoots, green green trees"

"Can you show me?"

He nodded happily and trotted into the back room. Following him into the gloom, she breathed in the moist air. "What's that making the water? Is this an irrigation feed?"

"Doc said yes, Paolo said no, Doc gave me one, and Paolo don't know."

An ache spread through her chest. "Anahera knew about the seedlings?" She shook herself, leaving the grief for later. "Is there a light in here?"

Jasper appeared at her shoulder, and she startled at his voice in her ear. "Why don't you make one for us?"

She stilled, heart flickering. His eyes were dark in the gloom, but kindness radiated from him. Her chin went up. She didn't ask to be different. Hadn't wanted it. But magic proved to be handy in fighting. Would be nice if it could help with less deadly things too.

Holding out her hand, she scrunched her face up. Did she even need to put her hand out? *God, how embarrassing.* "I wish for there to be light," she said, and without fanfare, a soft yellow glow lit up the room, spreading from just in front of her to fill the whole space.

"You missed a great opportunity to be biblical."

She closed her eyes, opened them and turned to face Ryder, her heart singing in his presence. "Didn't hear you come in. What do you mean, biblical?"

Jasper's voice floated through the small room. "Let there be light."

He stood in the middle of the plants with his arms out, bathing in the golden glow.

"Oh," she said. "Well I don't know if Faery magic and the bible go very well together. I might have to stick to wishing."

The warm light of her magic cast gentle beams over Ryder's face, and she accepted the drink he passed her with a smile that only ever came for him.

He brushed past her, staring at the rows and rows of

plants in Jasper's back room. The old man must sleep in the kitchen she realised. The air was too damp in here.

"This is amazing, Jasper," Ryder said. "Where did these all come from?"

"Deep in the Dust the seedlings cried, found them, grew them, here inside."

He raised his eyebrows at the old man. "They were growing outside the compound? Through the Dust?"

Their eyes met, and she knew he remembered the Valley of the Kings also. Hope blossomed, like the shoots of these plants. They weren't all edible, but if they survived the Dust then perhaps they could help hold back the deadly grey.

Ryder's face shone, and a smile teased the corners of her mouth. Maybe a future would be possible.

They left Jasper to his plants and his photographs. Outside, the night sky was clearer than she could remember. The Dust hadn't gone, but she wondered if she and Tama acted as a ward. Her dome reflected the light of the celebrations in the yard. Aesthetius said the shield would probably come down by itself in the next few days. She found herself grateful it still held tonight, when liberty felt too frail and small a beast to be left without shelter.

Ryder's arms came around her, and he pulled her back against his chest, dropping his chin to her shoulder. "So, Lark, I think we pulled it off."

She leaned into him, loving the strength of him, the warmth.

"You think?"

"Yep. We rescued the boy, didn't die, beat back the Fae. I'd say that's pretty good."

She laughed, and delighted bubbles floated through her veins. She went to hug herself then stopped. No, this wasn't a tight feeling, this was a giant feeling. She spread her arms out and leaned back on Ryder's chest, her face to the sky. Her eyes closed, and her smile widened, lifting her upwards.

"I feel happy. Like, actually happy. Not just 'everything's ok right now' or 'that was a kind of nice moment,' but the real deal. Happiness. Do you remember it, Ryder?"

She swivelled against him and looked up into his eyes. He gazed back at her, his own eyes warm with laughter and his mouth turning up on one side. "Who are you, and what have you done with Lark?"

She rolled her eyes, but her grin didn't fade. "Oh, so funny. But seriously, Ryder. Do you remember?"

He pulled her closer, and her soul rippled in a melody that sang out against the air and the shield above them.

"I don't have to remember it, Lark. I feel it. Usually when I'm with you."

Her hand caressed his cheek. She caught her breath at the wonder of him, that he would give himself to her so completely. She smiled so that she wouldn't cry and kissed him.

The night bled into dawn, and as the sun rose, she let the melody of her magic soar to the sky, punching through her shield and scattering the opaque dome like raindrops. They were not birds to live in a cage. She wound the magic around the compound, letting the melody play for the lives that dwelled within, letting it sing for the courage they would still need to show, then cast the notes up into the sky, meeting the dawn with a song of freedom.

ACKNOWLEDGMENTS

Bringing *Dust Bound* to the world has been one of the most important journeys I've made.

I want to thank my amazing family. My parents, Allen and Sandra Fraser, have read every single book I've written. Their belief in me allows me to shine. My brother, Raphael, has not only read my books but enthuses over them, which makes me so happy. My sister, Jessamine, not only cheers me on endlessly, but helped me write a query letter for *Dust Bound* early in the process—no small feat.

My sons. What can I say. From sneakily putting reminders to write in my phone, to letting me spend evenings intent on crafting a Dust blighted world, to reminding me that I control the journey I take. They are incredible.

I need to thank my amazing Critique Partners and Best People, Michael Roberts and Ashley Reisinger. They not only worked with me on my first draft of *Dust Bound* and every single revision since, but have been constant cheerleaders through every stage. They are the ones who listened to my meltdowns, my angst, my hopes. They are the ones who I run to first for brainstorming and reassurance. I could never have done this without them.

Kelly Andrew was the first person to read *Dust Bound* in its messiest, rawest form and was exceedingly kind to my terrified self. She was also the first person to draw fan art of my characters. A true friend and constant writer goals.

Robin Woodward proofread the final manuscript and kapowed my many comma errors. Any mistakes remain my own. Also, squinched is absolutely a word, Robin. I make it so.

Jonas Mayes-Steger, of Fantasy and Coffee Design, designed the most perfect cover I could have ever imagined. They are a magician.

So many people were invaluable beta readers at various stages of this book—Tiffany White, April Woodard, Erin Grey. Many others read chapters and gave welcome feedback —Chris Henderson-Bauer, Heather A. Lynn, Phil Williams, and Savannah Holland.

I also need to thank the amazing people in the #WriteFightGifClub, who cheered on this story from the beginning. Thank you for the sprints, the fangirling, the advice, and the fun. I will be forever grateful that I stumbled into the WFGC craziness on Twitter when looking for writing friends.

Paris Wynters acted as unofficial mentor after my unsuccessful 2018 bid to get into Pitch Wars, giving me invaluable craft and developmental advice on *Dust Bound* for which I am eternally grateful.

A very special thank you to Maura Fouhey, who read an earlier version of this and who has always been a huge supporter, encourager, motivator, and a very dear friend. Maura—I was thinking of you when I wrote parts of Lark's journey. I see her strength and resilience in you.

The roots of a book go very deep. The magical Sarah Rodgers walked and talked writing and books with me for a wonderful year. Her enthusiasm helped convince me that writing was something I could really take seriously, and I will be forever grateful for her friendship and the confidence she gave me to start writing this book.

My critique group, the Toasties - Michael, Ashley, Robin, Tiffany, and Brittany Kelley. I could not have got to this point without you all. Your support and love and friendship lift me up constantly, and you are a well of talent!

Finally a big thank you to *you*, for reading this book of my heart.

ABOUT THE AUTHOR

Clementine Fraser is an award winning romantic fantasy author. She lives in New Zealand with two boisterous sons and a giant doofus rescue dog. In her day job, she teaches teenagers to love history.

Writing in stolen moments at lunchtimes, after school, and in between children's bedtimes is not always easy (and requires a constant infusion of coffee), but is always worth it. When she is not writing or working, you might find her curled up in an armchair with a good book or trying not to kill the flowers in her garden.

Her core story is about vulnerability, and loyalty, and facing who you are and where you are with strength and dignity. Whatever the setting, this filters through into her stories. Fantasy in all its magical variations is the genre that captures her imagination and makes it sing.

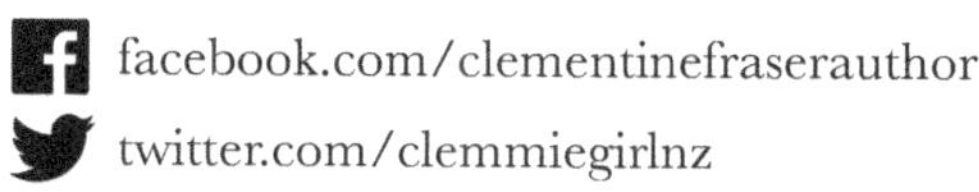

facebook.com/clementinefraserauthor

twitter.com/clemmiegirlnz